THE
CABLE DENNING
MYSTERY SERIES

JAMES P. ALSPHERT

GOLDEN THROAT
A CABLE DENNING MYSTERY

BOOK 1
PART 1

BY
JAMES P. ALSPHERT

TABLE OF CONTENTS
PART 1

PART 1

CHAPTER 1

THE MAN WITH THE GOLDEN THROAT

EAST OF THE MOON

Police sirens are unnerving. Case-in-point, even after years of hearing them cut through the night like screaming demons… harbingers of bad tidings, like coming home to your woman and finding all your belongings on the sidewalk—there's a place in your psyche that gets frayed with that desolate, forlorn sound traveling through your body like a cold metal snake. Life comes across as a constant surprise package of good and evil, a mixed concoction in a magician's bag of tricks, pulled from a dirty secret place and saved for a frenetic Friday like the one I found myself in this day. It was February 11th, 1927. My partner Mario Angelo and I had been called out to one of those gangland murder sprees, the kind the mob used to clean out their ranks when something went wrong. And something was really wrong that Friday afternoon as Mario and I stood with our boss, Sergeant O'Flaherty, looking at the pools of blood that had formed around two stiffs face down on Alameda Street in Chinatown. In fact, my cop intuitions told me it stank. One of the dead guys was a hoodlum who had become top banana in the local Mafioso…a guy named Ernesto Ardizzone. He had left his tracks all over this town, dealing in Prohibition booze, money laundering, extortion, speakeasies and white slavery. Oh, yeah, and bumping off cops who didn't go along with the Cosa

1

Nostra or the corrupt politicians downtown.

O'Flaherty was talking at us. "You'd be wonderin', boys, why they keep takin' each *other* down like this. Be gatherin' what you can about who's been doin' who in and why. And then tomorrow, you be checkin' with old doc Sandor down at the Morgue and gettin' me some causes of death post haste—ha! as if I didn't already know the half of it!"

"Yeah, sergeant...*east of Main Street,*" I said that, glancing over toward the colored paper lanterns hung over the shop doors above the wooden sidewalks. It always looked to me like the Chinese had this ongoing festive occasion with all the yellow, pink, green and red blowing in the afternoon breezes.

"What is it yer sayin' t'me now, Denning?" O'Flaherty probed. "East o' *what?*"

"Oh, it's just something I've observed lately, sergeant. We're getting a lot more murder cases east of Main Street." I looked up at the sky. "It's where the moon comes up, you know, right about there. Ever notice?"

"What a squirrely thing to be sayin', now. You better not be drinkin' any of that speakeasy hooch 'afore ya come on the job, lad. Irish or no, I'll have your badge for it!"

"I guess I'm just getting tired of beating the pavement down there on San Pedro and Central, chasing *long braids* in black hats for setting up their women as whores—at least today there's some excitement."

"Well, now, isn't that an almighty shame, Officer Denning? For bein' these three years now on the force, you're still a might impertinent, wouldn't ya be sayin'? Excitin' or not, you do what you're gettin' paid for. Check your tongue and be keepin' to the job at hand, Mr. Rookie." He surveyed the people standing around gawking at the bleeding bodies. "And clear these blood-thirsty Tongs out of here." He stomped away toward his car.

My partner Mario and I began raising our clubs and scaring off the local populace. By the time I heard the ambulance shrieking its way toward us, I found a little old Chinese lady, shriveled and trembling with age, bent over the smaller of the two fallen men. She possessed sparkling dark-brown eyes that were very much alive and complained when I pulled her up off the body that she had been rifling through. "You can't be doing that here, lady, they're police property now—and that includes everything found on their bodies. Did you steal anything?"

"Little man have something belong to me. You go find! He steal...you go find!"

I looked curiously at the little slip of a woman. "Can't do that, lady, I told you why—now scram and let us do our work here, okay?"

"*I no go!* Little man thief!" she persisted. "I not thief. *He* thief!"

Just then Mario came to my aid and pulled the woman away swearing, kicking and swinging at him. For a twenty-seven-year-old cop, life was a merry-go-round here on the fringes of skid row. You always kept coming around to the same place you were last week and the week before that. Sometimes faces changed and pretty little feminine things right off the boat from Shanghai graced the streets on my beat for a while. Some were seamstresses, kitchen help, promised mail-order brides and the like—but most of the real beauties ended up with some pimp selling them in thirty minute intervals for fifty cents a pop in back of a dirty dry goods store. And once in a while a drunken white man didn't think he got his money's worth and started beating up on her, until her fragile little body lay like bleeding pulp in a slaughterhouse. It was then that Mario and I would pick up the pieces. Beautiful black shiny hair, fine silken yellow robe with wide sleeves, her black skirt ripped and pulled up to her hips, her delicate painted face crushed in blood and bruises summed up the senselessness of it all and the depravity of human nature.

The ambulance attendants were just about to throw the bodies on stretchers and load them. I put my hand up to stop them. "Men…if you don't mind, just a minute…I…uh, need to check something." They stepped back. Mario was at my shoulder. I started rifling through the downed men's clothing. "Now, if you ask me, I'd say Ardizzone here was chasing this little guy—maybe the old lady was right." I found nothing on either man.

"What old lady?" Mario inquired, as if he didn't have a clue.

"The old Chinese woman you escorted out of here."

"Damn, there was something odd about that old crone, Cable. Like she had the energy of someone a fifth her age—ha! swore at me like a sailor and fought me tooth and nail! In fact, I had to handcuff her—over there, to the end post of that wooden walk near the *Canton Bazaar*."

"You didn't."

"Yeah, I did."

"Son-of-a-bitch, Mario—you're an *ox* and you can't handle a little ancient Chink? —c'mon, pal, you're pulling my leg, here."

"Shit, Cable, *you* take her on!"

I signaled for the guys from the county morgue to load the bodies. "I'll get to that in a minute. Here we are, Mario—at the crime scene. Does anything look out of place here to you?"

Mario looked around. "I don't know. *You're* the detective type. Remember me, I'm the guy you talked into joining the force three years ago—and I've been sorry ever since," he muttered. "So, Ardizzone was chasing the little guy for something he wanted, Jack Dragna's guys saw it as an opportunity to bump off Ardizzone, so they did. What's odd about that, Mr. Smart Cop?"

"Okay, you wanna know? First of all, why didn't Ardizzone

4

send one of his own goons to do the job—how much fire-power does it take to dispatch the little guy? Hell, you could've strangled him in an alley. Second, what were they doing in Chinatown? —and third, there was no trace of a gun either around Ardizzone or the little guy. If either of them was carrying a piece, they were confiscated by someone else before we got here." I looked at the Chinese gawkers still hanging around. "And you know as well as I do, the Chinks won't talk—even if they saw the whole damn thing."

Mario looked at the drying pools of blood as a Chinaman brought a bucket of water around from behind his establishment and began to wash the red away until it ran down the street in rivulets. "Well, you got me there, Cable."

Mario left and went over to a little teashop to get something to drink. I wandered over to where he had left the angry little Chinese woman. I spotted the silvery handcuffs shining in the afternoon sun okay, but it looked like the old woman had disappeared without a trace—and Mario's handcuffs were still locked! Crap, this had turned out to be a hell of an afternoon, I thought.

I was walking around looking for clues when I spied one of the most beautiful young Chinese women I had ever laid my eyes on. Somehow she looked too classy to be haunting the wooden sidewalks of Chinatown. I went up to her. "Do you *speekee English*?" I asked, noticing her flawless skin and perfect little body. She was dressed in a lovely red silken robe, pearl slippers and a golden barrette in her hair.

"No need to speak down to me, police man," she voiced in perfect English. "I see you looking at me. What is it you may desire?"

I wanted to say *her*, but I refrained. "I'm—I'm sorry—I, uh, I was just admiring your beauty. I haven't seen you here before. Are you new?"

"I think you would say, *just passing through*. I am...I am

looking for something I lost."

"Well, now, ain't that strange? Some old Chinese crone said the same thing hanging around two dead bodies earlier today—over there on Alameda Street."

"So I heard. Terrible how you humans kill each other…as if you did not know another way…"

"And you're not human?" I asked.

"I didn't—I didn't mean it like that," she sputtered. "I do not go around killing other humans."

Well, now the dame had captured my undivided attention. "So…ah…what exactly *did* you mean?"

"Highly evolved or cultured people do not sink to such primitive actions. In my land, I am a princess, you might say…"

"Ah, I see…" I said that, not knowing what this babe was getting at. "Well, anyway, as far as I can tell, we're human enough for the duration of this trip called life—and I don't see any way out of that. People kill other people for a lot of reasons, lady…mostly because someone else is in their way."

"Still very primitive, police man." Then she asked me a strange question. "Do you know where they take the bodies of the dead men?"

"Yeah, they usually end up at the County Morgue, south of town. Why would you ask that?" This was getting stranger by the minute!

"Thank you, police man." She nodded to me, turned away and left.

I took out a Lucky Strike and lit it. The sound of a lonely sax went wailing through my head as I took in a big drag and exhaled. Hell, just another babe, even if she was particularly curious—not to mention a knockout. But there was something about her I liked. Like a lot of other things you can't put your finger on. I bet to myself that little doll would be a fun roll in the hay. I kept telling myself a young cop had to take time out from this stinking world he lived in. After all it was 1927 and Prohibition had been in effect for seven years. But people still got thirsty and speakeasies thrived as much as open taverns ever did. Coming from an early life in the ghetto to Chinatown and Skid Row wasn't much of a jump. But what *was* it I liked in this cock-eyed world? I guess I went for *truth, justice and beautiful babes in red sequined gowns* singing their little hearts out in smoky dives in the middle of the night—a sultry voice singing *Blue Skies* while the rest of the world hid its dirty secrets in the dark corners. As a cop you could see the greed, corruption and intrigue from a front row seat, as well as the rest of the underbelly of so-called humanity, whether it was the emotionally trapped citizen punching out his girlfriend or my partner and I picking up the pieces of an accident victim—or even the boring everydayism of being a cop on a beat or on patrol car duty.

After the Great War in 1918 when Johnny came marching home to the tune of George M. Cohan's *Over There* or *I'm a Yankee Doodle Dandy*, the lucky ones had something and someone to come home to. The war's legacy was too often depression, suicide, and financial destitution—the wheel was turning too fast, spun by the wheeler-dealers on Wall Street and the bankers tucked away in their nifty million dollar homes off Mulholland Drive. It was tough for the returnees to get on board when someone else was pulling the strings, deciding who should prosper and who should be left to die in the dark shadows of poverty. Some kids were barely sixteen when they entered that bloody hell in the trenches, and they returned without professions or vocations, and little opportunity for a fair shake at education. And some came back from *The Battle of Belleau Wood* poisoned with mustard gas, shell-shocked, with no arms or legs, a burnt unrecognizable face or an emotional trauma big enough to sink another Titanic. Yeah, that was how the rich and famous used up the poor and not-so-famous.

ALL THAT GLITTERS

The next day Mario and I headed for the Los Angeles County Morgue. It was on West Temple now and the chief Coroner was Frank A. Nance, a guy who prided himself with burying more movie stars than any coroner in history. Nance ran a pretty tight ship. The principal floor doctor and chief autopsy surgeon was a sinister looking character by the name of Dr. Boris Sandor. He seemed to take delight in circulating among the dozens of corpses brought in every week, dissecting them and making, so I heard, rather colorful reports to his boss. Mario and I parked our Model T patrol car just outside and meandered around the stiffs looking for our quarry. Funny, it seemed death was the one great unexpected thing, for the rigid, gaunt faces, in all sorts of grotesque poses, seemed to say a single message in that semi-dark slab room: 'Help! I didn't expect this!' Many had their mouths agape and stayed that way as rigor mortis set in. Mario and I found Dr. Sandor and he led us to the toe-tags of a couple of hoodlums who had just been sacrificed with a lot of bullet holes in their respective *corpus delicti*, courtesy of the local mob.

One corpse was looking up at me with that cold, icy stare reserved only for the dead. That all too familiar glaze had already come over his eyes and Dr. Sandor probed and poked at the body until he was satisfied an autopsy would reveal what he needed to know. I couldn't imagine a guy who liked to hang out in cold city morgues and slice up the old meat before it gets cremated or put six-feet under. But Sandor loved it. When I asked him about it, he answered in his strange, Karloffian way, "You'll find, Officer Denning, that the dead will give you far less trouble than the living."

"So our sergeant wants Mario and me to follow up on this one—he's kinda piled up with a lotta homicide cases lately." Sandor grunted and walked off to attend other deceased residents. It seemed a lotta people wanted Ardizzone dead, not the least of whom was that poisonous viper named Jack Dragna, whose father and brothers also shared an equal mania for crime and violence. Suddenly the buzz is, Dragna's giving orders and taking over the family and their many illegal businesses, all the way from prohibition booze to white slavery. Oh, as I also said before, don't forget to throw in mowing down honest cops when *they* got in the way.

The other guy who got killed yesterday afternoon puzzled me. For one thing, the thug had no I.D.—and no fingerprints! He was a real John Doe. I asked Mario to lift the sheet covering this strange little man's body. He also didn't have a navel! Right away I went searching around for Dr. Sandor. I found him and led him by the arm to the corpse in question. Sandor peeled the sheet back and peered at the missing belly button but didn't raise an eyebrow. "So, doc, isn't it kinda weird, you know—no fingerprints, no wallet, no identification and uh… no navel?" I inquired of the pensive face.

"Yes, I—I, uh, took…notice of it earlier, Officer Denning."

"Well, you'd better take *good* notice of this, doc. There are a couple of pieces here that don't—don't, uh, quite fit."

"Officer Denning, just because something doesn't…. 'fit' into the norm of your everyday existence, you mustn't consider the anomaly mysterious." He smiled an all-knowing, devious smile. "Besides, there is always an explanation for everything. Surely, as patrolmen you must have deduced that when you have to piece together the elements of a crime scene…….the result of some murderous villain venting his viciousness on an unsuspecting society. I will give this cadaver every due consideration—and rest assured, all the pieces will fit when I'm through. Now, I suggest you busy young men upholding the laws of our fair city be on your way. Think… of the living…while you can…" Then he surveyed the room. "Look around, gentlemen, it is…such…a short journey, from cradle to…to grave, isn't it?"

Mario and I left and got into our patrol car. I looked across at my partner, who seemed unusually quiet. "This no belly button thing bothers me, Mario. If both of us hadn't seen that dead guy next to Ardizzone, I sure as hell wouldn't have believed you if you had told me."

"Well, fingerprints can be sandpapered off, Cable, and hell, for all we know, with these new fandangled medical things going on, he could've had an operation to get rid of his belly button, too." Mario mumbled.

"But why in the hell bother doing that?" I persisted. "It wouldn't surprise me if old Sandor found some other weird shit on that stiff."

"I don't know…and I really don't give a damn. Gangsters are gangsters—whether they're lying in a pool of blood on the street or getting paid off down at City Hall." Mario seemed unconcerned and nebulous about the whole thing, so I dropped it. Yet I had this gut feeling some more shit was going to come down the pike about this little guy with the big teeth.

"I don't think this is the end of it, either, buddy. I don't know why, but I've got hackles going up on the back of my neck just about now."

My gut proved to be right. The next morning Dr. Sandor called Sergeant Mike O'Flaherty. Mario and I roomed together off of Alvarado and we got rousted out of bed by O'Flaherty's phone call. He ordered us to meet him over at the Morgue, but since neither of us had a car, we caught a streetcar and made the quick trip. Mario and I were both tired from our all-night patrol duty and didn't particularly look forward to facing the mean-spirited, feisty sergeant.

"Well! About time, you two lackeys! I think you're a knowin' what this here thing is all about, now—don't ya?"

10

Old doc Sandor gave us a curious once over. "Of course they do, sergeant. Last night, both of these most efficient officers pointed out those physical anomalies in my presence. I believe they are to be…congratulated."

O'Flaherty grumbled something under his breath. "But that's not the half of it, boys. The doctor's autopsy revealed somethin' else that we kinda want to keep hushed, so he tells me."

Dr. Sandor led the three of us into a special side room with large jars with all kinds of body parts in them. It was not only grotesque but stank to high heaven. Then the doc took us to a medium sized jar, labeled #1602-Blinthe, and brought a small lamp to bear on it. "See? See how it glows, gentlemen. Pure, 24-karat gold. It seems our mysterious guest had a gold-lined throat. And now, you see, it just floats, there in the clear solution. Curious….and definitely unique, I might add."

"That's it?" O'Flaherty barked. "You brought me and two of me officers down here because some murdered thug has his throat lined with gold?"

"Well, so much for all of your pieces fitting together, eh, doc?" I said in a rather droll voice. "Explain this one away and we'll give you the Sherlock Holmes award of the year."

"Oh, fear not, Officer Denning, I shall…. I shall, and I do not take kindly to your…sarcasm. But I needed for you gentlemen to see it before I did anything else. I'm sure you… understand my precautions where such a delicate matter as this is concerned…and who knows…what twists and turns the clouded brain of man possesses? What mystery might be… shrouded…and what other blunt and horrible mischief might be unleashed? It is said, you know, murder and insanity are pale brothers."

I always thought Sandor a bit nuts anyhow, but he seemed to be increasingly teetering on the edge of insanity. Too damn many days and nights with the dead, maybe. Mario and I

11

wandered over to the jar containing the throat of the deceased gangster. I had noticed an indentation just above the Adam's apple, as if something had been lodged there but had been removed. But I kept it to myself. Just then O'Flaherty came up to us. "Before I leave, men, I wanted ya to know ya did the right thing here. As a matter of fact, I'd like to be trainin' ya for the homicide detective division. I'm lookin' to be runnin' short here in a few years—and bein' prepared now mightn't be such a bad idea. What would you be thinkin' about that proposal?"

"I'm game, sergeant," I said. "I've always had a yen for that sleuthing detail stuff…" I looked at Mario. "I can't, of course, speak for my partner…"

Mario nodded his head and then looked at his sergeant. "Yeah, sergeant why not? You know…it's been like that since the beginning—wherever Cable goes…well…I go. It's left from protecting each other's asses in the ghetto."

"Then so be it!" O'Flaherty crackled with his Irish accent. "I'll be seein' ya boys. Of course, you'll have to be takin' special classes in the field, observin', and with Lieutenant Karfosky—but I'll be warnin' ya this—he always keeps an iron horseshoe in his glove when he hits—and he's tough as nails, he is."

Mario and I discussed this opportunity as we took the streetcar home. We both knew it was a way out of being a flatfoot patrolman for life. We smiled and slapped each other on the back and soon Mario and I were back at home in our respective beds catching up on our sleep. After all, the dreaded nightshift came around soon enough.

CHAPTER 2

JAZZ ME A FLAPPER

Somewhere in the night that same lonely sax played a haunting version of *My Heart Stood Still* and my young man's imagination took me to Amanda Baxter's bedroom, and I was visualizing that amazing form of hers slipping on her night gown and wondering if she was thinking of me. The music wafted down the hill from a house above the dam. I could feel the sound wend its way into my ear like golden tones from sensual nights dancing with Amanda on the crowded floor of the *Café Montmartre* on Hollywood Boulevard. I had taken that dazzling dame up here to the Hollywood Dam at least three or four times before, but tonight she wouldn't come, saying she didn't want to end up marrying a cop, so I ended up listening to a concert of frogs instead. But that wasn't so bad. What was decent and good in you often came from that deep association with nature and the lessons she taught you.

But with pubescence the hormones start banging up against your brain and turn a young man's fancy to wondering what's really under a girl's dress when a windy day reveals a pair of pink panties, or when she bends down to pick something up and those lovely young breasts are revealed in all their glory and suddenly a deep, primordial instinct snaps you to attention. Then chasing frogs and dragonflies takes a back seat to that sexual curiosity that gets all men in trouble sooner or later. I didn't blame Amanda Baxter for not wanting to marry a flatfoot. In fact, I wasn't even sure I was the marrying kind. Sure as hell I couldn't support a wife and household on $168.00 a month! But then again, I was an honest cop. It was 1927 and some bluecoats were slithering, treacherous creatures, plying their nefarious trades in the underbelly of the fragmented, corrupt town below the dam—my town—Los Angeles. It was a city you loved to hate, yet the damn place was a strange harmony of contrasts. The darkest evil mixed with the highest good, and in between stood the rest of us, working our butts off for that piece of a decent life. The country was prospering as never before. Wall Street, the banks, rising corporative monopolies, and plain old greed gained status from lofty penthouses hidden in the dark hearts of men who had stepped into that slight-of-hand world of shadow and deception.

Prohibition had turned thirsty citizens into a slew of lawbreakers, giving rise to the speakeasy, vice, gambling, crime and corrupt politicians. The mob set it up and were in cahoots with the cops as "protection," making no bones about who ran what. And to add a further injustice to Mr. and Mrs. America, the stuff they served as libation was a virulent version of tainted death, known to rot out the insides of those who imbibed too frequently. Amanda's Dad smuggled in real gin from England, the true *Juniperus communis*, containing anise, licorice root, angelica and grapefruit peel. It was here that I began a life-long enjoyment of this beverage, with or without the tonic. At thirteen I began to smoke the green packs of Lucky Strike cigarettes, which were advertised as being 'good for you and relaxing as the day is long...' Well, I was never too sure about that, but I got hooked anyway. So my formative years bent my fate toward booze, smoking and beautiful, fast women—it was all part of what identified me to myself—and to the world.

But it was *music* that drew me like the proverbial moth to the flame and whenever I could I would take in a good ragtime band at a cheap speakeasy joint and get my foot to tapping, not to mention grabbing a gander at those sexy little flappers jazz-dancing the night away. I don't know where I got it from because no one in my family was particularly musical. But I had to have it, like I craved my Lucky Strikes. I never had a lotta dough, but for ten-cents a dance I would whirl around the floor with some cute babe who smelled of booze and perfume and sweat like a stale flower. Every once in a while I recognized a doll I grew up with in East Los Angeles, populated by the Irish, Italians, Jews, Chicanos and some other Eastern European immigrants lured to the American dream. Lincoln Heights was a tough and unforgiving battleground... the survival of the fittest, where either you had to win a fight or get the shit beat out of you three times a week. Across the river lay Little Italy and the Mics and Dagos had gangs that fought each other for no other reason than being of a different ethnic background. I hated that. And when times were really rough, and they always were, I grabbed a split baseball bat and whacked away at hoodlums trying to steal my mother's wash hanging on the clothesline. If it wasn't nailed down, they'd steal it in those days.

My Dad died when I was six. I cried a lot when he left us because he would be the only early male influence I would ever know. He was a tough Irishman, stout with steely blue eyes and chiseled looks. He drank with the best of them, swore like a sailor, but he was sharp as a razor and twice as strong and worked at the stinking steel smelters a few miles away. I think to this day it was the filthy, belching smoke, sulfides and cinders flying out of those ovens that killed him. My mother was a beautiful woman of Irish-Scandinavian descent with dark, roiling red hair. She stood tall and stately, had a great figure with warm, brown eyes that told you she cared, kind of like a gentle mother deer. She was a kind and intelligent woman, took in laundry and worked in a dry goods store to make ends meet. I had no brothers or sisters, but I remember my mother lying sick in bed with a swollen belly as infection corrupted a fetus fighting for its existence inside her. I was too young to remember it all, but I know she barely survived that one, and no more children were forthcoming.

But strange as it seems, my best friend, Mario Angelo, came from Little Italy. We bonded when I was twelve and he was probably about fifteen, when we were pitted against each other in a hand-to-hand fight, prodded on by some of our respective gangs in a makeshift arena in a wrecking yard. We came to furious blows and Mario busted me a good one on the side of the head. I went down. But I had some hidden fury in me, an Irish temper that once triggered, turned killer. So I rushed at Mario, screaming like a banshee in the night, jumped on top of him and pounded him to the ground. Out of blind rage I kept hitting him when he was down until he blurted out, "Stop! You win!" When I recovered my senses and looked down at this hapless young chap's face, filled with tears, blood and remorse, I knew we would be friends for life. The gangs were satisfied and slowly drifted away. Mario and I remained, sitting on the ground together. "Do you wanna come to my house for some lunch?" I asked the bleeding fifteen year-old. He nodded his head and from that day on we were all but inseparable. Even our families came to know and love one another and I got to experience Little Italy like few other Mics ever did.

TEN CENTS A DANCE

Well, one night, Mario and I went to this underground dump called *Gregorio's*, where the gin was eighty-proof poison. We went to laugh and dance a little, ogle the babes and check out the pickings. We were young and had a lot of steam to vent. Cops knew all the wild spots because the tainted police department was on the take and word traveled fast within the force. In fact, an officer could walk into a speakeasy in full uniform, order a drink at the bar and nobody would look up from his or her drink to give a damn.

We were pretty high when I noticed this dazzling number come out of the women's bathroom and survey the room. I was a pretty good looker myself in those days and brazen as hell when it came to approaching a dame. I winked at Mario and as we always did, we flipped a coin for her. I won. She was honey-blonde with wonderful blue eyes, stood about five-

five and wore an off-the-shoulder black blouse with a pleated, white short skirt. Her eyes invited you into the bedroom long before you spoke to her. As I said, I was gutsy as hell in those days and approached her with an over-estimated confidence. "Hello. Are you—uh, up to taking a few spins around the room—or do you belong to someone?" I asked, taking in her perfect figure, which I estimated was somewhere around 38-22-34.

"Do I look like a dog to you? I could never belong to someone, Mister," she snapped back at me with a low, warm voice. "But if it's a dance you want, you'll have to wait in line. I'm pretty well booked for the evening, and if you *do* get to dance with me, don't bring a collar."

"Oh. Well, I guess I'm at the end of the line, then, huh? And…by the way, I find I never have to use a collar, because a good dog just—naturally gravitates to her master."

She did a double-take on me. "You got a gutsy style, buster—maybe a little too big for your britches. Yeah, but I have to say, you do have an interesting patter. Are you an actor? I might like *that*."

"No, I'm not, but thanks. Maybe that's because I hear a lot of singers—and when I speak, I suppose words are like lyrics to a song for me—a musical poem, you know."

"Yes." She took a token reserved for the next dance and tossed it over her shoulder at the young man waiting for his turn. He caught it and looked strangely at the dish. "Sorry, I… uh, forgot I promised my musical friend here I'd—I'd, uh, try him out first. Will you wait?"

The young man nodded eagerly, if not gladly, glanced at me and then looked back at the dame. Then she took my hand and led me out into the middle of the crowded dance floor. The live combo had just started up with Gershwin's *Someone to Watch Over Me* and we started to dance. Mario Angelo was flirting with some little number he'd found, but glanced up at me long

17

enough to shake his fingers as if he knew I had the best the evening had to offer. And, you know, I did. "My—my name's Denning, Cable Denning," I said, not knowing quite what else to say. She was remarkably beautiful up close and those liquid bedroom eyes also contained a vulnerable innocence.

"They call me *Honey Combes*—my Dad's a beekeeper."

I laughed. "That's great! I do like your sense of humor—a good laugh. But of course, you're kidding me, right?"

She didn't respond right away but held me about two feet out from her body as she looked into my eyes. "No.... you didn't thank me for putting you at the head of the line, Mr. Denning—and remember, you owe me ten cents."

I reached in my pocket and dropped the dime down her ample cleavage. "Thanks, Miss Combes. I do remember kindness, believe it or not. Life kind of toughens you up a little around the edges, you know."

She seemed indignant. "Now, that was a cheap trick. You're a cop, aren't you? Only cops get away with that kind of crap in here." I didn't respond, but just kept dancing with her. Then she started singing with the band closer to my ear as she drew me in toward her. "*Won't you tell him please to put on some speed, follow my lead, oh, how I need...someone to watch over me...*"

Her voice was warm and wonderful, very musical and it gave me goose bumps. "Hey, you're a hell of a singer, you know? Now, why in hell aren't you doing *that* in some classy club somewhere instead of this dime-a-dance crap?"

"Because the money's good, regular and not everyone throws theirs between my breasts. And in case you haven't noticed, times are tough, Mr. Denning." I could tell she liked me. "But thanks all the same."

"I mean it—may I call you Honey?" She nodded that it was okay. "Voices like yours don't come along every day, you know."

"Oh, singers are a dime a dozen—may I call you Cable?"

18

"Nope." I shook my head, smirking at her and she laughed.

"Landing a job in this climate is like selling ice cream at the north pole. At least this pays my room rent with Zelda."

"Zelda?"

"Yeah, my roommate. She's a bit of a prude, though. Study… study…study. That's really about all she seems to do…to be a botanist, I think. You ought to see where we live—plants everywhere!" Then she grew serious and checked my eyes out again. "You didn't answer me. Are you a cop?"

As the music ended, I took her hand and we walked off the floor. I brought her back to where I'd found her, back to her panting young man waiting for his turn. But Honey Combes wouldn't let go of my hand. Then she put the back of her hand up to her forehead and rolled her eyes back as if she was going to faint. I caught her and she felt warm and right in my arms. "Please…Mr. Denning…will you take me back to the dressing rooms? I'm afraid I—I, uh, feel a bit weak."

I motioned to the seven or eight men waiting in line for Honey, to get lost and escorted her to a room at the back of the joint. There she suddenly recovered and went to a cooler for a glass of water. "You okay?" I asked, feeling some concern for the babe.

"Yeah, fine. It's just that—manhandling night after night can get to you after a while. You're a man, so I don't expect you to understand that."

"Oh, but I do. Did I, uh, 'manhandle' you tonight?"

"No. You were a perfect gentleman and even complemented my singing. I told you, I even like the patter of your voice, Cable."

"Well, thanks, kid. I'll tell you what. First things first. You're probably weak from hunger, so let me treat you at your favorite diner. Second, let's talk about a singing job somewhere—I might be able to fix you up."

Honey Combes said no more. She excused herself, went into a dressing room and came out looking like the girl next door—except she was still a knockout. She was wearing an off-white silk blouse with nothing underneath and her nipples stuck out like mini-thimbles from a sewing kit. "Now, don't get the idea I just traipse off with any guy who wears pants and treats me decently, okay? There's just…just something I trust about you. I hope I'm not wrong."

"Well, if I told you I was a cop, or even a rapist or killer—would it help alleviate your mind?"

She giggled. "Now I know you're on the level."

"Yeah, Mario Angelo, my pal out there—oh, crap! I gotta tell him we're leaving—he says I'm a *truth guy* but in the 1927 Los Angeles police department, that ain't the best badge to wear."

"So you *are* a cop!" Honey blurted out. "You see, I knew it! I suppose your buddy out there is, too?"

"Yep. Sinful young men on the lamb. So why would you wanna dump me over for a guy still wet behind the ears, a gangster who'll use and abuse you—like a lot of the guys who come in here? Wouldn't you prefer a tough guy cop raised in the hell hole of East L.A. where I spent my nights chasing down hoodlums with baseball bats?"

She snickered. "Damn, I like the way you talk, Mister. I think you're real, Cable Denning. I even like your name. *Mrs. Cable Denning*…how does that sound?"

She could've bowled me over. "I—I—uh, I'm probably not the marrying kind, Honey. I don't think I'm cut out for cutesy smiles after five p.m., or sitting in an easy chair listening to the phonograph until the needle gets stuck ad naseum, or reading the evening newspaper while the dearly beloved looks on across from you with her knitting needles."

"Damn, Mister, what a smooth talker *you* turned out to be."

I went over to Mario and told him I was cutting out with the doll. He winked at me and I went back over to Honey. She squeezed my arm as we exited *Gregorio's* and headed for a little diner near 5th and Grand. It was one of those converted 1910 streetcars and we found a comfy little table at the far end. We sat and the fat owner came over and tossed us a menu. Honey Combes didn't even look at it. "Now…isn't this about the time when the man gets all excited, anticipating that the lady may go to bed with him after he feeds her?"

I looked at her and smiled. "You know, you're quite a dame. Yeah, you're right, that's the plan, normally. But I work a little differently. I don't push it because it's a lot more fun being wanted…finding a place in some babe's head that eventually goes to her—her *other places*. And maybe sometimes, if both people are lucky, that feeling goes to her heart and triggers your own. Then…things…take on a different color now, don't they?"

She gazed at me as if my talking to her had smitten some place deep down inside. "I told you, Cable—the way you talk, you hypnotize a girl. How can I not fall in love when a handsome young policeman with an honest badge punches me in the heart without even trying?"

I took a deep breath, took out a Lucky Strike and lit it up. I had to look at myself honestly. There was something about the doll that didn't deserve my usual patter. "I'm sorry, Honey Combes, it looks like you had it right about me—you said it yourself—*smooth talker*. So promise me…after we finish up and I pay the bill…just let me take you home, shake my hand and say good-night."

She looked surprised. "Why would I do that, Cable?"

"Because it's all a game, kid. It's my Class-A set up line—put the lady off guard and hope to hell it gets you into her panties before the night wears too thin. It's like life, Honey, it's all a set-up. Any guy who tells you he doesn't want to fuck you until he can't anymore is a liar. And I'm no exception. Except now that I've blown my cover, it wouldn't be that much fun anymore, would it? Because…sometimes…people really do feel real feelings for each other. When I saw you walk out of that bathroom tonight, it was like you already fit into my body and I could feel your stomach and your breasts press into my chest like they'd always been there."

Tears welled in her eyes. I had definitely hit a sore spot. "God, Cable, you make me feel *naked* just sitting here with you." She sniffed in her tears. "I—I felt something the minute you came up to me, too—but I've become so jaded with—with men, you know, touching me and wanting me, paying for me to dance with them, and like you said, like hungry animals just wanting to screw me until they can't anymore—and then go home in the cold of just another morning." She looked at me and reached across the table for my hands. "I don't want just another morning, Cable. I want someone I love and trust and know will be there tomorrow…"

I took a big drag on my cigarette and put it out as the waiter brought our order. I pulled my hands back to salt and pepper my burger. "That's a pretty big order, Honey Combes. My mother always used to say that…she once had a dream. When she met my father, she felt that dream had come true. But life itself, the reality of hard times and struggle, take their toll and she ended up asking herself, how much of the dream really comes true?"

"Was she happy?"

"Maybe in the early years before I came along. My Dad died when I was six. We both missed the big galoot a lot. Love is a funny thing, babe. Most of the time you don't even see it comin', and the same holds true for when it goes away… sometimes it goes out with a bang like a flair of temper and bad luck, or sometimes it erodes slowly like a lonely tombstone, the wind…the rain…the years…wearing away the names written on the epitaph."

"God, Cable, how grim," she said. "I don't see it that way. I say live for everything you have *right now*, don't try to promise tomorrow, but work today to help the love be all you hope it can be. Then, as I said, there won't be 'just another morning' and so maybe we will—uh, *people* will treasure every single one of those mornings…"

"You…uh…you said "*we*". Was that a slip of the tongue? Or a proposal?"

She laughed. "Oh, you……yes.…and yes! I propose you take me home. But I'm not going to shake your hand and say goodnight. Unless you want it that way, Cable. Remember what you said just before we danced tonight—the thing about the dog that naturally gravitates to its master?"

"Yeah…"

"Well, by now you know I'm a woman, not a dog—but I am naturally attracted to you.…not that you're my master, mind you. Take it or leave it, Mr. Denning, this is a rare occasion for me."

I continued to play with her. "Sounds pretty good—but what's in it for *me*?" I taunted her.

She got up, came over to my bench and sat next to me. She grabbed my shoulder and brought my face around to hers. Then with those full, moist lips she kissed me ever so gently. I could feel mini jolts of electricity go through me. "How's that for openers in the first inning?" she quipped.

I kissed her back, a little harder. "What… uh…what are my chances of hitting a homerun before the ninth?"

"Lay the odds, Cable Denning, lay the odds…"

In 1927 neither Honey nor I owned an automobile. So we took the *A Line* streetcar from mid-town to Echo Park. These little yellow electrical wonders, noisy and smelling of burnt electricity from the motors, wound their way along streets and boulevards, back allies and short tunnels. Honey told me she lived on Preston Avenue near Ewing Street at the rear of a once-noble estate, now run down, facing the hills in the Echo Park district. "My Daddy really was a beekeeper," Honey was saying as we bounced along on our way to her place. "He thought I had naturally honey-colored hair, like my mother, so he named me accordingly. But I don't look anything like my mother—she's the salt of the earth type, calloused hands, and wind-blown."

"I assume your parents are still alive, then?"

"Thankfully, yes. They live in a little town called Willits in Northern California among the redwoods. Maybe you'd like to visit them with me some day? It's really beautiful up there."

I was still ribbing this beautiful and rare dame, sitting next to me on the yellow car. "Hey, lady, I hardly know you and already you want me to meet your parents?"

"You should feel flattered. I've never asked a beau to come with me when I see them, every two or three years."

"How old are you, young woman?" I asked, taking her arm and checking out her skin, which was pale white and flawless.

"Twenty-two. What about you?"

"Hmmm…. let's see now… September 13, 1900… that makes me—"

"—an older man. Lord, twenty-seven! I'm dating an older man."

"Funny, I don't recall anything said about dating. Are you sure you've got the right guy?"

She tittered. "Maybe…maybe not." Then she squeezed my hand. "But, oh, do I have this feeling about him…hmmmm…"

We got off near Preston and it was quite a walk up to a two-story home that had seen better days. There was a flight of stairs going up the side and we went up toward the rear of the main house. I was feeling my Lucky Strikes right about then. There was a small but handsome chalet, covered with vines. We entered quietly. "I'm not sure if Zelda's still awake or not," she whispered as we made our way down a little hallway. She led me to her bedroom, a quaint 12' x 12' ft. affair with a single bed and simple décor. She closed the door, lit a candle and turned to face me. "Well, here we are, Mr. Denning. Welcome to my humble abode."

I looked around in the candlelight. The room smelled of night blooming jasmine from a huge plant of the stuff just outside her bedroom window. "I never would have thought that tonight I would be taking a beautiful young woman home to her bedroom. Is it time to shake hands and say 'good night' yet?"

She came up to me and reached her arms around my neck. "It better not be." She upped and kissed me strongly on the mouth. "Will this do instead?"

I cupped her wonderful breasts in the palms of my hands, lifting them, feeling the warmth and weight of them as those marvelous nipples distended through her silk blouse. Every virile male who ever dwelled on this planet lived for this moment. This was the moment when he stood at the threshold of a whole new adventure with the mystery of the female of the species. His body sprang to life from his toes to his forehead, his spine tingled and his manhood swelled from the magic of her touch. "You're something else, babe," I said as I moved her quietly toward the bed.

"Mr. Denning," she whispered, "you must get a good night's sleep now, mustn't you? When are you on duty again?"

"Who can sleep when I hold the makings of a goddess in my arms all night?" Then I checked out her eyes sparkling there in the light of a candle. "Are you sure about this? You can't toss another token over your shoulder this time and tell the guy he's gonna have to wait for his dance, you know. And he can't get his money back after he's had that dance with you…"

She put her finger to my lips. "Shhhh…...!" Then she sat on the bed, lay back and pulled me onto her. All the rest is fairy tale, some kind of kinetic dream of passion and motion, thrill and sensation, elation and exhaustion. Her naked body was an exquisite thing and we blended together and curved around each other like the other half of a heretofore lost mold. Now we were found, rediscovered in each other.

All through the night I kept hearing that lonely sax from above the Hollywood Dam wailing in my ear, wending its way into some new and added layer in me. Honey Combes was a complete woman, a whole person, a truth person like myself. I would never regret one moment of my life spent with her. And speaking of truth, I considered myself to be the luckiest guy in town to have a sparkler like this beautiful woman kiss and caress every part of my body. Yep, April 21st, 1927 would be a red-letter day for a twenty-seven year old cop. Happy Springtime, Miss Honey Combes!

CHAPTER 3

TWO IRONIES IN THE FIRE

We had been up all night, sort of. After love making, we slept the sleep that lovers sleep, but when you're that young, it doesn't take long for the body to regenerate itself and the power of desire drives it again and again into the little death of ecstasy.

When the Los Angeles sun peaked into her bedroom window that morning, she was still wrapped around me, completely at peace. We slowly awakened to each other. "Good morning, Mr. Denning," she said with a very contented smile on her face. "Did you enjoy your evening?"

I squeezed her into me. "Yeah, you might call it that. I—I, uh, had this strange dream, though."

"Feel like sharing it?"

"There was this dame who made love to me non-stop, but every time we did it, we got closer and closer until she got glued to me, somehow. And…I awoke with that amazing feeling…the kind that dreams are made of and you never expect it to happen in this life."

She kissed me gently on the lips. "From the beginning I felt it, Cable. That's what my mother always said, that when it's the right guy, there'll be no question about you saying 'yes,' and that it's there from the beginning. And if it's not, it'll never quite work out…"

"I think I'm going to like your mother," I said, kissing her on the forehead and getting up. I had to pee and staggered my way down the little hallway to the bathroom. When I got back, Honey was already in her robe and out in the little kitchen, brewing up some hot coffee. Now, that was the kinda doll I could go a lotta miles with.

The breakfast nook was a card table with three chairs,

adjoined by a tiny kitchen with an icebox, a small cast-iron gas stove, a deep sink and a few cupboards.

We sat at the table, hardly able to resist touching each other every minute. "So, what I said last night before you brought me home to seduce me, still sticks. I'd like you to try out at a great little nightspot, *The Bella Notte*, out on Wilshire near La Cienega. The manager, Affonso Amadore, is a good friend of my buddy, Mario Angelo. He loves good music."

"Oh, Cable, you say I'm that good—but am I, really? I mean, I hear so many good female singers these days." I looked around the room. On top of the icebox stood a large wooden radio. This technical advancement had been out for only a few years and broadcasts were beginning to come in clearer and clearer.

"Would you mind turning on the radio—if it won't wake up your roommate?"

"She's gone off to classes, early." She switched on the radio. A nice orchestra version of Irving Berlin's *What'll I Do?* was playing.

"That's the future, babe. Three things can make or break you as an entertainer, as I see it. First, lots of people buy records. Second, lots of people go to the movies—and third, *radio* will help make you a star if you can get your records played on it." Suddenly I imagined I was in this wonderful night club and Honey Combes was on the stage in a dazzling gown, singing the Berlin song and people applauded and cheered as she finished and smiled that magical smile as she took her bow.

"That was great kid," I said, completely immersed in my fantasy.

"What was great?" she asked, puzzled.

"Your song. I—I was visualizing you up there on a stage singing that tune and people—well, hell, people loved you!"

"You really believe in me, don't you?" She came over and sat on my lap, putting an arm around my neck. Then she kissed

28

me so I'd remember what the previous night had been about. "What—what if I fall in love with you, Cable? Then where will I be?"

"You'll be in love…and maybe a little bit in trouble with a cantankerous cop who doesn't know which end is up when it comes to his heart."

"I suspected that. What does it take to operate on your heart? I always wanted to be a *love surgeon*."

"Well, I think you've already made the first incision. I can feel my—my heart…bleeding a little…is that a good sign, doc?"

"You bet." She put her arms around my neck. "And when I sing, I'll sing to you, Cable. But are you sure I'm good enough for that audition?"

"I've got a good ear, babe. All I needed was a few notes warbled as we danced last night. That's *quality*, kid. I mean, you've got a genuine *golden throat*. I can call a guy I know who works for a record label—I think it's Brunswick. Maybe we can make a few recordings through him and get some play time on the radio."

She held me tight. "God, I know I adore you already. I just never had anyone really believe in me. Yeah, men told me all kinds of things, promises, promises, you know, so they could screw me—but not Cable Denning—nope, he's the real thing—and he screwed me anyway."

We both laughed. "Well, I'm just honest, that's all. So, we've got you covered as a nightclub performer, a recording artist and radio singer. What other brass ring do you want to grab while we're on the subject?"

"I know this sounds strange, maybe, but I've always wanted to have a screen test. I mean, nothing serious, just to see me projected up there on the silver screen when they play back the audition."

"Hell, why not? I went to East High with Norman Weitzer, who is now a major talent scout for a new picture company they're forming. I think it's called 'RKO' or something like that. Norman knows David Sarnoff, who's head guy for the mother company back in New York, Radio Corporation of America. They want to get on the bandwagon of new talking pictures. The buzz is that Warner Brothers is gonna launch something big in a few months."

"Talking pictures? That means *singing movies*, doesn't it? If they're any good and not some passing fad."

"I've got this great gut feeling sound movies are gonna come in like gang busters and stick around."

"And just how does a flatfooted policeman know all this stuff?" she ribbed me. "Aren't you supposed to keep your mind on your beat?"

"Honey, this police force is so corrupt that there isn't a pie they don't have their fingers in, including influence with Louis B. Mayer, Jack Warner and some of those starlets who make a producer's comfy couch all the more comfy, if you get my drift."

"Oh, I get your drift. And speaking of which, last time I checked in with my memory, you said you were a policeman—do you ever go to work?"

"Yeah, I got the nightshift with Mario tonight. I've got to skedaddle pretty soon. Mario and I start at eight and maybe we can pop in to *The Bella Notte* and talk to *Affonso Amadore*."

Honey came up to me and whispered in my ear. "Thank you, for believing in me. Is there a chance you could come by after your *nightshift*, Officer Denning?"

"What's your phone number—can I call you?"

"NOrmandy 6851. I hear they have new dial phones now. I still have to crank mine from the wall."

"Well ain't we getting modern and all?" I laughed. "Down at the department it's changing over pretty fast. But in the patrol car we still have to get out and use a cop phone—or run into a building for a phone booth."

Saying good-bye that morning was a lot like tearing off a piece of your skin and hanging it out to dry. We were attached. It hurt. I don't know why, but the dame had found a way into me and I wanted her to stay there. "I had a wonderful time last night, Cable. You're a wonderful lover—powerful and yet gentle. Just as I imagined you would be with me."

"Yeah, well that's because I was on my best behavior—wait until the caveman in me comes out to play and drags you hair-first into the bedroom," I grinned.

"Oh, yeah? I think I'll be ready for this caveman," she said, grabbing my crotch and squeezing gently. "Please…call me."

That night I met Mario downtown at Central division and we picked out a patrol car. As with all of our fleet, it was a four-door black Model T Ford with a slightly modified engine, a canvas hooded top, chrome-trimmed radiator and shiny black spoke wheels.

Mario greeted me as we got in. He was stocky and stood just over six feet, a couple of inches taller than I. He was blessed with that Mediterranean black wavy hair, intense dark-brown eyes, full lips and a great smile. He was always a bit more serious than I. He liked to play the game straight and stick to the rules. He detested the crooked police department that posed in the name of law and order. We both felt that things needed to change ever since we joined together in 1923. Mario was three years older than I was and had been dating an Italian beauty by the name of Rosalie Elena Vecchio. She was nuts about him and when we went slumming, it was hard for Mario not to tell her. But guys have to keep some secrets, and, after all, he was still a bachelor. But I had a feeling—not for long. Rosalie Elena was twenty-five and didn't want to wait much longer to have kids, Mario told me. She had come from a family of eight and her mother had drilled into her that a woman's place is that of a homemaker, wife and mother. Period.

"Hey, you elusive Mic," Mario said as he hit me on the shoulder. "What in the hell happened to you last night? I got stuck with this hot little number who talked my ear off, kind of like Rosalie Elena. I saw you leave—did you go home with that damn good looker?"

"Yeah, you ghetto wop, doesn't sound like me, does it?" I said as I started up the car. "I—I, uh, hate to admit it, Mario, but I think I got smitten last night. I can't get the dame out of my head."

"Ha! Not you, Cable. I don't believe it for a minute. You were saying the same about Amanda Baxter a couple of weeks ago. Nope, lover boy, I don't believe you'll ever settle down, not as long as you can get all this free fruit and without the complications. Nah, you're just not the type."

I thought for a minute. Maybe Mario was right. Maybe I was sucker for knockout dames who had fun personalities and were great in bed. But Honey Combes sure turned my head. In a few days maybe I'd ease up on the whole thing. "So, what do *you* believe in, partner? Ever since that day when we were kids and I beat the shit out of your little Italian butt, I've never really known what's at the bottom of your well."

Mario mused a bit. "Well, it's pretty simple. A good job, Rosalie Elena Vecchio, a couple of kids, good friends like you, pasta and vino when I get home from work, Sunday at the park and a comfortable cemetery plot when it's all over."

I laughed. "Talk about simple, yeah! But what about other things—things like gods and angels, fairies and devils, planets and stars? And what about the murderous insanity that runs through humans? What about the worst violent acts we've seen that people do to each other? How do you explain that to your children?"

"Hey, you Mic! Remember, I'm a Roman Catholic. *God* takes care of all that shit. I'll stick up for the right thing and do what it takes to win. That's why we're cops, right?"

"Yeah, I guess." I was thinking about how corrupt it was on either side of the thin blue line. As much as I loved Mario, I knew I couldn't subscribe to religion, either. The same went for politics or the money rackets from Wall Street to Congress. I knew how crooked greed and temptation made people. In my line of work, I saw that people killed most often for money, sex, power— or all three. Look at those two stiffs down at the morgue being baby sat by the crazy Dr. Sandor. They got bumped off because one gangster wanted another gangster's power and money. So, bang! bang! you're dead! The new kings of the mountain, the Dragna family, would last just until the next more violent gang came along to put *them* on ice for keeps.

But deep inside there was always something niggling at me, something that knew there was more than this everyday crap of policing a city filled with morons, have-nots, the insulated wealthy, the entertainment industry's meat factory of human product mostly based on looks and sex appeal, and the artificial bullshit radio and newspapers threw at you, hoping it would stick. Then there were union riots, ballgame crowds, drunks crashing college sorority parties and domestic violence.

No, for me, there had to be something more. "You know, Mario old boy, I think I believe in things you can't see, like fairies and guardian angels, invisible dimensions, that we have stuff in us that we don't use—I mean stuff that could expand us, change our lives, make us grow to be more than the every-day crap we have to clean up after."

Mario laughed. "I have never in my life heard you talk like that, Cable Denning. You are one adventuresome son-of-a-bitch. But in a way we're the same, amico mio. The Catholic God is invisible, all-powerful, passes judgement on evil doers and urg-es us to use the gifts He gave us to improve ourselves. So you see, we're more alike than you might think, compadre."

The night went pretty smooth and as I was getting off duty,

I found a phone booth and called NOrmandy 6851. "Hello…" a sleepy female voice answered at the other end.

"Hey, kid, it's me, Cable—you still want a sleeping partner?"

"Cable! I didn't think you'd call. But yes—except I've already slept a few hours—so we might have to fool around a little before I can fall asleep again with you."

"You're pretty bold, little woman. You feel that safe with me?"

There was a slight pause. "Yes…yes, Cable. Come to me."

By the time Mario and I got the patrol car back and signed out, it was getting on to seven a.m. I told my partner I was on my way to Honey Combes' little bungalow and he raised his eyebrows again and shook his head. "I don't know…it just doesn't sound like my old womanizing pal Cable Denning."

"Yeah pal….I don't know either?"

By the time I arrived at her door it was around 8:30 a.m. I was surprised to see a stranger open the door. "Oh…hello… you must be Mr. Denning. I'm Zelda. Honey's taking a bath."

"Hi, Zelda. I'm Cable—just call me Cable." Zelda was the spitting image of the stereotypical babe hidden behind thick glasses who walked around with the body of one of Rubens' *Three Graces*. She led me to the kitchen and offered me a cup of coffee. All she had on was a thin bathrobe and her huge tits and nipples stood at attention like the Queen's Guard. It was mildly distracting as I tried to make small talk and drink my coffee.

"I—I, uh, understand you're studying to be a botanist—and if so, what made you chose that subject as a career possibility?" I asked.

"Easy. My Dad's Franchard Blodgett, creator of the world's largest strawberry. So, while he's focusing in on huge commercial fruit, I'm developing the next giant house plant that will become the rage of suburbia, U.S.A. Right now Honey's bedroom has been overtaken by a *Monstera deliciosa*, guaranteed to grow six feet high and four-feet wide."

"I'm impressed," I said as Honey came into the room, also adorned with nothing more than a bathrobe.

She came over and kissed me. "Good morning, Officer Denning. Are you hungry?" I didn't answer, but just looked over that beautiful body of hers.

"Uhhh…ha! I think I'd better get dressed for school," Zelda Blodgett said and excused herself.

"So? Am *I* the first thing on your menu this morning? From your glassy stare, it kind of looks that way."

I took a deep breath. "What more can I say? I'm a red-blooded, horny guy a lot of the time. I couldn't get you out of my head all night while Mario and I were on patrol. Stupid, right? I'm usually not such a dummy, falling for a dame after one night of around-the-world in the sack."

"Is that how you see me? Around the world in a sack?"

I laughed at her sense of humor. "Yeah, what else are babe's good for?" I ribbed her. "You see, for me it's babes, booze and Lucky Strikes—my big three, Miss Combes."

She came over and opened her robe right in front of me. "Here, buster, let's let a boob suck on another couple of boobs." She stuck those lovely, warm breasts up to my mouth. I licked them, fondled them and then started obeying the lady. The sucking response made her moan and she grabbed my hand and pulled me down the hall into her bedroom. Just before I lost all sense of reason, I got a glimpse of Zelda's *Monstera deliciosa*, but for the moment I was more intensely focused on Honey's *labia majora*.

That evening as Mario and I readied for our nightshift, Sergeant O'Flaherty called us into his office. "You're off the Ardizzone case. Don't be goin' back to pester Dr. Sandor, ya don't wanna know who the little guy was—and don't be askin' any more questions—got it?"

I glanced at Mario. "So you're saying that everything is now resolved to the department's satisfaction?"

"I didn't say that, Denning."

"May I ask then, what was it you did say, sergeant?" I persisted.

"Get outta here, now!" he shouted. Mario and I left with that feeling something was wrong but there was nothing we could do about it.

About mid-way through our shift we decided to play Rover Boys and sneaked into the County Morgue. As fully uniformed policemen we had no problem getting past the outer desk. But poking around and not being discovered by Sandor would be a challenge. We went into the records room and checked recent-deceased files with a flashlight. We found Ardizzone and learned he was released to a funeral home. That would be *some funeral*, I thought. Since there was no name, the little guy with the big teeth couldn't be traced. By now the county had probably burned the body. Anything of substance at all was the golden throat hanging in Sandor's suspension fluid in that strange, smelly room he called home.

We made our way down the darkened halls until we found the room. It was locked. Mario was an ace locksmith from his youth and soon he had clicked the door open. The flashlight revealed *#1602-Blinthe* was missing! My gut had told me that would be the case and that the corpse did have a name, Blinthe. Not an Italian after all.

"Mario!" I whispered to my buddy. "Guess where we're goin'

soon?"

"Knowing you, I won't even take a guess, Cable," he whispered back.

Luckily, we made our way out of the morgue safely and soon were parked by an all-night diner near 11ᵗʰ and Alvarado. "So this is the irony, Mario. That man with the golden-lined throat was housing a lot more than some fairy dust for the mob. I saw a larger than normal indentation in the lingual tonsil area, just behind where the tongue would be."

"You mean Blinthe or whoever he was had no tongue?" Mario asked, cutting his fork into a piece of apple pie.

"No, I didn't say that—but it's brilliant, Mario! Maybe the guy didn't have a tongue! Who bothered to check on our preliminary look-see?"

"So who's gonna tell you now? The dead don't talk last time I inquired. And there's probably no record of the poor cuss—especially if Sandor already cremated him down to ashes."

I thought quick. "Sandor. There's no one else. We've gotta shake up the old doc."

"He'll bitch to O'Flaherty—we might lose our jobs, Cable. Thanks, but no thanks. Why in the hell are you so curious about mob shit—especially when it comes to the dead ones?"

"It's more than that. Don't you feel it? There's a whole mystery behind this thing—and you know me, that's what I love best—rooting out the weasels and getting to the truth.'

"*You* go back and talk to Sandor. I'm your pal, but I've been doing a lot of thinking lately, Cable. I'm gonna marry Rosalie Elena and live a straight and narrow life. I can't be jeopardizing my future by running off on crazy adventures with you."

"Will you at least go to Ardizzone's funeral with me?"

"Why in the hell would you want to do that?"

"Because I want to be seen. I want them to know I *know*."

"Shit, man, they'll kill you. Sorry, Cable, I'm your pal for life, but some things I just can't do. I gotta start thinkin' about married life—and not just about myself—you know, kids and the whole shebang!"

We left the morgue that night all right, but what we were learning about this whole thing was beginning to stink to high heaven—and then there's all the things we *didn't* know.

IRONY OF THE BELLA NOTTE

Affonso Amadore was a medium-sized man with a big sincere smile and a carefully waxed moustache. He loved opera and the Italian and Neapolitan songs best, but non-Italian Americans paid most of his bills, so he had learned to enjoy the American Popular Standard tune, sung by a handsome young fellow or a classy babe with a low-cut sequined gown accompanied by a small combo of four to six pieces.

I was pleasantly surprised to discover Honey wasn't nervous when the streetcar let us off on La Cienega. The *Bella Notte* stood ground level, was decorated in fancy chandeliers, deep-red flocked wallpaper and a nice-sized little stage with two fixed spotlights hanging from corners in the back of the room. I introduced Honey to Mr. Amadore and he courteously took her hand and kissed it. "Signorina, I'ma hoping thatta you sing-a as-a nice as-a you looka....eh?"

"I hope so, too, Mr. Amadore," Honey said. "Do you have an accompanist?"

Amadore whistled and a tall, lean man came out from the kitchen. "This-a—this is-a our cook-a, eh? Signor Carlo Anselmo. He canna play anything-a you canna throw at 'im, eh?" he laughed.

Honey and Anselmo shook hands and went up to the stage.

He looked at the music Honey handed him. "Nice-a song… whatta key are we gonna play for da nice-a people-a, eh?"

"E-flat will do just fine, thanks," Honey answered.

Soon the two of them launched into a wonderful version of *It Had to Be You* and Affonso Amadore smiled. She started it slow, and made it into a romantically sexy song. For the second chorus, she stepped it up and I could see old Affonso tapping his feet. He *really* liked Honey. Somehow I could hear in her voice the lyrics were, at least in part, meant for me. '*I wandered around and finally found somebody who, could make me be true, could make me be blue, and even be glad, just to be sad, thinking of you…*"

All activity ceased in the restaurant when Honey sang. That was a good sign. I hadn't noticed until she launched into the slow part of the song, but standing in the background and leaning against a wall was a man who evoked something in me I didn't like and it turned my alarm system on.

Even the hired help applauded wildly when Honey finished. She had done a hell of a job and had all the makings of a real pro. Amadore came up and kissed her hand again. "Signorina! Signorina! Che bella! You are hired!"

I had been sitting at the back of the room when Honey thanked him and started to walk toward me. All of a sudden this guy who'd been watching her like a hawk came up and stopped her. "Miss—I'm sorry I missed your name, but I was very impressed with your singing. I'm Frank Laggore. Signore Amadore is wise to hire you. I'm sure you'll bring him a lot of business." He glanced over at me. "Are you with someone—or may I drive you home?"

"My name is Honey Combes, Mr. Laggore, pleased to meet you," Honey responded. "But yes, thank you, I'm with someone." Then she walked away toward me, the strange anxious man watched her every move. He stood about five-ten with a very white skin and clean-shaven face. He wore an immaculate suit with black-and-white patent leather shoes. He looked toward me and scowled, then turned and exited through the swinging kitchen doors.

"Babe—you were great! Didn't I tell you? It's that *golden throat*," I said as I got up and hugged Honey. Then I kissed her and got red lipstick on my face. I got out a handkerchief and wiped it off. "So, is this how you mark your men?"

I could tell that Laggore creep had upset her. "Thanks, Cable—easy gig here. I do like Mr. Amadore—but that other character—what in the hell do you think he was doing here in the middle of the afternoon? He gave me the creeps."

"Me, too, doll. I've seen the kind before. He works for someone in the mob, I'll wager, and maybe sells illegal booze, drugs or pretty white dames who have a lot of talent in certain places."

"Let's get out of here," Honey murmured.

"Yeah, and celebrate, kid." The irony at the *Bella Notte* that afternoon was the fact that I knew the more I plugged Honey into the entertainment world, the more I would risk losing her. It wouldn't even be her fault, it was just that people sold parts of themselves in the pursuit of their drives and ambitions. And some people, once pointed in the right direction, were unstoppable. I had a hunch Honey was one of *them*. But I believed in her, I believed in her talent—and sometimes we have to sacrifice our selfish desires for the bigger picture. That's how I felt about Honey.

We went to *Clifton's Cafeteria* downtown. We sat at a table on the mezzanine looking across from each other. She had a lot of love in her eyes. "You know, Cable, as much as I loved singing this afternoon, I was singing because of you—and to you. It wasn't even the job thing, but my heart was saying how lucky I am to have you—especially when that creep showed up and I was forced to make a comparison." Then she checked out my eyes. She was good at that. "I *do* have you, don't I?"

I took her hands and cupped them in mine. "You bet, babe.

I'm not sure just how it happened, but yeah, you're the tops on my list of dolls."

"List?" she repeated me.

"Just kidding. You keep me happy, toots. I can't even think of another woman right now. I just hope I can keep up with you. I have this feeling your career is gonna take off and leave me in the dust."

Her eyes misted a little. "No, Cable, I'm not made that way. I like balance. And I could not imagine not having your body next to mine at night—or sacrificing that opportunity to be shooting on a movie set all day with a bunch of ego-maniacs. I've seen them, some of them come in the club to check out the new babes in town so they can screw them while they're promising them the moon—and a starlet's contract."

"Sounds to me like you've got it together, sweetheart. I'm proud of you for doing your homework—and you're not even a cop, are you?"

"No, but you are—and that worries me. Is it something you're simply crazy about—besides me, that is?"

I snickered. "You got it. There are two things I love most in this world. Making love to you and chasing down bad guys and seeing justice done."

"Somehow I like the first part better. What will become of you, Cable? You know, it's getting kind of serious with me—I mean, the way I feel about you and a possible future—"

"—I don't think we can go there today, toots. The quick answer is a guy like me puts himself on the line every day, one way or another, gathering up the guts to take down another hoodlum when the opportunity arises. Trouble is, I'm fighting the mob and city hall at the same time. I never considered myself as marriage material. On my time off—even how *you* met me, I'm out boozing and womanizing at the local speakeasy—that's what I do—drink to numb myself from the reality of that high brick wall in front of me, smoke to hurry along the disease that might someday kill me—and play in the hay with beautiful dames who might also happen to sing. I told Mario that I might be getting hung up on you—but it's not a good idea. You see, babe, if I let my heart rule my head, I'll be in deep shit and there'll be no one to catch me in free fall when you go away or find that rich, handsome, educated dude that *didn't* come from the wrong side of the tracks—"

"—Cable, it would never be like that with me!"

"Please let me finish. Some lives are penciled out ahead of time, Honey, and mine is one of 'em. If you can enjoy me for now and stay in that magic, that sweet spot of warm nights and great sex, lots of laughs, a few drinks and most excellent companionship—then I'm your man—"

"—Cable! Stop, please! You *are* my man, like it or not, buster," she came back with her eyes misting and her voice firm. "There are some things not even *you* can control, Mr. Police Officer, so don't get so verbose and make me fall again for that fast patter and cover-up language you use to conceal a hurt I've seen deep inside of you that I didn't cause."

There fell a silence as we sat looking at each other across the table with the din of Clifton's Cafeteria in the background. "Damn," I finally said, "you're one hell of a woman, Honey Combes." I smiled at her and toasted her with my glass of water. "Am I, uh, to assume this is our first argument?"

"Never, Mr. Denning. There isn't time in life to argue. I just want you to love me—I can't make you do that. Even in magic moments when you are able to accept us, belonging to *us*, and no one else. I never thought of marriage as an option for us, Cable. And I don't think I can have children. The world is too cruel and I'd be selfish to wish that upon someone I love. I'm too damned independent and you are too…too much of a risk. I'd never know when they might be carrying you home in a pine box—and I couldn't be that bonded to you and have to say the last good-bye at a cemetery."

I looked at Honey Combes feeling a lot of love, because this moment was tearing apart all that insulation that kept me from freely giving of myself—and the security that nothing lasts forever anyhow, so what was I afraid of? "So…babe…thanks… thanks for that intelligent little head of yours. Yeah, I'm your guy, and if you'll have me warts and all, I think I can stick it out with you until—whenever, whatever—"

"—whatever, Cable. Don't think about it. Just love me. Because I'm going to love you, Mr. Denning. Somehow the rest takes care of itself."

I needed to change the subject. "I—I, uh, need to tell you something, babe. Tomorrow I'm going to a funeral—no, don't worry—it's not mine— yet. Some big thug with the local branch of *Cosa Nostra*. The reason I'm telling you is, that I'm kinda *off-the-record* involved in a mysterious case that started at the county morgue and is going to end up at Hollywood Cemetery tomorrow, I hope. I might be approached by some pretty tough players and if I'm threatened, it will tell me I'm on the right track. Now, if for some reason I don't call you tomorrow evening before you get to the dance club, call Mario." I took a pen and scribbled down Mario Angelo's phone number and handed it to her. "Tell him I was right about Ardizzone and the little creep that got it, but not to tell O'Flaherty—got it?"

She looked at me as she took the paper. "This is how you live your life? On the edge all the time?"

"Yeah, it gives me some fresh air, doll, a kind of high you can't get anywhere else—except maybe in bed with you. So you see little deaths occur around us all the time, some inside of us, some outside—and then someday it all catches up with you and someone's crying at your funeral."

"God, Cable, in a way I wish you wouldn't let me know what you're actually doing out there. It scares me just to picture you mixed up with those grease balls. I know some of them. They come into *Gregario's* and round up some of the girls for the night—you know, the big parties up on Mulholland Drive some gangster throws every night. They keep pressuring me to go, but I hate who they are and what they do to the women who don't have a clue about what's going to happen to them. Some of them disappear…just disappear, Cable."

"Yeah, I hear you, babe. You stay as far away as you can from those mugs. White slavery is one of their games, and pretty young dolls like you can easily end their days as a drugged-up sex slave in some wealthy Asian's harem."

"Oh, God, don't tell me that. It gives me the shivers."

I got up and took out some money to pay the check, and smiled at this lovely babe. "Well, on the bright side of the world, today was a *red-letter-day* for you, *Golden Throat*. I'm your number one fan, you know. I hope you'll remember me and autograph a picture for me when you're famous and the world holds you up there beyond my reach."

She took my hand as we walked downstairs to the cash register. "I'll never be out of your reach, Cable Denning. You're the only man I want to be famous for--and don't forget it."

We walked to pick up the streetcar. "I—I, uh, sort of had an important question to ask you. Neither of us discussed it, and I fault myself for not checking in with you the night we first—uh, you know… Anyway, you've had a constant spate of unprotected sex, in case you hadn't noticed."

She smiled and laughed lightly. "Oh yes, I noticed, lover man. But I can't conceive, Cable—something doesn't work in that department, it seems I don't have eggs that can be fertilized, if you wish a clinical description." Then she tapped me on the shoulder. "But keep trying anyway, Mister, the more you try, the more I like it." She stood up on tiptoe and kissed me.

We laughed and got on the streetcar. "Just let me know if I'm trying too hard—"

"—*hard* is how I like it, buster. Keep it comin', I'm your gal."
I took her home and then went back to my flat where I found
Mario fast asleep. Soon I had joined him. A couple of hours of
shut-eye was better than none, I thought.

CHAPTER 4

FUNERAL FOR ONE

At the last minute, Mario decided to attend the funeral with me. You never saw such formal pomp mixed with an ample serving of bullshit. Even the Dragna Family had the nerve to show up, dressed to the nines and brilliantly composed, standing back from the Ardizzone mobsters, friends and relatives. In 1927, the Hollywood Memorial Cemetery looked sort of like a golf course with mausoleums and tombstones. The L.A. mob was expanding and most of the local big shots attended. A few I had seen before. In fact, that slimy creature who showed up the *Bella Notte*, Frank Laggore, was standing with the Dragna clan.

Mob funerals always reminded me of a bad melodrama where everybody pretended, but you weren't supposed to notice. Guys in their ties and immaculate suits bulging from packing iron, stood piously with their hands folded in front of them innocently. Back where Mario and I stood, several bodyguards were standing in outposts looking for trouble. The service was Roman Catholic, and the priest did his thing with the words and holy water over the coffin as they lowered ol' Ernesto "Iron Man" Ardizzone into the earth. I'd never met the man, but when things began to break up at the gravesite, I noticed a few of the immediate family scoping Mario and me. We were on our way out to catch the streetcar when three of the goons ran up to us. "Thanks…for coming to Ernesto's last rites, officers. I'm Jack Dragna and I know you two are cops. I need to talk to you for a minute, if you don't mind."

"Yeah, sure, Dragna. We just came to pay our respects, seeing we've been scraping off Mr. Ardizzone's dirty work from the city sidewalks for some years now."

He called us aside and we walked to the protection of one

of those large pieces of granite where they laid to rest whole families. "Let's hope…a new era has begun, gentlemen. But I—I, uh, need to caution you both on one point. My family and I would consider it a favor if you and your partner stopped snooping around down at the morgue. You're never gonna find that missing thing you're looking for. If…you value your safety, and wish to continue serving in the Los Angeles police department with our blessing, I would take this advice…to heart. This must not get back to Matrangas nor should his business dealings with the police department be disturbed—he thinks it below our duty to warn off police officers, so I'm telling you on the Q.T." He started to walk away, then turned back to face me. "Oh, one other thing. We're gonna get very involved in the entertainment industry—so if you value your little squeeze, the dame who's gonna work for Affonso Amadore at the *Bella Notte*, I urge you to play it close to the hip, if you get my drift."

I looked at Dragna and then over to what must have been his brother Louie, and father, Attilio. Both of them had gangster written all over their faces, not to mention the family resemblance. But who in the hell was *Matrangas*? That was a name I hadn't heard before. "You know, Dragna, because we're in polite company today—oh yeah, and grieving about your plugging ol' Ernie and all—I won't cross that line and invoke your wrath. But I will say this….you know I *know*, and the cop in me is kinda like an old bulldog, he hangs on to his quarry by locking his jaws on it. And right now, my jaws are locked on certain *unsolved mysteries* down at the *rue morgue*, shall we say? I don't let go easy, Dragna. You see, fear is what you count on to scare people off—and if that doesn't work, they end up missing. I grew up with your kind—in fact, I used to *be* sort of your kind until I jumped tracks to the other side of town. So, you do your job, and I'll do mine."

Jack Dragna was taken aback by my boldness in the face of danger. Mario was tugging at my sleeve to get the hell out of the situation. "That…could be very dangerous to your health. There's such a thing as knowing too much for your own good. You're one hell of a gutsy guy, I'll say that—stupid, but gutsy. I kinda like your nervy patter. What's your name?"

"Denning…*Officer* Cable Denning to you."

"Well, Denning, in a way I'm sorry we've had this conversation and I can see we're not on the same side. For now, let's just say you're on my 'checklist' and I wouldn't push that envelope any further if I were you. It's liable to get you—well, you know what I mean. I hope I won't be seeing you around, Denning."

With that they moved off, leaving Mario and I watching the priest and his altar boys pack up his stuff and meander across the cemetery toward the chapel "Gees, Cable, what the hell? You're gonna get us killed, buddy! What craziness possessed you to talk to him like that? See? That's why I didn't want to come. Now I'm marked by the mob for being in collusion with you."

"I'm sorry, Mario, but truth is truth, and I have a funny thing inside of me, like an alarm, that goes off when I hear bullshit from big mouths like Jack Dragna. We can't cower under the pressure, pal, because if we do it means we're no better than they are—and what the hell more is the present police force than a patsy for those hoodlums driving away in their black Cadillacs?"

Mario reiterated he would not attend any more mafia funerals with me and we were on our way back to the streetcar stop when a man called to us from behind. We turned and there stood a very handsome middle-aged man with nice eyes and a good face. He cut a suave figure in a light-grey pinstripe suit and wore a nice grey fedora. "Officer Denning, may I have a word with you privately?" He looked at Mario who threw his hands up in the air with an expression that said we were never going to get out of the Hollywood Cemetery.

"Are you friend or foe?" I asked, somewhat flustered.

"Definitely, friend," he said in a light, warm voice. At closer look his eyes seemed fathomless, as if he looked right through me without even trying. I thought it curious, but I was young and still wet behind the ears in a lotta ways.

I asked Mario to hang out for a minute while the gentleman walked a few yards with me down the sidewalk. "Mr. Denning, my name is Joe Lorena, I am *consigliere* for the Dragna family. I cannot caution you enough about the danger you may have gotten yourself into today. I am also concerned about the people around you, like Mr. Angelo and your new friend, Honey Combes."

"How come you guys even know all about the dames I hang out with? Don't you ever mind your own business?"

"That *is* my business, Mr. Denning. I am counselor to the family, and as such, I must find out everything there is to know about certain parties that in some way or other affect us. Surely, you understand. And as far as Honey Combes is concerned, I suggest it is in your best interest to protect her by fading out of her life and not getting her involved in any of the forbidden fruit you seem determined to pick. In fact, I urge you to let your relationship with Miss Combes terminate so she does not become implicated in the future. Same goes for your partner, Mr. Angelo. You are about to walk a lonely road, Mr. Denning. I hope you hear what I say and take it in the best of spirits. As I said, my job is to conciliate, so let's keep the peace, okay?"

"You guys break me up! You go around dictating other peoples' lives, warning them, admonishing them—and it's all done with a smile, now, isn't it, Consigliere? C'mon now, what kind of dog shit are you feeding me here?"

Those warm, brown eyes looked at me like an alien checking out an earthling. "How can I get you to understand? You're young and fearless, it appears. That can be a lethal combination. You can't wage a one-man war against the family. Just as we are not in control of our lives, you are not in control

49

of things that happen in this city. Other forces mold what happens in the end, Mr. Denning. Please, I urge you, reconsider and drop the current girlfriend, the Blinthe case and lay low while you are disconnecting yourself from Honey."

"Suddenly you're on a first-name basis now? Who in the hell are you guys, anyhow? You got some gall, I'll say." I was also thinking of something else. "And tell me, who in the hell is this *Matrangas?*"

He looked at me with a little apprehension in his eyes. "He's—he's the man who pulls the strings from Chicago. His investments into our family are considerable. You might say, he owns us. But we don't like to look at it that way. He's powerful and dangerous to his enemies, believe me."

"Thanks for the warning, Mr. Lorena, but I'll take my chances."

I left Joe Lorena and joined Mario. Lorena stood there on the sidewalk, watching us. I could imagine what he might be thinking: *this poor cop is toast!*

BLOOD AND ELEVATORS

By the time we got back to our apartment it was late afternoon and I called Honey to tell her I was safe and sound. She seemed relieved and I told her I'd see her as soon as I could, but lots of stuff was on the burner just now. Mario and I went on patrol and it was about 2:30 a.m. when I called in to our station. We were dispatched to the Beverly Hills Hotel off Sunset Boulevard. Apparently some poor sap ended up dead in an elevator from being stabbed in key places. When we got there the management had sealed off the area and guests were required to take the stairs to their rooms. "Son of a bitch, Cable, this is the sixth homicide we've been on this week," Mario was saying as we entered the elevator. A very well dressed small man with broken glasses and a moustache lay in a pool of blood on the elevator floor.

"Yeah, you know the saying, Mario, when it rains it pours, and it's been pouring a lot lately in L.A." I bent down to examine the body. "Did they call the Coroner?"

"Yeah, I think. It's this kinda stuff that revolts me, makes me mad as hell that people go around bumping each other off—"

"—well, at least for the most part, buddy, they kill each *other*. Once in a while an innocent bystander gets it, but this—this is definitely organized crime at work." I turned the body over slightly. "Look…here…see how the knife wounds are perfectly made. With a very sharp blade directly into the heart from the right angle, and then into the gut a couple of times for good measure."

"You can toss it off, Cable—I can't. I go home with it."

"Then you should consider working an inside job—maybe you're not cut out for the terrible truth that all people are potential killers—and victims. Maybe that's why I could beat the shit out of you that day when we were kids. Admit it to yourself if you haven't got the stomach for it, Mario. And you know it's all right….don't sweat it. We all have our specialties. This one happens to be mine, that's all."

"Yeah, well, patrolling with you in a squad car is one thing, but these gruesome killings, night after night—"

"—hey! What's this?" I noticed a piece of paper clutched in the hand of the victim. I carefully pried it loose from his death grip. "Son-of-a-bitch, Mario! Look at this…I don't believe it—it's the label from Sandor's jar containing John Doe's golden throat! *#1602-Blinthe*! What in the shit is going on here, pal?"

Mario had seen the label stuck on Sandor's jar. "Crap, Cable! What are the chances of this showing up here? You don't suppose it—"

"—it was a setup, intentional? Nope, I don't think so. It's just a strange set of coincidences we happened to be the cops called to the scene first." I rifled through the breast pocket of the corpse. I took out his wallet. A Zurich automobile driver's license read…*Harold Eisenstadt*. "Crap, Mario, he wasn't even an American. Doesn't that sound odd to you?"

"The whole damned thing is odd to me," Mario responded, checking out the dead man's shoes. "He's also been in an area with red clay and not too long ago," he observed. "*Very* red. Here…look at this."

I checked it out. "Good catch, Mario. You see, maybe you'd be a good forensic investigator."

"Naw, I like it better out here with you. It's more hands-on. It's just the murders that kind of depress me. You know I'm thinking of marrying Rosalie Elena and having kids. What do I tell them about the world we live in?"

"Yeah, that's a big one, but we've already had this conversation." Just then the Coroner came in. We told him what we knew and left, except I told Mario to stay mum about the piece of paper I had tucked into my pocket.

When we got out into traffic, Mario was thinking about what I had done. "You know, that's withholding evidence, what you just did. It could be a major clue in cracking the case for the guys who follow up on it."

"I'm counting on just that," I said.

"What does that mean? You're not a detective, you know. You're just a cop and you happen to work for the police department—and that piece of paper should've by rights gone to the coroner and then on to the detective division. You're a three-year veteran, for God's sake. You know better."

"Is this a reprimand, Mario? Because if it is, I'm gonna tell you something. That piece of paper would sit in a file for months gathering moss while six detectives work on piled-up caseloads until doomsday. Is that what you would want, Mr. Seek-out-Justice cop?"

"No, but you can't take the law into your own hands, Cable."

"Then…my friend, who will? I was born with this sniffer of mine and a gut that tells me when something's right—and when something's wrong. And this whole stinkin' mess is wrong, Mario. If I don't take this bull by the horns, nobody will. You gotta remember, we work for cops who work for the mob who happen to be in bed with City Hall. So who's gonna do something about something they don't want something done about?"

Mario remained silent for a while and I lit up a Lucky Strike. "Well, I guess that's where we're different, you dumb Mic. So what are you gonna do now—become a two-man elimination team?"

"That's the easy part. Sniff out old doc Sandor and pin him against the wall. I sense—no, I *know* he's hiding a lot more than he's telling."

VAULTING WITH DEATH

The next night was a night off and I told Mario I was going to catch the enigmatic Dr. Sandor in his lair. My partner and friend feared for me, but understood that I had to do what I had to do. After all, our growing up together told us that if you didn't watch out for your own butt in our neighborhoods, you'd lose it—and just maybe your life. It was a tough, survival-of-the-fittest jungle, poor and struggling—so the poor stole from the poor a lot and when the pressure got too great for them to handle, they started beating each other up, unleashed testosterone on dirty streets littered with garbage and blood. I also called Honey and told her I might come by after my evening appointment, but I didn't tell her where it was or with whom.

It was about seven p.m. when I got to the county morgue and started tracking down Sandor. I found him in a basement laboratory, that place where he took the removed organs and such he wanted to keep and dropped them in formaldehyde. "Dr. Sandor," I called out as I approached him. The place had an echo and our voices bounced all over the place.

He turned around to look at me. He raised those huge eyebrows of his in surprise. "Officer Denning! You keep showing up uninvited, like a bad penny. But I *was* warned about you. Just recently, as a matter of fact."

I approached the tall, gaunt man. "Yeah, I'll bet it was Dragna and his gang. Seems I attended Ardizzone's funeral yesterday and found a curious assortment of hoodlums hanging around the coffin like grave robbers, ready to pounce when the coast was clear. You'd have been right at home."

"A rather quaint way to describe a funeral, Officer Denning. I notice that you are not in uniform—am I to gather…this is an…informal visit?"

"Well, not exactly, Sandor. You see, I've kinda got a problem. There's a stiff arriving any minute upstairs for you." I reached in my pocket. "I have a hunch he died for this. *#1602-Blinthe.* Sound familiar?"

"It was stolen, Officer Denning, from the sample room. I fear someone else, other than known parties, was seeking the gold-lined throat."

"Who was Blinthe? And why didn't he have a belly button? You'd better show and tell quick, doc, I don't have a lotta patience for bullshit."

"I don't know—a biological anomaly. He was nobody. I don't know who lined his throat—or why."

"Oh…doc…ya gotta come up with better stuff than that. I have this gut that goes off like an alarm bell when bullshit gets thrown my way. I'm kind of a *truth guy* and this whole Ardizzone and Blinthe thing doesn't add up in my book. But that's not what I came for."

"Indeed? There's more? Now you've piqued my curiosity, Officer Denning. Intuition, you know, can be...a dangerous thing. It would be one of the first things I would...*operate out* of a human being had I those...powers. 'Gut feelings,' as you describe, can be very misleading—and inaccurate as well. I'm a very busy man, so I would appreciate—"

"—there was something missing from the lingual cavity on Blinthe, wasn't there, Sandor? The gold lining was to protect whatever was housed in that nice little place safely tucked away in a dead man's mouth. You see, I've learned to put two-and-two together, Sandor. C'mon....you're a lot brighter than this! Or maybe....dumber than you look because whoever you're doing this for—and whatever you're concealing, they will eventually kill you for it. You must know that."

Sandor glowered at me. "A sleuth with...only partial knowledge...is very dangerous indeed, Mr. Detective. And assuming you are correct to some degree, what object could possibly have been lodged in the dead man's throat? And even if it were so, it's biologically impossible—he would constantly gag because the motor nerves located there in back of the tongue trigger the throat to convulse and the stomach to become nauseated. So I really don't know what you're talking about."

I knew Sandor wasn't the type who responded to subtle tactics, so I approached him and put my .38 in his ribs. "You're lying, doc. Things are exploding in my head because I know this thing is a lot bigger than you or me, somehow—and you have access to it. It either belongs to the city, county or a museum—or your mysterious benefactors—now what's it gonna be?"

"Threats...will avail you nothing, Officer Denning." He looked around the room, a strange stare coming over his eyes.

"Do you think I could have lived all these years among the dead and fear death itself? You are... mistaken, my foolish man. You can't play cat-and-mouse with me."

"Well, then, try this!" I said, yanking his arm behind him until he yelled out, his sound reverberating throughout the room. "Where I come from, coercion is an art, Sandor. So... what is it you stole from them?"

"Please!" he cried out. "I don't mind dying—but I cannot tolerate pain. All right, all right. But you must know, once you have seen what I have to show you, your life will be, for all intents and purposes—*over*."

"Let me make that decision, Sandor. Lead the way."

Still at gunpoint he led me to a vault on the far side of the laboratory. He knew the combination to the lock that sealed the door and soon it opened. He pulled a string and an eerie blue light bulb went on. Silently he approached a little metal box. He opened it. He withdrew an egg-shaped golden capsule about the size that would've fit nicely into that depression in Blinthe's throat cavity. It was finely etched with mysterious inscriptions. What was weird was that the blue light seemed to make the thing glow from within itself and the lettering showed up more clearly, even symbols that didn't appear until the blue light was applied. Sandor held it up to the light. "The *God of Our Fathers*...it is the Great Omnipresent...housed inside," he smiled a rather demented smile. "The secret of all life is etched onto a golden microfilm, painstakingly photographed from the original scroll."

"So what the hell does it do that's causing so much shit?"

Again, holding the capsule up against the blue light, he spoke as if he were mesmerized by its influence. He slid the capsule open, and took out a small bright gold rectangle. "Here! Look!" I came over and inspected both the outer capsule and the tablet inside. They were perfectly rendered although the tablet was miniscule. "The golden etched tablet is best seen with

The Blue Light of Noda. Photonos, the God of Light, and *Audianos, the God of Sound*, fashioned this unique communiqué to reveal the source of creation itself."

"Now you lost me, Sandor." I took my gun and put it in my chest holster. "Now you're talking mythological gibberish—and even if it were true, what possible value would something like that have to a bunch of hoodlums who run the streets of L.A.?"

"An unfathomable amount of *money*, for one thing. It is priceless. From the point of science, the scroll speaks of a new unit of light, a magical property—just now this year, named as *photon*, a basic unit of light that allows electro-magnetic interaction, thus forming *form* via intelligent *intent* in the cosmos. Einstein and others have been investigating it for a while, but they have not yet given it a name. Think of it, Denning—*the why and how of Creation* known, at last."

"You mean to say, this microfilm replica tells us the universe didn't happen by plain ol' incident and accident?"

"Precisely, Denning, precisely. No more guessing about the *origin of the blueprint of Creation.* However, it isn't a religious, but rather a scientific revelation."

"So, why are you telling *me* all of this, Sandor? And how do you know all this shit about it in the first place?"

"I have sources, shall I say? Mr. Blinthe wasn't exactly... what you and I might call *human,* you see. He possessed *other dimensional qualities* to which I gained access, quite by accident. Surely you realize, Denning, even *I* am delighted and surprised to learn of new things...new dimensions." Then he looked up to the ceiling and his eyes were aglow. "To transcend...to wipe aside man's pitiful little accomplishments and see...see the greater glory of a cosmos...filled with superior beings..."

"How do you know I won't take it from you now and make millions from selling it myself?"

"Because, you see, my dear man, part of my motivation is *science*—the other is profit. But…as I told you earlier, officer, you are a dead man, no matter how you slice the cake, now." In deep thought, I started to walk away and made the mistake of turning my back for a split second. Before I could react fast enough, Sandor hit me hard on the head with what felt like a lead pipe he got off the shelf and down I went for the count.

I was whirling in a vortex of sound and light and blackness all at the same time. I felt nausea and elation and pain. I came to in that dark vault of Sandor's. He must have slugged me, locked me in and left me for dead. Well, in the worst-case scenario, I wouldn't have far to go. Just upstairs to one of those slabs. My head pounded until I thought it would burst and I had a goose egg on the back of my skull big enough to excite a kid at Easter. I crawled toward the door. It was probably six-inches thick, made of solid metal and a lock suitable for a bank vault. The air was beginning to get a bit thick and I knew it would only be a matter of time before I'd suffocate—and then it would be all over. Or just beginning…..

Immersed in pitch-blackness can be a frightening thing for us surface creatures whose ordinary stimulus is visual and auditory. Now I had to depend on inner senses and my sense of touch. When one's head is banging and probably has a concussion—or worse—that isn't an easy task. I tried not to think of that moment when my body would consume all the air in that 10' x 12' vault, but it was getting harder to breathe so I tried to minimize my panic and how deep I inhaled. Like a wounded animal, I sat with my back against the vault door, waiting for the inevitable. When pain is so intense, one can't just start reminiscing about life and what you should have done and didn't, who you loved and didn't, what way it could have gone but didn't. But there were good things, too. I was awful young to be dying, I thought. Twenty-seven and I had only begun to know what I wanted to do in this life. Hell, the kids who went off to WWI were as young as sixteen and died in a forgotten trench somewhere on the Russian front, frozen to death.

Unbelievably, just then I could hear the clicking of the tumblers outside on the combination lock. Had that bastard Sandor changed his mind—maybe he didn't want murder on his conscience? Or did someone else regularly visit this inner sanctum? Soon the heavy door swung open and a flashlight spotted me on the floor. "Someone's been locked in here one-hundred percent alright." The little guy drew a gun and put it to my head. "You wouldn't be invitin' any trouble now, would ya? Because if you did, I would have to plug you one-hundred percent," he wheezed.

I could hardly speak I was in so much pain and exhausted. "Hardly. Sandor slugged me with something and I...I went down. I think I may have a concussion or I'm bleeding some-where in my head."

"Now ain't that one-hundred percent too bad," he sneered.

Just then, yet another man entered with a flashlight. I could see he was impeccably dressed, stood about six feet and his black hair shone in the light.

"What do we have here, Jinx?" a very warm, personable voice spoke.

"Found 'im on the floor, boss," the little weasel said. "Do you want me to put 'im one-hundred percent out of his misery? Seems the old doc tried to bash his head in."

The more refined man bent down to look at me. "Who are you?"

"De—De—Denning. Cable Denning. I'm—I'm a cop—Sandor clobbered me by...by surprise..."

"Clobbered...now that's a quaint word. Well, take it easy, officer. We won't have to worry about Doctor Sandor anymore. But you *do* worry me. Do you know why I'm here?"

"I'll...I'll bet the whole mob world...knows why you're here. It's the smell of money...pretty strong in here. So...who are you?" I was glad to be breathing good air again.

"I'm Matrangas. I am the major—you could say—'shareholder' in the Dragna family's chain of fine businesses. They do the work. I collect the profits. Simple, isn't it?" Then he studied me in more detail. "I...I can see you're probably not going to live much longer, so what I tell you really doesn't really matter. That walnut-sized gold capsule Dr. Sandor stole. Do you know where it is? Before he died, he gave us the combination to the safe—and informed us it was *here* we would find it. Is this the reason you will die today? Was it worth it?"

I chuckled to myself half in pain, half in delirium, cursing my luck. Of all my potential rescuers, why did it turn out to be these goons? "Sandor couldn't take pain, could...could he?" I labored under my breath.

"No, as a matter of fact. He died before he could tell me *precisely* where the capsule might be. I hate messy things like this, don't you?"

"I—I don't know. I clean up...after guys like you. L.A. streets are...are re-stocked...with corpses, courtesy of the... the mob...every day...."

"Los Angeles is truly corrupt, I mean, in an obvious manner. You see, I come from Chicago. A long trip to take care of dirty business. This one I preferred to implement *personally*. Isn't that right, Jinx?

"Yeah, boss, one-hundred percent."

"Yeah, I know...Dragna's consigliere briefed me...Lorena..."

"You know, I like Joe. He's an intelligent man. Without him, I'm not so sure I would have invested so heavily into the elimination of Ardizzone in favor of Jack Dragna and his people." Matrangas slowly directed his flashlight around the vault while Jinx stood by still brandishing his weapon. "So...Denning...do you know where the capsule is?"

"Yeah, I do—but—but you'll never find it," I lied. "But I'll make—make a deal. You get me…to a hospital…and I'll write it…on some… paper for you…when—when we get there."

"Why should I do that? Jinx and I can simply tear everything apart in this vault until we find it. Besides, if we take you to emergency, and you actually do survive your head injuries, we'll just have to kill you anyway before you leave the hospital—because now you've seen too much and know much too much. In fact, I'm still in Chicago, right, Jinx?"

"One-hundred percent, boss."

"Save yourself some…some time Matrangas before the competition arrives. *Those…are…my terms…take it or leave it.*"

"Well, I do have the combination to the safe and no one else does except Frank Nance, the coroner, and he would never set foot here, I'm told. I guess you might say it's a win-win situation for me, since Jinx will just have to kill you in your hospital bed when no one's looking. He's exceptionally gifted at strangulation, isn't that right, Jinx?"

"That's for sure, one-hundred percent, boss."

"Is it a deal?" I whispered, almost out of strength. Blood was seeping down my neck from the head wound and my shirt and jacket were soaked with it. I wasn't sure how long I *would* last, but I figured it was my only chance.

"My word is good, Mr. Denning. But I promise only one thing— and that is just to get you to a hospital. You walk in safely, sit down, write out the instructions— and we disappear— until Jinx comes back to perform his deed. And if you're wrong— and give us a bum steer— you'll be dead even sooner, capisce?"

They dragged me to the elevator and up to a back entrance to the morgue. Once there, Jinx busted a lock on the outer door and we escaped in a laundry truck in broad daylight.

The Los Angeles County General Outpatient Department

was jammed and seemed like a madhouse as they half-carried me into the waiting room. I kinda fit because so many people there were bleeding, banged up or in some kind of physical, mental and emotional disarray. As soon as I sat, Matrangas, who really *didn't* fit the scene, gave me a pen and a little notepad. I wrote what I remembered as being the little metal box containing the golden capsule. I hated to betray the little thing, but what was I to do? It was either it—or me. Weak and barely conscious, I handed the pad and pen back to Matrangas. "Good doing business with you, Mr. Denning. Remember, win-win for me, lose-lose for you, capisce? Isn't that right, Jinx?"

"One-hundred percent, boss," the little wind-up phono-graph said. Then they disappeared.

I had to get to a phone to call Mario and Honey. I had no idea what day it was or how many hours I dwelled in the darkness of that vault. I stumbled my way along a wall, down a hallway and almost fell into an office. A pert little brunette caught me. "Lordy, mister! Obviously you need some emergency services, let me help you back."

"No!" I said hoarsely. "I'm a cop and need to use the phone, miss."

"If you're a cop, then call me Clara Bow's grandmother," she said. "Now let me help you back out to take a number and stand in line. We are backed up tonight. Must be the moon."

I reached into my bloody coat and took out my cop's badge...which we had to carry even if we were off duty. The little gal apologized and let me sit at her desk to use the phone while she left the room to give me privacy. I couldn't get a hold of Mario but I was elated when Honey answered her phone. "Honey...it's me...Cable...I'm at County General...please... don't come...I need time..."

She was beside herself with anxiety. "Cable! Cable! I was worried sick! I've been going crazy—not knowing! You're injured, I can tell. County General? I'll be right there!" She hung up before I could say any more. Now she would be tangled up in my web. In my business it was called *guilt by association*. And I wasn't doin' too hot, either. So far what I'd found out wasn't worth all the lives and battle wounds. Then I fainted dead away on the nice little secretary's floor. Over and out.

SNUG AS A BEAR IN A RUG

To this day I'm not sure how it happened or what good Samaritan knew the score and helped me out, but two days later when I woke up I was in some quiet little bedroom in a small cottage in Big Bear Lake, California. It was cool but the sun was shining in through the curtains of a large window and casting a warm, yellow glow on the hardwood floor. How did I get here? Who drove me the 90 miles up the mountain? All I could hear was the steady ticking of an old alarm clock on a nightstand near my bed that read 9:30. I felt my head. It was bandaged and it was still pretty sore. My vision was okay and I could *breathe*, which is a hell of a lot more than I could do locked in Sandor's death-vault. I recalled the events as best I could, seeing Sandor, getting hit after he showed me what he called the *God of Our Fathers* golden capsule. Then just before I ran out of air and suffocated to death, in walks Matrangas and his henchman, Jinx, both salivating for the priceless golden walnut. We make a deal—I tell him where the late Dr. Sandor hid the damn thing—and I go to Los Angeles General Hospital… only to wind up in this place! Matrangas' promise was that the little weasel Jinx, would kill me anyway if I hung around. Someone knew the whole scenario and rescued me. But for what? What did I know that they wanted? I was beginning to think like a detective. I liked that about me.

Suddenly I heard a key turn and a door open. Someone was coming toward me. I was naked, had no gun and my head was still wrapped up like a mummy. In walked a white-haired man with a satchel in hand. "Officer Denning. Ah, I see you have returned to take your place among the living. I'm Doctor Gilbreth." He came over to the bedside, took out his stethoscope from the satchel and began to check me out. "Hmmm. Alright…pulse strong…heart beat…good. You do seem to be recovering remarkably well."

"Hello, doc. Forgive me if I look and act surprised—but how in the hell did I get here? Last thing I remember, I had passed out on a floor at Los Angeles County General Hospital. How long have I been here?"

"You've been here six days. I don't know much about the details at the hospital. Simply stated, I was contacted by someone in your department, a Captain Treadwell. He said they were sending you up here to Big Bear for recovery and would I be the attending physician during your stay. They also said you were in some kind of protected witness program. When you arrived there was an envelope filled with cash—more than enough to pay for the lodgings here, Ginny and my fees. That's all I know."

I had never heard of a 'Captain Treadwell' and cash in an envelope was not the way the bureaucratic police department worked. "Tell me—do you know a Mario Angelo or one Miss Honey Combes? Or my Sergeant, O'Flaherty?" I was still puzzled as hell.

"No, I'm afraid not. But you will be here for some time yet, Officer Denning. Your x-ray did not confirm the presence of any fissures in the cranium or undue swelling. But you do have a secondary concussion."

"So how long am I here for, doc? And who's Ginny?"

"She's your private cook and housekeeper. She'll be along as usual around eleven and then again tonight at six. She's very dependable. I brought her into the world, I did, not that many years ago." He threw me a professional smile and cleared his throat. He took a bottle of pills out of his satchel. "Now that you're conscious and functional, take two of these now and two in the evening. Pain pills may constipate you. Take an apple a day for the bowels. That should do the trick. You will be here for at least another two weeks."

"Two weeks! How in the hell am I going to stay penned up here with nothing to do except watch the sun rise and set and listen to the birdies chirp out there on the porch? And you know, doc, I have a question. Why, when a doctor prescribes dosages of medication, does he say take *two* of this and *two* of that? Why can't one pill contain double the strength?"

"An intelligent question. I don't know. Maybe the pharmaceutical companies make twice as much? I'll have to read up on that."

I was restless, I needed to contact people, get to the bottom of this murky mystery I was in the middle of. "Uh, is there a phone in the house? I gotta make a few calls."

"No phones. In fact, any undue stress on your brain is not recommended, Officer. I'm sure all the right people have been notified." The doc shook my hand and left, saying he'd return tomorrow to check up on me.

After he left, I got out of bed, put on some clothes and rummaged around the joint. The icebox had a few vegetables and fruit, some beef jerky and juices. I opened the front door. It opened out into a wooden deck and we were overlooking the lake, facing East, I surmised. I was dyin' for a Lucky Strike and a shot of good gin. But where in the crap would I get the gin in this Podunk place? What a hell of a note, stuck up here in Paradise without a pair of wings to fly me back to my City of Angels.

About eleven a 1921 Studebaker convertible drove up. A petite little gal about five-foot two got out, reached over the seat for a basket and came toward me. This little thing was a dish! She was probably about eighteen or nineteen, flapper-cut dark hair, happy blue eyes and a rather frizzy light-yellow dress that showed off her ample figure quite well. "Officer Denning? I'm so glad you're up. I never thought you'd wake up. I'm Ginny Fullerton, your food girl—and housekeeper. How are you feeling?"

I took a deep breath, inhaling this fresh new little lady with the dark-blue eyes and very red lipstick smile. "Thanks, Miss Fullerton. I'm doing a lot better. Especially, now that you're here. Please…call me Cable…just plain ol' Cable." All of a sudden I felt embarrassed. How in the hell did I go to the bathroom during all this time? "Did you, uh…also attend to my bathroom functions—I mean, one never knows about these things…"

She giggled as she approached me and opened the front door. "No, but I watched the nurse bathe you—Mrs. Crochetti—you never know…"

"Never know what?"

"When you might have to do that for a husband or children—you know what I mean, don't you?"

I was thinking about the enemas and peeing in my diapers I must have done in these past few days. It was a shitty feeling, to put in specific terms. But I chuckled it off. "Yeah, I guess I do. I don't suppose you could take me down to the local store so I can get some cigarettes. I'm goin' nuts with starin' at the walls. Not even a radio in the joint. I could use some gin, too. English gin, the best kind."

"I can bring a radio from home. Oh, but I don't think I can take you to the store. The doctor said complete and quiet rest for you—uh, Cable."

"Well, Miss—"

"—Ginny, please call me plain old Ginny."

"I'll throw in an extra ten bucks if you take me to the store. C'mon, kid, I'm chomping at the bit here…"

She put the basket on the table and turned to look at me. "Okay…but not a word to Dr. Gilbreth. He brought me into the world."

"Yeah, so I hear. Let's get to the store and come back so I can eat—I'm feeling a bit hungry all of a sudden." It dawned on me I had no money. "Hey, I haven't got any dough—the doc spoke of an envelope of the stuff for you—"

"—there's some expense money for you, here…" She reached up high into a cupboard and I saw those nice looking legs of hers almost up to her butt-line as the short dress lifted. "I don't know how much, though."

She handed me a plain brown envelope. I opened it. "Gees, Ginny, there's enough here for us to have a week-long party and invite the neighborhood!" I exclaimed. "Here's your ten bucks for taking me—"

"—naw, that's alright. I'll take you anyway."

"Well, thanks, kid—I can see you've got a good heart. By the way, is there a phone booth somewhere by the store?"

"Yep, right at the side of the building."

Soon that little Studebaker was rattling along the dirt road toward the highway. We turned south and drove for another couple of miles. What looked like a gas station, bakery and a general store stood on a corner under the shade of a bunch of fir trees. Ginny waited in the car while I went in and bought the goods I was desperately craving. I dumped them in the back seat of the car and told her I'd be right back after making a couple of phone calls.

I got a bunch of change from the storeowner and proceeded to pop nickels in the damn pay phone like it was a jukebox. First I'd call my boss at work. "O'Flaherty here."

"Sergeant—it's me, Cable Denning. You do know where—"

"—well, the saints preserve us! The little errant officer is talkin' again, eh? I'm a sayin' to ya, lad, someone higher than

67

me likes ya, for if 'twas up to me, I'd 'av sacked ya for leaving me with that corpse at the morgue and some other mysterious happenins."

"Oh, you mean Sandor. Well, that wasn't my fault. You don't think I killed him, do you?"

"Naw, I know ya didn't, lad, but ya gave me a headache, nevertheless. And speakin' of which, how is your skull these days? I see yer well enough to be speakin' to me now, aren't ya?"

"Sergeant, who is this Captain Treadwell? He seems to be that angel I know nothing about."

"Never heard of 'im, Denning. Somebody else pulled strings for ya, lad. Ya got one week to get back on yer feet and report for duty. I've put Paddy Larkin on with your buddy Mario Angelo for patrol. One week, Denning." He hung up and I was just as puzzled as ever.

I asked the operator for Mario's number and soon a sleepy voice came on at the other end. "Yeah, hello…"

"Mario—it's me—Cable…what the hell—"

"—Cable! Christ, man, am I glad to hear from you! How are you feeling? I didn't know what the crap to think when you went missing and O'Flaherty informed me you were badly injured and suddenly held in some 'protective custody' or something—and Dr. Sandor is dead. You didn't do it, did you?"

"Mario, you know that's not my style. Sandor conked me over the head with a lead pipe or something as hard, locked me in a bank vault to die."

"So, are you a cat or somethin', nine lives or what? How'd you get out?"

"Long story, Mario. I'm coming back into town next week. I'll fill you in. I miss you, pal. How's the evening patrol business with Paddy Larkin?"

"Shitty. He's an amateur who sniffs dope. With cops like

him, who needs gangsters? I gotta get back to sleep. I'm glad you're okay, buddy—see you soon. Call your little flapper, I think she's in love with you."

I hung up and immediately dialed Honey's number. "Hello…? Honey…it's me…Cable…"

There was a long pause at the other end of the line. "Is it really you, Cable? You're alive? And well? Healing? I think I went numb and died when I learned from Mario that they took you away. That day when you called from the hospital, I rushed as fast as I could on the streetcar, but by the time I got there, they said you'd been removed to a recovery house by the police department. I called your sergeant and he told me only that you were on some protection program or something." She couldn't hold it in any longer and she let go with the tears. "Oh, Cable—I—I thought you were dead and they were covering it up—God, I've lost five pounds! I knew you had gone to that Italian mob funeral—and when I read that some big boss, Matrangas or something like that was murdered, I thought somehow it had to do with you! And then all my lines got blurred and poor Zelda has had to put up with a grieving widow—and we weren't even married!"

I could've dropped my shorts. Matrangas dead! That meant that whatever he had, someone else wanted it worse, bad enough to risk killing the goose that lays the golden egg, so to speak. Matrangas was the mob's patron saint—why in the hell would they kill him for a microfilm scroll? Then it dawned on me. There was another joker in the deck, playing the same game but he was even more dangerous than the mob! "Hey, I'm sorry babe. I didn't mean to worry you. I'm healing up okay. I was hit pretty hard in the head, minor concussion, a few cuts and scrapes."

"Where are you? Can I come to you, Cable? God, I miss you so much and my body aches for you every night when I get home from work."

"I miss you, too, babe—a lot. I'm out of town in the mountains. You can't come to me. Secret crap and all, you know. Speaking of work, when do you start at the *Bella Notte*?"

"First of the month. Now that I know you're alright, I'm excited about my first singing job. You'll be there, won't you?"

"A pack of wild horses couldn't keep me away, Honey Combes."

There was another short pause. "Cable…I want you so…I want to be *Mrs. Cable Denning*…I realize women aren't supposed to do the proposing, but I want us to be together and one. Really together. Is that asking too much of a twenty-seven year old bachelor?"

I laughed. "Yeah, it is, babe, but it's the best proposal I've ever had. It's great that you care so damn much. But you know, when the guy is on the lamb from both sides of the law, it's kind of hard on the girl. Let's talk about it when I get back in a week or so."

"I love you, Cable Denning. Can you hear me? Can it soak through that thick skull of yours? Someone wants to be with you for all her life, my darling."

I didn't know how to answer. How did I use that word, *love*? I knew I didn't bandy it around carelessly like a lot of guys did. But I felt a lot of good things for this beautiful doll who I knew truly loved me. "I love *you*, Honey. Don't forget it. I'll be back in a few days."

"Cable…that's the first time you ever said you loved me. Do you realize that? My mother always said to praise the man who uses that word sparingly, because when he finally says it, he means it."

"I told you I'd like your mother. Yeah, doll, that's about it. I'll see you soon…I'll call again…"

"You'd better. Do you have a phone?"

"Nope. I'm at a phone booth. I sneaked out of the house

against doctor's orders in my housekeeper's '21 Studebaker. I had to stock up on gin and cigarettes."

"Cable, please don't kill yourself. Listen to the doctor. Is your housekeeper cute?"

"Yep, and pretty lonely up here in the mountains, I'd guess."

"Well, try to behave yourself…see you, my dearest…" She hung up.

I got back to the car and a smiling Ginny Fullerton. "Thanks for waiting," I said as I got into the rider's seat. "Would you like to celebrate with me? That is, if we can find some gin."

"Celebrate what?"

"*Life*, Miss Fullerton…life. Plus I gotta go back to the city in a week. Do you like British gin?"

"I've never had *any* gin. I don't drink much. My folks are pretty strict. You know, church, Bible commandments, stern uncles and aunts? But secretly, I'm willing to try."

"So, who bootlegs in your town? There's gotta be someone spreading the happy juice around. There always is, because the money's great."

"Give me twenty dollars," Ginny said, surprising me. "I might get into trouble. But I do have an Uncle Jack who sells really bad alcohol to the secret Lion's Club meetings, you know, back room stuff. And maybe I can borrow his table radio, too. He hardly ever plays it."

"Oh, yeah…and great on the radio, kid."

Soon we were back at the little cabin sitting at the breakfast nook, smoking and drinking, with the radio playing Irving Berlin's new hit, *Blue Skies*. "I hope I'm not corrupting you, Ginny," I said, laughing at her cough each time she tried to take a drag on a Lucky Strike. "How old are you, young lady?"

"I think you *are* corrupting me, Cable, but I like it. I'm going to be twenty in a few weeks." She giggled as she sipped from her glass of gin and made a terrible face. "Oh, it burns." She took another drag from her cigarette and coughed again. "I'm getting better, huh?"

"So what do pretty young things like you do for excitement up here in the hills?"

"Wait for some guy like you to come around so they can have some fun. Most of my girlfriends have already left the area for the city. I'm still here because my mother is a drunk and my Dad needs me to do the stuff my Mom can't do anymore. She drinks herself to sleep every night, after she raises Holy Hell with my Dad and me. She blames me for being born—that I was the cause of her downfall and it separated her from my Dad. That's how come I knew where the liquor was—my uncle Jack secretly supplies my mother."

Hearing a story like that always made me feel bad inside, like another beautiful flower would get wilted and ground down into the dirt of this life because of some ugly perversity in human nature that changes nice people into monsters. "I'm—I'm sorry to hear that, kid. Don't ever believe that you're less because your mother happened to crash and burn on the rocks." I took a big slug of my gin. I was beginning to feel a nice buzz and I could tell Ginny was enjoying herself, loosening up and letting go of all that crap religious and quasi-moral codes impose on people. "You got a boyfriend here in town?"

"Nope. No time, really. Taking care of the house and Dad, going to the store doesn't leave a lot of time for me. I was glad when Dr. Gilbreth hired me to take care of you. I really needed the money. My Dad used to be a preacher, but it drove my mother nuts. So he's a mechanic at Lang's Auto Repair. He's been there for years. Knows everything about cars, you know. In fact, he rescued my '21 Studebaker out there from the junk heap. I love my Dad.

Sometimes he sounds a bit crazy, still spewing from the

Bible when he's fed up with my mother's drinking and swearing. My Mom hates it. He doesn't want me to be like her, but pure and virginal until the roll is called up Yonder, I think. But he's the only solid thing in my life."

I lifted my glass. "Well, here's to your Dad, Ginny. Having a good Dad is always a fine thing," I said, smiling at her.

"Do you live alone in the city?" she asked, looking up into my eyes.

"Nope, I room with a buddy, Mario Angelo. I'm a cop, remember, days and nights get twisted around and sometimes I get confused where I am or what planet I'm on. Ever have the feeling that your life is going nowhere, but there's something else good and bigger around the corner? Well, I do. It's like you never quite know which end is up. Life and death come crashing down on you when least expect it—and after a while everything blurs—because things are moving too fast and life is moving away from you, leaving you in a squad car late at night with the sirens going on the way to scrape up the dead, the dying or the injured from off the pavement somewhere." I took a deep breath, then a drag on my cigarette. "And then once in a while the ticking in your brain stops and you're able to rest, or some babe holds you all night and you go away with her to some magic place…because it's where the both of you really wanted go…somewhere to escape the maddening sameness of everyday existence. And maybe, just maybe, you can wake up the next morning with a smile."

Ginny Fullerton finished off the rest of her drink, took a deep breath and shook her head as she smiled. "God, I love the way you talk, Mister. I mean, I'm a little embarrassed, but it—it kinda makes me feel—feel restless, like I want to go there, you know, inside a magic place with someone. Do you have a girlfriend in L.A.?"

"Yeah, I do, Ginny."

Her face dropped a little. A slow version of 1923's *Who's*

Sorry Now? came on the radio. "Would you…would you dance with me? I'm feeling so free, thanks to you, Cable. The last time I danced was in high school two years ago. I might be rusty."

"Sure, kid, why not?" I took her hand and we went out into the middle of the hardwood floor. I brought her to me and held her lovely young body close to mine as we slowly twirled around the room. "Hey, you're not bad. You've got a natural feel for the music—and rhythm."

She snuggled her head under my chin. "You're the best, Cable. I don't know why, but I feel so comfortable with you. I mean, like I trust you—and I know you won't lie to me—even about your girlfriend—or take advantage of me."

"Well, thanks, Ginny. I learned a long time ago, it ain't no fun unless both the boy and the girl are on equal terms—they both want what the moment offers. Otherwise, it's just notches on the gun for a guy."

"I know. I was a notch on some guy's gun once. Ronnie Dunlap. He dated me for six months and took me out to China Island one night just to seduce me. After that, slam-bam-not-even-thank-you, ma'am! It was over and he just called now and then to meet me for sex. I said I hated what he did. But it never matters to guys like that, does it?"

"It's a live-and-learn world out there, Ginny," I said, remembering all the guys I'd known like Ronnie Dunlap who took it out of their pants any time there was a chance to get into a girl's pants. "It kind of boils down to how wise you become through your experiences and what you're looking for—what do you want?"

She squeezed me tighter. "I want *you*, Mr. smoking and drinking policeman." She turned her face up to kiss me. I hesitated. Our lips were almost touching and her breath smelled of Lucky Strikes and gin.

"Hey, now, young lady…I'm a recovering patient, remember? My head hurts, it's time for my cook to fix us some dinner, don't you think?"

That broke the spell as the music ended. She tore away from me and took a deep breath, went over and poured herself another gin. "Well, so much for me being desired by you. No man has ever rejected me. Am I stupid, ugly or just plain not exciting enough? Or are my breasts not large enough or my thighs not hot enough for you?" The alcohol had gotten to her and her voice slurred a bit. I was beginning to feel guilty because I had started this whole thing to have a drinking buddy and someone to help break up the boredom of being locked up here 6,000' feet in the mountains.

"You look great, you feel great, you even dance with me great, Ginny. I just don't want to start something we can't finish. I know it sounds strange, but you know, I'm not a one-night stander—and I don't think you are, either."

She looked disappointed. "No, I'm not. I just wanted some of that magic you were talking about when someone holds you all night."

"Well, don't you have a curfew? You don't want your mom beating up on you if you come home smelling of cigarettes, booze and a man."

"I don't care. I know you're going to be gone soon—then all that excitement will go away—and I'll be left here driving down Big Bear Boulevard with all the fantasies that never came true. Do you believe you can fall in love with someone in a few hours?"

"Truthfully? Yeah…you can even fall in love in thirty-seconds with the right person. But as far as I'm concerned, kid, you got it right. I'm a fantasy, someone who won't be there when you need him. Correct me if I'm wrong, but my experience has told me that once a sincere doll like you gives herself to someone, she means it and it bonds her to him—maybe she even feels she belongs to him in a way…"

She looked down to the floor. "I'll prepare you some food."

"Sure, great." She took one more slug from her glass and emptied it. "Maybe if I got very drunk and pushed myself on you, you'd make love to me."

"Not a chance, toots. Thanks all the same. Tomorrow, Ginny, when this old mountain sunshine cranks up again, I think you'll be glad. I think you'll remember you could be with a man who *didn't* take advantage of you. You might end up remembering that you liked him for—for—"

"—please! Don't talk about it anymore." She made up a sandwich for me in silence, went in and cleaned up the bathroom and made my bed. When she came back out the sun had set and I had lit a candle that was sitting on the table. The radio was playing a bluesy version of *I Cried for You*, and I could feel it was going right through Ginny. I knew what she had to go home to, how she felt imprisoned by a troubled mother and a hard working but somewhat absent father.

She gathered her things and stood in front of me. "I envy your girlfriend, Cable. And I respect you wanting to be true to her. I'm sorry I was selfish. I guess I'll see you tomorrow, okay?"

She started to leave. "You're a good person, Ginny Fullerton." I checked out her face. She had been crying. "I—I, uh, hope you'll like me tomorrow."

She dropped everything in her hands and rushed over to me and almost knocked me out of my chair. She grabbed my faced and kissed me so hard it almost hurt. But it didn't, really. It felt good and warm and moist. She didn't say another word, but turned around, picked up her things and left, closing the door behind her.

I was a bit drunk and a little tired for my first day out of bed. I got undressed, took my pain pills and checked out my head. It seemed to be healing pretty fast. They say getting on with it, not babying things made them heal faster. I still had an ache in my head. But I knew Ginny Fullerton had an ache in her heart. Which was worse, I wondered? At twenty-seven

76

I didn't feel young anymore. The police force combined with my rough upbringing grew me up fast, so I seemed older than most guys my age. At least to me. And someone like that young dame stuck out here in the woods would have a lot of life to learn about yet. Maybe if I wasn't still a bit weak and doped up I would've taken her to my bed. But I don't know. Sometimes you leave things alone, things that your gut tells you is best for everyone. How many babes had I passed up as appealing as Ginny Fullerton in my life? Not many.

I drifted to sleep that night thinking about my benefactor, the party or parties responsible for saving my ass from the death grip of Jinx and Matrangas. But *who* killed Matrangas? My intuitions told me Dragna and his organized crime family didn't. Matrangas was their money pot. But who did him in... and why did they rescue me? What did I know that 'they' wanted to know? My mind was made up of bits of misshapen geometrical pieces like a jigsaw puzzle—and somehow they all had to fit together. So far they didn't and my mind was restless. It all started out so easy. Over and over I recounted the events: Mario and I visited the morgue to follow through on a couple of stiffs who were bumped off gangland style. One happens to turn out to be Ernesto Ardizzone, Don of the Los Angeles underworld, the other a non-entity named Blinthe, who happens to have a gold-lined throat and a space behind his missing tongue where some gold and priceless capsule called the *God of Our Fathers* was tucked away. Boris Sandor, the head pathologist at the county morgue, stole the great find. But when I discovered that fact, and Sandor slugged me and locked me in a vault to die, the doc himself got killed by a man named Matrangas, who was bank rolling the local mafia but hailed from Chicago. Add to that, subtle warnings at Ardizzone's funeral from Frank Dragna, new head of the L.A. gangs, and his consigliere, Joe Lorena. But my innate detective sense told me to eliminate all these guys from my suspect list. The biggest piece that didn't fit was the corpse Mario and I found in a pool of blood on the floor of an elevator at the Beverly Hills Hotel, one Harold Eisenstadt, not even an American. He was my number one lead. Why? Because none of the goons, not even Matrangas, got away with the *God of Our Fathers* capsule with all the fine mysterious hieroglyphics etched into it. Add to that…Eisenstadt held in his dead hand the label off the forensic lab jar that contained Blinthe's surgically removed golden throat.

I'd wager that when Matrangas went back to the vault with my written instructions to where the thing would be found, someone was waiting for him and Jinx, killed them, took my instructions, found the *God of Our Fathers* and escaped. Now, it came down to who in the hell was that—*and* why did they spare me when all the participants in this eerie mystery were currently pushing up daisies in Forest Lawn or Hollywood Memorial Cemetery?

CHAPTER 5

THE LEGEND OF CRAZY JACK

When I got back to town, things seemed to accelerate into a blur, the kind that whizzes by like a tornado and takes some of you with it. No one spoke again of "Captain Treadwell" or who it was that saved my butt from Matrangas' clutches. Weeks turned into months and months into the monotony of stagnant routine. I began to resent my job, especially when so many of the goons Mario and I arrested were back out on the street in days, no matter how heinous the crime. I lost heart in the so-called "system of justice." In 1928 you could buy a police captain's badge for $125 and everyone looked the other way. Yeah, there was trouble in my City of Angels.

There were fifty bordellos and three times that many speakeasies hidden in the twisted fabric of its core. Cops were on the numbers take, whether it was horseracing or gambling ships anchored off of Santa Monica. Clairvoyants, soothsayers, healers, mystics and miscellaneous occult shysters, ripped-off the gullible public and these scams existed where anyone hung a sign outside a house, apartment or pseudo office. Illegal immigrants from Mexico were brought in as slave labor to pick peas and other agricultural crops as ill-gotten water was piped from the Owens Valley into an arid region called the San Fernando Valley here.

In 1924, the residents and farmers in the Owens Valley area who had been screwed out of their hopes and dreams of using that water for an irrigation project to meet the needs of their farmland, revolted and the California Water Wars were born. These otherwise ordinary people with peaceful intent watching their farms dry up and become untenable, as an expression of their protests, blew up parts of the Aqueduct then and again last year. But there was no bucking the powerful players supporting this Aqueduct project. In March of this year the St. Francis Dam at the north end of Los Angeles County, collapsed and caused the second largest number of death's here in California since the San Francisco Earthquake in 1906

1928 saw the economy soar to new heights. Some warned there might be trouble ahead if the actual value couldn't meet the pumped up speculation numbers. But few paid much attention. Humans don't learn easily, and the hard times of 1907 and 1921 were just old newspaper clippings by now in 1928. Good-time Charlie was here to stay! Jobs were good, inflation minimal, food was cheap, cigarettes, booze and flappers were easily available. Why complain, as long as you were sitting on top of the bandwagon?

Honey's job at the *Bella Notte* was going great and she was attracting bigger and better audiences. I got her a screen test and the big muckety- mugs liked her. She was an up and coming starlet, being professionally courted by none other than Charlie Chaplin. He had just completed a film entitled *The Circus* and was beginning work on his next film, *City Lights*, and thought Honey (her screen name now changed to *Lana Loren)* a possible contender for a part in which she would play a blind girl. The film would be made with *United Artists*. A company that Chaplin himself—together with heavyweights of the time Mary Pickford, Douglas Fairbanks, William S. Hart and D. W. Griffith—formed in 1919 to retain better control, by the artists, of the qualities of good film making and the fair distribution of revenues. There was even rumor of a possible contract with *United Artists* for her. We saw less and less of each other and the down side of her singing at the *Bella Notte* was that those creeps from the dark side of the tracks frequented the place—I learned later, they *owned* it. Dragna's right-hand restaurant "business" associate, Frank Laggore, was not only hot to get into Honey's panties, but he did backroom deals at the restaurant. And that was no good.

Mario and I continued to have our differences as I got more

and more fed up with the way the police department did things. Some cops were naturally honest, a lot weren't. But all that was going to change one fateful night. Mario had finally married Rosalie Elena and she was pregnant within a few weeks of cutting the damn cake. But Mario was happy and that made me feel good, because he was a true friend. In earlier years I toyed with Mario's sister Francesca, but back in those days, you didn't play around inside the panties of a staunchly Roman Catholic girl without consequences. Pre-marital sex was akin to facing a firing squad with the family as chief executioner!

There was a secretive character known as *Crazy Jack*. Maybe a little borderline nuts…hence the name. No one knew exactly who or what he was connected with, but he was a legend down in Skid Row for knowing almost everything about anything. He would always begin answering your question by saying "I don't know! I don't know!" and then proceed to know everything there was to know about what you just asked him. I had consulted Jack a couple of times earlier in my rookie days. He told me then that I wouldn't last in the force, and my life would be a constant walk on the edge of danger, not all of it being *local in origin*, or however he put it. Mario and I had drawn dayshifts again and our lives were a bit more normal. But it was hard on Honey and me because she worked into the late hours and came home tired and needed alone time. So, we saw each other when it fit into both of our lives, which usually meant days off for either of us or Sundays and Mondays when she wasn't working. But despite all that, we grew together like peas in a pod and that little woman made me very happy. We could talk about anything, we took hikes, she cooked great food, darned my socks, introduced me to great new songs she was singing at the club, and continued to be the hottest little pistol I ever experienced in the bedroom. She still pressed me for marriage, and I still came up with the same excuses. So, after a while she gave up and just let us settle in to a space we could both live with.

I left Mario in the car listening to the newly installed

one-way radio. We could now receive short-wave transmissions within a few miles of the station house and squad car announcements kept us in the know about what car was doing what and where. I walked down a dirty alley to the Panama Hotel on 5th Street. The area was known as Hell's Half Acre and spanned roughly from San Pedro Street to Los Angeles Street. The four-story Panama Hotel had been built around 1908 and wasn't really that old, as buildings go, but for whatever reasons, it looked beat-up and neglected by 1928. I walked the four flights to Room #405. I knocked.

"Crazy Jack, it's me, you're ol' cop friend, Cable Denning," I said in a positive, penetrating voice. "Are ya in?"

There was a rustling behind the door. "I don't know! I don't know!" replied Crazy Jack's nervous voice. "I don't know—but ya can't come in, Denning...I'd be lookin' for Jack...down on the levy, down on the levy, down on the levy—but I don't know!"

None of what he said made sense to me. "Uh, Crazy Jack, I'm going to slip some dough under the door. I want you to take a streetcar tonight out to Wilshire near La Cienega—the *Bella Notte*, a nightclub—and size up it up for me, okay? I'm gonna be there about ten-thirty tonight. Can you make it a little later?"

"I don't know! I don't know!" he said in that wild voice of his.

"Well, if you can, I'll meet you out in the alley two doors down about eleven thirty. I'll look for you then, buddy. And, Crazy Jack...thanks..."

The voice behind the door kept repeating, "I don't know! I don't know!" but I had a hunch it was like a machine in his head, and while he was rattling off his stock and trade come-back, he was processing what he needed to know to answer the question asked him.

I re-joined Mario in the patrol car. He had just pulled off two or three guys attacking an old woman in the alley. He looked disgusted.

"How can humans be so inhuman?" he asked as I got in. "See that poor old woman lying there next to the wooden boxes? Three younger guys just started beating up on her because she had a nice new-looking pink scarf around her neck—and they wanted it."

"And they saw the patrol car with you in it?"

"Yep. Those creeps just don't give a damn anymore...not about anything. Let alone respect for other peoples' property... or the elderly...or the law for that matter."

"What can I say, Mario? Years before you married Rosalie, I told you your kids are gonna have to face the impossible enigma known as human kind. We all get thrown out there in the trenches. God, man, you remember the neighborhood we were raised in...shit, how much did your life count then? So what's changed, compadre?"

He started up the car and we pulled out into traffic. "So, did you find Crazy Jack?"

"Yep. Well, sort of. He didn't open the door for me but I slipped a few bucks under it and told him I'd meet him tonight at the *Bella Notte*."

"Why in the hell the *Bella Notte*? Can't you just see Crazy Jack pounding his fist on a lounge table saying, 'I donno! I donno! Now *that* is nuts, Cable."

"Not inside, but outside. I need him to size the place up with what he calls *the vibration*.... that's whether or not a place is okay and what energies might be hanging in it, around it, over it."

"You don't believe in that horseshit now, do you? C'mon, you've got more common sense than that."

"Is it any less difficult to believe in a God who punishes us all the time, sends dudes with fiery tablets to control other people, put camels through the eye of a needle—or sacrifices

His son because He loved the world?"

"The Bible's symbolical—"

"—and mythological—not to mention illogical," I said, a little steamed under my collar. "At least Crazy Jack says he's crazy and doesn't know anything. But somehow he knows everything I've ever asked him about."

"Hold on there! I think you've been reading far too many of those *Adventure* magazines…all that fiction and fantasy. We were unlucky for a while, finding all those gangland stiffs."

"You think we were? Well, Mario, old chum, I see it differently. I see it as signs of things to come, just like the *Great War* will most likely be the precursor of another world event which, I predict, will come in due time. War makes money and money is what people are all about."

"Geez….how cynical can you be! The world isn't like that, Cable. We're into the twentieth century here where civilized people are learning to do civilized things. Even the great minds said the Great War was the war to end all wars. I believe that."

I lit up a Lucky Strike. "Open your eyes, Mario. If you're gonna have kids, you gotta open your eyes and see how the millionaires run us peasants—and one of the best ways to grab you by the shorthairs is by war and manipulation of stock market prices."

"I don't know how Honey puts up with your negative take on everything. Put some faith in humanity, man. After all, you're one of us."

"Am I?" I laughed. "Someday remind me to prove it to myself, will you? A lot of the time I think I'd rather be something else."

Mario laughed back at me. "You're impossible buddy. But I love ya, and you're stuck with me."

I knocked him one on the shoulder. "Yeah, me too, pal."

The *Bella Notte* was jammed and Honey was hard at work

with a jumping version of Rodgers and Hart's *My Heart Stood Still*. She saw me come in and had reserved a little table up front. When she started the song the second time around, she motioned to the band to slow it down and she milked the tune for everything it had as she made love to me front and center. In the dark shadows I could see Frank Laggore standing there, probably burning up inside with the fever I knew he felt for Honey. I was uncomfortable with that man's presence, as was my little golden-throated singer. But it had just this very evening occurred to me that Affonso Amadore didn't own the club, but Dragna and his thugs did. And that worried me.

During a fifteen-minute break, Honey came to my table and kissed me gently on the lips. She was wearing a dark-blue sequined hip-tight gown with those marvelous breasts tucked tastefully in the upper deck. "Lipstick, you know," she said with a big smile. "Don't I know you, Mister?"

"Uh...what day is this? If this is Friday, I'm Rubio Genovese—if it's still Thursday, then I'm some old gumshoe you probably wouldn't be too interested in."

She took my hand. "It's Thursday, and I'm mad about the guy. I almost can't wait until he takes me home and pounds me into my pillow."

"Pillow pounding is extra, toots. Whereas just plain old pressing your head against the pillow while kissing is free of charge."

She giggled lightly. "You wouldn't happen to have a two-for-one bargain hanging around in your bedtime repertoire?"

"Hmmm....now let me see. Thursdays...well, I donno. You see, the pillow pounder has to get up to go to work at five a.m. Are rain checks in season?"

"Not if it's cloudy in the girl's heart, buddy. How about a compromise? I do you, you do me—and we do it together?"

I laughed. "Now you're talkin', doll. What time are you off?"

"Ugly over there has a party of twenty guys coming in at eleven." She motioned toward Frank Laggore. "The band and I have been asked to hang around and do a few songs for them while they're getting drunk enough to talk business."

"Do you know who these apes are?"

"Yeah, strictly Mafia. I think they own the club—and several more like it."

"You know, I just got that tonight. It's a pisser, Honey. I get you the job here, you're doin' great and all of a sudden it's a major meeting hall for the rank and file of organized crime."

"Will you wait at home for me? I think I'll need you after tonight, especially fighting my way out to the streetcar as Laggore stands in my way." "I'll tell you what, babe. I'm gonna see this guy called *Crazy Jack* a couple of doors down for a while. Then I'll be back and we'll go home together. I'll keep my eye on this Laggore character."

"Damn, Cable...I love you so damned much I think I'll die of heart failure over it," she said as she took my arm and squeezed it."

Just then a well-groomed inebriated man approached us. "May...may I ask the lady to...to...sing?...my wife and I....are celebrating our twelfth anniversary tonight. Do you know..."*I Can't Believe That You're in Love with Me*? I sang that...hic! to her...back when I was courting her."

"I think I know it, Mister—but I need to check in with the band. If they know it, I'll do it next for you and your wife."

"Bless you—bless you, beautiful lady." He bowed. "I stand... indebted." Then he turned and left, making his way to a table where a smiling middle-aged woman, looking very embarrassed, greeted him.

"Anyway, I'll be back, babe." I got up and kissed her on the forehead. "Yeah, I know...the lipstick..." As I left, I glanced at Frank Laggore, who threw me a quasi-smile and a hand salute. I guessed he thought I was gone for the night and he could continue to chip away at Honey with his suggestive and amorous intentions.

Two doors down from the club I cautiously walked into an alley. It was dark, so I stopped and lit up a Lucky Strike. The match light partially lit up a face against a brick wall down and opposite me. "Is that you, Jack?"

"I don't know! I don't know!" he intoned, his voice lower than when I had last encountered the odd man. "Not good— *Bella Notte! Bella Notte!* Not good!…but I don't know! I don't know!"

I was trying to interpret Crazy Jack's lingo. "You mean you sense some danger—or bad fortune for Honey hanging out in there? She's my girl…"

"I don't know! I don't know! Jack checked out…Jack checked out. You should do the same! But I don't know!"

"Yeah, I know the place is mafia owned and operated. I just found out, Jack. Should I take her outta there? It just seemed a perfect fit for my classy dame."

"I don't know! I don't know! Go back downtown…safer, better times—but I don't know!"

"I've got one more question. My partner and I came across a corpse at the county morgue some months ago. There was this golden capsule found in the corpse's throat… a thing called *God of Our Fathers*, supposedly containing priceless content. Knowing about it got me into some deep trouble, and I'm kinda interested in what happened to it since it got stolen from the morgue."

Crazy Jack remained silent for a short time. Then he approached me. "Cigarette! Cigarette!" I took one out, lit it for him and stuffed the pack into his coat pocket. He shook his head and looked at me. I knew he liked me—or maybe simply trusted me. "I don't know! I don't know" he exclaimed, his eyes widening there in the dark until the whites of them showed. "*Wonder Woman* knows. *Wonder Woman!* But I don't know! I don't know! Danger everywhere you go! Ask her question—tell her no lie…she will tell you…how goes the pie!"

"So who in the hell is this 'Wonder Woman?' Never heard of her."

"I don't know! I don't know! Clever as a cleaver—ha! ha! Very keeno can be Palladino. But…I don't know! The danger grows stranger…when you travel…travel by train…but I don't know! I don't know!"

I thanked Jack and noted the names *Palladino* and *Wonder Woman* in my head. I had no idea what 'travel by train' might have meant. I returned to the club just in time to catch Honey start up a very naughty version of *Makin' Whoopee* and knew instantly why every man in the joint wanted to undress her and take her on the spot. It was no wonder her popularity was soaring. She was a hell of a looker with a great body, intelligence and genuine charisma. That's what I had seen in her the first night we met at *Gregorio's*. Watching her there in the dark, I was thinking what a lucky bloke I was that she loved me and desired me. It could've been any Joe Blow, but it wasn't. What she saw in a discontented, on-the-fence cop with not much future for the big bucks was beyond me. But women are weird that way. You never know what they see in you that you don't even see yourself.

Thanks to the right and proper Signor Affonso Amadore, when Honey was through and the band began packing up and the goon squad retired to a private banquet room, the kindly manager escorted Honey over to me. "It's a good-a thing… Signor Cable…you wait-a now for our bella signorina. Dose-a guys-a, dey drinka too much—anda then—you know what I mean?"

"Yep, I sure do, Affonso…thanks." Just then Frank Laggore came out and approached us. "Mr. Laggore, haven't seen you since Ardizzone's funeral."

"That's right, Denning." Then he looked directly at Honey. "There's a piano in the banquet room, and we were hoping you'd sing a couple more songs, Honey."

She took a deep breath. "I don't get paid past midnight, Mr. Laggore. And frankly, you know, I've...I've been singing since nine."

He looked at me. "Too bad. Then may I take you home?" He said that to spite me, full well knowing Honey and I were lovers.

"Thanks, no. Cable will see to those...needs," she said, easing the knife into him a little more.

The streetcar ride home was simply a matter of holding hands and me ruminating on what Crazy Jack had said. One, the *Bella Notte* may not be good for Honey in the long run—two, the *God of Our Fathers* may be somehow connected to some gal named *Palladino* and a train trip would be dangerous.

"Have you ever heard of a gal called *Palladino*—or someone with that name mixed up with someone called *Wonder Woman*?" I asked the rather quiet and unusually sullen Honey Combes.

"Yeah, Cable—Eusapia Palladino, she's a famous Italian psychic. Some of the girls down at *Gregorio's* used to go to her for fortune telling and séances. In fact, she is *called 'The Clairvoyant Wonder Woman'*."

"You don't say!"

"Yep, she's in the phone book, I bet."

"Thanks, babe, you just solved Crazy Jack's puzzle for me."

"Crazy Jack?"

"Yeah, remember, the guy I told you I was meeting tonight, some really crazy guy who's tuned in to certain information beyond us silly mortals—work related, you know. He's kinda like a psychic snitch." I chuckled.

We got to Honey's place pretty late and we immediately undressed and went to bed. It was one of those still, warm L.A. nights and the bedroom window had been shut. I got up and opened it, then lay down again next to my golden- throated little love and lit up a cigarette. She seemed pensive as she drew invisible figures on my naked chest. "After all the loves of your life, Cable, will you remember me?" She took a drag from my cigarette.

"Hey, kid, I've never known you to smoke—not good for the voice, you know." She handed it back to me and I puffed on it. "Why would you ask me a question like that? I never think of any other babe except you."

She half-smiled at me. "I guess I'm just a bit melancholy tonight. While I was up there singing, I was thinking about you. It was the lyrics…they made me start asking *myself* the questions, as if from part of a diary I had written a long time ago. The words went like this… *'Why was I born? Why am I living? What do I get, what am I giving? Why do I want a thing I dare not hope for, what can I hope for? I wish I knew… Why do I try to draw you near me, and why do I cry? You never hear me. I'm a poor fool, but what can I do? Why was I born…to love you…?'"*

I lay there on the bed with my hands behind my head, look- ing up at Honey. "That's beautiful—but why so maudlin, doll? I'm right here, beside you. Honey, I'm still nuts about you— even after all this time. That's rare for me. What are you not saying? C'mon, come clean, there's something else here."

"I just had this vision, like I was seeing you at the other end of your life, after all the women you'd loved—and I was won- dering, would I still be the one? I got this feeling I wouldn't be around to see the end of your movie—"

"—babe! Stop it! What in the hell have you been drinking at that club? I've never seen you like this. In fact, it kinda scares me. What has caused all this kind of thinking from you?"

She took a deep breath and let out a sigh. "Who knows,

Cable? Maybe I'm getting my monthly trouble or something." Then she put her head onto my chest and lay her body over the rest of me. I could feel those wonderful warm breasts of hers flatten out against my skin and her warm mound rub on my crotch. "There's just this *thing*…like I can never quite get as close to you as I want to. I want to crawl inside of you, to stay safe and warm—and then you can take me out to play when you need me. There's this feeling…that…keeps me longing for something to be completed between us. And since I can't have children—"

"—are we back to the *Mr. and Mrs. Cable Denning* thing again? It started out to be *my* bag of excuses, now it's your agent's—you know he says marriage right now would stop your budding stardom in mid-ascension."

"I'd give it all up for a few acres and a ranch house in Mendocino or somewhere up there. But I know that's not practical. And you're still in a love-hate relationship with this God-forbidden city. What are *you* born to do, Cable? Do you even think about that?"

"Yeah, I've always known it. Help out the underdog, see truth as the only way to cut through the bullshit humans wanna dish out on each other. Find some kind of balance through justice when things need a little help along the way. That's why I hate being a cop in a crooked, rotten city filled with crooked, rotten cops."

"Why don't you quit and become—oh, you know, like a private investigator or something? Just be accountable only to yourself."

"Not a bad idea." I finished off my smoke and put it out in the ashtray next to the bed. "So…since we're playing the game, what are *you* born to do—assuming you know—and you can say it in fifty words or less."

"Born to sing. Born to love you." Then she lightened up and began to make love to me and soon we were lost in the ecstasy of youth and passion. Still, in the back of my head something niggled at me that didn't quite add up. After all, it's always the things that are never said that lie at the crux of that big human dilemma: who am I? where am I and who will go with me?

CHAPTER 6

CLAIRVOYANTS, SOOTHSAYERS AND WONDER WOMAN

When Mario and I reported for work that morning, I checked my message box as always. There were two items crammed in the box. One was a small envelope with a post office stamp reading *Big Bear Lake, California*. The other was a larger envelope with no return address. It simply read: '*Officer Cable Denning, Los Angeles Police Department, Los Angeles, California*. While Mario grabbed a cup of coffee, I opened the envelope.

'Dear Mr. Denning,

I am Captain Treadwell, whom I'm sure you will recall as your recent benefactor. It is in our best interests to meet in person. I beseech you, however, to maintain the utmost confidence in this matter. I know you have some concerns regarding the late Harold Eisenstadt. I am hopeful I shall be able to help you resolve any questions you might have. If you will be kind enough to meet me at 8:p.m. this evening where the Angel's Flight track terminates, on Olive Street. I shall look forward to meeting you personally.

Most sincerely,

Captain T.A. Treadwell.'

Now *that* was strange. I went down the hall and found Mario. I decided I wouldn't read Treadwell's missive to him. He sat opposite me, sipping his coffee with casual indifference. "Busy mailman this morning, huh? Two love letters for Cable Denning?"

"Naw, one's a training announcement." I held up the small

93

envelope. "Well, this one I have a hunch about." I opened it and started reading: "Yup, this one could be a love letter.

'Dear Cable, I've tried, but I can't get you out of my mind. I hope your head has healed by now. I'm coming to L.A. to visit an aunt next week, the 13th. Will you call me? PRospect 8134. My aunt's name is Alice Wardall. Please call me. I'll be in town a week or so. Sincerely, Ginny Fullerton.' What'd I tell you?"

"Who's Ginny Fullerton, anyway?" Mario asked, raising an eyebrow.

"Oh, she's a little doll I met while I was recuperating at Big Bear Lake. She was my cook and housekeeper."

"Did you fool around?"

"Well, I guess if you call having a few drinks, a smoke and a dance or two fooling around, then I guess we fooled around."

"And Cable Denning resisted taking her to his bed?"

"I was tempted, buddy, and she was hot to trot in that direction. But something stopped me. She was such a decent kid; I didn't want her to have a bad memory hangover."

"Since when did that ever stop you? You would have fucked my sister if the family hadn't protected her from you."

"That's not true. We were young and Francesca was a hot number, even if she was your sister. But I wouldn't have crossed that line, Mario, and you know it." I laughed. "No Romeo wants the whole damn Catholic hierarchy after him, especially for just a piece of tail."

Mario snickered. "Yeah, I guess you're right, pal. I know you respected me, and my family. But, shit, you might as well have fucked her after all—she ended up hot and pregnant anyway, by some slimy paisano across the river."

"Yeah, I went to the shotgun wedding, remember? I can still see your mamma giving the new son-in-law the evil eye." We both laughed.

The patrol car shift was rather uneventful for a change and by seven o'clock I had called Honey and told her I had this appointment, but not to worry. She worried anyway. Women have an invisible perversity in them, but when its little head peeks out, a guy sure finds out about it.

As instructed, I took the 1901 cable car from the bottom at Hill Street and got out at the top of the hill on Olive. I looked around. No one. The fog started to come in with a slight chill that went right through me. I was standing on the curb, when a shiny black Packard came squealing around the corner…coming right for me. I jumped back toward Angel's Flight and the car came to a screeching halt in front of me. Two goons got out and approached me, their hands loaded up with iron. One got behind me, the other stayed in front as they escorted me over to the Packard. I was unceremoniously pushed into the back seat with one goon on either side of me. I couldn't make him out in the darkness very well, but the rider in the front seat had a bottle with a handkerchief he was dousing with something. He handed it to one of the other mugs and before I could react, he slammed the wet handkerchief in my face. I choked and gagged, but just as I went out I recognized the familiar odor of chloroform.

I was caught in a yellow cloud, running and screaming, but no sound was coming out of my mouth. I ran in desperation from something unseen, but I knew it was there, behind me, and I took my chances hurling through the thick, yellow fog-like vapor. Then I fell out of the cloud onto the pavement of a dark alley. As soon as my eyes could focus somewhat, I saw two shiny black shoes. Attached to them was a man in an evening tuxedo, wearing a black overcoat on his shoulders without his arms in it. A large white scarf was wrapped around his neck and he was smoking a cigarette through a long, black holder.

"We could have crushed your already damaged skull, Officer Denning. But, you see, I am merciful, on the side of the angels.

We only administered chloroform in the hopes you would not suffocate or suffer cardiac arrest. You didn't, I see. Good for you. Yet, on the other hand, you are relentless, meddlesome—and definitely laced through and through with *evil*."

I tried out my voice. "Are you…ahem!—are you…Treadwell?"

"Treadwell does not exist, nor did he ever.

It was simply a ploy to fool your stupid police department. Money can buy anything—and does."

I sat up, still gulping for fresh air and feeling a bit woozy. "So…there's just one question…why didn't you let Matrangas' idiots kill me in the hospital?" The rather tall man with a very thin face helped me to my feet and dusted me off.

"Every so often a perfect foil—a dupe, if you will, appears on the scene to help us. You see, Officer Denning, contrary to your detective brand of logic, neither Mr. Dragna *nor* I ended up with the priceless golden capsule. It is true, I intended to intercept Matrangas when he got back to the morgue. But someone else beat us both to it. By the time we had killed Matrangas and found the empty metal box per your instructions, we could hear the police sirens and so we were on our way."

"So you think I know more?—you're barking up the wrong tree, Mr.—"

"—*Damianos*, Isaiah Damianos."

"What a fucked name," I said, expecting a kick or a punch any second. "How did your mother and father dream that one up?"

"I am Greek and Etruscan—*Isaiah* means 'salvation of the Lord,' and the *God of Our Fathers* must be returned to its sacred hiding place."

I was trying to figure out what this guy was all about, who he worked for or whether he was an 'independent' dishing out his own form of vigilante justice. "So now you're telling me you're a religious nut on his way to saving the human race from some unspeakable horror locked in that gold-etched microfilm?"

"Not a horror, Officer Denning, a knowledge so profound that it would be impossible for the human race to comprehend. Besides, the small golden-etched tablet is *not* a microfilm. It is the original ancient coding—and it must be restored to its original resting place, until its proper time comes. I am a guardian of that quest and am pledged to return it...or perish in the pursuit."

"Well, then, get in line, Damianos, everyone's died *so* far. But why did you spare me—or was that someone else?"

"No, we spared you because anyone who has looked upon the *God of Our Fathers* can be led to it by a vibrational *scent*, if you will." He leaned into my face with his own and lowered his voice. "You have seen it, haven't you?"

"Yeah, the gods *Photonos, Audianos*, the source of creation and the whole shootin' match. But I'm not the only one who saw it. So did Sandor—a lotta good it did him—he's dead. And as far as I'm concerned, the only 'vibrational' bloodhound I've got in me has a good nose for booze and broads."

"Your crassness will not avail you any benefit, Denning. And I might add what makes the *God of Our Fathers* so unique in this world is the fact that not only is the source of creation explained—but *why*."

"Then you've read the microfilm..."

"No."

"Well, crap, have *you* even *seen* the damn thing? After all, you're the appointed overseer, right?"

"There are many of us, but none have ever been privy to look upon it, especially in the blue light of Noda. You are the only living being we know of who has laid his eyes upon the precious golden capsule. We have watched you, studied you, concluded you are of truthful character—and thus charge you with the task of finding and returning the *God of Our Fathers* to our Order"

"I'm really confused, Damianos. Blue light of Noda? Do you take me for a hocus-pocus sucker? First you almost kill me with that dope in the handkerchief—and you're damn lucky I don't have a weak heart—and now you're asking me—or is it commanding me—to hunt down this sacred icon of yours that's supposed to contain unfathomable knowledge."

"I couldn't say it better myself. We are willing to compensate you handsomely. Money is not significant in and of itself to us. All we ask is the safe return of the *God of Our Fathers*."

I *was* rather intrigued by the thought of taking on the role of true detective free of the confines of the police force. "So, if I even think about doing this stint for you guys, how do I get out of the monotony of the good ol' Los Angeles Police Department street patrols?"

"Simple. As we did before, we will arrange an extended *leave of absence* through Captain Treadwell."

"You mean the guy who doesn't exist?"

"Precisely. Well….what do you say, citizen Denning?"

"How soon you forget, Damianos—or should I call you *Captain Treadwell*—remember? Your cordial invitation to have this meeting face to face—and the little matter regarding one Mr. Eisenstadt…?"

"Very well. In the early 1500s, Pope Julius the Second, known as the 'warrior Pope', hired a group of mercenaries from Helvetia, today known as Switzerland, to aid Julius in a battle of military might against the principality of Bologna. With the mercenaries' help, the pope was victorious. Afterward on January 22, 1506 he requested that these men officially make up a small but powerful guard, to be known as the 'Swiss Guard' to permanently protect the Pope. Now, among these men was a sort of '*Knight Errant*', known as *Orson Amadis, Knight of the Flames*. He did not remain in Rome but wandered the hills of Tuscany. There he came upon some ancient ruins and far in a cave, buried in a deep chamber, he found a large golden neckpiece with many trinkets adorning it. One of those '*trinkets*' happened to be the lost *God of Our Fathers*. From that moment on, the lineage of Orson Amadis was sworn to the protection of the precious and priceless gift of the gods. Eisenstadt was one such descendent. He traced the stolen capsule to the gold-lined throat of a Roman Catholic-raised gangster, named *Blinthe Rettini*. When he turned up dead in a gangland execution spree, Eisenstadt discovered Dr. Sandor had stolen the capsule from its hiding place in Rettini's throat. But the slain man's corpse had no identification, no fingerprints and no navel—all of which had been altered to protect what he housed behind his tongue."

"So now enter two ignorant policemen, and one of them happens to see a jar containing Rettini's removed throat section, but it's marked *Blinthe* because that's as close as Sandor could come to discovering Rettini's identity. Eisenstadt tears off the label in the hopes he can find *Blinthe*—or what's left of him—assuming it's his *last* name. But Sandor doesn't want to share any of the loot, so he follows Eisenstadt and bumps him off at his hotel in Beverly Hills, in the elevator, no less."

"Indeed! You think like a detective who knows his sequential logic, Officer Denning. So is it a yea?"

"What if it's a nay? Do I still get to keep my life?"

"I cannot answer for that, Officer. Let's just say a 'yea' would extend your life…"

"And you can save my job until I've completed the assigned task? And what if I fail—what if the damned thing isn't recoverable?

"I guarantee you will return to full reinstatement of your job. On the other hand, failure to accomplish the task may indeed result in your ultimate demise."

"Oh, that's great. I like my choices. Let me see…one, I'm dead…two, hmmm….I'm *dead*. Which one would you choose?"

Damianos laughed as he urged me toward the awaiting Packard at the end of the alley. "Some souls are just *picked out*, it seems, Denning. I, somehow, have great confidence in you. And, indeed, if you are destined to fulfill this objective, then know the gods have led you thusly—and smiled kindly upon you. Now, tell me true, weren't you really rather bored with your job as a lowly patrolman?"

He had me there. The excitement of this new adventure made my blood flow, kicked up my adrenals and made me feel alive again. "Okay, count me in, Damianos. Just give me a couple of days to get my affairs in order, okay? I mean, I have to say good-bye to Mario and someone I'm very—"

"—Honey Combes, Lana Loren—those names…are they not priceless?" How in the hell could these guys know all these things about me? Crap, next it'd be the manufacture's label on my shorts! "By the way, I do apologize for roughing you up earlier. It's the hired help nowadays. Even though I have to admit the chloroform was my idea. Had I left it up to those fellows in the car, they would've used baseball bats instead."

On the way back, Damianos sat in the back seat with me and I began to warm up to this odd but personable character. I don't think he was more than maybe forty, had very amber eyes and light hair, well groomed. He gave me a phone number that I must share with no one and to call within 48 hours for further instructions. Where in the hell would this next chapter of my life take me? As 1928 was coming to a close, could it be my life was, too!

It was one of those days when the Santa Anas blew hot and dry from the mountains to the east. Whatever was in those winds made people feel restless and irritable. Could be why Honey and I had a disagreement of profound proportion and I found myself feeling less and less in the center of her life. The Hollywood agency that represented her had urged her to change her look along with her name. So, when Honey Combes officially became Lana Loren, her hair became a shoulder-length platinum with a flip on the bottom, her eyebrows got thinned and those warm blue eyes and lips of hers were suddenly set off with enough make-up and color to disguise an Egyptian princess.

Anyway, this makeover thing bothered me. You know how men are, a bit on the territorial side. I just didn't want my woman becoming someone else without at least consulting me. She said she did—I said she didn't or I would never have gone for it—hence the impasse which left a sour taste in the mouth of our relationship. I also wondered how that transformation might affect her image as a singing entertainer at the *Bella Notte*.

For whatever silly reason, I decided to take Crazy Jack along with me to my appointment with Eusapia Palladino, the famous psychic *Wonder Woman*. We had gotten off the trolley at Main and 37th Street and had to walk a couple of blocks to Madame Palladino's parlor of mystique, which turned out to be a little old house set back about twenty-five feet from the sidewalk.

On the way to Madame Palladino's, I was trying to communicate with Crazy Jack, which often wasn't that easy. "So, Jack," I was saying, "since you steered me on to this broad, tell me what to expect. I mean, I've never been to a soothsayer or fortune teller, or whatever she is, before."

Crazy Jack popped his neck and raised one shoulder higher than the other and jerked it. "I don't know! I don't know! You mention the dimensions...but I don't know! I don't know!"

"Dimensions?" I said, giving Jack a strange look.

"I don't know! Other rooms...like you find...in the mind, but I don't know! I don't know! Cigarette!"

He was always mooching Lucky Strikes off me. I took out the whole pack as I always did, lit one for him, took one for myself and tucked the rest of the pack in his pocket. I lit up and we continued our walk. "So, you need to know I got a free ride to chloroform city the other night. Some strange guy hired some goons to kidnap me off the street, dope me up and spit me out once I promised the head mystery man I'm going to birddog out that *God of Our Fathers* golden capsule thing. Now I'm kinda stuck, Jack. Got any feelings about that, Crazy Jack?"

"I don't know! I don't know! Sounds like a fanatic from the attic—but he won't hurt you—but I don't know—someone else might! Ha! ha! I don't know!"

"You talked about a train trip or something the other night when we met near the *Bella Notte*. Any more thoughts on that?"

"I don't know! I don't know! Maybe you'll miss the mark if you take the Lark by night—sent by woman to find a woman—but I don't know! I don't know!"

We reached the front of the house that belonged to one *'Eusapia Palladino: Psychic Wonder Woman,'* so stated the large rickety white sign with black lettering. I told Crazy Jack to wait for me outside. "I don't know! I don't know! They might see me! But I don't know!"

"Who might see you, Jack?"

"I don't know!—them…" He looked across the street. "*Them*. They're everywhere—they want to catch me, but I don't know! I don't know!"

I rapped on the door and soon a very short, rather frumpy looking woman stood before us. "Madame Palladino? She nodded, looking us over. I'm—I'm Cable Denning—and this is Crazy Jack, my friend." We must have looked quite the pair, a cop and a down and out bum from skid row.

"Yes, please come in." She led us into a very small living room. I was looking for a crystal ball, a mysterious cornucopia or a big megaphone to call up the dead, but I saw nothing. She looked at Jack with some disgust—he probably smelled somewhere between sweat, tobacco and garlic. "Would you be kind enough to wait there on that chair, by the kitchen table?"

"I don't know! I don't know! The *Photes* might get me! I don't know!"

Madame Palladino looked up at me, then back at Jack. "The Photes?"

"I don't know! They're everywhere! Invaders! But I don't know! I don't know!"

"I think you'll be just fine, Crazy Jack," I said. "If you need me, just call and I'll come help you with the Photes, okay?" That seemed to comfort him a little. I was escorted to a seat at a small round table. "Will you be comfortable with only candlelight, Mr. Denning? Didn't you say you were a police officer?"

"Not if I can help it," I joked. "But, yeah, I play at it. Don't like it a lot anymore. Got discouraged by all the chicanery going on in the force these days, particularly since Prohibition. By the way, I was under the impression that Eusapia Palladino was much older."

"You are speaking of my aunt, who died in 1918. I took her name when I began to use my powers here some years ago. Her sister, my mother, was equally gifted with seeing through the dimensions of time and space. My mother trained me and I guess successive generations become more educated and better at what their forebears began."

"I see," I said, feeling awkward, wondering what in the hell I was doing in a spiritualist's living room. "So, you know why I came?"

"How could I? I require something that belongs to you." Her mouth was tight and small, she was a bit over-weight and stood no taller than five feet from the ground. Her eyes were dark-brown and her nose slightly flattened. Her hair was short, thin and non-descript, while her eyebrows were dark and thick. I figured her for about thirty-five. "Perhaps a memento, some keys, a wallet?"

"My wallet!" I kidded her, "you mean *you* want to get at my wallet before your bill does?"

She did not laugh. I guess she was lacking in that certain lightness of spirit that humor can bring to a situation. I handed her my keychain. She lit three candles on the table before us. One was white, one red and the middle one… black. I'd never seen a black candle before. She closed her eyes and started swaying with my keys in the palm of her hand. "Your journey is frightening, rewarding, violent…yet…full of…of love, Mr. Denning. How strange this should be so." Then I heard a bell ring and I looked around. "Not from this world, Mr. Denning. Do not be alarmed. We are being visited from the other side of the veil."

I looked around for any sign of a bell. None. "Veil? So where's the sound coming from if not from this dimension?" I asked, baffled.

"Everything is manifest in everything else. Good and evil are opposite sides of the same coin. We must not run from evil, but walk into it, greet it as we would a friend who is lost and ill-intentioned toward strangers. That is why we light the black

104

candle, Mr. Denning. Sin is necessary in order for redemption to take place."

So far I wasn't comfortable with any of it. And I worried about Crazy Jack out there in the kitchen itching and scratching. He did that a lot. He probably picked up some fleas or lice from that dump where he lives. "I'm only here because Crazy Jack out there has a record for being psychically accurate. But I don't personally believe much in the occult crap."

She didn't look up but continued with her eyes closed. "Please…you must be silent now. The spiritual universe does not care whether or not we believe, Mr. Denning. It just *is*, whether we accept or not." Then she went into what appeared to be a deeper trance. Then her voice changed into what I could swear was someone else! The voice became low and eerie, and spoke in measured tones. "*That which you seek lays hidden in a night of knights in a castle far away. The Deus Patrum Nostrorum must rest in its rightful place. You are chosen of truth to bring it there. Humans must not access it. It cannot be destroyed by human hands. Others will attempt to kill you for it. It will protect you through the Asian Virgin of Nymphaea Ou. What must be destroyed is the icon photograph inside the capsule. The golden egg itself is the true Deus Patrum Nostrorum. Go to a city by the large bay, facing west, look to the west that leads to the East. Look to the west…that leads to the East…*"

Then my hostess jerked herself out of the trance. She slowly opened her eyes and looked at me. I could hear Crazy Jack in the background mumbling, "I don't know! I don't know! I think they're here—but I don't know!" It appeared the "photes" had caught up with him and it was time to take him back home.

"That is all we can bring you today, Mr. Denning."

"That's it? If you're really Wonder Woman, how can I pull a wonder out of that scant amount of information? That voice—was it really you disguising your own? C'mon, you can tell a young cop with a nose for detective work."

105

Madame Palladino seemed insulted. "Yes you are young, and you are also quite arrogant. I was not present during the channeling, so I cannot say what was told you. But give me my twenty dollars and please leave with your friend. If…what was told to you does not prove to be true—I will refund your money." We walked to the kitchen to fetch Crazy Jack. "When my grandmother left Naples for Bulgaria, she had mastered levitation, elongation, raised heavy tables into the air with thought power and played musical instruments remotely. I can do the same. For two hundred dollars I could give you a complete demonstration."

I handed her a twenty-dollar bill. "That's more dough than a policeman's salary can afford. But as far as what I heard here today, I've got no choice but to believe you, Madame Palladino. Out of curiosity, I'd sure be interested in seeing some of what you just mentioned, though." I looked at poor Crazy Jack sitting at the table, itching and scratching, twisting his neck around and around. "Well, Jack, are you ready to hit the road?"

"I don't know! I don't know! The *Photes* came in! They're waiting outside—to grab me—but I don't know—photes! Bad!"

I looked at Madame Palladino with a raised eyebrow. "Sometimes gifted people see things ordinary mortals do not see, Mr. Denning. Your friend may indeed see through the veil. He led you here, didn't he?"

I couldn't argue with that, so I took Crazy Jack by the arm, thanked Madame Eusapia Palladino and left. We walked to the streetcar line stop. An accordion player with an old cigar box at his feet stood across the street playing *I'm Always Chasing Rainbows* and it hit me pretty hard because it was one of the songs my mother used to play on our little wind-up phonograph when I was a kid…and suddenly I was ripped back to melancholy nights watching my mother sit on a beat up old cushion chair listening. Only she played the Chopin version, a solo piano. Sometimes I was embarrassed to go home and visit her. Just across town, you know, to a land of tough times and poverty. I wished I could help her better her life situation. But she said she didn't want to change anything. That she would live and die on that same street where I was born. For a minute I got homesick. I must see her soon.

On the streetcar home, Jack was nodding his head up and down. "I don't know! I don't know!" he was chattering under his breath.

"If this Palladino broad was on the level, Jack, then I've got three major challenges here. One, how in the hell do I figure out the riddle of what is meant by the capsule being hidden in *night of nights in a faraway castle?* What the crap does that mean? Sounds like some fairy tale shit to me. Second, this weird stuff about an Asian virgin, of all things, from *Nymphomania* or some such place—and third, what city has a large bay facing west? Los Angeles Harbor?"

Crazy Jack put his finger to his temple, "I don't know! But maybe you'll find it so, where the redwood grows! But I don't know! I don't know!"

"Redwood? Ah, you mean Redwood trees."

"I don't know! I don't know! Ferries cross the channel—hide and seek, find the peak called twins. Ha! ha! But I don't know!"

"Well, Crazy Jack," I said as we stepped out of the streetcar on Main street "The only city in California that's big enough and has a bay near Redwood trees is San Francisco. Maybe that's it?"

"I don't know! I don't know! Never been! But my sin comes creeping in to say I never knew! 'Cause I don't know!"

I took Jack across the street to a little stand and bought him a couple of tacos. He relished them and I stood with him watching the noisy, dirty traffic make its way along the crowded streets across from us. I noticed that the little Mexican gal who waited on us somehow looked like she didn't belong. Soon Crazy Jack got restless and I gave him carfare and thanked him for his help. He left and I could hear him mumble to himself as he inspected the coins I had given him. "I don't know! I don't know!"

I threw my wrapper in the garbage can by the concession when suddenly the little gal behind the counter said, "Are you Mr. Denning?" I was floored. How in the hell would this petite little gal know me?

"Depends on who's asking and what for?" I said.

Her accent was pretty thick, but she was pert and had a hell of a figure, as well as those warm, dark eyes Latinas are known to show off in the pre-bedroom ritual. "Will you please follow me? It is safe to know me. I am only a messenger for someone."

"And how in the hell did you—or anyone—know that Crazy Jack and I were getting off the streetcar here on Main Street—at this particular spot? It could have been anywhere in the city, lady."

"Lo siento mucho, señor. I just follow my instrucciones. Por favor, follow me." I checked my pocket for my .38 but had left it at home. I followed my gut and the little señorita to a phone booth. There she tossed in a nickel and told someone at the other end I was present with her. Then she hung up.

"Please wait, señor. Look over there. Allí. Someone will pick you up," she said, looking up a rather dark alley.

I was thinking about what clues would lead me to that unknown city I had yet to discover. "Is there a travel agency near here?" I asked of the pretty little lady waiting with me.

"Sí…mi hermana, Señorita Moreno, has *Todo el Mundo* across the street, over there. She can get you ticket to Sud America—or anywhere!"

I decided to skip out on the arrival of the mysterious surprise package and told the lady I'd be across the street. I walked in to a green and yellow painted room with a potted palm tree in a corner. Behind a small desk stood a larger version of the young Mexican woman across the street selling local food. But this lady was a dish, from A to Z. She wore a bright yellow skirt with matching blouse, stood about five-six, had those same tantalizing eyes her sister possessed and a figure that belonged on the inside of the Police Gazzette. Her face was beautiful, with a gorgeous aquiline nose and full lips... slightly pouty. Her shiny black hair was up in a bun with a silver barrette holding it together.

"Hi, there. Uh...your sister across the street directed me here. I think I'm interested in a train trip. I'm just not sure where yet."

Her voice was warm and charming. "Señor, I am Adora Moreno, at your service." I sure wish she meant that in all departments. This gal had something that turned a switch on in me. "How can I help you?"

"Well, I've been presented with a mystery, you see. Maybe you can help. I need to find a city facing west with a large bay, Redwood trees growing nearby, maybe some hills or mountains close together that look alike, a fairyland castle nearby—oh, yeah, and an Asian virgin called *Nymphomania* or something like that."

The beautiful young woman looked at me strangely. "Have you been drinking—I mean too much tequila, señor? I never have customer oh, so—so extraño!"

"No, I like gin and smoke cigarettes and chase beautiful women, but...no, I'm not drunk, Miss—Miss Moreno."

She came out from behind her desk. I had a feeling she was as drawn to me as I was to her. She extended her hand. "*Entonces*, it is a pleasure to meet you and let us see if we can find your city by the bay, a fairyland *castillo*, some *montañas* like twin breasts—and one Asian virgin."

"I'm—I'm Denning—Cable Denning…" I said, shaking her hand. A jolt of electricity went through both of us. We registered it with our eyes and it took a few seconds for us to recover. "I—I, uh, sure would be grateful if you could help me out. You see, this isn't exactly a pleasure trip."

She looked me over. "I can see, you are a mysterious—and maybe dangerous man." She went back behind her desk and took out a folder. "Come, Señor Denning…*venga aquí* so I show you." I came around to where she stood behind the desk. As she leaned over the map, her ample breasts fell forward and the loose blouse permitted me to see two marvelous cantaloupes just right for the picking. "Ay, *aquí*—here! *San Francisco* has everything except *el castillo* I believe. Here you have big bay, ferry boats to carry *la gente*, facing west *al océano*. Probably you find your virgin *aquí*—in Chinatown! Big trees with red bark grow across the water in Muir Woods *Parque Nacional*. No other *ciudad* has all those that meet together, Señor Denning. You want to buy ticket on the Owl, the Lark or the Daylight?"

I thought about what Crazy Jack had said, something about a Lark.. "Thanks a bunch, Miss Moreno. I think I'll take the Lark. I owe you a dinner or something—you have helped me mucho, señorita."

"Con mucho gusto," she replied. "When, señor, do you wish to depart?"

"I need about three days to wrap things up with my sergeant, and take care of some miscellaneous business."

Adora Moreno began to make out the ticket info. I couldn't help being attracted to the babe. "Ah…. you say *sergeant*—are you in the army?"

"No, I'm a cop just about to go on a business leave of absence."

"Oh, you do not look like policeman—more like *private detective*, señor. One who walks en la noche in overcoat and brown shoes with a nice fedora." She laughed a wonderful laugh and I echoed her.

110

"You know, you're not the first person to say that to me. Maybe someday I'll get out of the force and become a private dick."

"A what?"

"A private dick—that's short for detective—I don't know how the term came into being. Anyway, it means, like you said, a private detective."

She got a little red in the face. "Oh, well, señor, where I come from, *private dick* means private okay, but not what you're saying…"

We both laughed. "Yeah, I know that one, too." Then I looked at her. "Life is so strange. I walk in here and find you, Miss Moreno—and I'm completely taken by surprise—and delighted. I know it may seem a little forward of me, but may I call you Adora—a lovely name, by the way."

"Sí, if I can call you Cable—okay?"

"Yeah, sure. Cable's fine. Would you…uh, would you consider having lunch or dinner with me sometime soon?"

She looked up at me, a smile crossing her face and her eyes shining. "Like you say, señor Cable, *la vida es extraña*. You walk in…and I also look at you—and I breathe better…like I know you before I even meet you."

I was touched by this young woman's frankness. "Do—do you have a boyfriend or husband—marido?"

"Sí, once upon a time, un esposo. But like a lot of Latinos, he beat me and contrall—ah, contrell—"

"—controlled you, Adora."

"Sí, gracias—control. Ahora I am alone. I left him in San Diego two years ago. And mi hermana, me and mi madre open *Todo el Mundo*." She finished writing up the ticket info and I paid her.

"I think it was your hermana who led me into a dark alley to

111

make a phone call about twenty minutes ago."

She was looking at me. "She is restless, my sister. Did she do anything dishonest to you? Oh, I know, sometimes she does sneaking things. But she is good. How you say, silly…"

"No, she was on the level. Probably got paid a couple of bucks to follow me today and then report to certain parties who wanted to know my whereabouts."

She looked at me more deeply, into my heart, into my spirit. "How long…does it take…to fall in love with someone, Señor Cable?"

I winced a bit, thinking about Honey. "Please, just call me Cable." I took a deep breath. "Probably about thirty seconds if you're the right one," I said, looking into her eyes, mesmerized by the sincerity that poured out of them. "But if you're looking at me as a candidate, I ain't the best choice, Adora. I smoke, drink, look at pretty skirts a lot, have a doll for a girlfriend— and currently live on the edge of extinction. Your sister can vouch for that if she's seen the kind of company I keep lately."

"I did not think you were available to love, Cable. But that does not stop me from what I feel, eh? We cannot always stop—what we—feel…for somebody else, no?"

"No, you're right about that, Adora. I—I, uh—I want you to know I kinda feel the same as you do. You took me by surprise. But it's the wrong timing, kid, and nobody knows it better than I do just about now. I was drawn to you the minute I saw you behind that desk. But then again, what hombre in his right mind wouldn't be?"

She reflected quietly. "*Gracias.* So…what is my sister up to?"

"I don't know. It was very strange. When I went to a food stand for a few tacos, she waited on me and then asked me if I was me. The next thing I knew I was following her down an alley to a phone booth—"

Just then in walked Isaiah Damianos. "Oh, Mr. Denning. I

waited in the alley for you. Flora told me you might be here. Hello, you must be the sister Flora was talking about."

I knew Adora had picked up the tension Damianos brought in with him. "Hola, señor. What can I do for you?"

"I—I'm here for Señor Denning, señorita." He looked at me. "I believe it would benefit us mutually if we could talk in my car. Por favor?"

"Yeah, as long as you've got no odorous surprises this time, Damianos." I walked over to Adora. "Very glad to meet you, Miss Moreno." She slipped a business card into the palm of my hand.

"If there is something else—I can help you with— call me, por favor..." I shook her hand and left with Damianos. We crossed the street, went up the alley to his car.

Damianos opened the door for me. I got in. "So...Flora Moreno tells me you went to see one Madame Palladino, a respected soothsayer of sorts. You went with an odd little man who appears a little unbalanced mentally. We do not know him. Then she followed you to this little Mexican food stand."

"Why the tail, Damianos? I thought you trusted me on this crazy journey you've more or less mandated I am to take. Remember, the only reason I'm doing this is to get you off my back and get out of going back to work as a cop for a few days. By the way, you've gotta come up with an expense account for me—I ain't shelling out any more dough for you and your cause until you start paying your way."

He took out a wad of greenbacks from his pocket, counted me out ten crisp one-hundred dollar bills. "This will get you started, Mr. Denning. Now...tell me what you know...so we can amicably account for my expenditures. Does that sound fair to you?"

"Yeah, okay. It comes down like this. Crazy Jack tells me about a trip by train, and Palladino's name, so I go to see her.

She tells me about a city by the bay, twin peaks, redwood trees, an Asian virgin and a fairy tale castle somewhere nearby. Totally baffled, I ask your little spy if she knows of a travel agency. She and her sister run the one across the street where you found me. Adora Moreno solves my immediate dilemma. *San Francisco* comes up in neon lights, so I buy a ticket in three days. Can you clear it with my boss within that time so I can get on with it?"

"Good work, Denning!" Damianos exclaimed, quite excited at how fast I worked. "You've got the makings of a true detective. Yes, I can clear it with your superiors. By all means, take the trip and keep me posted." He reached into his breast pocket and handed me a piece of paper with a phone number. "Here, call me as soon as you've got something. Please keep any and all details confidential—and share them with no one."

He thanked me, opened the car door for me and I left, thinking what a crazy day this had been. Tomorrow would almost be a relief to go to work one more day and tell Mario and Honey about some of my new adventure. I would drop in to the *Bella Notte* tonight and see Honey.

CHAPTER 7

DANGERS ON A TRAIN

The place was packed and noisy and the blonde singer up there on the stage almost seemed like a stranger to me. I could not get used to the makeover Honey had allowed in order to change her theatrical image. She was singing a fine version of *After You've Gone* and it reminded me of a character in a yet-to-be released novel by an ex-Pinkerton employee named Dashiell Hammett. Rick St. John, a police storywriter, told me about a tuberculosis victim who smoked and drank too much and was creating a tough gumshoe character named *Sam Spade*. A tentative title for the book was *The Maltese Falcon* and just the concept of it fired my young man's imagination. A pulp fiction magazine, *Black Mask*, was considering a finished book for serial publication. Anyway, *The Maltese Falcon* reminded me of the teetering romance Honey was singing about. It held a kind of irony in the lyrics: '*After you've gone, after we break up, after you've gone, you're gonna wake up…*' I would've liked to do that just about now, be gone, just disappear. Things were piling up on top of me like the pyramid of Cheops. But there was something in my blood that got excited when danger and adventure met at the pass like two forces clashing at the crossroads, pushing me into the land of the unknown and mysterious.

Honey finished her song and came over to the bar where I stood. "Fancy meeting you here," she said in that wonderful voice of hers filled with wit.

"Well, you know, I came in to hear some golden-throated little songbird and all I get is a blonde blackbird."

"Harping on that again, are you? You look like something the cat dragged in, Mister—too many nights out away from home?"

"Too many nights away from someone who's hardly ever

available anymore, is more like it," I quipped back.

"What's a matter, copper, you afraid to enter a dark room late at night? The lady might even welcome a secret lover who comes and cums but hardly stays anymore."

"It's the price of stardom the lady pays. The secret lover is simple and uncomplicated, loving and horny for her."

"There's nothing simple about him, buddy. He's about as simple as a thousand-piece jigsaw puzzle. What part do you put where?"

"He'd probably be pretty happy just putting the part that works best right up into her—her finest places, if you know what I mean."

She smiled and gave me that tit-for-tat expression of hers. "Touché! As a matter of fact, I'd settle for that tonight, if the gentleman's available."

I hugged her and kissed her on the cheek because I had been trained never to muss the lipstick. "He's kinda beat, but he's available. What time does the lady get off?"

"Midnight, Mister. Can you wait around?"

"I've got that 5:00 a.m. Reveille, you know. It's hard pulling an eight-hour shift chasing bad guys after a night of skin wrestling with a pretty babe. Is there any possibility of a rain check?"

"Hey, Bub, you never used to complain. Am I not putting out to the man's satisfaction or something? Maybe I should get a guy whose hours are more like mine—what do you think?"

"I've put in for a job on a different planet, babe. I've got some stuff to share with you. What if I go to your place, grab a little shut-eye and then lay it on you when you get home?"

"I'd rather you just plain *lay* me, Mister, but if it's as important as you say it is, then okay...but before you go, I've got a new song for you."

"That's great, *Golden Throat*," I said, smiling across to her. "I'm sorry our lives have gone in such diverse directions lately."

"Where in the hell did a two-bit cop like you get such a vocabulary, anyhow?"

"Salvation Army, used words are on sale Mondays and Thursdays," I chuckled. "Could you use some spare used words? I got lots of 'em."

She kissed me gently on the lips and went back up to the bandstand. The band started up and she lit into a Ruth Etting song that knocked my socks off because I knew it was meant for me. *'Love me or leave me, or let me be lonely, you won't believe me, but I love you only...I'd rather be lonely than happy with somebody new...'* Honey was singing her message to me in no uncertain terms. I felt she loved me for keeps, but life had torn some of the fabric and we were limping a bit these days. *'There'll be no one unless that someone is you....I intend to be independently blue....I want your love, but I don't want to borrow, to have it today, and to give back tomorrow...for my love is your love...there's no love for nobody else...'* When she finished I whistled and applauded until I knew she could hear me and smiled my way.

On my way home on the streetcar I was reflecting on Honey's amazing song and delivery when suddenly Adora Moreno came seeping into my mind. I couldn't explain it, but I knew we had some kind of magic going on between us. I could still feel the electricity between our fingers when we shook hands earlier today. That's the kinda stuff people talk about in romance novels and erotic fantasies everyone would like to take into their heart of hearts. Rarely is it ever experienced, I thought.

I decided to pop off at the flat I shared with Mario before going to Honey's. Since he'd married Rosalie Elena he wasn't around much. But some nights he'd sleep in closer so the ride in wasn't as demanding. Every guy needed down time alone.

Mario was sitting up in bed in his T-shirt listening to the radio. He was a burly guy and the hair on his chest bubbled out of his shirt like a dark ink splotch. I told him I was taking another leave of absence. At first he got pissed because he hated working with my alternate. Then he calmed down as I explained the truth of my predicament.

"Take me along, Cable—I'll smash that Damianos character to bits and get you out of those jaws of coercion. Good cops are heroes, Cable—and I'm one of 'em for you, buddy."

"Thanks, pal," I said, going into a dresser drawer and taking out a fresh pack of Lucky Strikes. "But I think I need to go this one alone—they could bump me off if they suspected I was bringing in someone else. Plus you're a married man now—with a baby in the oven."

"Have it your way, buster. You know, you're acting more and more like one of those independent new breeds of private dicks. When will you be back on patrol with me?"

"Three, four days—tops. Once I procure what they're sending me after, then that's it."

"And this is still about that *golden throat* thing at the morgue?"

"Yep. Seems to some it's like the most valuable collectors' item ever."

"Ehhh…who can figure? Well, call me if you need me."

I tapped Mario on the shoulder and left. By the time I reached Honey's it was already eleven thirty. Surprisingly, Honey's roommate, Zelda, was still up, sitting at the kitchen table. As I walked down the hall toward Honey's bedroom, she called out to me. "Oh, Officer Denning—would you come here a moment, please?"

I walked back toward the attractive girl with the thick glasses. "Well, hello, Zelda—what's up?"

"I have a sliver from my *cycas revoluta*—and I can't see the darned thing up close—even with these glasses. How're your eyes?"

"Cycas who? Sounds like the Mexican Revolution has come and gone in your backyard, huh?"

She laughed. "I really like your sense of humor. Here." She showed me her finger and I asked her to move to better light. She led me down the hall into her bedroom. It was small and filled with all kinds of flowering cactus plants. She handed me a pair of tweezers, sat on the bed under a bright lamp and I sat on the bed next to her. "How does someone like Honey attract a wonderful man like you?"

I raised my eyebrows as I picked away at the sliver slightly under the skin on her left thumb. "Because she's young and beautiful and intelligent," I answered, concentrating on the task at hand.

"And I'm old and ugly and dumb?"

"Of course not, Zelda. That's not what I implied. You asked me, I answered. I don't think you're old or ugly or—"

"—and she's really good in bed, isn't she? I hear you two a lot and I know she's making you very—very happy in there."

I laughed. "Shame on you—for listening. But I guess I can't deny it, kid. Honey's got the right chemistry for me. Everyone's different, you know."

"How would I be able to land someone like you?" She had only her robe on, and whether it was intentional or not, she leaned forward as I pulled her hand a bit more toward the light. As she did so, she revealed her ample bosom to me as they hung dangling against the white terrycloth. "How does a woman display herself to someone she might be interested in? I mean, I'm such a bookworm—I don't even think I have a sexual personality."

I pulled the sliver out. "Ah, there you are." I got up to go but she pulled me back down onto her bed.

"Please—may I call you Cable?—I really don't have a clue…"

"Well, Zelda…attraction between opposite sexes is usually made up of two things. One, chemistry and two, cosmetics. I think girls who get a lot of guys or attract a lot of men for whatever reasons, make themselves up—like Honey does when she goes out to sing or dance—you know, she wears a lot of makeup. But the chemistry part is a little more elusive…you either have it with someone, or you don't."

She took her glasses off and continued to lean forward, still exposing her full breasts to me in plain view. "How endowed does a girl have to be before a guy notices?" she asked in an innocent enough tone.

I quickly glanced at her breasts. "Ah…I—I think you are more than adequately endowed, young miss."

"If I make myself up, leave my glasses at home—and gussy up with a sexy dress—will you take me out on a date?"

"Well, I'd do it for you, Zelda. But I do have to check with Honey."

Then she hit me in a lonely, sensitive place, for I knew there were a million Zeldas in the world for every Honey Combes. "I've—I've never been on a date. If you can teach me how…I mean, how to behave, maybe I can be attractive to someone—do you think?" She leaned back, giving me relief that I wouldn't have to be tempted by those large, welcoming honkers of hers.

"What about the guys at school? College should be a neat place to meet someone who might be attracted to you."

"They're all geeks, like me. You know, boneheads. *Your* life is exciting and that's because you're exciting, Cable. Most guys are boring. Of course, maybe I'm boring, too. How can we help who and what we are?"

"Well, we can't very well, I'd guess. Seems we're born the way we are and maybe we can change a few things here and there—"

Just then Honey walked down the hall and saw Zelda's bedroom door open and me sitting on the bed with her roommate. "Aha! The hen's barely gone and the rooster's playing with the chicks, eh?" she laughed.

Zelda flushed a little. "Oh, Honey—it's my fault. Cable was getting a sliver out of my thumb that I couldn't. And we started talking about guys. Would you let him date me, so he can show me the ropes sometime?"

Honey raised her eyebrows. "Well, what's been going on here?" She glanced at Zelda's open robe. "That's up to Cable, hon, but it's okay with me. I don't think you could have a better teacher than old flatfoot here."

"Hey, thanks, kid!" I said, chuckling.

I bade Zelda good night with the promise that one day I'd take her out for dinner and a dance. She seemed thrilled.

Honey came in from the bathroom completely undressed except for her panties. "Laggore pestered me again tonight—something about me singing for a big birthday bash for one of Dragna's lieutenants. Also, I got a call about a meeting at United Artists with Charlie Chaplin. I'm rather jazzed about that. If I get that part in *City Lights*, Cable, my career will be made…made…made, big guy!" She came over and pushed me onto the bed, jumping on top of me. "Now…with my lipstick, rouge and powder gone, you can muss me up all you want. Where do you want to start? I can think of several places—what about you, handsome?"

Before we made love that night, I told her I was going away in a couple of days. I tried to communicate the whole scenario without it sounding dangerous, but Honey's instincts were powerful and she sensed a lot more was going on than I told her. "Don't go away to die, Cable—I know you've been feeling us drift from each other. For me, baby, there is no other man. I am devoted to you and want you to come home to me. I know it would be of no use for me to try and convince you to stick to being a safe daytime policeman and we could live happily ever after. But I see it in your eyes, that restless thrill that comes from you being released into danger and the unknown. I don't even know how I know that. I just do."

I kissed her so she'd know I heard every word. "Thanks, babe, for not being possessive of me. I fly best when my wings are untied, you know. And you've done that for me. I'll be back in a few days."

Then she asked me something curious. "Cable…is there someone else? I just got this feeling today. Like someone's on the horizon and it's changed the energy between us. Stupid, huh?"

"There's no one, Honey Combes. You know me, I always look at pretty skirts and maybe flirt now and then. But I do come home to you because the fit is so good and I love who we are together."

She turned the light out, and we blended together under the sheets in a wonderful union of bodies and hearts. "Are you really going to take Zelda on a date, officer?" That was the last thing she said as she began massaging my private parts to attention. The rest was excitement and bliss. Who knows why certain people come together—or what they discover in each other that changes their worlds?

The next morning Sergeant O'Flaherty called me into his office and informed me that Captain Treadwell had requested I go on special assignment. He dismissed me with an odd look, as if he suspected I'd been pulling strings upstairs to gain these opportunities. If it were only that simple.

For whatever reasons, I followed through and called Adora Moreno before Mario and I headed out. I forgot how early it was. "Sí…halo?"

"Sorry to call you so early—Adora—this is Cable Denning.

We met yesterday, remember?"

There was a slight pause. "Oh, gracias, Cable. I was afraid I never hear from you. I am happy you call."

"I—I, uh….I was wondering if you wanted to have dinner with me tonight—and maybe a little dancing? I get to my joint about six, need to wash off the day, shave, and put on some clean clothes. How about around seven-thirty? Where do you live?"

"I am afraid, Cable. I think about you all night. I am afraid I am being in love with you. Tu comprende, señor?"

I hesitated, not knowing exactly how to respond. "I feel it, too, Adora. But if we just run away from it, we'll never know exactly what it means. Maybe things will have a whole different outcome than we think."

"I don' think so, Cable. When you touch me—then it is all over my body, the spark—and I feel myself….falling…sí, *yo caer*."

"So you don't want to have dinner with me?"

"I did not say that. *Mi corazón, es levanto…Yo pienso, sí…* I go with you. I live just above *Todo el Mundo* with mi madre and Flora. Seven-thirty I am ready for you." There was a short pause. "Cable?" Her voice was soft, vulnerable.

"Yes?"

"Por favor, be gentle with me. I ask only that."

"Of course, Adora. After all, it's only dinner and a dance or two. Besides, I'm going away for a few days—to San Francisco, remember—you sold me the ticket?"

"Sí…not with that strange man, Señor Damianos?"

"No, by myself, babe…on special assignment for the police force…"

"Oh," she said, as if that didn't figure in her head.

"See you tonight, Adora…"

123

I hung up thinking about the rush in my stomach that woman evoked in me. It was like I desired her and wanted to weep with her all at the same time. It felt crazy. The rest of the day went okay and when Mario and I got back to the station in our Model-T, I was looking forward to going home and getting cleaned up. Mario was taking the trolley all the way back to East L.A. and Rosalie Elena.

As I got to the stairs leading up to my flat, I saw a familiar figure standing in the shadows of the dimly lit hallway. It was Crazy Jack. He approached me. "Cigarette! Cigarette!"

"Hiya, Crazy Jack." I performed the usual ritual by giving him a Lucky Strike and tucking the package into his musty coat pocket. "What's up?"

"I don't know! I don't know! Oh, bird fly high—under sky! Birds on train skin you alive in five—but I don't know! I don't know!"

"What're you telling me, Jack? Danger on the train? Yeah, well, I've already suspected that. I can feel someone doesn't want me to reach San Francisco—at least alive. So I'm packing my .38 with a good supply of ammo—just in case. Is that what you came to tell me?"

"I don't know! I don't know! Plenty...plenty...throw off... the black hat...and celebrate—celebrate your new fate—not too late! But I don't know! I don't know!"

"Look, Jack, I'm kinda in a hurry here. Tell me if there's anything else I should know." I took a five-dollar bill from my pocket and tucked it into his. "Two days from now I'm on my way to—well, I don't know what the hell I'm on my way to. A ride to Chinatown? Where will it take me, Jack—can you tell me that?"

"I don't know! I don't know! China...China...doll...pretty thing...might sting! But I don't know! I don't know!"

I thanked Crazy Jack and ran up the stairs trying to piece

together the weird things this man was prone to say. Most of it didn't make much sense, but I got the danger on a train thing and the possibility that if and when I find that Chinese virgin, all may not be as it seems.

I got to 424 N. Main Street. It was a three story stone and brick building called the Pico House. The top floor was all residents and the ground floor was all small shops. I rang the doorbell underneath the sign that read, *Todo el Mundo Travel* at the ground floor. An attractive, matronly woman with black and silver hair tied behind her opened the door. "Señor Denning? I am Elisa Moreno, Adora's mother. Por favor, come in…"

"Good to meet you, Mrs. Moreno. Nice little business you have here."

"Gracias, señor. Please wait here. Adora will be out in un momento." She was a handsome woman and walked proudly. I was wondering if she had sacrificed her life for those two lovely daughters when one of them came walking through the door from the back of the building. She was dressed in a light-yellow dress with white heels, gloves and a lovely black onyx necklace and a light coat to match her dress. Her hair was pitched slightly to the side in a handsome bun, not unlike the one I had seen when I met her the day before. I was awe-struck by how naturally beautiful this woman was. "You're a knockout, Adora," I said as I walked forward to greet her.

"Knockout?"

"Yeah, like the most beautiful thing I've seen all day."

"Gracias, Cable. I am ready. Do we go now? You meet mi madre, no?"

"Yeah, and I liked her right away. Goodness pours out from her all over the place. No wonder you turned out to be such a fine lady."

"I am lady? Con mucho gusto, I am lady with you. Do we go?"

"Yeah, we go…"

With my bit of extra loot, I thought I would take her to Montmartre Nightclub…a hot spot with a nice band led by Vincent Rose, at 6757 Hollywood Blvd. It had been awhile since I went dancing there with Amanda Baxter, but I heard the food was good, the atmosphere ritzy and the band played songs of the day. Not to mention the celebrities that usually frequented the place. I had forgotten to make reservations but we were shown to a nice table near the back of the restaurant and all we had to do was walk through a large opening to the lounge and the music. We sat as the waiter did his usual and left the menus with us. "So, babe, what will it be? I'm hungry as hell—I think I'm going to order a steak for a change."

The lovely lady in yellow looked across at me. "I forget to tell you, you look beautiful también, señor."

"Well, thanks, Adora. I guess once I clean up at least they won't throw me out of the joint, huh?" I laughed.

She smiled, those warm brown eyes burning a hole in me as the candlelight set them to sparkling. "*Qué extraño*, Cable—I am nervous. Lo siento mucho. I do not mean to. It has been long time since when a man take me out. But I enjoy to dance."

"Just try to relax, hon. What do you feel like eating?"

"I have no *apetito*—maybe a little something to drink?"

I hailed down the waiter and ordered a lime seltzer water. It was tough not being able to have a good couple of shots of alcohol. But then I just remembered I had a flask of gin in my coat pocket. When the drinks came, I poured a couple of shots in both of them. In a few minutes, I could see Adora's face relax as the booze warmed her up a bit. We drank for a little while, I finally got her to order a ravioli plate while I went for a New York steak with all the trimmings.

The band began to play a very danceable version of *You Took Advantage of Me* and I took Adora's hand to lead her out onto the dance floor. Again, we both got hit with that spark of magic something that went right to certain places instantly. She reacted as if she'd just gotten an electric shock and had to take in a deep breath to continue walking beside me. "You…you felt it again…?" I asked her, checking out her eyes.

"Sí…yes, Cable. It is so difficult…before when I meet you, I breathe easy, now I cannot breathe when I am near you."

"We both feel it, lady. I think the song they're playing is appropriate. It's called *You Took Advantage of Me*."

"Okay, so I take advantage of you—or you me?" she said.

For the first time I took Adora Moreno into my arms—and it felt good. She jostled her body into mine until the fit became perfect and when I leaned over a little, she put her cheek next to mine as we twirled slowly around the floor. "Well, what fits best? I could take advantage of you because I know you're vulnerable and your eyes have told me it's been a long time between guys in your bed. Or, you could be planning to take advantage of *me* now, couldn't you? Women plan and scheme and make it look like it was the guy's doing all the time."

"Sí, pero…I would not do that to you. For me, it has to be *equal*."

"Do you remember why I'm taking you out this evening?" I asked.

"Because you want to make love to me," she said in no uncertain terms.

I was a bit taken aback. "Well, that may be at the bottom of things, doll, but originally it was to thank you for helping me find the city where all the clues came together. And preparing my train ticket."

"*Por nada*," she laughed. "For you, I would buy a ticket for around the world—if you would let me come with you…"

I squeezed her tightly as we spun around the floor. "That's a

127

lovely thing to say, Adora. You don't even know me. I'm a lowly cop, barely out of the rookie stage with a private investigator's instincts. I told you before, I drink alcohol too much, smoke cigarettes, chase after pretty skirts and have a girlfriend named Honey Combes who tames my bedroom manners. She's a professional singer and aspiring movie actress."

She looked saddened a bit as the music ended and we went back to our seats. "She is high in the world…beautiful and talented, no? Oh, and…I am only another woman you meet. But I cannot complete—complar—"

"—*compete*, is what I think you're trying to say. But this isn't about competing, Adora. It's about two people who just found each other in this crazy world and they're trying to figure out the pieces. Why? Why would a dame like you and a guy like me feel sparks fly when we touch, or why does your body fit into mine like it was born there? And why is it when I look at you, all thought of anyone else is suddenly taken away from me?"

The alcohol had begun to affect her a little and she relaxed somewhat. "You speak—*tu habla la cancion*, like a song to my heart…I am sorry I am so extraña with you esta noche—but I think I am falling in love…I tol' you on *el teléfono esta maña-na*. And…" She twirled a finger inside her glass. "…you have a honey—not me. So…I must not fall more…" She looked intensely into my eyes. "As you say, long time…I am close to a man, Cable. I am built up like—what you say?—"

"—a dam…."

"Sí, a dam. If I do not spill it out on you—or I see you or even talk to you—I will die, señor, simple…oh…*yo muera!*…"

"So maybe we shouldn't see each other after tonight. I'm—I'm sorry, Adora. Neither of us saw this coming. But it's my fault. I asked you out. I don't wanna lie to you. Sure, I wanted to thank you for being so helpful with my trip and all—but as I said, down deep there's this fire in my belly that won't go away and its name is *desire*—wanting you, lady. So there you have it. My truth. I always want to tell the truth, Adora. That's why I told you about Honey so you would know another woman takes care of certain needs and helps absorb the shock of being human, making it a bit easier to get along in this insane world."

"*Yo comprendo.* I did not mean *esta noche estar triste*, Cable. I am sorry. Ahora, we are both sad. Maybe you take me home? I don' like me much just now. What you say—no fun to be with, gringo." She tried to lighten the moment, but it didn't work for her. We ate in silence. I paid the bill and we caught the street-car back to her place. I walked her to the front door. She stood there looking up into my eyes, checking out my face, my lips. "If I kiss you now, Cable, I will be lost. I am breathing hard, trying not to fall into you anymore. *Por favor—*"

On a savage impulse I grabbed Adora Moreno and thrust my lips hard onto hers. She melted into me as if all the idle talk had suddenly crumbled before the altar of passion and desire. She clung to me as if her last breath depended on it and I held her to me under that transom as if I never wanted to let her go. When finally our faces separated enough for us to look at each other, I could hear a lonely sax playing in the night, the same one that haunts me when life holds a bitter irony of all the things that might have been. "I had to do that…it was building since the first minute I saw you in that store in there."

She melted back into my arms. "Sí, I know—I needed you to do it. My heart, my woman have…have *pulsed* for you *todo esta día.* Now, as I tol' you in *la café*…I *am* lost…in you, Señor Denning. What to do?"

I took a deep breath, found my cigarette pack, took one out and lit up a Lucky Strike as we stood there. "Yeah, beautiful Adora—what to do? I don't suppose if either of us, uh, walked away…it would change anything, do you?"

"You are the truth hombre—what does your truth tell you?"

129

"That I want to spend a month in bed with you and never leave it except to take a bath and eat."

She sighed and looked at me with an expression that penetrated the wall I had built around me to keep most people out. "Me, too. Will we do that *algún día*—someday?"

I boarded the Lark just before midnight. The steam rose from the engines as they rested like giant dragons on their rails. There was something exciting and mysterious about a train station in the middle of a big city. People from all walks of life were arriving, leaving, greeting one another, while others walked alone out to the taxi stands. Honey was singing *The Man I Love* in my head and it haunted me somewhere inside because I knew things were different between us. Even if the intention was still there, things move on in ways we can't control, just like that belching, steaming behemoth up ahead. Maybe somewhere in another dimension things stay in that state of bliss two people wanted for each other, but I doubt it. I think everything changes and you can't stop the world from turning, spinning us into the unknown, the next surprising minute, the entrance to the door up ahead or a smile that changes your world.

When I checked in at the ticket office to pick up my passage, the clerk informed me my ticket had been upgraded and I was to have a drawing room sleeper instead of coach, which I had originally paid for. I questioned the man how it might've happened, but he told me he had no idea, it just showed up that way. I wasn't sure whether the favor was a deathtrap or a courtesy because my gut told me some things were going to come down on that train which would try to prevent me from completing my trip to San Francisco. I doubted it would be Damianos, for why would he double-cross himself? But if not him, who?

Every face was a stranger as I boarded Car #27. The Lark was supposed to take 13 hours and travel through the central valley of California, making very few stops along the way. I asked the conductor to point the way to Drawing Room 6. The porter looked at me with surprise as I stood before the door about to open it. But he didn't say anything. I reached inside my coat for my chest holster and put my hand on my .38, just in case. The room was dimly lit. The tiny bathroom door was shut and a light shone through a crack at the bottom. Just then the door opened.

"It is not, señor, a ticket around the world—and we do not have a month to spend in *la cama*, but this is next *best thing*?"

Adora Moreno ran to me and I was glad to feel her warmth in my arms again. "Adora! How in the hell?—"

"—I could not spend any more days away from you, querido! It is now or never, Cable. I bought the sleep-car ticket —and mi madre and mi hermana will see to the agency while we are gone." She checked out my eyes. "You are not angry with me, no?"

"No, beautiful lady, no. I—I, uh, just didn't expect it, that's all. And you may be putting yourself in harm's way. This is not a pleasure trip—or at least it *wasn't* until you showed up—nor is it about police business."

"Yo Sé. It is about Damianos' secreto, huh? How you say, *danger excites this señorita*."

"You, too, eh? I thought I was the only one with that disease."

"So you think Damianos cause trouble? *Un hombre misterioso*."

"I can't say yet. I don't think Damianos wants to stop me— just yet. I have a feeling there are some other tough hombres plying their trades aboard this train, though."

"I come to help you stay *seguro*—safe." She melted into my arms and turned her head up to kiss me. I couldn't resist the dame. There was some other force at work here, something that drew me to her like the sea to the shore.

"So now it's truth time, Adora. You know about Honey. You know I want you like a bull in heat. I don't know how long any of it will last."

"*Ahora*…now…is all we have *en toda la vida*. I cannot see beyond *este momento*. All I know is I desire you so much I cannot contain it, Cable. I mean to hurt nobody, even your nice *chica romántica*."

"Then it's settled. I won't tell that part of myself that's got the moral conscience—that way, you get a brand new guy without guilt."

She laughed and touched my leg with her warm, open hand. I don't know what it was about the doll, but I got chills when she touched me. I led her over to the bunks as the train began to pull out. I could hear that wonderful, familiar and lonely whistle. It was like that melancholy sax that keeps playing in my head. It pulled me somewhere, but I didn't know whether it was past or future. Just a place where longing sits in your stomach but you can't figure out what it is and why it's there. But it's always there.

"These bunk beds will never do," I said, taking my shoes off. I was thinking of Honey. What was I doing? I hadn't been with another woman since we began seeing each other. Yet it was like a hand on my back, pushing me toward this beautiful creature whose smile and laughter and sincerity drew me in like a magnet to hot metal.

"Double-deck—you on top, me on bottom—okay," she laughed. Then she began to unbutton her blouse. "I am *temeroso*—afraid—a bit…will you help me? I like you to be the man…and I will be the woman who *entrega*, surrenders to her hombre, okay?"

I said nothing but continued where she left off and slowly undid the buttons on her blouse. Her chest was heaving and those wonderful and full breasts of hers stood firm as I touched them through her bra. Shivers went through her and she sighed. Next I began to unbutton the four large buttons on her skirt. When it fell to the floor and she stepped out of it, I could understand why men go insane over a woman's body. Adora Moreno's body was perfect. She got the idea and began undressing me. By the time we were standing in the sleeping car totally nude, we knew nothing would stop us from making love. Hastily we grabbed all the blankets, cushions and pillows we could and put them on the floor. She pulled me down onto her. "Oh! Rock-a-bye, baby!" she said, realizing how swaying and bumpy the train ride was.

"Speaking of which, can you have babies? I mean, I don't have any—any, uh, protection to prevent—"

"—sí, I can have babies." She brought her lips to where they barely brushed my own. "I want ten of your babies, Cable."

"Oh, God, Adora…I think there's a stop in Fresno. I can buy some—"

"—no! Señor Denning," she whispered. "I want nothing between us except *amor, mi amor*."

"Adora…do you realize what you're saying? I mean, a baby could change our whole lives—we're coming into the middle of a Rudolph Valentino movie here—you know, the Sheik and all?"

"He never use anything."

"It's a *movie*, babe, not real life. I don't think you know what you're saying here. I mean, look, kid, I don't want to use anything either…"

She looked at me with those melting brown eyes of hers. "…do you trust me, mi amor? Do you feel how—how heavy is my breath? Can you know how I ache for you since first I see you? *Por favor*, Cable…"

Her breathing was labored and her gorgeous breasts were prickling with goose bumps as her nipples became rigid. She

133

pulled my mouth onto hers and we started climbing to the moon with fireworks going off on all sides. As I entered her there came such a joyful release of pleasure that I probably will never forget it. She was the perfect everything for me. Our parts all fit together the right way in the right places. There on the floor of a speeding train, clicking and clacking and rolling, two people found each other and neither would ever be the same again.

We may not have broken any sex-marathon records, but we managed to make love a good three or four hours. Finally I sat up and leaned against the bunks. I reached into my pants pocket and got out a pack of Lucky Strikes. I lit up and offered Adora one. "Smoke?"

She was beaming and contented. "*No fumo, gracias.*" Then she felt herself between her legs. "Ay, you make me sore, big man. But I love it."

I chuckled. "Well, you can never say you didn't *want* it, young woman. I think that's part of being re-initiated into love making after so long a time. We don't have to do it anymore, you know."

She scooted over to me and kissed my private parts all over. "*Hombre malo*…you better not leave me alone. I want you until I cannot walk anymore, *mi muchacho bonito.*"

"That's fine with me, babe, but I'm more expensive as the day wears on, you know. So…you might pace yourself a bit."

She hit me lightly on the shoulder and laughed. "*Nunca! Nunca! Nunca!* Never will I keep myself from wanting you… and having you…"

We were about four hours south of San Francisco when we made our way to the dining car. Being an overnight train, it was open all night and we sat down to an immaculate white table-cloth with cloth napkins and real silverware. We were hungry and ate heartily. "All that—uh, exercise, makes me hungry—what's your excuse?"

"Some hungry man already ate me—so now *yo tengo hambre, toro.*" She smiled at me and lit me up with those warm brown eyes. "And you were *el toro pasion*, Señor Denning. And you left your smell on me. I am now smelling like your—your *producción total.*"

I looked across the small table at her. "Well, how else does a bull mark his territory?" I said, winking at her. She giggled out loud. How did I get so lucky in this life? I guess I could've asked that same question about Honey—and did, if I recall. To have that specialness just *once* in your life was rare, so twice was more than any man could expect. Yet here I was, looking into the beautiful face of a woman I'd met only days before who desired me with a consuming passion and ardent love few are equipped to deal with. I hoped I would be for Adora. She deserved *good* in her life.

During our meal I noticed a couple of men sitting at different tables who had been glancing at me from time to time. One of them looked like a gangster that worked for Frank Laggore through Dragna. They called him *Crank Sotto*, because when he was young he broke his arm twice while crank-starting his car, so I'd heard. I knew about him because he had a police record two miles long and was probably a hit man for Dragna and his newly organized crime syndicate. Him I'd have to keep my eye on.

The other fellow appeared to be quite elderly, a stern but kindly look sat in the middle of a nice face that sported a silver-white beard and moustache. He could not have been more than five-five and possessed a piercing twinkle in his eye. I noticed a cane leaning up against the wall near to his seat. Across from him sat a much younger woman. My observation told me it was not his daughter, but perhaps a wife or care-giver. Soon the young woman got up and helped the old man on his feet, handing him his cane. They made their way unsteadily toward us on their way out of the dining car. He glanced at me curiously and nodded his head in a greeting as they exited.

This intuition of mine was working overtime. Crank Sotto was still watching me and I had the feeling something was gonna happen any minute. We finished our food and I escorted Adora back to our sleeper. I told her to lock the door and let no one in unless she knew it was my voice at the other side of the door. She cautioned me to be careful. I kissed her and left. I knew I had to draw the lizards out of their cages, so I found a remote place between two cars, at the coupling transom. There I lit up a cigarette, opened and secured the half-window and leaned on the door watching the dawn come up. A porter came by and said passengers weren't supposed to open that door and lean out. It was dangerous, especially if another train was coming on the track next to you. I told him I couldn't stand my own cigarette smoke and I needed the fresh air. He mumbled something and went on his way.

The hairs on the back of my neck began to prickle as I waited for what I knew would be the inevitable confrontation with whoever it was who set me up for a patsy. I was thinking about the reality of getting back to L.A. and how I'd face Honey as if nothing ever happened between Adora Moreno and me. But I had lived long enough to know that energy shifts in people when the dynamics change and we are creatures far more tuned to each other than most people acknowledge. It was like waiting here for the next 'thing' to happen. Somehow I was tuned to it and my body was preparing minute by minute.

But I didn't have to wait too long. Through the sliding door came Crank Sotto followed by none other than Frank Laggore! "Officer Denning—or should I say the mysterious *Mr.* Denning?" Laggore said, his snake-like stare checking me out.

"I didn't know you were a train fan, Laggore," I said, spewing out a little venom of my own. "Crank and Frank on a field trip, huh? Charming…"

"Mr. Dragna wanted to know if you knew where a certain missing item is—and you certainly are elusive—and keep unexpected company. You know what I'm talking about, I presume?"

"Yeah, but I don't know where the missing item is. It's either one nut case or another that's following me. Get lost, Laggore, I never liked you before and I don't like you now...or your goon."

"Mr. Sotto, did you hear that?" Laggore drew a gun. Crank Sotto did the same. "Since the mysterious Mr. Denning doesn't know where the object in question might be, he also may not know that he's going to have an accident very soon. He's going to fall off a moving train while smoking. Bad habit. Never picked it up myself."

"Well, then, shoot and get it over with. I'm bored with you guys and I'm about finished with my cigarette. So, if you don't mind, I'd like to get back—"

"—to your little Latin lover? Whatever would the charming Miss Combes say back home, I wonder? I think she thinks you're a true-blue Johnny boy, now, doesn't she? Well, imagine she won't have to worry about that anymore at all now, will she?" He laughed a sick laugh. "You'll be one of those uncounted *missing persons*."

"Yeah, maybe so, Laggore, but I know you've lusted for her so long your dick hangs out when you're around her—and that ain't pretty, you lousy punk. Bumping me off is one way to clear your way to her — so why don't you shoot — I'm — I'm kinda tired of waiting around for you spineless pieces of shit."

Laggore bristled. "Not nice, mister, I think I need to wash your mouth out with Life Boy soap—you're gonna need an extra life. But...we're not going to shoot you, Denning. Then it wouldn't look like an accident. No, Crank is going to come over and confiscate your firearm before we push you from the train traveling now at about sixty miles an hour, I estimate. What do you think?"

"I think it'll take both of you to take my gun away. Hoodlums like you two never change—you live in fear and act in anger—because you're really yellow inside just like the color of that stripe down your back," I said, gritting my teeth. "So come and get it!"

Sotto started toward me, but he was slow and I kicked him in the gut and he dropped his gun to the floor. Before he could recoil, I grabbed him by the hair, slammed his head against the stainless steel bottom half of the door and tossed him out the top half. There was a scream and a terrible thud as I realized I had thrown the man right into the path of an oncoming freight train. Laggore went white and began to tremble. I knew he wasn't the tough guy he pretended to be. He was one of those cheap gangsters who rode on other people's shirttails and played yes-man to the mob.

"Now—now I'm going to *have* to shoot you, Denning!" I ducked as he fired, but he grazed my shoulder and I felt the pain of the bullet carve up some flesh through my clothes. Before he could fire again, I lunged at Laggore and grabbed his gun hand and smashed it against the side of the transom. He yelled in pain as I brought him to the floor and stomped on his hand until I could feel the bones break in his fingers. I took his gun and threw it out the window. I could feel the train was slowing as I dragged Laggore to the open half-window I had tossed his accomplice out of.

"The trouble with you guys, Laggore, is that you're pampered and you're not tough enough. I was raised in the land of kill or be killed, buddy. So guess what, you're taking a ride on your *own* railroad!" I stuffed him through the window and tossed him out onto the tracks below. Unless he hit his head or something or suffered the same fate as Crank Sotto, I didn't think the fall would kill him, as by now the train had slowed to less than maybe forty miles-an-hour. I hoped that was the last of Frank Laggore—for my own sake as well as Honey's.

I made my way back to Adora's compartment just as the train came to a stop. I knocked. "Who is?" she inquired as I had instructed her. She was a good girl.

"It's me, babe, open up…"

"How do I know? You could be pretend hombre, eh? Give me what police call—uh, 'living proof.' I must know that first."

"You're gonna know a knuckle sandwich first if you don't open up—now!"

She opened the door and saw my bloody left shoulder immediately. "*Ay, mi amor*! *Qué pasó?!* I get train doctor."

"No, Adora. I've got to keep this quiet. There may be another group on the train—other than Dragna's goons."

"Dragna? Who is Dragna?"

"Never mind. Too much to explain now. It's just a surface wound and maybe you can wash it for me before my shoulder stiffens up or it infects."

Adora was fast. She said no more and went into the bathroom, prepared some cloths and warm water. She had me strip to my waist and sit on the toilet. She carefully washed my wound and dressed it as best she could. Trouble was I had brought only one coat that now had a bullet rip on its top and was stained with blood. "I bring your suit top to train valet—or what you call pott—port—"

"—porter. You stay here and lock the door, I'll go."

"But you are weak, and shot, *querido*."

"Listen to me, Adora. This isn't the time to argue and I told you I didn't want to get you involved in this thing in the first place, okay? So, please, if you don't mind, stay here until I get back."

"I will always mind not being close to you, mi amor. *Pero, yo comprendo.*" She hugged me desperately around the waist and kissed me as I departed. I was wishing I had a drink when I remembered my little flask of gin in my left coat pocket. It was there and uninjured. I got to the dining car and made my way toward the kitchen. The breakfast coach was starting to fill up with people and I got some curious looks from folks who saw the bloody shoulder and the slightly disheveled coat. I asked for the head chef. He was a jaunty looking black man. "Yes sir! Yes sir!" He saw my shoulder. "Me oh my, mister. You okay? What can I do to help?"

"I need something to sterilize a superficial wound. Do you—uh, cook with alcohol or the like?"

"No, siree, it's Prohibition—and we's not allowed to do some such things. But I think Alexander's got just what the doc ordered. Can you wait here, Mister?"

I sat at the last table in the dining car, just at the entrance to the kitchen. Just then I noticed the old man and his caretaker enter and mine was the only table available. I started to get up and give it to them.

"Oh, no, sir, please don't move." He studied me and sized up the situation immediately. "They say a couple of people left the train in a hurry back a ways. And I can see you're—you're wounded, son."

"Uh….yeah, word travels fast now, doesn't it? I suppose that's why the train's stopped?"

"By the way, I'm Dr. Jedediah Penn. I think you had better come to my compartment and let me take a look at that. It looks like a bullet tear—and lead has a way of poisoning the body, you know."

I extended my hand across the table. "Denning—Cable Denning, Dr. Penn. Yeah, that'd be swell if you could see to this. Thanks."

I told the cook I was in good hands and we left. "By the way, this is my lady-in-waiting and my day-and-night nurse, Polly Parker."

"How do you do, Miss Parker," I said, looking over the medium-sized young woman of about thirty. "What, may I ask, does a lady-in-waiting do these days?"

She seemed embarrassed. She spoke with a German accent. "Vell, I suppose she vaits. Perhaps for da right man to come." Then she hooked onto Dr. Penn's arm tightly. "But my doctor is my man today, Mr. Denning."

"Pshaw! Never heard such nonsense! She's building her hope chest along with her chest just the same as any other red-blooded healthy female her age. But, she's modest…you know how that goes…"

"Yeah," I said as we arrived at Dr. Penn's compartment. Polly Parker led me in after she was sure the doctor was comfortable and seated where he could examine me.

"Please to take your shirt off, Mr. Denning," Miss Parker said.

As I sat down, the old man with the penetrating blue eyes and silver hair, beard and moustache looked me over. "I'd say, Mr. Denning, you live dangerously and wager a guess you might not live long enough for this here wound to completely heal. Lord knows, what possesses men to commit violence upon one another."

"Well, doc, it's like the spin of the ol' wheel, you know. Life deals you out a hand and molds you pretty well. And you take it from there. I came up pretty tough, but thought the good side of the law was better, so—"

"—you became a policeman, right?" Dr. Penn looked through his spectacles at Polly Parker. "Polly, will you fetch me the denatured alcohol, please? And, oh, get me one of them there pain pills for Mr. Denning."

"How did ya know? Is cop written on my face or something?"

"Yep, a *kind* of cop. But if you're a policeman in uniform, you're in the wrong business, young man. Police business is politics and politics is corrupt and therefore, police must be corrupt by the very nature of who runs city hall. That said, it doesn't mean there aren't good men in the police force. Like you, some believe in fairness, law and order."

I was impressed with the wisdom of this old guy. I thought of Mario Angelo. He was one of those. The guys that put it all on the line in order to fulfill the letter of the law. "So…so, uh, where did you practice medicine?"

"Truth be known, lad, I'm not a medical doctor—although I took a medical doctor's internship at one time, a hundred years ago. No, I am a Doctor of Ancient Antiquities. I study the mysterious and buried past of civilizations which bear… little resemblance to our present mad house of industry and twentieth century war machines."

A shock of realization went through my body. I knew in that minute that something or someone had led this man to me—and I to him! Call it Fate, if you like, but this was beyond coincidence, I thought. What are the chances? Was there really something in the universe that pulled like souls together to ride shotgun with each other for the duration? Crazy, but somehow true, I was beginning to comprehend.

"May I ask you a question—ouch!" I exclaimed as Dr. Penn doused my shoulder with alcohol.

"Hmmm….let me see, yeah…I think this will not infect now, Mr. Denning. I would say .32 or .38 caliber? Were the two men you *catapulted* off the train less than desirable personages?"

"I'd—I'd, uh, say that, doc. Organized crime. L.A. is becoming a cesspool of it, as you said, on both sides of the blue line."

Just then there was a knock at the door. I noticed the train was still stopped. "This is the Southern Pacific road deputy.

142

Will you come to the door, please?" Right away Polly took my hand a led me to the bathroom and closed the door behind her as she went to the main entrance door and opened it. "Ya?" she said in her cool German accent. "Vat is it?"

"We are looking for a man we believe killed one man and badly injured another. Have you experienced any strange activity or seen anyone who might appear desperate, most likely a criminal type?"

Polly had a great sense of humor and this was my first introduction to it. "Vell, take a look at Dr. Penn here, officer. Does he look desperate? Or perhaps, he has hidden a criminal somevere?"

The man glanced in at the sedentary doctor, pretending to slobber and be asleep in his chair. "No, ma'am, but when we reach San Francisco please report anything that might be helpful. There was some blood found smeared against the stainless steel wall between coaches."

"Oh, dear, officer. Ve vill surely be on da lookout for a desperate criminal. Sank you for doing such a good job."

"You're welcome, ma'am," the railroad man said and departed.

Polly opened the bathroom door and peaked in at me. "Are you, Mr. Denning, da desperate, criminal type?"

"Yep," I said, chuckling. "You never know who you're being kind to these days now, do you?"

"Put your shirt back on, Denning, and talk to me. I am curious about you. Since I came to your aid, perhaps you will have the courtesy to extend to an old man....some exciting moments of your life..."

I sat opposite the doc. "Well, I think we may have something very much in common, Dr. Penn. You said you were a doctor of antiquities, right?"

"Correct. I have ventured to days ripped back in time, to

civilizations more advanced than ours of 1928, to stupid men and women who destroyed their cultures and themselves, not to mention leaving only shards of broken memories for their progeny. So...Denning—"

"—Cable, please call me Cable..."

"Okay, Cable...why is it you ask of my vocational specialization?"

"Okay, here goes. I think this might raise an eyebrow or two. Have you ever heard of a golden capsule called *God of Our Fathers*?"

The old man looked at me in disbelief. "*The* 'God of Our Fathers'? Lord, Cable, don't play games with an old man. That golden, priceless walnut is said to contain ordination of the universe—and very, very old. What do you know of it? And how came you by this extra-ordinary knowledge?"

I told Dr. Penn the whole story from the start, including Sandor's greed and right up to last night when Dragna's goons were preparing for my funeral. "Now I'm on my way, maybe on a wild goose chase, to Frisco to trace down a Chinese woman who may know the whereabouts of the capsule. All we do know is that since the night Sandor was killed, there's been no trace of it. Neither Damianos, Dragna or whoever else may be after it, it's disappeared."

"And you're going by a psychic's clues?"

"Well, really Crazy Jack was the first to clue me in. He led me to Madame Palladino, the Psychic Wonder Woman."

"Crazy Jack? No doubt a trusted acquaintance, I presume. But I have actually heard of Eusapia Palladino, Cable. No less a man than Sir Arthur Conan Doyle of Sherlock Holmes fame validated her as being able to contact his dead son and attended a séance in 1922 after her death, where she came as a spirit through the medium. Since Palladino died in 1918, you're current Madame may be an imposter."

"She says she's a niece, just took the same name. So, doc—"

"—just call me Jed, Cable. It's too late to pretend…that I am anything but an old man hanging on to his last days, anxious to hear an exciting story—that might make his blood roil once again…So what's next?"

"As I said, the Chinese woman, if I can find her. What other clue do I have? Right now I'm shootin' in the dark, doc."

"So it seems…so it seems…humans never get it. *Everything in creation works together*. People kill each other, eradicate the natural world, invent new chemicals to poison populations, even fight over the ridiculous premise of ethnic, political and religious differences."

"You won't get an argument out of me on that count. I see it around in my job. Criminals run for high office and win—then laugh all the way to the bank."

"Speaking of which, I hear under the table that a certain political rebel is being groomed to take over Germany—have you read a book called *Mein Kampf* by Adolph Hitler?"

"Believe it or not, I'm a reading cop, but haven't read that one. Yeah, I've heard of the book and this Hitler guy. But Europe's a long ways away."

"Is it? I wonder. My many years exploring antiquities and human nature have brought me to one conclusion: never trust a human. I have grave reservations about his policies. In particular, his acrid description of what he calls '*the Jewish peril*' should affect everyone with decent sensibilities. Even Polly gets the shivers seeing what he thinks, says and does with the 'new revolution' in her native land."

"Well, I'm not an authority on ethnic differences, doc, but I was raised with Spics, Mics, Dagos, Mexes, and Polacks, not to mention Krauts. In my neighborhood, they all hated each other by virtue of their differences. My best friend, Mario Angelo—we met over a fistfight to the death—and I won,

145

spared my knuckles from beating his face in and we became life-long friends. I don't know. I think it's the *individual*. And this Hitler fellow, if nobody listens to him, he'll end up like the rest of us, passing specters in the night of men."

Dr. Penn looked at me, studying my eyes and my face. "How did you become so perceptive, Mr. Policeman? Precisely my own view. It's how we greet the individual. Just like our meeting today. Propitious, wouldn't you say?"

"Yeah, I'd say." Then I thought of Adora back in the sleeper wondering what the hell happened to me. "I've-I've gotta go for now, doc, Miss Parker. Thank you both for your kindness and hospitality, perhaps we'll meet in San Francisco—"

"—Cable…I think we need to meet soon. How about tonight? I think I might know whom this Chinese woman is you seek. And you need to tell me all you can about the *Deus Patrum Nostrorum*. Polly and I are staying at the *Sir Francis Drake*, a brand new hotel on Powell Street, off of Union Square, that has just had its gala grand opening. Will you join us?"

"Hmmm…so you know its Latin name, too, eh? Maybe you're right. Right now *I've* a lady-in-waiting in Car #27." Then I came back to the present. "Yeah, I can do that. But I probably should bring my lady. She knows very little of this…"

"Then perhaps you should leave her behind? Too many ears, and it might be for her own good. I will send Polly out to a movie. What about eight p.m.?"

The Lark had resumed its northward journey and I teetered my way back to Adora's compartment. I knocked. "Hey, kid, it's me." There was no answer. I tried the door. It was open. I walked in smelling a rat somewhere in the works. There was a sign of a scuffle and my little Mexican's purse lay on the floor, it's content strewn about. I went to the head conductor and told him the situation. He said he'd not heard of any kidnapping on his train, but that it had been a strange journey, with

146

the deaths of two men and all. He promised to alert all porters and other assistant conductors to be on the lookout. My mother had always said in times like these when you don't know what to do, just do nothing. I went to the club car and ordered a seltzer. When no one was looking, I poured in a goodly amount of gin from the flask in my pocket. I settled down and took a big gulp, thinking about what could have happened to Adora Moreno. There was a babe in a tight black wool skirt a few stools down from me. She had been giving me the once-over. She smiled at me. I smiled back. That was all she needed to get off her stool and come sit next to me.

"You look forlorn, Mister, like you've lost something."

"Yeah, as a matter of fact, I have. But I don't want to talk about it."

"Okay, okay, just trying to be friendly. It's a long and lonely trip to Frisco when you're alone and not too many folks are willing to talk to a single woman without thinking—"

"—you know, lady, I'm really not interested in a sob story at the moment. You'll have to forgive me, but I'm not very good company tonight—today—or whatever it is."

"Today, Mister. Okay, I'll go, but may I ask you a question first?"

I was a little distracted and impatient. "Yeah, shoot…"

"Are you a cop of some sort? You look familiar. I work at the Beverly Hilton in L.A. and I think the night some poor man was murdered in the elevator you were one of the presiding policemen. Right?"

"Yeah, right. So what's that got to do with anything?"

"I thought you might be interested in other things that were found in Mr. Eisenstadt's room."

Now she had piqued my curiosity. "How—how would you know where that stuff went? And why didn't the cops claim it when the coroner went over Eisenstadt's room? Are you a thief—or are you one of those tails the syndicate or whoever has sent to keep an eye on me?"

"No," she snickered. "The unclaimed properties department, known to you as Lost & Found, is under my jurisdiction. You see, I am the official assistant manager of the hotel. I must confess, I went through Mr. Eisenstadt's room before the police arrived and, uh, shall I say—*secured* certain items that looked rather curious to me. And maybe of value. After all, a girl has to make a living, you know."

She was fairly tall and slender, wore a gold-leaf necklace and fluffy white sweater with a couple of medium-sized boobs filling things out pretty well. Her hair was a dishwater blonde with a few threads of grey and her skin was good but she wore a lot of makeup. "Why are you telling me this? First of all, I could arrest you for confiscating police property. Second, you could lose your job and even if I bought your story, lady, I'm a cop and couldn't afford to pay your price—even if I wanted what you have to sell."

"Yes, but maybe you know someone who could afford my price? I'm not unreasonable, Mr. Policeman, just a woman with a good business sense. I watched you with the old man and his caregiver. I also saw two men who have strangely disappeared tailing you toward Car #27 late last night."

"What were you doing up so late?"

"I'm an incurable insomniac. I was smoking in the area between Car #'s 26 and 27 when I noticed you walk by as I entered my sleeping compartment. Two men followed you in succession. Since I was only a few doors up from your confrontation with these men, I heard the ruckus and suddenly the two men are gone—zip!" She snapped her fingers and smiled at me. "And now there's just you…"

I closed my eyes. This was all I needed. A nosy dame with

a yen for extra bucks through extortion. "What's your name?"

"Anne—Anne Banning. What's yours, if I may ask?"

"Denning…Cable Denning. So what do you want—even if you could prove I was in that transom at the designated hour. It's your word against mine."

"Well, not quite, Mr. Denning. You see, I consulted the porter who warned you not to open the half-window door and lean out. So now we have two witnesses." She sighed like a cagey old cat that had cornered the mouse and was about to pounce.

"You know, your timing is really bad, Miss Banning. But I must admit you'd make a hell of a detective. Female detectives are rare."

"I did a stint once in a department store as a shoplifter's worst nightmare. I was good at it." She looked at me. "You're a pretty handsome young man to be mixed up in all this. What are you going to do, throw me off the train, too?"

I laughed under my breath. "You know, that's not a bad idea. Double-dealers like you need to be brought to justice, Anne Banning."

She squinted her eyes and smiled. "I just *love* men who play rough, Mr. Denning. Are you…are you, uh, rough in other departments of your life—like love making, for instance? I might be interested in that as…partial payment…"

I swallowed down the rest of my gin-laced seltzer. "Maybe some other time, Miss Banning, but I really can't afford you-- or the time just now. Plus, I'm looking for some dish who has, coincidentally, also disappeared. You haven't seen a dark-haired Latin doll around, by any chance?"

"No," she said coldly. "Too bad. I'd make it worth your while and we've got a couple of hours yet before we step on to that platform in San Francisco."

"Thanks, but no thanks." I got up to leave. "See you around."

"Aren't you forgetting I know too much—I could forewarn the San Francisco Police Department that a dangerous killer is—is on the loose and on his way to their city by the bay."

"Go ahead, call 'em. I'm just not that interested at the moment. In fact, I don't think you'll cry wolf, Miss Banning, because you spilled some of your own beans. Remember how naughty you were in stealing police property out of a dead man's room before the authorities arrived? I don't think extortion or blackmail would work for you just now."

"But I like being naughty, Mr. Denning. I was hoping you'd be naughty with me."

"Not this time, lady. I'll be on my way now, if you don't mind." I left Anne Banning sitting there at the bar, her face perplexed.

For a while I wondered aimlessly around the train, car after car, checking out the dining car, the lounge and observation and reading car at the rear of the train. By the time we chugged into the Oakland station, I was internally distraught. Why did the silly dame risk herself—and me by coming aboard? But then I thought about the great sex we'd had and the beautiful woman who owned that body which satisfied me so damn much. Truth was I missed her. I missed her voice, her sincerity, the way she kissed me and how she wrapped herself around me without fearing that one day we might not be an item anymore, but a memory. Maybe that was what already had happened. I stood at the gate to Track 11 where everyone who was aboard the Lark exited. Desperately I searched for Adora. She had vanished.

CHAPTER 8

CURSE OF THE RED DRAGON LADY

I took a ferry across the bay to San Francisco. From the deck I could see the fog spilling over those twin peaks Crazy Jack had told me about. I was about to disembark when a slight man came up to me. "Mr. Denning? Have you lost someone? If you want to see her alive again, I suggest you take a street car alone to the *Hotel Verona*, 317 Leavenworth Street, Room #417. Don't ask any questions—and you never saw me, right?" The man disappeared off the gangplank. I dared not follow him.

After I asked directions to the Hotel Verona, I caught a streetcar. It stopped a few blocks from the hotel on Market St. and 7th. I got out and walked briskly to a six-story, typically San Francisco-style affair with the bay windows, located on the corner of Leavenworth and Eddy with a large vertical sign on the corner of the building. It wasn't a dump, but it wasn't the Mark Hopkins, either. I asked the elevator boy to take me to the fourth floor. Like all old hotels, there was a quiet feeling mingled with a must from the carpets as I walked down the hallway to Room #417. I reached for my .38 as I knocked. Soon a small man in a black suit and white silk tie with a gun in his hand opened the door. "No, Mr. Denning—I would ask you not to reach for your gun. Miss Moreno is shaken, but well. Please, come in." His voice was raspy and sinister in tone, and he possessed a strange accent I didn't recognize. He was obviously well spoken and educated. "The gun, if you don't mind."

I handed him my .38 as I entered. Immediately I saw Adora gagged and tied to a chair. I went to her. "Babe…are you alright?" She nodded in the affirmative with very bright eyes that lit up the room with alarm. "Untie her and take that gag off, then we can talk. She won't scream or run as long as I'm here." The man did exactly as I asked him.

Adora got up and ran into my arms, tears streaming down her face. I held her and rocked her a minute. "Cable…*esperé, querida!*—I wait--and then they come and take me away—"

"—shhhh!" I said, comforting my little Latina. "It's okay, babe. I'm here now and we'll be outta this mess pronto." I looked at the medium-sized man with the bright brown eyes and clean-shaven face. "What is it *you* want?"

He looked me up and down. Then he saw how I protected Adora. "Touching, Mr. Denning. I am glad to see you. You are famous already. Within the past few hours, you killed two men, visited with a renowned professor of ancient antiquities, you were unavoidably propositioned by a meddlesome wom-an—and now you stand protecting the object of your affection. That's a pretty full day, wouldn't you say?"

"I'm fashed and tired, buddy. If you want anything out of me, you're going to have to let me freshen up and rest a bit. I get very resistant and stubborn when I'm pushed to the limits."

He smiled a cunning smile. "Oh, dear, we can't have that, now, can we? I'll tell you what. To show you how generous I am, I will surrender this room to you and your señorita. It is now almost 2:00 p.m. I will return at six." He reached into his pocket and handed me my gun. "To show how civilized I am and that I trust you—to a certain degree—I am returning your revolver. Do not try to go out or escape. I have a man at the door. The fire escape will be watched. Order any food you wish—or valet service— I will pick up the tab. After all, you are a special guest here at t he Verona." He turned his back on us and left.

Adora held me tighter. "Oh, *mi pobre hombre*! Ay…I nev-er think I see you once more. Those terrible people stole me. When we get into train station, they take me all way back to last car and force me to jump tracks, where we sneak away. I look for you, but I cannot scream. They tell me they kill you if I scream—or try to run away!"

"It's alright, Adora. I'm here now, doll. I'm just glad you're safe. I worried myself sick. I couldn't figure what happened or where you might've gone to, but I knew something was up. It seems everybody wants what I don't even have."

"What you mean?"

"Oh, it's too complicated to tell you now. I told you before we left L.A. you were putting yourself in harm's way…and guess what? Here we are in the middle of a doozy of a mystery with heavy hitters at bat. I'm sorry you got mixed up in the middle of all this."

She snuggled into me. "We take bath and rest together, okay?"

And that's exactly what we did. We threw our clothes off and I ran a bath as the beautiful naked lady let her hair down. When she turned to face me, it was like seeing an incredibly sensual Latin fantasy, a woman so perfect and warm, direct and unassuming that I could only imagine it was a dream and one day I would wake up and it would all be gone. As tired as I was, I could feel certain parts of my body swell with the visual delight she was presenting me with. "Oh! Oh!" she tittered. "Señor Grande get happy!"

We both laughed and climbed into the bathtub. She sat between my legs bubbling on in a happy voice. "I tol' you I am excited *por mucho peligro*—and you live with much danger."

I reached around and cupped her large firm breasts with my hands. I had soaped them and my fingers slipped over those wonderful nipples of hers until her whole body began to sing with chills. "Well, babe, it seems you came to the right place if you want danger. Just crank up my phone number and you got it. Why aren't you afraid with all this shit happening?"

"*Por que?* Because I am with you. That is why."

"So many characters coming out of the woodwork. Don't you wonder what's it all about?"

"If you want to tell me, okay, Joe, but if not, okay, *también*."

"Why?"

She reached around in back of her and massaged my balls. "Because I am in love, Cable. *Completamente*. No thing I want except you. *Para toda mi vida*."

I leaned her body back into mine and drew my arms around her exquisite body and perfect tan skin. "For all of your life? That could be a long time, babe. In case I ever forget, Adora, I want to tell you now. I'm crazy about you, doll. I don't know how it happened. I only know it did and here we are."

"Sí, here we are, señor." She leaned back into me and I buried my face in her abundant black hair.

Just then I thought I heard a sound coming from the living room. I put my lips to Adora's ear to quiet her. We sat motionless. "Maybe the maid or something," I said, still a bit cautious. But since no one came storming through our bathroom door, I assumed for the moment we were safe. "I guess it's okay. I thought I heard something rustling around out there."

We go through life maybe on two or three cylinders, when we could be firing on all eight. The car we start off in comes complete with engine, transmission, wheels and steering wheel. But sometimes parts are missing, or malfunctioning, like a bad carburetor or the spark plug wires got switched somehow and the motor doesn't work right. Like Crazy Jack. It brings up the question of who's okay and who's nuts in this world, no matter what walk of life they show up in. When I look at the people I'd encountered in the past few months, I shudder to think how many of them seep out of dark shadows from brains that are twisted or misfiring, like those sparkplugs and causing havoc to all who cross their pathways. I could go back all the way to Dr. Sandor, Matrangas, Jinx…his twisted little henchman… the sexually frustrated and treacherous Frank Laggore, Jack Dragna and his sinister big crime mentality, the mysterious Isaiah Damianos—and Lord knows whoever else was lurking

154

out there in the mine fields of evil and dark, shaded brains, perverted because their wiring wasn't right and when the ignition sparked from the twist of a key, nobody was safe. Maybe even *I* was a bit nuts. But at least I knew it, and maybe that made the difference.

Adora and I got out of the tub and dried each other off. It was a wonderful feeling being treated to a rare timeout of serenity and lovemaking. There was nothing about this woman I didn't like.

We went over to the bed and were about to jump in it when something caught my attention out in the living room. I told Adora to stay put and I ventured out for a peek. There on the floor lay the dead body of a woman. Only this woman I knew. I recognized Anne Banning's black skirt and white sweater with the gold-leaf necklace. "Don't come out here, Adora," I cautioned.

"*Qué pasó?*" she asked from the other room.

"You don't wanna know, kid," I said, as I came back in. I got a blanket from the bed and took it into the living room and covered the remains. I noticed an unfolded note on the corpse's chest. I grabbed it and came back and sat on the bed next to a nervous Adora. "Out there…a gal I met on the train while I was looking for you. She was implicated in all of this somewhere along the line. Anyway, they killed her. She's out there staring somewhere up into eternity."

"Cable! We are next? If I die, I wish to die next to you, no one else. *Ay, yo espero, querido!*"

"I don't think they want us dead just yet, doll," I said, looking at the note. "*A reminder we mean business. Miss Banning's demise is the result of someone knowing more than she should have…*"

"*Ay, mio Dio!*" Adora exclaimed under her breath.

"Nothing we can do about that," I said, looking at the bed covers pulled aside. "We still need to rest, corpse or no corpse

155

in the living room." We fell into bed together, holding on to each other. We were both exhausted and 6:00 p.m. would come all too soon.

But it was a restless sleep for me. I was in a golden Chinese palace being chased by a bunch of opium smoking thugs. But one in particular was sober and dressed in black and wore a fedora, and from his sleeve drew a handle-less hatchet. He was trying to get a bead on me so he could throw that deadly thing. Then in came this knockout of an Oriental babe in a bright-red outfit clear down to the ankles. She was medium in height but very slender with golden slippers adorning her feet. She motioned to the Hatchet Man to stop chasing me and he did. She ran and I followed her into a dark tunnel, like the mouth of Jonas' whale with little red lanterns hung here and there. At the other end of the darkness we came into a beautiful cavern, glowing red and gold. A strange looking object descended from the roof of the cave, maybe fifteen feet above us. The beautiful lady was wearing a pure golden necklace. She took it off and handed it to me. She motioned for me to put it around my own neck and stepped back. The object above us descended, as if by magic, for I could see no strings or wires attached to it. It slowly came down until it was at chest level with me, directly opposite the golden neckpiece. When next I glanced at the lady in red, she stood completely nude and got down on her knees and motioned for me to do the same. As I did, I began to feel a scintillation around my balls and penis. Then I awoke to Adora's hand holding the very parts I was dreaming about. I tried to shake myself completely out of the dream, but it lingered and I recalled much of the detail.

When we were both fully awake an hour or so later, I tried to fill Adora in on all I could. But it didn't even make sense to me. But I did tell her about the meeting with Dr. Jedediah Penn and Polly Parker, and the appointment I had with him tonight at eight. Adora took it well and it was true she felt stimulated by the thrill and excitement of a dangerous undertaking. Who would've known?

We dressed just in time to hear the key turn in the lock. The door opened and there stood our strange host with the odd accent. "Ah, I see you have rested. Good." He glanced down at Anne Banning's body. "I see also you read my note. That was just a reminder…that I am not, what you Americans would say, *kidding*, Mr. Denning. I am also sorry for your young and handsome paramour here, but she simply must be eliminated when our business is concluded."

Adora clung to me and her fingernails dug into my stomach as she clutched me. "So, whatever your name is—if death is what you deal in, then you might as well deal me in, too. I've got no stomach for misfits like you. The world isn't big enough. One of us has to go."

"That…can and will be arranged. Soon. My name is *Nazar Ravna*, my mother was Turkish and my father from Calcutta. So that makes me, like you, Mr. Denning, a mix of ethnic backgrounds."

"Okay," I said, taking out a Lucky Strike and lighting it up. Adora stayed close to me. "What's your line, Ravna? I suppose it has to do with that damn capsule I know so little about and have no clue as to its whereabouts."

"Ah, *au contraire*! But you *do* know much. Let me refresh your memory. Please, will you and the lovely lady sit on the sofa while I take this chair and sit opposite you? Notice I have no gun. That's how I wish our relationship to be, Mr. Denning. Without violence…at least for the moment." He drew up a chair and sat about six feet opposite Adora and me. "Now, will you tell me all that you know? Many have already died in the pursuit of the object in question, as you have witnessed. In a way, you have helped me. By eliminating Mr. Dragna's dispensable creeps, as you might say, and putting off Mr. Damianos—and *we* have eliminated Miss Banning here—you have cleared the way for us."

"Now, tell me…just who is '*us*'?"

"I regret I can say no more about 'us' and what we represent. Just know that the capsule is highly desirable and we are prepared to pay handsomely, maybe even spare your girlfriend here—*if* you come up with the precious treasure, give it to me personally with no questions asked—and be on your way, free to go wherever you wish, financially set for life, so to speak."

"Do you think I'd fall for that, Ravna? I don't think you're that stupid, why would you think I am? You know as well as I do that anyone on either side of the blue line gets killed for knowing too much."

"But being a procurer, you will not know what the golden capsule contains or what its timeless inscriptions read. You see, as a plain and simple 'delivery boy,' you know nothing more than the lad who delivers the morning paper and throws it on the doorstep. You have no idea as to the content of the newspaper now, do you?"

I was looking down at Anne Banning's body. "A question, Ravna. How in the hell did you get Miss Banning's body in here without being detected? After all, it's broad daylight and you had to come up an elevator somewhere."

"We are *professionals*, Mr. Denning, and service elevators containing a large cart filled with fresh linen could certainly contain a body at its bottom, could it not?"

"Yeah, I guess so." I put my cigarette out in the ashtray next to the sofa. Adora was staring at Nazar Ravna. It was almost as if she were seeing something in him I wasn't. "So, you gotta know I've got an eight o'clock appointment with Dr. Jedediah Penn at the *Sir Francis Drake.*"

"Charming!" Ravna exclaimed. "I'm staying there as well. New posh hotels are one of my passions. The smell of everything brand new—doesn't it excite you?" He cleared his throat. "Now… I am delighted you are meeting with Dr. Penn and you may go with my blessing. He will enlighten you as to the power and content of the capsule—and perhaps the whereabouts of the Chinese lady we all seek at the moment."

"So you're looking for her too, eh? My, my, I do hope she isn't so elusive as to prevent you from obtaining the object of your desire."

"Thank you. I am certain not. However, I hear she transforms herself into a dragon now and then, or some other demon or personage when she is threatened. She is very powerful, not one to be trifled with. Therefore, it is best she come to you. I am certain she knows of you already. The Chinese community has secret ways, just as our Order does."

Adora and I took the streetcar to Union Square. *The Sir Francis Drake* was an elegant affair that sparkled with that atmosphere the rich bring to their haunts. We checked in with the desk clerk and had him announce our arrival to Dr. Penn. We were told to take the elevator to Room #1218. The elevator was outfitted in brass and gold trim, with real tile floors with 17th century scenes hand-painted on each 12" x 12" square. When we reached the twelfth floor, the operator indicated we turn to the right. We found #1218 and I knocked. Polly Parker opened the door. "Good evening, Mr. Denning." Then she looked at the beautiful Adora Moreno. Sitting on a deeply cushioned golden sofa sat Dr. Penn, his legs covered with a blanket. He wore thick glasses and was reading when we entered.

"I—I, uh, had to bring my lady, doc. Some things happened that we didn't expect, including a murder in our room, not to mention the appearance of a rather odd character—"

"Murder, eh? It does seem where you go, danger follows— I know him—*Nasar Ravna*—he is no one to sneeze at, so they say. How do you do, young lady." He took off his glasses and examined Adora. "My, you are a most beautiful young thing. How lucky can one man get in his lifetime? I am Jedediah Penn…"

"This is Adora Moreno, doc. She was a surprise passenger when I embarked from L.A. I would never have invited her—"

Adora walked up to the seated doctor and extended her hand. "—*Con mucho gusto, Señor Penn*," she said. "I am happy to meet you." One could tell there was an instant rapport between the two.

"*Sí, con mucho gusto, también, señorita. Lo siento mucho que está teniendo la mala suerte cuando vas a venir a San Francisco. Pero, yo beso su mano...*" He reached for Adora's hand and kissed it.

She was delighted he spoke her language. "*Bueno, tu hablas español. Este gringo aquí—él no sabe nada,*" she laughed.

Dr. Penn looked up at her with stern admiration. "You are in great danger, señorita. I will do all I can to protect you. But for now, Cable and I have much to speak of. Will you go to a motion picture with Polly? This lady is my trusted caretaker and confidante."

Polly Parker came over to where we stood. "Vee ladies are not vanted here. Vill you go to see a picture vit me? Do you like Greta Garbo? I vould like to see *Mysterious Lady*, you might like?"

Adora looked up at me for approval. "*Sí. Me gustaría, señorita. I go with you.*" She leaned up and kissed me and the two women soon left our presence.

"What a beauty!" Jedediah Penn said. "How do you rate to make love to such loveliness? Even in my best years, I did not command such a wench."

"Just lucky, doc. She was an unexpected gift in my life. Sometimes I can't believe God still makes such honest and lovely creatures."

"Yes." He studied my face. "I think we shall like one another, Cable. You are not without deep sensibilities. I admire that. At the same time, it is what has brought down upon you this terrible curse of danger—and perhaps an abbreviated life. Often, you must realize, the good die young. Especially the ones who seek out *truth* as their measuring stick. You are such a person, aren't you? I can see it in your eyes—and the fact that you attract such an innocent, beautiful soul as that of Miss Moreno's."

"Yeah, thanks, doc—truth *is* the one thing I fight for. Between you and me, I'm even having a difficult time not feeling guilty about Adora being with me, because I have another gorgeous doll back in L.A. who's been my only squeeze for a long time. And I never cheated on her. Until now. I don't know what it is about Adora, but I found her irresistible. And I think she felt the same toward me—you know, we just gravitated to each other like magnets."

"She's completely in love with you, Cable. It's written all over her. Sometimes, it's—it's like the game of *musical chairs*. One moves until the music stops and then you find a seat until the music starts up again—and when the music stops again, there you are, somewhere else, in a different seat with someone else smiling up at you with love and vulnerability. Then, also, sometimes you may not find a seat and then you're out of the game. Though I very much doubt that happens to you."

"Yeah, something like that, I guess." I lit up a cigarette and the doc motioned for me to sit beside him. "So…what have you to fill me in about this Chinese dame who's supposed to be a virgin nymphomaniac or whatever?"

"Well, first of all, legend has it that she's a virgin because of her—how shall I say—*other dimensional status*. It seems some beings come to us from other places, other than the normal three-dimensional world. I suspect this lady is one of them. As far as the *'nymphomania'* you describe—that's a misnomer. The term really applies to another part of the legend of this lady built on fact. The *lotus flower*, in this case, the species *Nymphaea nelumbo*, is said to have virgin seeds that had lain dormant in a dry Chinese lakebed for over 1300 years. When an exceptionally wet winter came upon the countryside, the new waters from the heavens awakened the seeds and resurrected our mystery lady."

"Oh," I said, trying to put all this "other dimensional" crap I'm hearing, into some semblance of common sense. "So, I'm to assume this lady is not a common mortal, really is a virgin, but doesn't hail from these parts of the known world?"

"Yes, exactly. She is also said to be the *protectorate* of the *God of Our Fathers* and as such, will stop at nothing to keep it safe. But she has her limitations, too. For example, it is said she cannot appear easily amongst humans without being adversely affected, her energy partially drained."

"Oh, poor dear," I joked. "Whatever should she do for companionship—if not good sex? I don't buy it, doc. A woman's a woman's a woman in my book—hair, tits, pussy and desire."

"Don't you think that's a bit crude, Cable? Women are persons as well, you know. They are not less than you, even if the Christian babble says she came from one of Adam's ribs. I think the old Jewish boys wanted to subject woman to their beds, child-bearing and preparing food. Patriarchal control. But other beings have different make-ups and agendas. I suspect this mysterious Chinese lady to be one of *them*. You know, history does speak of the Amazons, the other extreme of patriarchy—but even today we can observe levels of matriarchy in the Berbers, Taureg people, Basques, Sardinians—so it has not completely died out. Dominant current religious doctrines, such as Christianity, Muslim and Jewish are patriarchal. Woman is relegated to what I mentioned earlier and few male egos can tolerate a dominant female."

"It's funny…I find I kind of like the submission part, though. Like Adora looks to my every mood and move and falls in line with it."

"Do not mistake humility and grace for subservience, Cable.

Your Adora is an exceptional person, you must honor that. Her woman surrenders to you out of youth and passion. A woman in love gives up a part of herself for the gift of conception." He looked at me, winking an eye. "I'll bet she's told you she would like to have your babies, true?"

I marveled at this wise old man sitting next to me. "Yep—how'd you know? That's exactly what she's told me, like she could have ten of my kids."

"You see? It's nature's compulsion in woman. It's not right or wrong, just the natural state of things. Man wants to inseminate, woman wants to receive his seed. Just that simple. That's what makes the world go 'round."

"By the way, would you take Adora back to the train station and send her back home? I can't risk losing her—especially since Ravna said he'd kill her as soon my work was done here and the Chinese thing was over."

Dr. Penn studied my face. "Yes, I'll send her somewhere with Polly under the cover of night. Then she can catch the eight o'clock Daylight Limited in the morning."

"Thanks, doc. I've gotta work alone on this one, as you know."

"You're a brave man, Cable. Lord knows what dangers lurk out there for you. But I will stay on until you are finished here. I have a feeling you might be needing me at some point."

I thanked him again and by the time the women had returned from the picture show, Jed Penn had told me all he knew about my next quest. He said he didn't know how all the players tied in. Were Damianos, Ravna, and the Chinese lady all playing the same game? I knew Jack Dragna and his gang were in it for the money, so I wrote them off. There were still a few untied ribbons. Eisenstadt came to mind.

When Polly and Adora entered their eyes were red. Obviously they had been crying. "Ah, no doubt a moving movie, I dare say," Dr. Penn observed.

"Ya…ya…Garbo vas a spy who fell in love…and lost her… lover…but she killed a man because she loved another. That is stupid! Undisciplined!"

Adora looked at me with pleading eyes. "She fall in love… and die inside. *Por qué la vida es complejo*. Why is love never simple?"

"Well, well, well, a Kraut and a Latina who get along. How fun is that?" I said, winking at Dr. Penn. "But I'm glad you enjoyed." I looked at Adora. "Babe, I need to talk to you privately."

"Use my bedroom," Dr. Penn said.

I took her hand and we found ourselves alone simply looking at each other. "I see your *expresión. Qué paso, Cable?*"

"I'm sneaking you out of here tonight to take the train back to your Mama and your sister. This is no place for you."

Tears welled in her eyes. "And if I never seen you again, amor? How shall I live? I am part of you now. *Por favor*, let me be dangerous lady with you. If I die *en tu abrazo—entonces, es suficiente*. It is enough for me."

"I can't let you do that, doll. I'll be back in a few days. Hey, look at me—I've got nine lives—and I've only used one or two so far," I chuckled, trying to lighten the moment.

"*No creo*, Cable. I saw that man who hates…and kills…"

I took her into my arms and kissed her. She clung to me as if it was her last breath. "*Te lo ruego*—I beg you—*regreso*, return to me, mi amor."

I worried about some of Ravna's goons keeping a watchful eye at the station, but I gave her some money and Polly Parker promised to take her in tow and make sure she boarded the Daylight. I thanked Jedediah Penn and told him I'd keep him posted. Adora's last words to me were three poignant, forlorn-sounding calls down the hallway as I headed for the elevator. "Cable?…Cable?…Cable?"

I made my way out of the hotel into the night. I could hear that lonely sax again…playing through my head as street cars and traffic noises permeated the streets and alleyways. A dense, low fog crept along the sidewalks as I made my way toward Market Street. I needed some sunshine just about now. Suddenly I was homesick for Honey. I could hear her singing *Blue Skies* and that filled me with hope that all of this was just a dream and I'd wake up next to her with a bright L.A. day coming through our window. "*Never saw the sun shining so bright, never saw things going so right, watching the day hurrying by, when you're in love, my, my how they fly…*"

I got back to my room at the *Verona* and sure enough, Nazar Ravna was waiting for me. "Where is your *amor*, Denning? Did you leave her somewhere? I cannot imagine you lost her again…"

"No, Ravna, she just seems to have disappeared. You know, she went to a movie with Doctor Penn's caregiver—and zip! they decided to stay out and maybe see the picture again. You know how it is."

"Yes. I know how it is. But I will deal with your deceptions later. First, tell me what the good doctor shared with you regarding the *Sacred* and our mysterious Chinese lady."

"It's simple. First of all, nobody knows whether she has it or not. Not even Dr. Penn. Second, she seems to be some kind of legendary creature, not really human."

"A *shape shifter*. That's what they're called."

Yeah, how'd you know?"

"It's my business to know these things, Denning. I was beginning to like you. Now I don't know. Ordinarily I would have you destroyed for having disobeyed me by hiding your little señorita. But we always find what we're looking for."

"If you touch a hair on her head, Ravna, I'll make things so complicated for you, they'll have to carry you out in a straight-jacket before you can figure it out. Do you think I go for all that bullshit you're giving me—like the Chinese mythology that a woman can transform herself, or that she even exists? What do you take me for?"

"What does Dr. Penn believe? Did he not tell you what I've told you?"

"Yeah, and then some. About some dormant seeds in a lakebed coming to life with rains that broke a draught—and this 1300 year-old babe coming to life among the seeds. Oh, yeah, like I believe in Santa Claus and Dracula."

Ravna kept his composure. "Okay, Denning, I'll make a deal with you. I won't touch your Latina lover if you continue as planned—at the very least investigate if such a person exists in Chinatown. Ask around, hang out in the unsavory places—and if you survive it and return with the golden capsule--I give you my word I will leave your señorita alone and just kill you. By then you *will* have known too much and you'll be too great a risk. I'm sure you understand these things, after all, you work amongst the very slime that creeps out from under the rocks in Los Angeles. Is it a deal? I'm being very generous, you understand…"

I lit up a Lucky Strike. "Sure…but what about Damianos? After all, he was the one who sent me here after I got the compass directions from Crazy Jack and Madame Palladino."

"Mr. Damianos is a religious fanatic. He wants the *God of Our Fathers* to be returned to what he considers 'its rightful place.' But I see it differently. And we, I remind you, are much more powerful than the Catholic Church. They come in at a distant second to us."

I took a long drag on my cigarette. "So we play it your way for now. Go home and leave me alone, will you? It's been a tough day." I looked down at the floor and saw that Anne Banning's body was gone. "What…uh…what happened to the late Miss Banning—was she hanging around too late at

166

night? She did proposition me on the train, you know."

"Miss Banning has served her purpose for this lifetime. She is safely on her way to a crematorium. We don't like to leave... how shall I say it? Tell-tale signs?" He got up to go. "You drive a hard bargain, Denning. In a way I admire you for it. You are not a sniveling coward as are many men. I sense you are not afraid to die. But that you're just choosy about how you will die, does that sound somewhat accurate?"

"Something like that. Good-night, Ravna. I'll start out in Chinatown in the morning. How do I get in touch with you?"

"Oh, you mustn't ever worry about that. We'll be getting in touch with *you*. Every step of yours will be observed. I promise I will not kill you until I face you. It is my way. I am not a coward either, Denning. I face those I am about to kill."

"Kinda like the old gladiators, eh?"

"Yes, good analogy. Good-night, and good hunting..."

He let himself out. Now I was thinking of poor Adora in a confused state, in hiding all night and having to take that long ride back to L.A. by herself. I was already thinking of us in the past tense as I heard Honey's voice sing the lyrics to what I was feeling. Just days ago when I had first looked at Adora Moreno, my heart did stand still. I had never seen a woman so beautiful in real life. *'I took one look at you, that's all I meant to do, and then my heart stood still...'* I drifted into a restless sleep hearing Honey's wonderful voice sing a song that tugged at my heartstrings and memories. How could one man screw up his life in so many ways?

THE HATCHET MAN

It was November 19th, 1928 and the San Francisco air was crisp. A whopper of a storm was brewing out of the northwest from the Gulf of Alaska, bringing rain and a wind that smashed the ocean's breakers up against the shoreline like an invading army of thundering gods. But I was going the other way, on an open-air Powell Street cable car toward Grant and Bush Streets. I had heard that once the "Zhongs" endured a two-month immigration clearance on Angel Island, they came to settle here in this densely populated little city within the city. But I wasn't a tourist on a curiosity tour. No, I was going for the highbinders, the opium dens, the "parlor houses" of ill repute—and to watch out for the Hatchet Man. These guys were a highly skilled breed of assassins, pledged to the Tongs to carry out whatever was ordered by their superiors, no questions asked. The traditional weapon for dispatching an unsuspecting soul was a handle-less hatchet hidden in the sleeve, quickly taken out and thrown with great speed and accuracy. I was wondering if the dream I had was a precursor to an encounter with one of these unsavory characters.

I got off at Bush St. and walked to Grant Street. There was a famous landmark at the entrance called The Dragon Gate and it arched over the street as one entered. My first task was to find someone who spoke English. By the time I got to Stockton Street, my task seemed impossible. I mulled among throngs of Asian faces—and you know, most of 'em *did* look alike to me! Mario Angelo had pointed that out to me one night we were patrolling the Chinese village in L.A. I suppose we all look alike to them, too. Sounds, sights and smells filled my senses. Even the shop signs were in Chinese, but some did have both languages posted. Finally I spotted a likely candidate, Zou Du Lee Cleaners. I entered and a very mild mannered older man approached me from behind the counter. "What you want? You got tickee?" he asked in that marvelously clipped speech pattern.

"Ah, no...I—I, uh, I'd kinda like to soak up some of your culture—I mean the real thing. Like bars, opium dens, prostitute hangouts, places like that."

He looked at me oddly. "No bar in Chinatown. Opium den in Stockton Street—you look to rent lady?"

"No, not actually. I just wanna sample the atmosphere."

"Go Lung Hou's—good Chinese food. Ask for *Charlie*. He help."

I thanked the nice man and left. I elbowed my way through the crowds. The Chinese weren't any too polite when it came to push and shove. I guess they were used to it. *Lung Hou's* smelled like home cooking, Asian style. I couldn't remember when I ate last, so I bellied up to the food bar and pointed at a couple of dishes I could more or less recognize. As I paid the man at the register I asked if he knew *'Charlie.'* I knew he understood me, but pretended he didn't. He pointed out to a patio in the back of the noisy joint. I put my food above my head and sandwiched my way toward the patio. One good thing, the Chinese are mainly shorter than I was, so I could maneuver over a crowd of black heads without too much difficulty.

I found a small empty table in the shade of an old olive tree. Damn, the man at the cleaners was right—Lung Hou's food was good. I stuffed my two plates' worth of food pretty fast and could've used a cold beer to wash it down. I tried to hail a waiter but he couldn't hear me over the din. Then a nice young man approached me.

"I understand you have difficulty here. I am Bojing Cheung. May I sit?" The young man was probably about twenty, neatly dressed and quite handsome. It looked like his blood was mixed with a little Caucasian along the way. His hair was cropped short and he had a nice smile.

"Sure, anyone who can converse with me. I feel like I'm downtown Peking or something here," I said, chuckling. "Can you get me a beer?"

"Certainly. We have best Chinese import beer here. *Tsingtao* very good. Made in *Qingdao*. I have one with you, okay?" I gave him some money and he promptly returned with two beers in hand.

"Well, that was fast—what'd you do—steal it?"

He laughed. "No, my father is Lung Hou. We have family restaurant. I work here since I was eight. My name in Chinese means *'I win admiration and have good luck.'* Now I am in San Francisco State college to learn taxidermy."

I did a double take. "Taxidermy? You'll *need* some good luck for that."

"Yes. Very lucrative. Rich man pay big to have stuffed favorite dog or bear he shoot. You know what I mean?"

"Yeah, I never looked at it like that. Sounds promising." I poured the beer into my glass and started to drink. "Blah!" I exclaimed. "This crap is *warm*!"

"May I ask what is your name?"

"Denning…Cable Denning…call me Cable," I said, making a face.

"Cable Denning, nice name. All Chinese beer is warm. In 1903 it was introduced into China by an English/German brewery based in Hong Kong and their original recipe became the standard quality that Tsingtao Beer is known for today."

"Oh, I see. I'll drink it, but I'm sure not used to it." I took another deep sip. It wasn't so bad the second time around. "I'm looking for a guy named Charlie. You see, I'm—I'm here for some research on the underbelly of Chinatown—you know, the opium dens, houses of ill repute, gambling houses, places where the highbinders hang out."

Bojing Cheung studied my face. "Why would you want to go *there*?"

"Isn't that as much a part of your people's lifestyle as anything else?"

"Yes. I will say you're right. How's my English?"

"Swell. At least we can communicate. So, do you know this Charlie?"

"Yes. But he does not stay when he buys food here. He pays for it and walks away to an opium parlor on Stockton, *Soc Ti Lao*. I think he gets high on sweet smell of smoke alone," he laughed.

We spent some time with young Bojing filling me in on life styles here in Chinatown. But when I mentioned possibility of a young mysterious Asian virgin who might also know a Hatchet Man, he drew away from me and a frightened look came over his face. "Was it something I said, or do I have beer all over my face—what?"

"It is bad luck to speak of the *Living Lotus, Nymphaea Nelumbo*," he said in a foreboding tone. "I must go now. I wish you well, Cable Denning." Just like that he was gone. I must have looked like a stranger in a strange land, because I got a lot of weird looks from the locals as I got up to leave. Granted, I did stick out like a sore thumb, being the only Caucasian in view most of the day so far.

Bojing had described the opium 'parlor', as he called it. But when I found it and entered, it was a *den*—maybe even a cave—etched into the basement of a flower shop above it. I'll bet they sold a lot of flowers for funerals because I'd heard a lot of these guys down here don't get back up topside alive. Small cots were strewn helter-skelter, and beaten little men with beaten little faces lay on their sides, sitting up or on their backs, sucking away at that sweet, acrid dope. I had studied the green bud-pod with the leaking latex at the police academy and knew that morphine and heroin were by-products of this infamous little poppy. Once hooked, it was a near impossible journey back up to the surface of life, like Orpheus in Hades, the journey had many risks and few made it out alive.

The filth and smell were so bad I didn't think I could stay, so I turned around and started to walk back up the steps when a light touch tapped my shoulder. It was a very old man with a black cap, long, stringy white beard and moustache. He motioned me to follow him. We went through the living corpses to the rear of the den. There was a thick, small door near a corner. He opened it and motioned me in. Suddenly I was in a royal court…at least compared to what I had just seen. Other kinds of smoke, the real tobacco kind, mingled with shouting voices at different gambling events, beautiful young women dressed to the nines adorned some of the men while others hid away in dark corners on little tables lit with small red candle lanterns.

Then my host spoke—and very articulately. "What bring you to see Charlie? Charlie not here. You dangerous man to be here, *fan kuei*."

"Don't tell me, those are not nice words, now, are they?" My patience was wearing a bit thin. "What in the hell does *fan kuei* mean?"

"It mean *ocean ghost*, white man. Lucky your eyes not blue."

"What does that mean?"

" It mean white man with blue eyes most treacherous."

"Well, then, if we can get a drink and I can light up a Lucky Strike, we can toast to my natural brown eyes then, can't we—and then I'll *really* be dangerous."

The old man looked at me strangely. "You cannot stay here. We have one rum with triple sec. Then you must go."

"But I just got here. Rum and triple sec—you Chinks are pretty sophisticated after all—or at least some of you."

The old man glowered at me. Something I said must have offended him. He seemed to be quite respected in this house of ill repute, for he snapped his fingers and right away a pretty little thing dressed in a tight-fitting yellow outfit came over. He spoke in Chinese to her and she left. "Like most white men, you are offensive and walk with pomposity. We Chinese, even transplanted to United States, remain humble and require the simple to bring us happiness."

"Well, whoever you are, I couldn't agree with you more. Outside of being a little 'pushy-pushy' out there on the street, I'd say you guys are somewhat more humble. Do you think it goes with the breed?"

"Do not be facetious, my race has lived longer and grown wiser than you. One day, when the rule of the white man is over, the Chinese will dominate this planet."

"How in the hell do you have such a vocabulary for such an old, ignorant looking coot?"

"I have mastered all languages of the earth. I learn engineering and build railroad over the Sierra Nevada mountain."

"Now you're pulling my leg. They started that at the end of the Civil War, 1865 or so. It killed a lot of them. You look old, but not that old, Mister."

"Not matter." Just then the lovely little Asian waitress brought our drinks. I reached into my pocket to pay. "No pay. I have good credit here."

"Well, thanks, Mister—you do have a name, I presume?"

"No name. You tell me, ocean ghost, what you come for—I think I know, but I must hear it from your mouth. Speak with your lips, I no hear perfect."

I finally lit up that cigarette. I lifted my glass to toast my very strange guide. For a spark of a minute I could swear I saw the old man's eyes change color. Naw, a trick of the red candlelight. He lifted his glass with a very stern countenance. Of course, the Chinese are always serious, aren't they? Well, except for maybe Chinese New Year in February when they all get drunk. "Well, do you want the truth—or do you want me to skirt around the gory details and simply tell you I'm soaking in your culture?"

He studied my face carefully. "You…are truth man. Not lie

easy. Now speak with your lips, look at me with your eyes when you tell me…"

"Okay, here goes. Talking about railroads, I got railroaded into finding this rare golden acorn, pod or capsule—whatever it is—called *The God of Our Fathers,* okay? It's supposed to contain the origin of the blueprint of creation and *why* something or someone bothered making the universe—let alone humans—so it's the Great Omnipresent, or some such thing—I mean, that stuff's not my line. I'm a cop in L.A. I don't like what I do, so I got roped into finding this thing. A couple of psychic people pretty hooked up to something or other, guided me here. They told me a lovely Chinese virgin who came from a lotus seed at the bottom of a dry lake knows where the damn thing is." I took a deep breath and a slug of my rum and triple sec, which was quite potent. "And that's why I'm here. I haven't got a clue where to start looking except in these pits of damnation and vice."

The old man sat back in his chair and I saw appear on his face the first semi-smile he'd cracked since we'd been talking. *"Fen de Fuqin.* The lost precious was stolen from the Cave of the Seven Truths. A legend, I say to you. Chinese occult know all this. You are stupid to pursue. Finish drink and go home. You young, handsome *fan kuei.* Why waste life? Much to live yet."

"It ain't that easy, stranger. I neglected to mention a few things, such as the death toll this thing has already cost us *fan kuei's* and personally, there is a very beautiful young woman whose life is dangling there in the dark unless I come with something real soon. You see, I can't make heads or tails of who's who chasing this thing around. There was Dr. Sandor who was half science, half greed, and when I saw the little thing glow under the blue light—"

"—you see *Fen de Fuqin?* In blue light?" His eyes widened.

"Yeah, that's how old Sandor could see the etchings on the

outside. Of course I understand a microfilm etched in gold is inside. It'd have to be awful small to get stuffed into that little capsule."

"You dead man."

"Aren't we all—sooner or later?"

"Not good you be here."

"So, are you gonna help me?"

"Huh?"

"The Chinese virgin and all—can you steer me in the right direction?"

He studied me for a final time. "You go tonight to House of Black Hand. Down stairs to basement."

"You guys sure are into basements..." I chuckled.

"Not laugh. First place by Dragon Gate. When sun set."

"I've heard of the Black Hand, alright, but it wasn't Chinese. I thought it was at the beginning of the century—Serbia or someplace like that."

"Unity...or death...it mean nothing funny. Hatchet Man must not know."

"Okay, okay...just trying to warm things up a bit. I'll be there."

The old man said no more and departed. My pretty little waitress motioned that I follow her. She led me to a back door and let me out, saying nothing. The whole thing was getting creepier by the minute. The old fart knew about the *sacred capsule,* the virgin—and the Hatchet Man. Just that in itself sounded like a lethal combination to me.

Just about sunset I made my way toward the Dragon Gate. I was listening to Honey singing somewhere deep inside. It was like she was in my ear, reminding me to come up for air, that life and love and something good still existed out there, fighting its way to the surface. *I Can't Give You Anything But Love* was coming in loud and clear. I guess in the end of things, that's all we've got. Something of ourselves to share, and I knew Honey was true-blue, and even though I knew she'd be tested by the world and tossed to the wolves of Hollywood sooner or later, she was made of better stuff and she'd survive it. Between singing at the club, making records and a movie career, her life would hardly be her own. I knew it was easy for me to be selfish about it, demand more time of her, hand her a male ego ultimatum. But that wasn't my style. After all, I was the one who introduced her to the world she now found herself circulating in. And yeah, there'd be wolves in sheep's clothing trying to get into her pants, guys with lust in their groins for another notch on their guns, all on the pretense of assisting her career. An old story.

At dusk I was searching for some clue as to exactly what first building by the Dragon Gate I was supposed to enter. The old man forgot to mention left or right? Then I saw a figure beckon to me. It was the building on the north side of the gate. It wasn't exactly the Hall of Supreme Harmony in the Forbidden City of the Ming Dynasty, but it looked kind of fifteenth century with all the gingerbread on the roof and all. I entered and a young woman in plain black led me silently down a flight of stairs to the bottom floor. But this basement was a far cry from the opium cave or gambling hall I was in earlier in the day. This interior was exquisitely decorated in reds, gold and blacks. A huge bright burgundy carpet fit the room wall to wall. The young woman took me to a wonderful heavily upholstered chair. She left and I sat and waited.

Soon a man in a deep black suit with a fedora entered. He approached me but did not speak immediately. Instead, he went into a chest and withdrew a string of incense. He lit it with a match and came over to me. He began swirling the damn thing above my head. I had the distinct feeling I was not supposed to speak until spoken to. For some reason, while

176

he was doing it, I was thinking of my little Latina lover. What a brave and adventurous soul she turned out to be, I thought. Adora Moreno would've made a great life mate for a private dick—they could actually work in tandem. The key to it all was the lack of fear. The minute you fear, I'd learned, is the minute you attract what you're afraid of. Adora seemed to have the same makings inside that I did in that regard. She was a swell dame and I hadn't a clue as to where our intimate relationship would end up. I only knew that she had already given me some of the sweetest moments of my life. And for Cable Denning, that was saying something!

"I am the one you fear," he finally spoke up, his voice deep and clear. His English was remarkable. He was a bit pudgy and his black robe was too big for him. The sleeves hung draped over his forearm. His eyes were so slanted that I thought they were closed some of the time. "I am the one you dreamed. The old man feared me. You do not?"

"Well, it's kinda hard to fear what you don't know, now, isn't it? But I am amazed you remembered you were in my dream. How's a thing like that work? Now let me see, you're probably the Hatchet Man—and a member of the local branch of the Black Hand, right? But you can't kill me unless your superiors obligate you to that assignment, am I batting five-hundred so far?" I realized I was goading him a bit.

"Never mind. I am cleansing you for your audience."

"My audience?" A shiver went through me. I just got it. I was going to be introduced to the mysterious "she" of virginal fame. "This is a nice place you have here, but it's a bit chilly for a fun time with some babe."

"You disgust me, like all white men disgust me," the chubby man in black said. "You *fan kuei* all alike. Every female mean something sexual to conquer. Do you know who I am—or was before I committed myself to the Black Hand? I was executive of successful import company."

"Bully for you, Mister Hatchet Man. You guys are ridiculous. All these secret clubs and organizations—I did that as a kid in a tree house when I was eight. Why don't you grow up and have a life?"

His face turned red as he reached up his sleeve and brought out the head of a hatchet. Uh oh, I thought, I'd done it now! I got up and ran for the nearest exit toward the rear and it was just like my dream. The Hatchet Man began to chase me all around the damn place and just as I was forced into a dark corridor at the end of the rear hallway, I caught a flash of red in the subdued light and out stepped a most gorgeous babe in a shining silk outfit with golden dragons embroidered all over it. She put her hand up and the Hatchet Man stopped, also exactly as in my dream! She said nothing but motioned for me to follow. We got into a gold-plated elevator and we ascended three stories. I was still so out of breath from too many Lucky Strikes and being chased around by the 'Mad Hatchet Man', that I had to bend over while the lady went forth and lit a few very large red lanterns.

She approached me slowly. She carefully looked me over. "What is it in the mind the heart cannot understand, Mr. Denning?" she asked. "You have pursued me for the sake of pursuit and capture—rather than for truth."

I was floored by the dame. She stood about five-five, slender but shapely, her eyes slanted in some sexy way I can't quite explain, while her thick, black hair shone in the dim light of the red lanterns. Suddenly I felt humbled in her presence, like I had been a smart shit all day and now it was time to stop. I stood there out of breath. "You're right, but first of all, thanks for saving me from your goon out there. Your Hatchet Man is a bit testy, you know." She didn't comment. I couldn't believe I was actually in her presence and she really did exist! "How'd you know my name and may I assume you—you are the virginal Red Dragon Lady I have heard about for quite some time now?"

"You may assume what you like," she said as she faced me, checking out my eyes. "I am *Lei-tao*. We have met before. In your Los Angeles…on a street in Chinatown. You flirted with me one day, when two bad men were killed on your streets."

All of a sudden it hit me—yeah, the babe who seemed out of place that Friday afternoon when Ardizzone and Blinthe got it. "Oh, yeah, I remember…I thought you were a knockout."

"A knockout?"

"Yeah, a real dish—you know, beyond pretty…like beautiful."

"Thank you." She sized me up, then walked away a few paces. "I am the guardian of *Fen de Fuqin*, the Sacred. To put your mind at ease, I reclaimed the capsule from inside the bank vault and began to return it to its home. But too many evil forces were blocking my passage, so I hid it securely in a location within a day's journey of here."

"*Fen de Fuqin*? So that's *your* name for that damned golden capsule?"

"Yes. It must be returned to…to its proper place. But, as I have told you, now it is safely hidden somewhere."

"Ah, the fabled magic castle, huh? How come you speak such damn good English, probably better than mine?"

"I have mastered all languages of the world. Remember, 'I study engineering and I build railroad over Sierra Nevada mountain'?"

Now I was really stumped. "You mean…it—it was *you*—the old man?"

"Yes. Nazar Ravna discovered that when he and his *Oculus Pyramis Mandatum* tried to abduct me. I *am* a shape-changer, able to transform into any organic form I wish at will."

"Well, let me tell you, lady, *that's* the best trick I've heard of in my entire lifetime! And what in the hell does this *Oculus* thing mean? You're not pulling my leg now, are you?"

She smiled at me. I had an inkling that this lovely creature was not completely free of prurient desires and that she was just a little bit attracted to me. Or maybe it was just my fantasy. "No. There is no time for that. In Latin, Ravnas's Order is translated as meaning *mandating eye of the pyramid*. Before very many of your years, you will see how far they cast their shadow as reference will be made of their Order on the very backs of your paper money that you exchange every day without even knowing it. You and I—us—are in a dilemma. I understand you are in the middle of this by seeming coincidence. But the natural order of things does not work that way, it is *intentional*. All of life is a classroom. What have you come to learn, Mr. Denning?"

"Cable…please call me Cable. Uh…I don't know…let me see…I came up the rough way and I'm not sure that it didn't warp me in some way, like toughen me up and cover up some of my emotions. Maybe that's what I need to work on. What do you think?"

"You are extra-ordinary, Cable. Call me Lei-tao. *Love* is always the best place to begin the great journey of learning about what we might contain as beings."

"I'll second that." I was thinking of that wonderful little body and that China doll face of hers without the Red Dragon Lady's clothes on. "May I ask…are you…are you really a virgin as legend has it?"

"In your sense of the definition, yes. I come from a very different dimension than you. I cannot have sexual intercourse in the crude manner of overt physical contact with the opposite sex such as you do."

"Well, then, do you have sexual feelings—l mean, like normal women?"

"I do not know what you mean by 'normal,' Cable…but yes, I feel desire to receive love and erotic sensation—but it cannot happen by touching someone. It would revolt me—or—or

180

turn me cold and rigid."

"I see," I said, lamenting the waste of all that luscious looking babe. "That's too bad. But on the other hand, maybe it has its merits, too. Let me tell you, in the past few days I've been battered around so much in my head, emotions and body, I'm still trying to find which end is up." I stood there looking at her beautiful face. "You don't look like the horrible Red Dragon Lady I was told you were. Am I missing something?"

She laughed mildly. "No. You see me now as I have chosen to appear to *you*. You saw me as the old man. I was even the old lady searching the bodies of the dead men that day. Then I changed back into a form you would be attracted to, so you might tell where they took the bodies. There are many other forms I can take that would terrify your limited mortal perceptions."

"Yeah, but why such a dish? You don't make it easy on a guy to do business with you, you know. Ballsy young cops like me live like a bull in a China shop…pardon the expression… careless and clumsy."

She avoided answering me. "You must rest your body now. Stay here with me tonight. Tomorrow I will show you something special about the *Fen de Fuqin*." She showed me to a plush sofa in the middle of her gold and red living room. Then she left me without a word. Just thinking about her, a love song started playing in my head. Honey was singing *My Heart Stood Still* somewhere in the recesses of my mind's ear and I wished it was Lei-tao, and maybe somehow it might be prophetic, for a few minutes later, as the song was humming in my brain, Lei-tao walked down a hallway from her shower room totally nude! If one can fall in love with the backside of a babe, I figured he was really hard up or the gal really had something. I had never seen such a perfect and exquisite back. I wondered if she had done this thing on purpose? I lit up a cigarette and sat on the sofa, trying to collect myself and review the day's happenings. Phew! Today had been a corker.

But complete rest was not to be. I was dreaming about Honey and she was singing her little heart out at the club, a sassy version of *Someone to Watch Over Me*, the same song she sang to me out on the dance floor at *Gregorio's* the night we met. In a way, I wished I was there watching over her right now. But the dream got pretty intense as I was reliving a terrible night in '27 when I shot and accidentally killed a gangland big player, one named Vincenzo Drucci. The mob had vowed to get back at me, but the crooked cops in the force would've done it for the syndicate except for one thing. Someone didn't want the favor pulled out of the magic hat—at least not yet. Mario had kept telling me the Jewish Mafia wanted Drucci dead, so they owed me one. Maybe it was them that kept the specter of death away from my door. Anyway, the dream got pretty intense as I found myself running around desperately trying to protect Honey from all the guys who wanted to screw her *and* own her. We were in the *Bella Notte*, and all of a sudden a whole bunch of guys who looked just like Frank Laggore showed up, dodging here and there, looking for Honey. They came out of the kitchen, from behind the stage, in the front door—all of them with guns drawn. I fired away at them, but as soon as one dropped, another one showed up just as mean and intent on getting to Honey. Just then a stranger came to my assistance. It looked to me like the brains behind the Prohibition money making machine, one known as Arnold "The Brain" Rothstein. He was known to the underworld as the *Moses of the Jewish Gangsters*. I needed someone to deliver me to the Promised Land just about then, and even though we'd have to forego the burning bush and God's commandments for the moment, I was glad to have him aboard, firing away at the bad guys right beside me. But they kept multiplying and soon Honey came running out of nowhere calling out my name. I ran to her but it was too late as the punks turned their guns onto her and filled her full of lead. She went plunging to the floor as I screamed out her name, "Honey! Honey!"

The next thing I knew it was morning and a beautiful Asian female was looking down at me dressed only in her thin red-silk morning robe. "You dream of past and future because you are haunted, Cable. You cannot help the pathway of others. Be present."

I rubbed the sleep out of my eyes as I sat up on the sofa. "And good morning to you!" I muttered. "Hope you slept better than I did."

"I do not sleep. Not in the sense you do. I go away into a state of being elsewhere. Now I have come back for you. You must wash and dress. Today we will take a journey. Shall you be prepared?"

"I don't know. Depends on where we're going and how long it takes to get there—and is it dangerous? Frankly, Lei-tao, I'm kinda tired of 'dangerous' for a while. Can we have 'mysterious' and maybe 'fun' for a change?"

She laughed and took my hand to help me up. Her hands were ice cold, like a corpse down at the city morgue. I chuckled. "I hate to say this, but don't you have any blood circulation? You feel like a tray of ice under a champagne bottle."

"I am sorry. It takes a little time for this body to warm once I have been away from it. As I said, during the night I go away. My body goes into a state of—of…there is a word for animals—"

"—hibernation. I'd hate to be your husband. The poor guy'd freeze to death and they'd find him in the morning ready to float out to sea like an iceberg. If you ever have a lover, you've gotta do something about that, kid."

She giggled. "I love your humor, Cable. Laughter heals. I am glad you can take things so—so lightly when most humans would be falling apart at this time from all the pressure."

"Say, I've got to use your phone before we leave. I need to

check in with Ravna. He'll kill Adora if I don't let him know I'm doing at least *something* about procuring the *Fen de Fuqin*."

"There are no phones here. When you come to meet me for our journey, Wong Lo San will take you to phone booth. He will also escort you to where I shall await you. I must go to prepare now."

She started to go. "Uh, you're not leaving me with that goon downstairs?"

"We must not be seen together. Dangerous for both of us. Wong Lo San is trustworthy."

"I don't know, considering he was the guy who pulled out that hatchet head from under his sleeve last night and started chasing me around your lobby."

"Go now, Cable, get washed and dressed." Then she walked away.

Good ol' Wong Lo San directed me to a phone booth where I called both Dr. Penn and Ravna. I told Jedediah I was fine and on the trail of something big, including the precious capsule people were so willing to die for. When I talked to Ravna, I found him a bit irritated that my detail was so sketchy and that if by tomorrow I didn't have the object in question in his sweaty little hand, he'd have Adora blown away with a few bullets in her lovely head. I came back that if he did that, he might never see the golden priceless again. He backed off and I assured him I was in negotiation with the honorable Lei-tao, the Red Dragon Lady herself. He was sufficiently impressed with that information, but what cinched it for him was my usage of the original name of the golden acorn, *Fen de Fuqin*. I promised him I'd call him by tomorrow evening because I was most likely taking a short trip with the beautiful Red Dragon Lady.

Wong Lo San led me down Bush Street toward Stockton. "Lei-tao tells me you're not such a bad sort, besides being a killer, murderer of men, women and children, enforcer of prostitution, gambling, drug addiction palaces and immigrant female slavery," I poked at the man.

"I hate man like you," he stated with a toxic vehemence. "You also put curse on Red Dragon Lady. She is not same since you arrive. You corrupt her with erotic thoughts and behavior. She is pure—and must stay pure."

"You know, old boy, I think you're jealous because she doesn't want you in her bed. I mean, after all, who was it that spent the night in her quarters—huh? all night, laughing and drinking and making love—"

"—stay quiet! You are insult to men! Beside, you lie. She cannot shape into your kind of woman. I am thankful for that. Say no thing more."

And so I didn't. We got to the same old opium den I had first entered the day before. He guided me downstairs, past the hopeless men rotting away in their bunks, into the gambling hall with the richly dressed men and whores, and finally through a third door. But this one was painted a shiny black and had a lock that required a large, complicated key that the Hatchet Man withdrew from his robes and applied to the lock. Finally it opened. "You go. Wong Lo San hope he never seen you again." Then he departed.

I walked through the black door and it shut behind me with a solid sound. I was thrust into a night of pitch-black nothingness. Then out of nowhere one candle was lit inside a small red lantern. I walked cautiously toward it. I didn't suspect any treachery from Lei-tao, but you never know—life can be tricky. "Come, Cable," a voice spoke from out of the darkness. "Come sit here, at the table." I fumbled my way to a small black table where the red lantern sat.

"Lei-tao—I—I can't see you, but I know your voice. So, I'm sitting. Where are you?"

"I am sitting in front of you but you will not see me." I looked around. Now that my eyes adjusted to the light, there was another object on the table. It was a tall golden cup filled with red and gold liquid. "What in the hell is this stuff?"

"It is I, Cable. I have become the essence form I am in the liquid universe. Drink me, and we will take our journey together."

"Gees, lady, I'd really like to trust you here—but you know, I'm just not used to drinking *people* down like that. How do I know it's not poison and you're *zai jian* to me? Are you sure this is the only way? I mean, I was thinking of a cable car ride or a short train ride or something—"

"—you know some Chinese. *Zai jian* means good-bye—and we have barely said hello."

I looked around the room. Her voice was coming from everywhere at the same time. But I had to move on it. "I read it. So…where are we going, if I may be so bold as to at least ask that?"

"To the *Cave of the Seven Truths.* It is my birthplace when I incarnate from the Lake of Lotus Pod. I have shown it to only one other earth soul. Will you drink now, please?"

I took the golden chalice in hand and drank it all down without tasting it. What the hell, I thought, today was as good a day to die as any other. Interestingly, the stuff tasted sweet and warm on my lips and I began to feel euphoric. "Whoa! You taste pretty damn good to me, Lei-tao. Does the rest of you taste this good—I mean that with no offense, of course."

She didn't answer, but the room began to spin and I was whirling up through the ceiling, higher and higher and watching my body sit there by the red lantern at the same time! I could feel a hand take mine. This time we both had the same temperature and floated faster and faster until all I could see were colors upon colors whirling through my consciousness.

I was forced to close my eyes as things accelerated faster and faster. Somehow I wasn't afraid and I don't even think my heart rate increased.

Next thing I knew, Lei-tao and I were standing in the middle of this magnificent multi-colored dome, towering maybe a hundred feet above us. But what was really weird was that the entire surroundings pulsed with golds, reds, greens, blues and indigos. "Welcome to my birth home, Cable," Lei-tao said, looking at me with a smile. "Here I was born forever. Here is where the untouched *Fen de Fuqin* sat for thousands of your years. Then sorcerers who intended chaos and confusion upon your earth plane found a way to transport the Sacred Golden One to the world of men. There, the terrible Order of the *Oculus Pyramis Mandatum* got possession of it through an evil other-dimensional creature called *Tsaga*...you knew him in human form as *Blinthe*. He was to benefit greatly by turning the *Fen de Fuqin* over to the Order. The golden capsule contains a sacred, etched golden tablet copied from an ageless vibrational parchment. That is the key to the symbols on the *outside*."

I was using my natural detective sense. "So what's the golden capsule say?"

"Nothing visible to you, but it contains the *Tone of Creation*, the one sound the universe was made from. The terrible men of the *Oculus Pyramis Mandatum* were aided by this alien mischief-maker, named *Tsaga*, who could fly up to the beginning of the first sky. When he captured the *Fen de Fuqin*, he brought the knowledge of the *Blue Light of Noda* with him. This is how the golden capsule is read and magnified. It was what you beheld when Dr. Sandor showed it to you in his vault—where I reclaimed the precious one."

"That's quite a lump of info to take in at one time," I said, wholly perplexed and puzzled. "So you killed Matrangas and Jinx?"

"I have told you I appear in many forms—and at all costs, must protect the *Fen de Fuqin*. That day I was a black dragon."

"Hmmm…I see…so you weren't kidding. You'll have to forgive me, I'm—I'm, uh, just not used to this shape-changing thing."

"I understand. You are a three-dimensional creature."

"So what are the seven truths you spoke of?"

It is the origin of my own being, not only what I was taught, but what I was in *non-consciousness* before awakening into form. She pointed to a rock in the ceiling of the cave. It lit up a deep red. "The vibration we are taught is 'WE ARE POWERFUL AND MIGHTY SPIRITUAL BEINGS IN A PHYSICAL WORLD, AND WE LIVE WITH DIGNITY, DIRECTION AND PURPOSE.' Next she pointed to another rock and it turned a lovely deep red-orange and glowed so brightly that it filled the room. "'WE CHOSE TO COME HERE FOR SELF-BETTERMENT, AND FOR THE BETTERMENT OF OTHERS.'"Then she pointed to a rock far in the distance and yellow beamed out everywhere in the giant cavern. "'WE WERE ALSO CHOSEN TO COME HERE. A LOVING FORCE TRUSTS AND BELIEVES IN US.'" Next, Lei-tao pointed to a rock well over to our right. A lovely green-yellow stood out. "'WE POSSESS MANY GIFTS AND TALENTS.'"Then she pointed to another rock in the distance to the left. Suddenly the room filled with a warm, magical blue glow. "'WE CHOSE TO BE HERE AT THIS TIME—NOW. WHEREVER WE ARE, WE ARE NOT LOST.'" At the next motion of her finger into the air, a beautiful blue-green began to emanate from this cavern of indescribable beauty. "'WE EXISTED IN OTHER DIMENSIONS BEFORE, BEAUTIFUL, SAFE, ALL EMBRACING. WE ARE PRECIOUS THERE, EVEN NOW.'" Then her hand swept across the very heavens directly above us and the room filled with the most incredible light I had ever seen. The space between my eyebrows ached with a kind of joy I could never explain to myself, let alone anyone else. It was a purple, or indigo color of such magnificence and depth that I fell into it while I stood there with Lei-tao. "'WE WILL RETURN TO OUR BEAUTIFUL DIMENSIONAL WORLD, AND LEAVE BEHIND THE UNIQUENESS OF OUR DIVINE MARK.'"

Those messages issued by the colors from her lips resonated in me like a pinball hitting all the bumpers at the same time. My lights went on deep inside and I felt how shallow and limited we humans were who dwelled upon the earth. And wherever I was right now somehow amplified the best parts of me, made me see there is a limitless something in every one of us that lies there asleep at the very core of our being. I could never be that wise in the ordinary day-to-day existence—on patrol—with Mario Angelo and I taking a chronic shoplifter back to the station house for booking. That pedestrian world suddenly paled before this, the magnificent *otherness* I was also.

Lei-tao took my hand and pulled my body into hers. "Now I can touch you, Cable. Now I know you have endured the vibrational test and the cave has not rejected you." She hugged me amidst the warm splendor of the multi-colored cave. "Now... do you want to have some pleasure?"

"Yep, that's me. Mr. Pleasure...does this mean we—we, uh, get to explore each other in slightly more intimate ways?" I still had a hankering for this lovely, mysterious creature.

"You might say that. But please remember, I already told you we cannot have the kind of physical intimacy you are used to."

"Yeah, you did. That part's too bad. I was kinda hoping you'd give it a go. But you did explain it would mess up your vibration or something. So...uh, how we do this thing?"

"We go to *The Center of the Sun*. We become wholly natural...naked. We kneel and face each other and by concentra-

189

tion, allow each and every cell in our bodies to come to life, to stimulate us until together we experience *the Little Death*. It is the way of the Tantra from what you know as ancient Sanskrit."

"But isn't my body still back at the ol' opium den?"

"Yes. But *you* are here. And you bring with you the memory of your body. So it manifests. Whatever you can image, Cable, you can become."

"Easy for you to say. I've still got trouble shaving in the morning when I've got a hangover, no matter what I imagine in my head."

She ignored my ridiculousness. "Are you ready?"

"I'm not too crazy about going to the center of the Sun part. Won't we be burnt to a crisp within a wink of an eye?"

"It is symbolic, Cable, for walking into the *Room of Impossible Light*."

"Oh, that's even more exciting." I took a deep breath, wishing I could have my last cigarette before taking what might be my last walk with this babe—or anyone! "Alright…lead the way, doll."

She took my hand and it felt good. In that second I trusted her and realized she would guide us to new places that I must be willing to explore. Or else I would end my life like any other bloke, stiffened to hardness by a constrained world of emptiness, longing and concealed desperation.

We walked to the very middle of the glowing Cave of the Seven Truths. There the Red Dragon Lady began to turn gold before my eyes. It was a warm, heated gold and it spread from her to my body until both of us were glowing like golden iridescent candles against a sky of endless beauty. She let go of my hand and sank to her knees. I did the same, sitting on my knees about three feet from her. "Close your eyes, Cable, think of me, think of desiring every bit of me, all of my female self, all of my mind, all of my spirit—think of combining with me into complete Oneness. Feel the connection…we are never separated…now rejoin in consciousness with me…bring me to *the little death* as I do the same for you."

To this day I can't completely explain it. But whatever happened in that Cave of the Seven Truths that day, changed me forever in ways I may never know, given the stupid default systems humans are made up of. First I could feel my feet begin to warm. I concentrated on Lei-tao's feet, for I felt her thoughts were directed to me by a ritual pattern of some sort. Then I could feel my lower legs and knees come to life and it made me take deep breaths. Soon my upper legs were filled with the energy and when it hit my genitals it felt like someone had just rung the bell at a carnival sideshow. I could hear Lei-tao begin to moan and I knew I was getting pretty good at this focus thing. With my eyes still closed, I imagined her beautiful dark mound lighting up, swelling, pulsing, the electricity shooting through us both as my own genitals took on a powerful jolt and my manhood came to spectacular attention as my balls tightened. By the time the energy had moved up past our stomachs, I, too, began to moan without being quite able to control it. When my focus hit her wonderful, young and firm breasts, I was breathing in and out like a wolf in heat and I was tempted to open my eyes and watch those lovely little nipples stiffen and stick out like bright-pink ornaments hung on the morning Christmas tree. When this mystery woman and I reached the throat and head places, we broke loose with cries of ecstasy that seemed to echo into forever, the sounds went out to every space in the cosmos yet never left our presence. Not before or since in my life, had I experienced such ecstasy.

Then the golden light that filled us dissipated and I instinctively inched toward Lei-tao as she fell into my arms. Our bodies were dripping wet with perspiration but our minds were alert and euphoric. "Thank you, Cable! She said breathlessly. "I knew you could do this with me—I just knew."

"And thank you, babe. I think you just spoiled me for a human existence, though. How can I ever have a mortal woman again?"

"You will. In the human condition, you will forget. And you will live on without me, as I must live on without you. What has been added is that you will pass some of this *golden walk to the Center of the Sun* onto others that they might be lighted by your presence. This is how we silently grow and learn from others. This is my gift to you, Cable."

I woke up on the floor of that dark room with the little table and the single red lantern. "Lei-tao?" I called. "Lei-tao?" I felt my body. It was still intact and nothing hurt. "Are you here?"

"Yes, Cable. But the cup is tipped and you must right it so I can re-form into it and regain my physical self."

I saw the goblet next to me on the floor. I got up and placed it on the table by the glowing red lantern and sat. "Okay. Shoot..." I couldn't believe it as the bottom of the chalice began to fill again with the bright red and gold liquid. Soon it rose like a mist up out of the container and spread around the room like a beautiful fog. Then Lei-tao's complete woman's body formed out of that fog and she stood before me...perfectly wonderful...perfectly naked. "Happy to see you again, fellow traveler. Do...do you, uh, need to put some clothes on? Now that I've experienced *the you in you* I think my human man's desire is tweaked. But what an adventure, toots! How am I gonna ever top this one?"

She giggled a little. "You won't have to. Some of it I have erased already. You will take away only the essence of our experience together. Otherwise, you might go mad trying to equal your experience with other earth-grounded women." She went to a dark corner and slipped on a red outfit that was hidden there.

"Yeah, I'll drink to that." I looked around. "Speaking of

which, I could sure use a mighty potent drink just about now."

"We will go back to my apartments. I will go first. You follow in ten minutes. We will drink a celebration, Cable. You have accomplished much this day."

"I have? So what about the Seven Truths?"

"They are reminders and speak of our sacred roots. Do you remember most of them?"

"Naw, not really. They're a bit over my head, kid. You see, I'm still a caveman in some ways—the guy who sucks in his gut every day as he goes to work in that silly blue uniform and badge, someone who walks his talk but runs into the bullshit that the unjust of the world dish out—someone who'd rather be amongst the smoke and din of a crowded nightclub, watching a pretty babe with big tits and a red-sequined gown warble a couple of great tunes. I live in the realm of what is and what *could* be, willing to take the chance because life is a brief trip anyhow and it doesn't take a genius to figure out if you start out at the bottom of the money-ladder, chances are you ain't gonna be having lunch at New York's Stork Club or playing polo on a twenty-grand horse anytime soon. So you see, you do the next best thing, take your sword in hand and slash away at the untruths and injustices in the world, help out the poor and under-privileged, rescue a damsel from being beaten to death by her boyfriend, help that old lady across the street and draw your gun when danger threatens, shoot or be shot, kill or be killed, eat or be eaten. That's the world I live in, lady, the one where the battle never quite ends, where love and sex become all muddled up together and children still cry on street corners when Mamma gets mugged in the dark, where the underbelly of the world rules with its diabolical greed and lust, where people like Ravna and Matrangas or Laggore spread a violent sickness like a virulent plague that won't go away because they own the store and run it smart, because the populace is too dumbed down to notice as it struggles just to make ends meet providing food and a roof over their heads. And that…that's called the school of hard knocks, kid."

Lei-tao stood there. "If a shape-changing woman could love a mortal man, Cable Denning, I would love you. I have never heard a man speak as you do. Your mind is bitter but your heart is wonderful. We must go now."

CHAPTER 9

THE REACH OF THE BLACK HAND

About 600,000 people died between 1918 and 1920 of the Spanish flu in the United States. It hit every income strata, every family, every walk of life. Now, ten years later, it was as if it never happened and it faded like a memory of something that happened on another planet. Life has that capacity, to go on, to not look back if the nightmare was worse on the road behind than one could imagine on the road ahead. Lei-tao told me I would forget her in time, that whatever I had shared with her this day would fade from me, drain out of my memory as every day existence pounded its drum in my ear. Maybe it was true. Maybe there is a failsafe mechanism in humans that unless your heart is broken, most things we recall don't amount to much. Perhaps a fond childhood memory or someone you loved who isn't around anymore filters through our brain cells now and then. But survival was dependent on the *immediate* on those days, and no matter how crazy something might have appeared to be, the inexorable march of time buried it along with the other dirty laundry in the basket we keep under the counter marked 'once upon a time.'

I went down the stairs and crossed the basement room toward the golden elevator. Wong Lo San caught up with me from out of the shadows. "You are to be searched, ocean shadow," he said, as he stopped me. He threw me against a wall and slapped the palms of his hands all over my body, giving my genitals an extra-hard whack. "That to remember me by, white ghost. Go, and may the Curse of the Red Dragon Lady be upon you."

I was smarting from a case of whacked balls. "Thanks, you ugly son-of-a-bitch. You're a cowardly bastard for a Hatchet

Man. You fear and that's why you hit me. You fear you will never have what I have already experienced with your mistress. Well, let me tell you, buster, you never *will* have that privilege. You know why? Because you come with a pre-set gearbox of meanness, and until you lighten up and let go of what you can't change, you'll always be a cheap henchman." He raised his hand to strike me. "Go ahead, hit me again if it makes you feel better. You Chinese are supposed to be ancient and wise, but you know what? I see you as fearful and stupid, breeding like rats in a filthy sewer of your own making. Even if you could rule the world one day, your kind will perish because you fucked your way to oblivion along with the rest of the planet."

He put his hand down. "Go, piece of white crap, and do not let me see you again, for surely, I will kill you when next we meet."

I went to the elevator, got in and pressed "4". Soon I was in Lei-tao's gold and red living quarters again. She was sitting on the plush golden sofa I had slept on the previous night. She was wearing a very light pink see-through nightgown. She sat with her legs crossed and a long, narrow crystal glass in her hand. I was still a bit bent over from the pain in my groin. "What happened, Cable?" she said, alarmed at my strange gait.

"Oh, nothing much. Your hatchet boy down in the lobby doesn't like me much. He searched me and punched me in the balls for good measure."

"Oh, no…I'm so sorry…" She got up and came over to me. She scooped my balls into her left hand and almost instantly all my pain ceased. "Wong Lo San is bitter. He feels demoted in the web of things. What he does not know is that he has not learned the first lesson he came to learn. He will need many, many lifetimes to accomplish that, I would say."

She let go of my balls and I was sorry. It felt pretty good. "Yeah, well, let's not talk about Wong Lo San anymore, okay? I think I've had my fill of him in this one lifetime I've got right now."

She escorted me to the large sofa and sat me beside her. "Now that I trust you, Cable, I must ask you a favor. I must ask you to seek out and retrieve the *Fen de Fuqin* from its hiding place. Then you must return it to me so I may put it back to where it will be safe."

"Aren't you forgetting a thing or two? Say I retrieve your precious sacred, how do I sidestep the Order from killing Adora, myself and anyone else in the way? You do know everyone and their brother wants the damn thing? Did you say it was supposed to be filled with that *Tone of Creation* thing or something? Oh, yeah, and what's to prevent those bogeymen creatures from returning to your Cave of the Seven Truths and stealing it again? I'd hate to go through all that effort only to find I was dead meat at the other end anyhow."

She smiled at me and raised her crystal glass to me. "You are so perceptive, Cable." She got up and poured me a drink from a different bottle than what she had been sipping from.

"What, I don't rate to drink equal with the lady?"

"No, it's not that. What I drink in this bottle would kill you. I do not eat or drink as you do. This is liquid gold plasma and dissipates into my body before it reaches my stomach. I cannot eat your food or drink. I have some very aged brandy here for you. I hope you like it."

"Oh," I said, a bit perplexed as how these beings lived. I toasted Lei-tao and drank down a little of the brandy. It was so smooth that my whole chest lit up when I drank it. I got out a cigarette and lit up. "Thanks, Lei-tao. I'm—I'm just not used to dealing with other dimensional creatures you know. As I said, you'd make a hell of a difficult wife or lover."

She laughed. "If I could, I would be your wife, Cable. I think I love you, I mean, in your language, your way of loving someone. I am sorry I cannot participate. But now you have 'had sex' my way. Did you like it?"

"I'll never forget it. It's just different, that's all. I liked the part about raising the energy from the genitals up to the solar plexus, into the heart and way up there in that purple place I felt. Yeah, and thanks for loving me, your style. I like you a lot, too."

She cleared her throat. "Now, to answer your questions. First of all, I cannot retrieve *Fen de Fuqin* because I must leave immediately tonight...my energies are depleting, and it takes several of your weeks for me to regenerate in order to return. Taking you on our journey took most of my reserves. But I wouldn't have traded it, Cable. That said, I do not know the answers to all your questions. If Ravna or even Mr. Damianos is still seeking the *Fen de Fuqin*, then your mortal lady is safe."

I thought for a minute. "You're forgetting the fact that at the end of *this trip*, I'm supposed to deliver up—or Miss Moreno dies, and as I said, God knows who else. How do we circumvent that little reality, Red Dragon Lady?"

"*Toggth*. For a short while he can replicate the original *Fen de Fuqin* and get away with it. But you must get the original to me as soon as possible. He will fashion a three-dimensional duplicate. But it will only vibrate in that state for so long. And once I have the real one, I must extract the microfilm and replace it with the *Tone of Creation*. In that moment, *the sound of the lotus returning* will be heard and the duplicate will disappear."

"Now who in the hell is this *Toggth*? You sure know some weird dudes." I took a big drag on my Lucky Strike and had a big swallow of my very smooth brandy. "And when whoever has it discovers the fraud, I'll be right back where I started, won't I?"

The Red Dragon Lady thought for a minute. "*Toggth* will appear to you when the time comes. *Toggth* knew the *Fen de Fuqin* was hidden in the throat of Blinthe, until other evil forces discovered it and thought they had killed him for it. But when your Dr. Sandor stole the golden capsule, Blinthe's body evaporated. Toggth is a substance-master, one who can create dimensional matter into any shape or form. But it will last for only a limited time. We can hope once the duplicate is put away, the deception will not be noticed."

I almost choked on my drink.*! No wonder Blinthe disappeared from the table next to Ardizzone's body at the morgue that night. He really did!* "But I saw a dead man on that slab, some little guy with no fingerprints, no belly button. He was as human as you and I…." Then I stopped. I realized Lei-tao was not one of *my* kind. "I think you've got me playing a game of Russian roulette here, lady. I've got five blanks and one live shell in the chamber. When I click the gun stuck to my temple, I've got one chance in six that I'll blow my brains out. I don't much like those odds."

"Please, Cable. Let's say it works." I was looking at that beautiful body of hers through the see-through nighty. "As far as the evil ones returning to the Cave of the Seven Truths, it is now protected with the Vibration of the Spheres. You see, we do have lots of help, despite those who intend harm."

"Okay, let me get this straight. While you're recuperating your energies, I find and retrieve the capsule. Somehow I get it to you. In the meantime your master alchemist replicates the *Fen de Fuqin* and I get that when I hand you the real one, right?"

"Correct."

"Then I go back to living my life just as though nothing happened, right? What about Dragna and his gang, Damianos and whoever I *don't* know about who's after the capsule? I've got this feeling that Ravna will be first in line to grab it and it'll be him and his *Oculus Pyramis* Order that'll get first dibs. So, at best, Lei-tao, we're buying some time here." I finished off my brandy, feeling a little lit up from the near-pure alcohol. "What a chump I turned out to be. All for a dame—whether it's you or Adora—it's my balls that drive me, let's face it."

"No, Cable, not just that. You're very strong and live without fear for yourself. There is nothing you can do about others who may step in harm's way. What you do not see is that we are all part of the fabric."

"Well, not if I cause the death of someone else in the *fabric*. What if they didn't ask for it? What if I got them implicated accidentally? Like Adora—"

"—you don't know souls, Cable. Each has its own pathway of intent."

There was a long pause as I lit up another Lucky Strike. I took a deep breath and let out a sigh. "So…where is this thing hidden?"

"It *is* in a castle on top of a hill above a little village in California called *San Simeon*. The castle was built by a newspaper tycoon and contains many very old artifacts and collections. Among them, in the Hall of Flags, is a medieval knight's armor standing on a pedestal. Remove the left glove, and near the elbow you will find the *Fen de Fuqin* wrapped in a doe skin."

Finally I got it: the riddle was never "night of nights" but "*knight* of nights!" Madame Palladino's channeling was correct. "Truthfully, Lei-tao, I think the chances of complete success are about one in a million. But I'm so damn wrapped up in this thing already, I've nothing to lose but my skin, I suppose. What the hell, life is short anyway."

The lovely Red Dragon Lady glowed in the red candlelight. Her dark eyes shone out at me with much admiration, her lips poised on that wonderful mouth so perfectly. "*You* are a one-in-a-million, Cable Denning."

I leaned closer to her. "I know you said I might defile you, but how much harm could one kiss do? May I kiss you?"

"I—I don't know…no one has ever kissed me."

"Are you still a virgin, then?"

"Not really. Not around you, Cable. I gave something of myself to you in the Cave of the Seven Truths when we made love. I cannot take that back. So perhaps in the ethereal sense, I gave my virginity to you."

I bent my head forward to her mouth, my lips nearly touching hers. "So, permission requested, beautiful Dragon Lady—may I kiss you?"

"Permission granted..." She said that and ever so tenderly brought her lips to press on mine. They were a bit cool at first, but soon warmed up and clung to mine for the longest time. When our lips separated she sighed and took my shoulders between her gentle arms. "My first kiss...it felt...so wonderful, Cable. And it didn't deplete me. I feel...stronger, reinforced in your world...thank you for kissing me...perhaps again sometime?"

"How about right now? I've always said it has to be the right kiss, kid. I'm not exactly your prince, but at least I didn't turn into a frog, did I?"

She smiled and tittered a soft sound. "No, you didn't—nor did I evaporate into nothingness. When first we met, I told you it is love, Cable... love is the great perfecting moment, the one that binds us in unity and makes everything good, inside and outside—even pleasurable."

"Well, damn, I'd hope so." I moved in to kiss her again. This time she drew away.

"I—I am afraid...I do not want to become a mortal woman...or think like one, tied to uncertainty and desire. Please... let it go...and remember the one perfect kiss we have shared." She rose up from the sofa. "I must leave you now. Wang Lo San will escort you out. He will not harm you. I have forbidden him to hurt you."

"Well, my balls still smart a little. If that wasn't a painful enough—"

"—please…go now. And thank you…thank you for who you are…and for entering my life. I will see you at the other end of the adventure."

"Oh, one thing more. How do I gain access to this castle at San Simeon? Who in the hell owns it?"

"It's called *La Cuesta Encantada* and owned by a newspaper mogul named William Randolph Hearst. He is very well known and involved in Hollywood. Maybe someone you know of can help you gain access. I will send you some magic to help you." She turned and walked down the hallway.

That night, I returned to my room at the Hotel Verona and found everything in order. I called Ravna, reassured him that although I didn't have the golden capsule in hand at the moment, I was sure to have it within a week or two. He grumbled that I'd better be on the level and he'd be in L.A. in a few days to get a report first hand. He also informed me that one Isaiah Damianos had met with a most unfortunate accident and now resided at the bottom of San Francisco Bay, rent-free. That hit me pretty hard because I was just getting to like the bloke. And if I didn't deliver that damned *Deus Patrum Nostrorum* pretty soon, I might be renting a place at the local cemetery. Ravna informed me that the Church was out of the picture for the time being until they sent their next emissary to procure what Ravna wanted more than anything else in this world—and reassured me he was determined to get it.

I also called the Sir Francis Drake and spoke to Dr. Penn briefly. I caught him up on whatever I could make sound believable. I left out details like shape-shifting, transcending my physical body, visiting the Cave of the Seven Truths and being revealed the seven secrets, having tantric sex with an ageless Chinese virgin and discovering the whereabouts of the *Fen de Fuqin*. He asked me to drop in and see him, but I told him I would be taking the Daylight Limited south in the morning and needed the shut-eye. He said he understood and we'd re-connect when I needed him.

LAND OF THE EXTRA-TERRESTRIALS

Every once in a while people hear of strange stories about aliens, the non-terrestrial kind, showing up in faraway deserts on a starry night, or an encounter by a person who at best may be of questionable character. But since my very bizarre and other worldly experience with Lei-tao, I was beginning to change my tune. It made sense when you really thought about it. How could so vast a universe only be populated with a single species of odd, war-like creatures bent on destroying each other—a kind of intelligent life form that bred ceaselessly and lived divided by culture, language, religious belief, politics and ethnic differences? No, there had to be more. There had to be advanced civilizations out there somewhere, whizzing around in spacecraft that proved Einstein's space-time theory, that light and velocity could be altered so that maybe beings and inter-stellar spaceships could go from one point to another in a blip of time. I still couldn't explain how I left my physical body and traveled with the beautiful Red Dragon Lady to a dimension certainly not in my local neighborhood. I recalled I was twenty when I began to read about the laws of relativity. Something in the whole thing made sense, that gravity creatures might somehow be electronically capable of overcoming the limitations of three-dimensions and find a means of travel that easily transcended taking the Southern Pacific Daylight for fourteen grueling hours over a couple of steel tracks traveling at top speeds of maybe seventy miles an hour.

Talking about which, I got back to Los Angeles safe and sound from one of the most bizarre experiences of my life only to find the pedestrian existence in the police force a farce. Once I had a taste of the Incredible with a capital "I", everything else seemed boring. Well, almost everything else. As soon as I got back, Sergeant O'Flaherty scheduled me for regular daytime patrol duty with Mario. I called Honey, but she had been hired for a bit part and was tied up in a picture show rehearsal, but would be back singing at the *Bella Notte* the following night. So I called Adora to make sure she was okay and she told me she was very happy I was back safe, missed me terribly and she had a bad cold and I had best stay away for a few days until she was well enough, although she was anxious to see me as soon as possible.

After my first shift with Mario, I told him I was bored with the whole police business and that my trip to San Francisco was an eye-opener. I didn't say any more, but what I was really thinking about was a way to get hold of this William Randolph Hearst character and find a way to penetrate the hallways of Hearst Castle in San Simeon, which seemed about eight hours by car from L.A., according to my California map. I was about to leave the station after I had said good-night to Mario when a familiar face with a cute little body came down the hallway toward me. "Hello, Cable. Did you get my note? I thought you might call me at my aunt's."

"Ginny—Ginny Fullerton, my little Big Bear Lake love affair, how are you?"

"I wish…love affair…you don't even know I exist now, do you?" she admonished me. "Did you forget everything I might have meant to you?"

"Tell you the truth, kid, I was in Frisco for a few days. On business, for the police department. You okay?"

"I have to go back in two or three days. I was hoping we could get together and you'd show me the Los Angeles *you* know. So far what my Aunt Alice has shown me is b-o-r-i-n-g, and I hate hospitals."

"I—I don't think you'd like my part of the city, Ginny. Besides, I'm sorry but your timing isn't the best. You see, I'm on this sort of special assignment and it's gonna take up most of my time."

She put her head down and seemed genuinely disappointed. "I'm—I'm sorry. I was really hoping—"

"Well, the least I can do is take you out for a hot dog and milk shake and take you back to your aunt's place."

She perked up a bit. "That'd be nice. Thanks. Where can we go?"

I took her to a little joint at West 1st Street and Figueroa. It was one of those stainless steel jobs with white paint inside and stools at a long counter. We sat and ordered. All the time Ginny was looking at me in that manner a young inexperienced woman sizes up a man. "You did read my letter, didn't you?"

"Yeah, sure, kid. It was nice. I'm sorry I'm just so damn busy now."

"Well, it's still the same for me, Cable. I really *can't* get you out of my mind. I don't mind telling you, because I know you prefer the truth. And *that's* the truth. There's nothing I can do about it. I know you have a girlfriend and all, but I'm stuck on you." She blushed. "There…I said it…and I'm not ashamed I said it."

I looked at the attractive little lady sitting next to me. "How old are you now, Ginny? Seems you were going to have a birthday pretty soon…21?"

"No, twenty-two pretty soon. I turned twenty-one a long time ago, remember, it's going to be 1929 pretty soon."

I lifted my milkshake and toasted her. "Well, happy birthday anyway, Ginny," I said, smiling at this little gal who had traveled so far to see me. "Many more—and may you know only happy ones."

"They'd be happier with you—I mean, if you weren't with someone and all. I so enjoyed the time together in that little cabin near the lake. Remember me smoking your cigarettes—and drinking gin for the first time? That was so much fun. I was hoping we'd do it again sometime."

"I'd better get you home pretty soon. It's getting dark and if I remember right, your aunt doesn't live in the ritziest neighborhood."

She leaned over to my ear and whispered. "Will you take me to a hotel?"

I looked at her in amazement. "Ginny! Did I hear you right?"

"Just for a few hours. My aunt is a nurse and works until midnight. She doesn't even get home until after one in the morning. We could even go to her place. I have my own bedroom. I stole some of her French Champagne, just in case we got together, you know."

"Now, Ginny, you know I think the world of you and all but—"

"—please! Just once! I promise, I'll never ask you again. If you don't want me to love you, I guess I'll find a way talk myself out of it. But my body isn't as agreeable and I know you can't feel it, but I'm trembling inside right now she wants you so bad."

"She?"

"My body...she has a mind of her own. When she gets restless, I sort of have to take care of myself, you know—"

"—I don't think I wanna know anymore, Ginny. Now, tell you what. I'll pay the tab and take you home on a streetcar. Then, once I know you're safe and sound, I'll leave. Is that clear?"

She was a stubborn young woman. "I'm twenty-one, Cable, for God's sake, am I not desirable or something?"

I didn't say anymore but paid the bill and we took a streetcar up to and along Temple to Alvarado. The house was on Clinton Avenue, near Queen of Angels Hospital where Ginny's Aunt worked. We walked along old picket fences and ramshackle housing until we finally came to one Ginny turned into at 2147 Clinton. We walked down a driveway to the rear of the house. She went to the back door, took a key from under the mat and opened the door. "Please, Cable, at least come in and see where I've been living these past few days *thinking* about you."

I followed her in the little house. She led me to a tiny bedroom with a single bed and little brown painted dresser with a mirror. "So…this is where you live?"

"Yep, nurses don't get paid very much. My Uncle Charlie died three years ago in a car wreck. He drank a lot."

"I'm sorry. Does your aunt get lonely?"

"I don't think she has the time." She came to me and tip toed up to my chin and kissed it. "Please…have one drink of my aunt's Champagne with me? I think it's before Prohibition, like 1919 or something."

I looked directly into Ginny's pretty blue eyes. "Kid, I'm a police officer, I know the law and I could get tossed in the hoosegow for even being alone with you in this house, let alone drinking with a minor."

"Cable, where have you been? As I said, I'll be twenty-two soon. I'm just as much a woman now as I'll ever be, here, wanna see?" She opened her blouse and exposed her wonderful young breasts to me. "And if you're interested in the rest, that's just as grown up, too." She lifted her skirt and showed me a pair of yellow panties through which I could see her dark, inviting womanhood.

"What are you trying to do, Ginny? I mean, I really like you. But you're putting me on the spot here."

"That's exactly what I want to do. Don't you see, you'll probably never want to see me again as long as you live. And you don't have to live with me, but I do. And I wouldn't want to live with me without knowing that I'd had you—even just once."

I sat on her little neatly made single bed. "I can't do this, kid. Whoever taught you that when a guy says 'no' he doesn't mean it?"

She came and sat on the bed next to me. "Because some things are meant to be, Cable. And this is one of them." She got up and fetched the Champagne from another room, came back with the green bottle.

"Here…will you open it? I'll be right back."

Reluctantly I opened the bottle slowly. Warm champagne is especially volatile, so I grabbed part of the bottom sheet to the bed and when the cork popped off, some of it bubbled into the sheet. I took a swig out of frustration and desperation. Then Ginny came bouncing back into the room. Only this time she was without her clothes and a bath towel hung around her, barely covering her breasts and pussy. She approached me and reached for the bottle, and as she did so, the towel dropped to the floor, revealing her clean, white young woman's body. "Do you know what happens to young women when they have unprotected sex?" I asked, my own manhood beginning to stir, as if it had given up the battle to refuse this charming young thing.

"Not to worry…I just finished my monthly time two days ago. My aunt told me years ago that it's somewhere in the middle of my cycle that I can get pregnant. Heck, I wouldn't even mind *that*—if it were your baby."

A shudder went through me as I imagined being stuck in the hinterlands with a cute little thing and a papoose in her arms bawling away the night. I was thinking of a new song that came out last year. *My Blue Heaven* had lyrics that were enough to put the heebie-jeebies into any red- blooded American male.

208

Just Molly and me, and baby makes three, are happy in my Blue Heaven…' "How about just fooling around a little? You know, some good making out like a Saturday night date in your little Studebaker."

She pulled me up from off the bed and then went to her knees as she undid my trousers, reached into my boxers and took my already rigid manhood into both her hands, caressed it and began to lick it in long strokes with her warm tongue. Soon it was in her mouth and she was moaning about the pleasure it gave *both* of us. I could feel the nerves in my lower back bring chills to my buttocks and I knew things were happening I would be hard put to control. I tossed off my shirt, took off my shoes and britches. I lowered Ginny onto the bed, spread her legs and put my head between them as I repaid her affection with my own brand of tongue language. She writhed and moaned below me with that ecstatic look of pain such a pleasure bestowed. Slowly I moved my tongue up her soft, young skin, up past her belly button, stopping at her tight warm breasts. Her nipples were stiff and hard and as I massaged them with my fingers, I moved my mouth to her lips. It felt damn good as this infatuated young woman darted her tongue into my mouth and soon I was astride her. She let out a short cry as I entered her, but from that point on she seemed to be in some sexual delirium that captured both of us and sucked us both into a state of excited pleasure. I worked her until I could fcel she could take no more without exploding, so I grabbed her buttocks and thrust my male member as deep as I could into her. She let go with a fevered yell and I soon followed as we consummated a delicious moment in the frenzy of that wild, primal instinct.

For several minutes afterward we lay together in complete silence. As my manhood began to deflate, I could feel the warmth of our wet juices pour out the sides of her vagina. My ear was by her mouth as she spoke. "God, Cable, I never had a climax before. I heard about them, but—but it's nothing like my girlfriends described to me. It's so…so incredible with you I don't want it to ever stop. If I move to Los Angeles to live with my aunt, can we see each other? I mean it. I know about your girlfriend and all—"

"—it can't happen, Ginny," I said, a little sad for both of us. I kissed her. "It's not that you aren't wonderful, little lady, you are—but I've got so much crap on my plate just now, including Honey. Try to understand, my plate's full, Ginny Fullerton. It's bad enough you talked me into doing this tonight."

"You didn't like it? I finally got to feel that magic place you told me about in Big Bear that night we danced, remember?"

"I loved it, babe. And I sure hope you're right about your period. The last thing I need right now is to worry about you being—"

"—it's fine, Cable! Trust me. I know my body pretty well… even better after tonight. Do you realize the only other sex I'd ever had was with Ronnie Dunlap forcing his way into me—and it lasting for less than a minute before he came all over himself?"

I chuckled. "Well, sometimes teenagers have to, uh, kinda 'kick-start' their love making skills. It takes time. Even I was clumsy in the beginning."

We unglued from each other and she pushed me onto my back and started licking me off. "So you won't forget me, Cable…" she said with a mischievous smile.

"Oh, I won't forget you, Ginny. You can count on that."

"Good. Because I'm going to move to L.A. anyway."

That night was a restless one. Mario had been staying more and more with Rosalie Elena and since she was expecting their first-born soon, I assumed he'd probably give up our little ramshackle apartment in the not too far distant future. Ginny Fullerton invaded my space for a while as I reflected on a very erotic evening with a sexually hungry young woman. But she was a good person and I had enjoyed her refreshing personality and more than abundant womanhood. What a lucky guy I was in this life, I ruminated. Over and over again, beautiful dames with great bodies and desire for me came into my life and all I had to do was be there, at the right place at the right time and open my mouth with a few words that told them who I was to the best of my ability.

But what was really haunting me was the unsolved mystery that began with the *golden throat* of a strange dead creature named Blinthe. According to Lei-tao he was one of the other-dimensional bad guys who helped steal the *Fen de Fuqin*, and never really existed on this three-dimensional world of ours. But how could he be when Mario and I saw his dissected golden throat floating around in that jar in Sandor's little room of anatomic horrors? And that's not to mention that little body lying there in the morgue without a navel or fingerprints! But as I drifted into a fitful sleep, I felt Lei-tao's wonderful presence and she was telling me about something when this little gnome of a creature shows up and starts talking to me. He told me that as soon as I got the *Fen de Fuqin* to him he'd fashion a vibrationally equivalent duplicate. Of course he didn't mention how I'd gain access to Hearst Castle and find the medieval knight's armor and all.

I awoke with the alarm clock clanging away in my brain. I washed and showed up at the station in time to see Mario drag himself in. We exchanged nods and got our uniforms on, grabbed a cup of java and a cigarette and slid into our Model-T for the day's workload. It was one of those stupid days when everyone in L.A. seemed to be in a fender-bender as more and more automobiles filled the already smoky, clogged streets of the city. Gasoline engines produced a kind of blue-black exhaust that smelled half of burnt cylinders and half raw gasoline.

Thanksgiving was in a couple of days and I had called my mom to tell her I'd spend the day with her. Honey had promised to journey to her folks in Willits, but I couldn't afford the days off, so she was going by herself. Tonight would be the last night to see her for a while and she had been gone from the *Bella Notte* because of a film shoot she'd been doing. Tonight she would be returning and I knew the mob that controlled the restaurant would be anxious to have her back. When I told her about the untimely death of Frank Laggore she actually seemed relieved but knew there was a lot more to the story than I was telling her. There were a lot of strangers on that train. There was Adora Moreno, also the now deceased Anne Banning, Laggore's horror of a sidekick, Crank Sotto, and the coincidentally convenient Dr. Jedediah Penn and his German caretaker, Polly Parker.

I walked into the *Bella Notte* about nine-thirty. It was packed with late night diners and boozing, noisy celebrants. Honey was singing *The Man I Love* and although she couldn't see me, I could feel she was talking about the ideal man she wanted me to be. *'He'll look at me and smile, I'll understand. Then in a little while, he'll take my hand…and though it seems absurd, I know we both won't say a word…'* When she finished I walked up to her. She grabbed my hand and led me backstage, grabbed a tissue out of her purse, wiped off her lips and threw them onto mine. She kissed me deeply and passionately, and just like the song, never said a word. Finally I had to speak up. "Hey, babe, glad to see you."

She pulled back and looked at me. "You've changed. You've lost weight. What else do I need to know?" she quipped with her usual sense of humor.

"Well, if you must know, I gathered a harem full of Arabian beauties, met a Chinese virgin whom I seduced, almost got killed by a Hatchet Man, made love to a teenager from out of town and had a dream about an alien creature who's gonna lead me to a castle in the clouds someday."

She laughed. "Maybe half of it is true, darling, but I missed you anyway. Can you stay with me tonight and take me to the train station early before you go to work? The train leaves at six from downtown."

"Sure."

"And speaking of castles, Charlie Chaplin, Mary Pickford and Doug Fairbanks have invited me to Hearst Castle for a weekend. Seems the newspaper bigwig, Hearst, has a movie star girlfriend—you may have heard of her, Marion Davies?"

The floor almost dropped out from under me. How weird life is—or was it planned that way? Was Lei-tao pulling psychic strings and opening doors in her secret world? I pretended not to be too excited about it all. "Nope, never heard of her. Hearst Castle, eh? I've heard of it. Do you think you might need a bodyguard on the trip?"

"What a great idea, Cable! Yes, I'm sure Charlie won't mind. He promised to talk about *City Lights* with me. Damn, Mister, if I get that role, I can name my ticket in Hollywood—do you realize that, Mr. Policeman?"

"Yeah, babe. I'm proud of you. You've already come a long way. How was that picture you just shot?"

"Boring. I hate these stupid little roles. The director says it adds to my credits. Talking about harems, it was some silly Valentino-like thing. I think the producers just liked to see me with almost no clothes on."

"So do I," I quipped, putting my hand on an ample breast. "Crap, Valentino's been dead a couple of years now—don't they have to move on?"

"You'd think so. Hollywood is slow to new trends. They're still stuck in the silent era. Talkies, like you said, are going to be the future."

"Well, when are you through so we can go home?" I asked.

"I've got two more sets. I've got a surprise new song for you. It's a new Jerome Kern tune I hear he wants to put in a new show. He just hasn't found the show yet."

"So, what's the name of the tune?"

"*Yesterdays*. I love the lyrics. It's almost like I've already lived them, but then I'm really too young to have lived them, aren't I? Kind of crazy, huh?"

"Yeah, babe," I said, feeling inside that Honey and I were already leaning toward those yesterdays that used to be and our tight togetherness had already begun to unravel. But maybe it was up to me to stop it. Maybe if I put the brakes on my restless balls and settled down with her, we'd pull back together. But some things you can't stop, you can't put the brakes on because everything has an expiration date written on the inside of the package.

Honey was wearing a warm, fall-colored gold and orange gown with light-green trim and pearl shoes. The dress was cut low so her feminine assets could be easily admired. It was more or less the policy of the house. The mobsters loved Honey and drooled for her on the sidelines, but never touched her. Only Laggore had wanted to invade the henhouse and take away the prize hen. Now he was gone and apparent peace had come to the *Bella Notte*. I wouldn't know for some time just how wrong I was, but it goes to show…a false sense of security is just another word for a stick of dynamite with a long fuse.

When my beautiful Honey Combes, now increasingly known as *Lana Loren*, stepped up behind the microphone and blasted the audience with *When the Red, Red Robin Comes Bob, Bob Bobbin' Along*, the crowd went nuts. But when she launched into *Yesterdays*, an unusual silence fell upon the room and Johnny Origin's velvety piano background provided all the accompaniment Honey needed to sell the song to tears. I think even her eyes were misting by the time the song ended. A tumultuous applause arose that night at the *Bella Notte*. Lana Loren had arrived!

I kissed Honey good-bye at the train station and watched the Daylight chug out of the train yard, its huffing and puffing belching black smoke into the morning air. I turned and went to the trolley stop and caught a streetcar down to the station. I knew it was early, but I called Adora. Her mother answered and told me she was groggy, but she'd come to the phone. When she did, I asked her if she'd like to spend Thanksgiving Day with me at my Mom's. She said she would be privileged to do so, but she had to divide her day between me and her own mother and sister. I agreed and I'd come by to pick her up Thursday morning around nine. Damn, I missed that beautiful, sincere and sensual young woman. Tall and elegant with a warmth that called out to me, I could tell that part of me was hooked on the dame. But it wasn't just about sex. It came with another call, the one deep inside that asks you why in the hell can't you settle down with someone so wonderful? Why can't you be happy with one doll in your bed so you can wake up together and smell that first cup of coffee in your robes?

The sun shone a dreary half-light and the fog was burning off from the ocean's nightly visit as Adora and I rode the #10 Line out to Lincoln Heights. I had forgotten how ramshackle and run down my old neighborhood was. Adora was familiar with early poverty, so she knew the score and shared with me the most humble of beginnings. She was holding my hand tightly and had her cheek against my shoulder as we rode. Finally, when we got off and walked the three blocks to my old trappings, the sun came out a little brighter. We came to the rickety old wooden stairs that led up to the porch. My mother was already watching at the screen door awaiting us. She opened the door and I greeted her, taking her into my embrace and kissing her strong all over her wrinkling face. "Ah Mom!

Good to see you!" I hugged her. "This is Miss Moreno—Adora. I'm glad we're doing this. It's been too long." We brought a bag of things that I knew my mother liked, including pumpkin pie, coffee, spices, and whatever else I could think to stuff into it.

"Yes, it has, Cable…sometimes I think you've forgotten you have a mother—who's still living. Miss Moreno—"

"—*por favor*, Mrs. Denning, call me Adora." My little Mexican lady came forth and extended her hand to my mother. "*Con mucho gusto, Señora.*"

"Okay, Adora. Happy to meet you, too." I knew my mother. She sized up every broad I ever brought to the house and made severe judgments on them later. She looked at me. It's an interesting phenomenon to see your parents shrink as they get older. In fact, everything in the house seemed small. Her eyes were still laced with the surprise of life, that blow it hits you with when dreams shatter and death comes in singing "*I've Got You Under My Skin.*"

"I'm sorry, but I couldn't afford a turkey, so we're having good old Irish lamb stew, and apple pie, if that's okay."

I looked at Adora. She smiled. "Yeah, Mom, great. Everyone else is having turkey anyhow. I'm ready for something different—and probably a lot more delicious." I came over to her and kissed her on the cheek. "And nobody…I mean *nobody* makes lamb stew like you."

"Sí, *mi madre y hermana* have roast squash pudding with sweet potatoes in guava. So I like anything you serve, Señora Denning. *Gracias.*"

We visited for a while, but it was Adora's gentility and graciousness that pulled my mother to her. In all my life, I had never heard her ask a person to call her by her first name, but this day she did. "Please, Adora, call me Flo or if you prefer, Florence. I would like that."

"*Sí, Florence.* That is Irish, no? Like this hombre here?" she giggled.

My mother laughed. "Yes—at least half of me, Adora. My mother was Irish and my father was from Norway. He got lost in Ireland and kissed my mother at a dance one night, so I heard tell, and that was that."

I looked across the table to Adora whose beautiful eyes seldom left me all afternoon. My mother's warm brown eyes were observing it all and I could tell she felt the warmth between Adora and me. "So, Mom, how are you feeling?"

"It's terrible getting old, Cable. New aches and pains, now my ankles swell in the morning. But, what is one to do?"

"Is there *un médico* you go to, señora?" Adora inquired.

"Doctors? What can they do? Break an arm, he can set it. Break a leg, he can fix it—but break a heart—and there are no cures in his bag, Adora."

Adora and I looked at each other. It was the first time I ever heard my mother speak of never getting over my father's death. In that minute I realized a big part of her life also stopped on that day. *"Lo siento mucho, señora. Dolor del corazón, que triste.* Sometime, pain in the heart never heal. So *la vida es muy difícil."*

"Well, guys, we can't mope around in that kind of mood all day, can we? The apple pie was great, Mom—and I brought some bootleg rum to wash it down with. Let's all have a toast to the lamb stew, the apple pie and the turkey we didn't have and the wonderful time we *did* have."

I got out a bottle of cheap, lousy rum and poured a bit for the ladies. We all toasted. But soon it was time for Adora to go, for she had promised her mother and sister she would spend the remainder of the holiday with them. My grey old mother sat opposite me, next to Adora. She looked directly at me with those wonderful brown eyes of hers. "Son, this is the finest young woman you have ever brought to meet me." She took Adora's hand and held it. "Forgive me, Adora, but I must speak. You see this lovely young Latina? She is in love with you *forever*, Cable. She will make you the finest wife any man could have on the face of this earth." Then she looked at Adora. "Am I right—or is it only an old woman's well-wishing for her son?"

Adora had tears in her eyes. "No, señora, I love your son with my whole life—in front of you—I say this." Then Adora looked into my eyes...my heart. "*Te amo para siempre.* For always and always...I love him..."

All three of us sat there with eyes misting as if part of time stood still in that moment and it would mark a place somewhere deep in each of us, like someone carving love's initials into a Valentine Tree. I didn't know what else to say, so I just whispered under my breath. "Thank you. I thank both of you."

By the time we left mother and our little old house on Alta Street, she and Adora were hugging good-bye. Adora started down the stairs and I went up to this little old lady who birthed and raised me. "I love you, Ma," I said. I slipped a twenty-dollar bill in her hand. "I'm sorry it's not more, but these damn cops are still fed scraps these days."

She drew my head forward so she could whisper. "Make a life with this woman, Cable. She will settle your restless heart—like I did your father's. I never told you how happy we were together. I couldn't wait for him to get home each night so I could feel his body hold me, his rough whiskers, his whiskey breath—I loved all of him. So does this woman...for you, Cable—she adores all of you. One like her will not come again in your life." She let me go and Adora and I waved good-bye from the sidewalk as we walked to get the streetcar.

When we got to *Todo el Mundo,* Adora used her key to let us in. I told her I couldn't stay and I thought it best if she spent the afternoon with her family without me. It was dark in the big room and the blinds were drawn. She backed me up against a wall. "*Por qué, señor?* You no like me anymore? I come to your mama. You come to mine. But first I want to come."

I could hardly believe the brazen boldness of this beautiful creature. She lifted her skirt and undid my belt. Then she reversed our positions, with her buttocks against the wall. She spread her legs and boosted me into her. As I pumped her against the wall, she moaned and whimpered in low tones so as to not alert her mother and sister. She clung to me like she was growing into my body as part of me and I got bigger and harder until I thought I would drive her through the wall. She let out a short shriek, which happened to be enough to alert her sister Flora. Adora immediately pulled her skirt down, leaving me there dripping, facing her in a quasi-embrace while Flora looked on in amusement. "*Flora! Vaya para ahí! Por favor!*"

The sister dodged back inside the door to the living quarters. I cleared my throat, still a little out of breath. "Uh…what heading do we put that under—caught in the act?"

She laughed as she grabbed my wet, shrinking manhood. "Ay, muchacho!" She wiggled in place. "I am so happy…you satisfy me *mucho, mucho!*" She put my hand back up under her dress and I could feel the hot, wet fluids still seeping out of her. "This…is naughty, no? *Pero, Cable,* how I love it—you make me free—*libertad!*"

We spent the rest of the day until early evening visiting Adora's sister and mother full well knowing our secret passionate act was now well documented by Flora Moreno. But what the hell, I thought, life is what it is and great sex is also just exactly what it is—incredible—maybe that should have one of those capital "I" letters as well.

I got back to my little flat. It was pitch black. I pushed the "on" button to the light switch on the wall. Nothing happened. I lit a match, but before it did any good, someone grabbed me from behind and held me in a hammerlock. "Good evening, stupid policeman," a familiar voice said to me there in the dark. Then on a bedside table he lit a small candle I kept there for emergencies. "Did you think I would allow your insults to continue unpunished? You live in fear thinking of me?"

"No, you piece of crap," I answered defiantly, "I forgot you the day I got back to L.A. I don't think much about yesterday's shit, you know."

Wong Lo San came forth and slapped my face while the goon who was holding me tightened his grip on my neck. "You *will* remember what I give you tonight, one who destroys. My mistress become ruin because of you. You and your sex desire make trouble for all. Black Hand say 'punish this man so he remember...' So now I do this...with pleasure, shitty policeman."

"Well, you'd better hurry, squat face, it's getting late and I have to get up in the morning. You know how responsible these shitty policemen are."

"Make fun, die harder."

"You're a coward, Wong Lo San. If you got your idiot here to release me and faced me man to man, then I might say you'd be spared by your ancestors from a very harsh judgment."

There was a pause. "My ancestor not to do with this. But you right, I should face man I kill. It is way of Hatchet Man." He barked out an order to the man holding me and he released me, pushing me to the floor. My neck hurt and my breath had been compromised. "Now you get up on knees." The Hatchet Man's shadow silhouetted against the far wall. I could see him slowly remove that terrible axe without a handle and hold it in his hand. "Now bow head so I have perfect split of skull."

I kneeled there on the floor. What a hell of a way to end Thanksgiving Day, I thought. Just then two strange sounds emanated from another part of the room and both the Hatchet Man and his accomplice fell to the floor. I looked around. I saw no one. Then a little creature came out of the shadows holding what looked like a bean shooter. "Not too late, I trust, Mr. Denning," a very nasal, low voice spoke. "I am *Toggth*. The late members of the Chinese Black Hand are dead. This tube shoots deadly poisonous darts, dipped in a very toxic liquid from a plant in your Africa—or is it South America—I always get them mixed up. Yes…South America…Colombia. I prepared the poison myself. I learned it from the *Noanama* tribe of the *Choco region*. It comes from the black-leg frog, which is really green and yellow with black on its little suction cup feet. Effective, wouldn't you say?"

I was still rather stunned. I got up and faced the little creature who stood about four-feet five, maybe. His skin was rough, his nose sharp at the end and bent. His eyes were a kindly non-descript dark color and his body seemed filled with lots of unkempt long silver hairs. He had no hair on his head, however, and his ears were pointed. "Well, thanks, Toggth. Phew! That was a close call! I'm sure glad you decided to come by tonight. Did you know these guys were coming by to do me in?"

"The beautiful and ever-gracious Red Dragon Lady directed me to come to your aid. She knew. You are protected by her, Mr. Denning. Consider yourself very fortunate. She can be a viper when crossed. Obviously, you did not cross her. She tells me you went with her, *trans-migrated* with her, to the Cave of the Seven Truths?" "Yep. A hell of an experience. I think the world of your mistress. In fact, Lei-tao and I had this little thing going—"

"—I am not here to hear of your prurient assaults on our world, Mr. Denning. My instructions are to tell you that as soon as you receive the you-know-what, you are to hand it to me and I shall give you a *vibrational duplicate*. In securing this necessary time, our esteemed Red Dragon Lady will employ me to remove the etched microfilm from the golden capsule and replace it with the Tone of Creation."

"I have a question, if you don't mind. Weren't you this guy, Rettini or Blinthe Rettini—or something? Anyway, the corpse my partner and I saw at the city morgue that night, you know, we saw your golden throat and after old Doc Sandor removed the larynx, I spied the cavity where the precious cargo must have originally been stored—temporarily of course."

"Of course. Rettini or Blinthe Rettini, as you say, never really existed on this plane of existence. They were projection bodies without corelife."

"Corelife?"

"Yes, the center of animated consciousness in a physical body was absent in Blinthe. Only the gold was real. He was a thief, one of the dark ones."

"I see. So what's next? You know I dreamed all this."

"Shhh…...!" Toggth said as he motioned me to the floor. "Someone comes." He blew out the candle and we lay on our stomachs on the floor. My front door opened and in walked Nasar Ravna followed by none other than Jack Dragna. A couple of henchmen stood at the door with guns drawn. Everyone tried the light switch but just as with my experience, nothing happened. One of the goons took out a flashlight. As soon as Ravna saw the two bodies on the floor he dropped to his knees to inspect. "Denning?" Then he turned the bodies over and saw the dead Hatchet Man and his accomplice. "It's someone else. It appears Denning didn't make friends with the Chinese element. So maybe he's still alive."

What puzzled me was that here we were on the floor not three feet from the bodies and they didn't see us! Then I felt this warm sensation pulsing through my body and I knew little old Toggth was putting a disappearing spell over us.

"So who are these guys?" Dragna asked.

"Hell if I know. But I'll tell you this. Wherever Denning goes, death follows. I don't know what it is about the guy. Even I have this strange unhealthy respect for him."

"You're blowin' smoke up your ass, Ravna. He'll die just like

222

anybody else. But he's got to see this thing through so I can get my dough and you can get your precious golden thing, or whatever the crap it is."

"Now all we have to do is find the son-of-a-bitch. We had him tailed with that Mexican señorita to his mother's house. Then he took the babe home and stayed a while. I was told he came here."

"Don't worry, I've got six men on it. Denning is too damn dumb to know his number's up. He has this attitude—as if he were important. What he really is, is *dead*—and soon! I felt that chip on his shoulder at Ardizzone's funeral that day I met him. He's cagey, but a lousy cop. Just give him enough rope to hang himself."

"These two Chinamen belong to that Red Dragon Lady, no doubt. But why would she double-cross Denning? He told me they were on good terms and delivery was imminent."

"Was what—*imminent*?"

"Imminent means it's coming down the pike, inevitably. I get impatient with uneducated rabble like you and your two-syllable thugs . *Deus Patrum Nostrorum* represents the best the mind can be in this or any other world. If the *Oculus* doesn't get it back very soon, I will begin to hold you responsible, Jack Dragna, and start eliminating your happy little family of dummy hoodlums. Do you comprehend that?"

"Stop threatening, Ravna. So I'm working with you, okay? You can call me all the names you like after I've collected my cool million bucks right off Uncle Sam's press. So, in the meantime, what're we gonna do about these stiffs on the floor?"

Ravna bent down to look at the bodies. "Leave them here for now. Denning's got to come back sooner or later. He's a cop. He'll get his people to clean it up and keep it hushed."

"Yeah, you hope. So what's next? We still haven't got the object of your affection, Ravna."

"For the moment, I'll let Denning buy some time. He's… he's never far away from…from my thoughts," Ravna said pensively, taking a final look at the remains of the Hatchet Man and his goon.

They left and closed the door behind them. "How in the hell did you do that?" I asked Toggth, marveling at the invisibility act.

"Redistribution of energy is relatively easy. You see, objects that can be seen must generate or reflect light. When no light is present emanating or reflecting from them, they're invisible. Very simple, as I see it."

"To you. It's way above my head, I'm afraid." Then I sat on my bed as the little creature stood by, his eyes were glued to watching me. "So here's how it has to go, old boy. First, we gotta get rid of these bodies. I don't want them hanging around smelling up my rug. So, either I get the police involved, call Lei-tao and tell her what happened or—"

"—or the fleshy dead things can simply disappear," Toggth said, snickering a little under his breath.

"Disappear? Another one of your magic tricks?"

"Sort of, I would venture to say. Why don't you let me take care of it? No traces, the less you will be—how is the American colloquialism—*bogged down*."

"That'd be swell. Okay, that's taken care of." I got up, took out a Lucky Strike and lit it. Toggth coughed.

"How can you suck that poison into your breathers? You humans are intentionally self-destructive now, aren't you?"

"You might say that, Mister. But for me, it's always been booze, broads and cigarettes—and oh, yeah, music. I wouldn't wanna live without music."

"Tones…frequencies…harmonic combinations, ah yes… health-stimulating sounds with rhythmic patterns…good

224

for you. Better than that terrible stuff you inhale into your breathers."

"Yeah, well, my 'breathers' are doing okay. You keep to your job and I'll do mine, okay?" I was a little impatient with his nattering. The overload on my person at this particular juncture of my earth life made me feel like a pack animal ascending a mountain loaded down with three times my weight! "So, now, the matter of your precious golden capsule. It just so happens, my girlfriend—"

"—*one* of your girlfriends. You mustn't forget the attractive Mexican woman and the little mountain girl—you even made overtures to someone you could never have, my Lei-tao—"

"—hey! Whose life is it here, anyway? Can you mind your own business?" I went to my little kitchen and grabbed a bottle of gin and poured a big one. "You like a drink?" I asked the little humanoid creature.

"That is also a poison. Especially, how you make it. Sometime I will make you up some genuinely pure spirits."

"Like the kind Lei-tao drinks—the stuff that disappears before it hits your gullet?"

"Yes, something similar. So…you were saying…?"

"Yeah, by odd coincidence, Honey is going with this movie actor character, Charlie Chaplin and a group of movie stars to Hearst Castle up north, on the coast. You do know the rest?"

"No. Was I supposed to?"

"You mean you don't know where the damned thing is hidden?"

"Lei-tao did not confide that to me. I suppose that was her way of keeping fewer beings in the equation. But she told you, obviously?"

"Yep. So I pose as a bodyguard and tag along boyfriend when we go to San Simeon. I grab the capsule, get back, you contact me, and forge the replacement thing you talked about—I get it to Ravna, he pays Dragna—and bingo! we're home free!"

"Seems simple. The trick is, as Lei-tao must have explained to you, getting the gold-etched microfilm out of the capsule and replacing it with the Tone of Creation—counting on the fact that wherever Ravna has hidden it, when it goes poof! disappears, it will not be detected for some time to come. In the meantime, as you say, Mr. Dragna and his underworld people will be a million earth dollars richer. One thing remains unsettling to me."

"And what might that be?" I drank down a big slug of gin. I made a terrible face the stuff was so bad. Bootleg hooch was a concoction of poor grade juniper berries, rye flour and a few herbs that were available, tossed into a tub of cheap, raw alcohol. The damned stuff wasn't even distilled. I had a tough gut, but every now and then it would burn the crap out of my stomach.

"The Church. It is very powerful, Mr. Denning. When they know Damianos is dead, theirs is an anger to be reckoned with."

"Call me Cable. I hate formality when I have to converse with someone long term. So as far as Damianos' Catholic Order is concerned, we're just gonna have to cross that bridge when we come to it. If I think about it now, I'll go more nuts than I am already."

CHAPTER 10

A CASTLE IN THE CLOUDS

Honey was still gone, but I had to get out and go down for a breath of fresh air after I said my good-byes to Toggth. I had to run away from a world that bound and strapped me to the seat of conformity, took my wild and free spirit and pressed it like a dead flower between the pages of my life. And nothing quite did it like the sound of a pretty babe singing a Gershwin tune backed up by a sexy sax, a tinkling piano and a warm bass tying it all together. I thought I would head up to Hollywood Boulevard again to the *Café Montmartre* where I had taken Adora dancing…and for a moment I lingered on the memory of how luscious she felt in my arms that first time I held her. I'd also heard that radio networks were trying to establish a phone line feed to broadcast live from locations like this. But what really piqued my interest to go was I'd heard there was a hot new singer there tonight, by the name of *Misty Sheridan*, who sang with the band at the microphone, looking like every guy's fantasy in a low-cut dress.

It sounded like the perfect alibi for me to escape from the dead creeps in my room and for Toggth to do his thing and get rid of them for me. So I took a streetcar into Hollywood, got off at Hollywood and Highland and crossed the street to 6757 Hollywood Boulevard. There was still a pretty good crowd filing through the entrance.

The *Montmartre* took up the whole second floor of the building. I found out that it had been purchased and built in 1923 and was pretty much responsible for starting the Hollywood nightlife, much to the chagrin of many of the local residents who didn't want movie-types makin' hay in their town after the sun went down. The interior was all marble with Spanish tiled floors, a potted palm on the right at the foot of a stair case and on the left, a glass cabinet with a combination of figurines and expensive liquor bottles. People usually came with their own flasks…but I heard there was a bootlegger on-hand in case the flasks went dry. The marbled stairs led up to an arched shaped doorway with ornate openwork wrought iron and the name Montmartre across the top. The ceiling was slightly domed with carved wood. The inside was classy alright, with textured wallpaper, imported carpeting and chandeliers. The tables went right up to the dance floor which was already pretty crowded with folks kicking up their heels. The area of the dance floor had a suspended square shaped cover with draped fabric in robin's egg blue with gold drapes to the floor at each corner. The band was at the back of this area sounding in good form.

The place was crowded at the tables too and noisy with laughter, talking and smoke clouds roiling up into the air. Then the band stopped and an announcer asked everyone to take their seats which they did obediently, knowing something special was coming. The lights went down and a quiet anticipation fell over the place. Then a single blue spotlight shone on the center of the dance floor where a microphone stood alone. Then from one side, one of the most striking women I had ever seen, walked into the spotlight and took her place at the microphone. *Misty Sheridan* stood statuesque in a dark pink tight-fitting dress that was cut so low a full fifty percent of her upper bosom was exposed.

I sized her up to be about my age or a little younger, she stood about five-foot six and had blue eyes that smiled on one hand, but carried in them a sullen sensuality. The drummer started in with a quiet snare beat and then the band began to play the introduction to what I recognized as Irving Berlin's *All By Myself*, so I stood in the back of the room and just listened.

One could just tell this babe's life was a bit out of joint, something in her tone, something told me a restless, searching heart pumped under her marvelous breast. I couldn't put my finger on it, but I knew it was there and that's what made her, at least in part, a mesmerizing songstress. By the time she had sung *'I'm growing so tired of living alone, I lie awake all night and cry…nobody loves me, that's why…'* I was sure every guy in the joint wished he were in Misty Sheridan's bed and taking care of her loneliness. I was no exception. But I had my hands full right now and so I could enjoy the lady's talents without secretly panting for the dame when she wasn't looking.

As she finished, the well-deserved response rang out with whistles and enthusiastic applause. But as soon as they cleared the dance floor, the band started back up and people went back to dancing and smoking, drinking and blabbing at their tables. I made my way to the bar. The least I could do was to buy the fine young woman a drink. I asked the bartender how I could manage it and he told me frankly that I should buy the drink anonymously and I'd be better off. I asked what her favorite beverage was. I winked at him, full well knowing no alcohol was served in the club—*legally*. "Aged Kentucky whiskey with a twist of honey and boiling water in a snifter on the side," the bartender said. "That'll be six bucks, Mister." I thought the price excessively high but paid it and let it go at that. He told me he'd deliver it to Miss Sheridan before she went into her last set for the evening.

I'd been standing at the bar next to a handsome but some-what life-worn woman of about fifty, I guessed. She was look-ing at me. Obviously she had been drinking some of that Prohibition hooch that polluted the brain and gave one that glassy stare with a kind of inarticulate, stammering English prattle. "It was the shots that killed him, you know," she was saying, as if I had known who 'he' was. "Two and a half years without a man in your bed is a long time, Mister. Do you have a man in your bed?"

"No, lady, I'm not into men. Who are you talking about?"

"My husband. He served in the war. Healthy—healthy a man as you ever want to see, ten years ago. During the plague of 1918 they…they started shooting him with something that eventually… killed him."

"I'm sorry, ma'am," I said. I had heard of the for-profit drug companies stuck with so much vaccine stock after the Great War that they spent big money to throw fear into the population to get inoculated before the next Spanish flu epidemic. Trouble was, a lot of people didn't need the damn shot and the result was often a terrible disease as a side-effect. "What, if I may ask, did your husband come down with?"

She took a stiff drink as if girding herself for what followed. "He…he began to get headaches and threw up in the morning. Then…then he started being mean and irritable, listless…you know, no energy for work, job, even sex with me, his wife. It was like his brain was going away along with his body. It was called…some terrible…thing…I'm trying to remember…I'm sorry…I've been drinking, you know. Another one of the government's mistakes you encounter ev—everywhere. And you can have all the booze you like, if you can afford it. Hic! How's that for corruption, Mister?"

"Yeah, I'm a cop. I know. I see it every day, lady."

"Joyce…my name is Joyce. But I donno where the joy part is in Joyce anymore…do you see it in my aging face?"

I felt sorry for the broad. I looked at her kind, light blue eyes. The pain of too much too soon was written all over them. "No, Joyce…you look fine, just take it easy on that poisonous hooch you're drinking."

"You're a cop and you're not going to…to arrest me—hic! from drinking illegal alcohol here—here at the club?"

"The world's illegal, Joyce. You can call me Cable, if you like. I think your husband's disease might have been *post-vaccinal encephalitis.*"

"Yeah! That's it...Cable...what a strange name...but I like it...I don't suppose you're interested in a drunken old broad who's lost her way now, are you? I'm probably rusty, but I might be pretty good—pretty good in bed."

"Well, thanks all the same, Joyce. But I've got my—my, uh, hands full with girlfriends lately."

"Well, I'm too old for you anyway—that's—that's what you're really saying, isn't it? I'm too damn old—I'm even too damn old for...for me!"

I had noticed that the bartender had been good to his word and brought Misty the drink I had bought her. She was sitting with some of the band members. One of the guys was familiar to me. I'd seen him around town a lot. He was a black man... brilliant and though he was young, he seemed to be a well-respected jazz piano player and was always in demand. Soon, as Joyce continued to hold me captive, I watched the beautiful Misty get up and walk over toward the bar. She moved like a proud cat, smoothly with those great buttocks doing all the right moves inside that skin-tight silken gown. She came up to the bartender with her drink still in hand. "Who...who bought me the drink, Charlie?" she asked him. The bartender reminded her he preferred to keep the secret admirer anonymous for fear fifty guys would be hitting on her all at the same time, which the management discouraged.

For whatever reasons, I spoke up, revealing my identity. "I—I, uh, confess, Miss Sheridan. It was I—my name is Denning... Cable Denning...and I'm a cop moonlighting tonight as an appreciator of great music well performed. I—I, uh, truly liked your Irving Berlin."

She looked at me strangely. Her voice was soft, feminine with a nice breathiness to it. "You...you even know the composer?"

"Yep. Ever since I was a kid I've been in love with music—

some people take drugs—well, I do smoke, drink and chase skirts—but no dope does it like music for this guy."

She seemed intrigued. "It's nice to know, Mr. Denning, at least some of my audience is educated."

"Oh, he's educated all right, young lady," my inebriated bar companion spoke up. "He even knew what killed my late—late hus—hic!—husband! 'Post-some-or-other enceph...iss. They shot him...shot him to death...with medicine. Now, tell me, doesn't that strike you....strike you as being very—very strange...when a government kills people trying to prevent a disease?"

Misty Sheridan had no idea what we had been talking about. "She lost her husband a couple of years back. She's still grieving—and claims that the 'cure' in the form of inoculations actually killed her husband," I explained.

"It really doesn't surprise me. My aunt lost her husband the same way. He got back from the war, they told him he'd avoid the Spanish flu of 1918 and so when he took the shots it killed him."

"You see? I told—I told you so, Cable Denning." She looked the two of us over. "I—I have to go home now. The house is empty and lonely, but I have to sleep. Will I see you again here, Cable? I like you—you're—you're a good man, even for a cop—cops are crooked in Los Angeles—are you a crooked cop? I hate crooked cops...you never feel...feel safe anymore..."

"Yep, I'm afraid so, Joyce. I'm as rotten as they come, drink gin and tonic, smoke too much and chase pretty women when I can."

She laughed. "Oh! I'll bet you're not that bad...if I were younger...I'd like you...in my...life...Cable...lady....good-night now..." She grabbed her purse from off the bar and disappeared into the crowd.

"Well..." Misty Sheridan said, studying my face. "So you're

a cop moonlighting as a customer, huh? I haven't seen you in here before."

"Oh, I've been here once or twice before, Miss Sheridan, but on the nights they only had dancing. I do need to say how much I enjoyed your singing—and all the rest of you that comes in that package you're wearing."

She laughed. "I can see you're a man who says what he feels and doesn't mince words, uh, was it Denning?"

"Cable…call me Cable."

"I've got to go, now. I have another number coming up. Will I see you again sometime? I always like it when I've won over a new fan."

"Well, you sure won me over tonight. When you're up there singing, a guy can take that ride to fantasyland…imagine all the dreams he ever dreamed with a babe can come true with you, because he can feel it…feel the electricity run through him as you sing…right down to his shoes and make him feel his life's been incomplete until now. Then he wants to take you home, own the heart and body that lives underneath that dress you're wearing, tear down the walls of pretend and become a haunted thing of desire and passion, longing and lust." She looked away for a minute, searching over the crowd as she leaned against the bar. She was breathing deeper and that ample bosom of hers heaved right along with those wonderful lungs.

"I've—I've, uh, never heard anyone talk like that, Cable—please call me Misty. I mean, I've got no come back words."

"It's okay, I blab a bit too much sometimes. It's part of what I do. So, you see, Misty Sheridan, that's the kind of emotion you stir up in some guys. You make 'em want to know you… the whole you…but have to realize one day that something so exquisite can't be owned, maybe borrowed, begged for, stolen or left dead in a penthouse because you won't let anyone else have her."

She leaned forward toward me. "Is that how *you* feel toward me, Cable? Are you so possessive you would murder me after you have me so no one else can?" She sipped down the rest of her drink. "That was good, thank you. I enjoyed talking to you."

"No, Misty, that was just a general statement. Actually, my emotion plate is pretty full just about now. I don't mean just babes, but my cop work has recently taken me into some pretty serious crap."

"I'm sorry. I've got to go now." She extended her hand. It was a bit cool. "Will I see you again? I hope I do….I mean I *really* hope I do. Maybe we could have a drink together sometime. I like the way you talk, Mister. And maybe you'd like to know a little more about me…oh, and there's one other thing you should know, just in case."

"And, uh, what might that be?"

"I'm not into men. I have a female lover and those needs are well taken care of. But that doesn't prevent me from enjoying the company of a man, now, does it?" Then she walked away, those marvelous buttocks doing that dance in her tight dress. Well…that took me by surprise. I always thought when I heard of a homosexual woman as knock-out gorgeous as Misty Sheridan, that it was a terrible waste of a good woman—that some handsome, virile man could be taking care of that wet, warm womanhood of hers the way God intended. Oh, well, live a little, learn a lot…

As I left the place, Misty had begun to sing a sexy version of *Rock-a-Bye Your Baby* in a way that made it a million miles apart from the Al Jolson version, which always smacked of the black minstrel parody he did so well. Well, maybe someday when Honey was off and making a movie somewhere, I'd come back and catch Misty Sheridan singing something wonderful at the *Café Montmartre.*

A few days went by and I felt restless waiting for Charlie Chaplin to call Honey and tell her when old man Hearst was inviting the United Artists bunch up to the castle in San Simeon.

Finally the day came and Chaplin said it was okay if I went along and that a few other folks would be in his limo party, including a little blonde number by the name of Virginia Cherrill. Honey suspected the little tramp was tramping around, screwing his favorites and maybe whoever slept with him the most during the filming of *City Lights* would end up being the co-star. Honey told me it definitely would not be her. *City Lights* was the story of the usual bungling tramp with a big heart who befriends a blind flower girl on a street corner. Eventually he falls in love with her, robs a bank with a buddy and uses the money to pay for a sight restoration operation on the flower girl. He gets caught and put into prison. But Chaplin was stuck and didn't know how to end the story. He never used a script and sometimes would dream up an idea and re-work it for weeks at a time while the cast sat around bored to tears until the genius tramp came up with the solution. But I guess you couldn't knock the guy, he'd had one hell of a track record with that same character over and over, re-working his subtleties until something new or original was achieved. Chaplin told Honey he was absolutely convinced that *City Lights* would be his best picture ever.

One night after I got off work and had said goodnight to Mario, I was approached by someone I vaguely recognized. He was the man who pursued me that day after Ardizzone's funeral. Yeah, Joe Lorena was his handle, if I recalled rightly— *consigliere* for Jack Dragna's mob.

He walked up to me. "Officer Denning." He extended his

hand. It was a warm handshake. "You may not remember me—but I'm Joe Lorena—we spoke some time ago. A rather awkward day, it was—"

"—after you guys bumped off Ardizzone and some other non-entity. A funeral, Lorena, a perfect place for guys like you to hang out. Just dig a bunch of holes and push 'em in as you go."

"That's uncalled for, officer—and it isn't what I came about today."

"So what brings you by?—I'm tired and busy these days. And frankly, I don't have much patience for hoodlums. The last time we met you warned me off and told me I was in deeper shit than I thought. Guess what? I'm in even deeper shit now."

I was looking directly into those fathomless eyes of his. That was the one thing I'd noticed before. He wasn't a bad sort of character. What in the hell was he doing as the talking head for the syndicate? "I realize you are. Maybe I can help. But this isn't about my business life, officer—"

"—cut the bullshit and call me Cable, okay?"

"Cable, then…it's about Honey Combes, now Lana Loren. I need to talk to her and since the two of you—"

"—oh, yeah, you're the guy who knows everyone else's love life, aren't you? Do you get off on the sexual comings and goings of active, young people? I remember now…you mentioned Honey the afternoon we met. So whatta ya wanna see her for?"

"I would like to have a private conversation with her—with you present, of course. Nothing hidden or ulteriorly motivated, I assure you."

"Well, now you've got my curiosity piqued. What possible connection could you have with Honey?"

"Please, Cable. Call me Joe. I would like you both to be sit-

236

ting when I share with you what I need to communicate to Honey."

"Sounds strange to me, Joe Lorena. But I'll ask her. Worst she can say is 'no.'"

"But I must see her. It affects her entire earth life. And you—"

"—earth life? You sound like a science fiction writer. What kind of crap do you read?"

Of course I could tell him about the weird shit that'd already been spinning into my life. Things like the *Fen de Fuqin*, my ultra-dimensional trip with Lei-tao in the Cave of the Seven Truths, Toggth's arrival and his weird stuff, not to mention the now-deceased Hatchet Man, etcetera. "Just a fifteen minute audience. That's all I ask."

"Well, Joe, I'll do my best. I don't even think she knows you, does she?"

"Yes and no," Lorena answered, making the mystery deeper.

I told him I'd ask Honey and he gave me a phone number where I could reach him. It was already Saturday and I thought I'd go home, clean up and go catch the last part of Honey's performance at the *Bella Notte* and then take her home. I said good-bye to Lorena and got to my little flat. Toggth had done a good job of "disappearing" the Hatchet Man and his goon. I checked my mail and there was a postcard from Chinatown, San Francisco. The front was a hand-colored picture of the Dragon Gate. I flipped it over and read a very neatly printed script in red ink. "Naughty man kill Hatchet Man...Hurt her pride, now she cry inside..." It was unsigned and I thought for a minute that it could've come from Lei-tao. But why would she write? Besides, she was off in some other dimension getting recharged or regenerated or something like that.

I washed up, put on some clean clothes and was combing my hair when the door buzzer rang. I reached in my dresser drawer and took out my .38. I crept over toward the side of the door. "Yeah? Who's there—and it better not be the bogey man."

"I don't know! I don't know! Let Jack in."

I opened the door and welcomed one of my favorite, crazy characters. "Hey, there, Crazy Jack—long time no see. You sure nailed things on my San Francisco train trip. Between you and Madame Palladino, who needs fortune tellers, eh?"

"I don't know! I don't know! Cigarette! Cigarette!" he insisted, as he always did around me. I went to my dresser drawer, took out a fresh pack of Lucky Strikes and tucked it in his pocket. Then I offered him one of mine from an open pack. "Want one now? Here..."

"I don't know! I don't know! Face of Mars like other stars—over your head—but not dead...but I don't know!"

"What are you saying, Jack—no comprendo the lingo, buddy."

"Man you see...no strange key to Honey Bee! But I don't know! I don't know! Look at eyes, deep surprise—when you realize...things are new...and only few...can know...but I don't know! I don't know!"

"Let me see here now...man I see...that must be Lorena... face of Mars—not dead? Something to do with Honey—my singing girlfriend?"

"I don't know! I don't know! She be smart to quit the ark—for music find a new palace to sing a song—but I don't know! I don't know!"

"Crazy Jack—are you saying, as you did before, that the *Bella Notte* is not a good place for Honey to hang around?"

"I don't know! I don't know! Someone die—who knows why? If bell be rung, Honey Bee get stung. Help her now—someone come who is not dumb—but I don't know! I don't know!"

"Wanna take a ride out to the *Bella Notte* right now with me? I'll sneak you in the side entrance so we can watch Honey from the wings. Do you like American popular standards—like what they play on the radio?"

"I don't know! I don't know! Music a poem, rhyme in time… make Jack think of a happy time… but I don't know! I don't know. The *Photes!* The Photes are coming!"

"You're still going on about that, eh? Just *when* are the photes coming, Jack?"

"I don't know! I don't know!" He was puffing away on his cigarette. "Good cigarette! You are good to Crazy Jack, Cable Denning."

"Well, Jack ol' boy, I aim to please. And you're just as good a people as anybody I know in this world. Never let anyone tell you different." He hit me affectionately on the shoulder and we left together.

Jack and I rode along on the streetcar. People looked at us and shunned the sight of Crazy Jack. Me? I liked the guy, maybe a screw loose here or there, maybe even his chemistry was out of whack, but you know, he was truer than many a friend others might have in this world. And isn't that what really counts? Sometimes we get our priorities mixed up, like who's crazy and who isn't, who's good looking enough even though she may be empty inside, or who's gonna be there for you when the chips are down and most of your so-called "friends" disappear? It was an issue the ego wrestled with—how does a guy not be attracted to a gorgeous young dame with a great body, fun personality and an intelligent enough head to get you the grocery store? And if she's musically talented, well, in my book that's the icing on the cake, the thing I couldn't resist if they tied me to an Inquisition stake and set it afire. I'd still be up there yelling and burning that *music* was the one thing that kept me sane, kept me alive in the world, brought me the smell of the barroom floor with all the memories in the sawdust you could dream up for a thousand years, the smoke-filled room with the jaunty laughter of people loosened up from the stupidity of taking ourselves too seriously on this nutso planet. Yeah, that's when I secretly came alive…and add to that a pretty babe with a body that shows through a skin-tight gown, glowing up there on the stage in a see-through show of movement, color and sound. Yep, that was better than going to the picture shows for me.

Crazy Jack and I entered the club from a side entrance Honey had shown me. It was dark and Honey was singing this knock-'em-out rendition of *Can't Help Lovin' That Man of Mine*. She was so sexy tonight and the lyrics wrapped around her like warm silk in a Swedish steam bath. Crazy Jack was mesmerized by Honey's performance and never said a word during her song, but twitched his wrists like it was the only way he could be without being totally still.

When Honey wrapped up her tune I took Crazy Jack by the sleeve and pulled him toward the stage where Honey stood accepting the applause she so richly deserved. "Honey Combes—what, are you living out of Harlem these days? Baby, are you sure you're a white girl?" I laughed.

She came down and hugged me, took a double-take at Crazy Jack and I hugged her back. "I don't know, big boy, could be there's a little black blood circulating around in my tonsils," she quipped back at me.

"This—this, uh, is Crazy Jack. Remember, I told you about him before. He's kinda—kind of 'hooked up' to the psychic world. Helped me a lot with the San Francisco adventure."

Honey was never prejudiced and accepted Jack as I accepted him from the start. "Good to meet you, Jack, I'm Honey—you can call me Honey. Which reminds me, Cable, you know you've never shared with me most of what happened on your San Francisco escapade."

"The photos—the photos are coming!—they'll get you—

go…home…I don't know! I don't know! Cigarette!"

Jack had gotten very nervous all of a sudden. I took out a cigarette from the pack I had given him and lit him up. I looked at a puzzled Honey. "He—he, uh, keeps talking about these 'photes,' creatures or something I've never seen. So we kind of go along with him, you know."

Honey looked out into the crowd. "Do you see any *photes* in the audience, Jack?"

"I don't know! I don't know! Everywhere! They're everywhere! But I don't know! I don't know!"

The bandleader motioned to Honey to return to the stage as the crowd was getting restless and wanted more of her. If Jack and I had felt our collars get warm with Honey's arrangement of the Show Boat song, we hadn't heard anything yet as she launched into the hottest, most sensual version of *Makin' Whoopee* I'd ever heard. When the notes reached their naughty ends, the crowd went wild and many people at their tables stood up to hail the new songstress diva, the new queen of the American Popular Songbook.

On the way home on the streetcar with Crazy Jack sitting across from us, I could feel Honey's body still perspiring from her night of hard work. "Cable, will you marry me?" she said out of the blue.

My mouth was put out of commission. The only thing I knew how to do with it at that minute was to make light of the situation. I looked across at Crazy Jack. "Do you think I should marry the girl, Crazy Jack?" I asked of my friend.

"I don't know! I don't know!" he cried, tears welling in his eyes as he clenched his hands together and started rocking back and forth.

"I guess that's a no—or maybe?" Honey purred with her wonderful sense of humor.

Jack's unshaven, grisly face showed a rare emotion I had not seen before. "Go home now…but I don't know! I don't know!"

We let Crazy Jack out downtown. Before he left he put his hand on my shoulder, his arm shook as he spoke. "Funny…ha! funny tilt brings guilt something maybe eighty—but I don't know! I don't know!" Then he got off the streetcar. Honey and I looked at each other as we also got off and transferred to another streetcar. Again, what in the hell could Crazy Jack mean?

When we got out near her place, we walked along in silence for a few minutes. "You didn't answer my question, Mr. Policeman," she said, squeezing my hand.

"That's because I have the same answer Crazy Jack had," I said, wincing and hoping that my answer didn't upset Honey.

"That's what I thought. You know, Cable, for me it's getting closer to *now or never* because I don't want to live a life with you hanging out in some dirty little flat—when you could hang out in *my* dirty little cottage with me and Zelda," she snickered half to herself.

I made a big sigh as we walked along. "You know how I feel about you, babe. That's not it." Of course I was also thinking of Adora Moreno in that particular moment. "It's a crazy time, Honey—for you, for me—new dice have been tossed across the table and I don't know what'll come up—boxcars or snake eyes."

"What if it's something in between? My life is getting crazy, too, Cable. I need an anchor…someplace to go that's really comfy and filled with love and put together by the two of us. A real *home*, my darling man." She stopped and held me. Then reached up to kiss me. Her warm lips told me she was in love and completely mine, present and accounted for. What made me hesitate? Any other bloke in his right mind would jump at the chance to be with a dish like Honey. Why was I so removed in my heart and mind? It wasn't that I didn't love her. I did, and when we were together she was a delight—in all ways.

242

"Maybe it's just me, babe. It's true, I haven't told you a lot about what's been going on—because I didn't want to alarm you. But a lotta shit's piling up around my door just now and if I involve you, I'd be endangering you unnecessarily."

She looked intensely into my eyes. "You mean it, don't you? You're in big trouble, Cable. What can I do?"

"Stay clear for a while. I've got to deliver this *golden capsule*, the *Fen de Fuqin*, the Chinese call it. And everybody and their uncle wants it—and they're all playing for keeps. Actually, I'm lucky to still be alive. And please….that's all I can say for now. The less you know, the better…."

"Gees, Cable…I don't know about you…one minute you're a bored flatfoot, the next thing I hear is that you're mixed up in some bloody mess with some treasure and a bunch of violent people!"

"It just happened that way, doll. I didn't ask for it."

"Yes, you did, Cable. Your restless spirit had to find a way out of the police world. So you found this. And it turned out to be a hell of a lot more than you can chew now, didn't it, Mister?"

"Maybe…just trust me…and oh, by the way—some Mafia consigliere that I met at Ardizzone's funeral made a strange request of me today."

"Yes—what's that?"

"He wanted to meet you and said he had something he needed to talk to you about…in person."

"*Consigliere?* What's that and what's his name?"

"He's kind of the spokesman and attorney for the mob. His name is Joe Lorena. Actually, I kind of like the guy. It puzzles me that he's mixed up in the middle of organized crime. Something just doesn't fit."

"And he wants to see me?"

"Yep. So he says. How do you feel about that?"

243

"I don't know. I guess so…if you're around when we meet."

We got to the front driveway of Honey's place. I noticed a man standing in the shadows. As soon as he saw us, he put out his cigarette and approached. "Cable…I apologize for showing up unannounced, but what I have to say can't wait." Then he looked at Honey. He extended his hand. Without hesitation and looking up into his eyes, Honey took it. "I'm Joe Lorena. I know you are Honey Combes, also known as actress Lana Loren, right?"

"Right, but what do we have in common, Mr. Lorena? Cable tells me you're one of the local syndicate's kingpins. You know, at the *Bella Notte* I deal with the mob all the time—the drooling henchmen, the snake-eyed little dons, the backroom meetings filled with smoke and violent intentions—so what's your racket?"

"All of that is true. But I'll explain. If we can go to a private place, the three of us, I would be very grateful. If in ten minutes you don't think I'm telling you the truth or what I have to say doesn't make sense, please tell me and I'll leave and never bother you again. Is it a deal?"

I looked at Honey. She seemed okay with this man. I couldn't figure it. After all, this guy was a complete stranger who she wouldn't even be talking to without me along. Yet she was comfortable and relaxed around him. "Cable? Are you okay with that? It's fine with me."

I nodded my head in the affirmative and we walked up the stairs to the back of the main house to Honey's little cottage with the berserk vines growing all over it. It was very late and Honey told us to go into the kitchen nook so we wouldn't wake up Zelda. Honey made us a cup of tea. I put a little gin in mine, but Joe Lorena declined, saying water was fine for him. There the three of us sat, looking at each other. "So…ah…my role here is to shut up and listen, right? So just pretend I'm a paid-off cop eavesdropping on one of those secret meetings, okay?"

Joe Lorena was a little nervous and had to stand while he spoke. He looked down at Honey who sat quietly with her cup of tea. "The only way to do this is to start at the beginning. Now, I will say some very strange things to you, Miss Combes. Please try to be open minded. This isn't easy for me." He took a deep breath. "Now…first of all, I wasn't born on this planet—or dimension. Believe it or not, there are many alien life forms here on your planet. Of course, one must also realize that there are millions of kinds of *humanoid-like* beings that exist throughout the universe. It doesn't matter where I come from. What does matter is my relationship to *you*." He checked both of us out. So far, we sat there looking like we were a riveted audience watching a science fiction movie, but wouldn't believe any of it after we came out of the movie house into the night air. "One thing my species discovered, when we arrived a long time ago, was that we couldn't *interbreed* with your kind… your species. So we devised a way. Why? Because our intentions were good. We wanted to infuse some of our advanced knowledge into your *bloodlines* so your kind would stop being so primitive and warring with each other, dividing yourselves by political, ethnic, religious and personal prejudice. We found a way by gene-splicing the chromosomes, but we realized that any offspring as a result of that pairing would create a hybrid child who cannot reproduce. Humans do it when they cross a horse with a donkey, for example—the resulting *mule* is a fine, healthy and good-sized animal, but cannot reproduce."

Honey looked at me. But something had come over her. She studied Joe Lorena's face and seemed to find no fault. "So, what you are saying, Mr. Lorena, is that I am one of those beings— and that's why I can't have children."

Joe Lorena looked at me. I shrugged. "Yes! Thank you for intuiting that! It will save a lot of anxiety as to what I have to say next."

"Oh, do go on, Lorena. I haven't been this entertained

in ages," I said a bit facetiously. "I'm certainly no Doubting Thomas here, but aren't you stretching things a bit and—"

"—Cable!" Honey cut me off. "You promised to keep quiet." I shut up.

"Almost twenty-three years ago I fell in love with a highly intelligent and beautiful human woman. Her name was *Lorena Brockmore* and she came from a very successful family and fortune. You'll notice, my own birth name would not suffice—*Ilt Kneklp*—so I eventually adopted an everyday American *Joe* first name and used Lorena's first as my last. So…here I was, in love with Lorena Brockmore—and she with me. Our love tryst was wonderful and I wanted to integrate into her family by marriage. But I was secretly an alien, not even human by the customary definition of the word and I was a no one with no traceable background, so I was rejected. However, Lorena wanted to have my child once I told her who I truly was. She was an adventuresome woman, full of wit, bright-minded, slim, dark-haired and beautiful like you, Honey. With her senses slightly dulled—and with her consent—I took her to one of our under-the-mountain clinics and she was artificially inseminated with my seed." He stopped and then smiled at Honey. "*You* are the living product of the joining of that seed and your mother's ovum. All during her pregnancy your mother sang and sang and sang until she nearly passed out singing operettas and popular songs of the day. But something went terribly wrong." By now Honey's eyes had welled with tears and I knew she knew, she had already guessed the rest of the story, but let Joe Lorena finish. "Some human women become poisoned with the half of the chromosome that is vibrationally so different than the more slowly evolved human chromo somatic makeup that they become deathly ill—and perish…" Joe Lorena's own eyes misted. "You were born perfect—the ideal success story of millions of years of evolution crossed into one being. But your mother paid the greatest price of all. She died two weeks after your birth. At least she was able to enjoy you that long, holding you in her arms, cuddling you, kissing your fat little cheeks."

Honey could hold it no longer and burst into tears. "Please! Stop! I can't take anymore—I know what you say is true— I've—I've known it all my life but couldn't tell anyone! I didn't even know *how* I knew. Now you—"

Joe Lorena came over to Honey and extended his arms to her. "—I'm all you have left, Honey. I always dreamed a little dream of you, trying to imagine what you'd look like now. And here you are, as stunning as your lovely, intelligent mother. I realize it's a dismal legacy, and if it weren't for me, she would be alive today." He paused and sniffed in his own tears.

Honey sucked in the tears. "Yeah, but I wouldn't be around, would I? And I must have enough of you in me to know there's—there's *more to everything* then we can imagine." She took Lorena's hand and clutched it. "I don't blame you. Love is love, Joe, anyplace."

Lorena bent down and she grabbed his head and cried into it. He embraced his daughter. "Thank you—thank you, Honey, for understanding! I've lived so long with it, this secret—and the pain! Can you accept me? I know you were raised by your adoptive parents and you love them and they love you very much. They chose to keep the adoption a secret from you. Please don't blame them."

Honey began to dry her tears. "I won't…I can't…they've been so good to me." Then she let go of Joe Lorena's hand and looked up at him. "But you are my father, the one who truly sired me, and that blood is in me, I can feel you, read you, know your truth as you speak."

Joe Lorena didn't know what to do next. "Well," I said, totally out to lunch by now on some planet of my own. "Why don't we have another cup of tea and maybe we've said enough for one night. Might I suggest that the two of you meet privately for lunch or dinner sometime?"

Honey stood up and went over to the little stove to boil more water. "There is one question I have…"

"Anything, Honey…anything I can answer that'll help you…"

"How did you get mixed up with crime…I mean…Jack Dragna and those horrible low-life men who rob and kill and steal beautiful young women for export, never to be seen again?"

"I needed to make a lot of money to help support our *alien cause* here on your planet. In that respect, crime pays. I know it sounds terrible, but I don't have the same moral codes as you do. Not that I approve of taking life, kidnapping and extortion. It's that my cause is greater than the sum total of the parts that my business life takes me into."

We were all exhausted from the emotional roller coaster and the incredulous content of Joe Lorena's tale. Honey and I escorted him to the door to say good-night. I liked the man— or being, or alien—or whatever or whoever he was. It really didn't matter to that part of myself that took individuals as I found them and made a character analysis based on that perspective. Nothing else…if I liked them I did, if I didn't, I didn't. My brave Honey hugged the humble man at the door. I couldn't imagine how he held all that inside of him all those years. "Don't be a stranger, Mister," she said. "I may not approve of what you do for a living, but I think I kind of like you anyway," she said with a wry smile.

Joe Lorena left and we fell into bed together. "You know, Cable, he had a lot of nerve," Honey was saying just before she drifted off into a restless sleep. "Using my mother's name. *Lorena*…just think of it, my real mother's name was *Lorena*. And, Cable…?"

"Yeah?"

"My Dad's an alien…" I drew her into my arms and we slept.

Chaplin had ordered two black Packard limousines and we started off very late on a Friday night in late December. We were to celebrate New Year's Eve at the famous ranch in the middle of nowhere on the central coast of California. Again, somehow strings were pulled at police headquarters and I was given "protective assignment" for a week. Mario was pissed at me for being absent so much, but I told him I'd level with him when all this crap blew over.

William Randolph Hearst was a reclusive man who nevertheless found time to pitter patter around the Hollywood set by trying to control Louis B. Mayer at Metro-Goldwyn Studios. Although married to an ex-vaudeville entertainer who bore him five sons, Hearst philandered with a lovely young blonde actress named Marion Davies. Hearst was so enamored with the young lady seventeen years his junior, that when he was rebuffed by United Artists, he went and started his own studio, working in conjunction with Paramount, called Cosmopolitan Pictures. In 1923 there was a falling out with Paramount and he teamed up with Goldwyn Pictures, which a year later became part of MGM. Working closely with Louis B. Mayer proved to be a mutually advantageous venture. The bloodline Hearst had come from was started by a guy named George Hearst who at forty married an eighteen year-old girl, one Phoebe Apperson. Old George was born in 1830 and got gold fever in the 1850's, made a killing and never worried about money again. William Randolph Hearst was an only child and had a penchant toward newspaper publishing. He took over the *San Francisco Examiner* in 1887 and built his empire. In 1895 his mother financed his purchase of the failing New York Morning Journal and Hearst soon entered into a heated rivalry with Joseph Pulitzer, a feisty Hungarian and his newspaper, the *New York World*. Both Hearst and Pulitzer had mastered the style of sensationalism soon called '*yellow journalism*'...in glaring contrast, in 1897 the owner of the *New York Times* created the motto "All the news that's fit to print".

The buzz was that Marion Davies was already at the *La Cuesta Encantada* for our holiday and was an ideal hostess. According to Honey, rumor also had it that Chaplin and Davies had a secret thing going now and then, an affair the jealous and protective old Billy boy probably didn't know about. But that was life and people did what people did, based partly on their instincts of lust and desire, insecurity and curiosity, and partly on the boredom the rich enjoyed until with nothing to do, they played with fire in a paper house.

We had driven all night. Honey and I were in the back seat with Douglas Fairbanks and Mary Pickford was up front with the chauffer. Fairbanks drank a lot those days and his swashbuckling days were pretty much over. Ten years before he was Hollywood's most popular silent film star. It was his son, an equally dashing Douglas Fairbanks, *Jr.,* who was the new star on the block. He had done some silent films with Loretta Young and Joan Crawford, was dating the latter and they were going to do a picture together soon called, *Our Modern Maidens*. It looked like the handsome bloke could pick out any maidens he chose with those connections! Chaplin, Virginia Cherrill and another very rich and famous comedian, Harold Lloyd traveled in the lead Packard.

It was damp and the little two-lane highway was fogged in with mists from the sea. But as the sun began to break through from the east and we approached the tiny hamlet of San Simeon, Honey awakened me to behold something none of us may ever live to see again. As if in a fairy tale movie, the thick banks of fog began to part at the top of the ridge above us. Suddenly as the curtain of fog drew away, an enchanted castle loomed out of the mists into the sunshine. Even Doug Fairbanks looked through blurry eyes and said he'd never seen the likes of it. The white castle with the two Moorish towers and palm trees scattered about, contrasted against the green slopes and pine dotted mountains of the Santa Lucia. We were all awe struck by the time we reached the summit and through the last gate in full sunshine. A few miles below, the blue Pacific Ocean shimmered in the morning light as the fog bank pulled back out to sea. For a minute it seemed like I was coming home to something I couldn't quite remember. But I wouldn't forget what we saw that day.

The castle was massive with the most spectacular outdoor swimming pool I'd ever seen. Scaffolding told one the castle was an ongoing project and some areas were as yet not completed. As one walked through the gigantic main doors, a fireplace big enough to have a picnic in stood directly across from us. To our right was a huge dining hall where there were flags from all countries of the world. Old paintings and tapestries hung from the walls. Of course, what I was looking for was my knight in shining armor, probably lurking somewhere in a dark hallway in this gothic potpourri of a building.

William Randolph Hearst, Sr., was a fairly tall man, a little paunchy with a rather austere face. He greeted us all with an enthusiastic smile and told us right up front, that all smoking was to be done outside the castle, it was obligatory to attend feeding at the trough at 8:00 p.m. and there was no alcohol served in his castle except one drink per person at dinner—nor was any to be found at any of the three wet bars. Prohibition was an absolute with the old boy. The blonde and friendly Marion Davies came down from the second floor and spoke to a couple of servants before she approached us. When she came closer, I could see blue-eyes on a nice face and she had a pleasant voice. She was probably the quintessential flapper who was commanded by her lover boy to perform costume dramas before the motion picture camera. I saw her as light-hearted, positive, intelligent and could understand where a lover other than the newspaper magnet was in order. She had a deep need to love and be loved…it appeared to me.

We were led up a flight of stairs while our luggage was traipsed up to the second floor by the many castle employees. If folks were not married, each got a separate room. So Honey and I had to live under that pretense, as did Charlie and Virginia Cherrill. Doug Fairbanks and Mary Pickford were married, so they got one communal room. One could see how easy it was to play musical beds in this joint, with all 172 rooms playing a slightly different role.

Almost immediately I began a self-guided tour, looking down corridors for my knight. Standing in front of the main library entrance stood a wonderful specimen, one that Lei-tao must have shape-shifted and gained access to when she hid the *Fen de Fuqin*. The armor was a brilliantly shining silver-gold and at its base there was an inscription that read, *"Augsberg Tilt Knight, c.1580."* *Tilt* and *eighty* were two of the clues that Crazy Jack had given me as he departed that night onboard the streetcar! That guy was hooked in to *something*—but what?

I knew I'd have to wait until very late to do my prowling without alerting any of the other guests, including Honey. That'd be a trick since she insisted that I sleep with her once dinner was over and we were ready to call it a night. Honey and I were very tired and so as soon as the coast was clear, I sneaked into her room with the afternoon sun lighting up the green hills to the east. In the distance I saw a small herd of African zebra and then remembered Fairbanks had told us Hearst had created a complete zoo, with animals from around the world. What money can't buy! I thought to myself.

"Cable…maybe you can ask Mr. Hearst if we can honeymoon here…and we can invite my father and a few friends?"

Why do dames put pressure on a guy when he's already told her she's just gonna have to wait until things simmer down. I had called Adora before I left and wished her Happy New Year. She was sad we could not see each other and mentioned that was one of the repercussions of being a lover and second on the string. 1929 was supposed to be a prosperous year for everyone concerned, except maybe the average Joe-blow like me who never really knew what life was like without struggle. "That again, eh, babe? When the time comes, I'll ask the ol' boy myself. But in the meantime, can we simply enjoy each other where we are now?"

"I'm sorry. I don't know why, but lately I've felt so insecure. Are you sure you don't have your eyes and balls intent on someone else?" She asked that, searching around in my eyes for the truth. But in the end, I was always good at truth. "You can tell me, it's alright. I gander at good-looking men all the time who come into the *Bella Notte* and hit on me. But I won't act on it because I'm in love with you, Cable Denning. Sometimes I'm not sure you get that part."

"Can't we just rest for a while, babe? It was a long, uncomfortable ride from L.A. to this Mediterranean Mecca in the middle of nowhere."

"You're avoiding my question, Cable. Is there or isn't there?"

"What's with you, Honey?" I got a little upset. I hate being grilled. "Okay—okay—'cause I don't want to insult your intuitions. So there was this Chinese doll named Lei-tao. You wanna know about her? She was a shape shifter, called the *Red Dragon Lady* and lives most of the time in other dimensions. She's a virgin and can't have sex like we do. So we had tantric sex in the *Cave of the Seven Truths* and I came all over the rock floor." I stopped and took a breath, opened a window and lit up a Lucky Strike. "Now…does that satisfy the lady? There's truth for you…suck that in."

Honey's mouth was agape as if her tongue suddenly got paralyzed with a ray gun from a science fiction novel. Then she laughed. "Cable…damn, you probably did date one of those Asian princesses—okay, I believe that. But please, let's not add any bullshit to embellish it, okay? So you got lonely, went out for a couple of drinks, right? And you didn't screw her, did you?"

"I told you the truth. *Tantric sex* is filling your whole body with healthy energy. You just happen to stop along the way at the genitals and give them an extra revving. That's it, doll, take it or leave it."

"I'll leave it, thanks," she said in a droll tone of voice. "Okay… okay…let's just let it be…I'm going to believe what I feel and you're going to tell me you believe whatever you experienced is what happened. I can buy that."

"In light of what you experienced just before we left—one Mr. Joe Lorena and all—I thought you'd be a little more open minded. You do believe that, don't you—about him being your Dad *and* an alien?"

"I have to. I felt it all my life."

"Are you gonna tell your foster parents?"

"I don't think so. They're getting older and why distress them? I understand why they did what they did. I might do the same if I were in their shoes. Funny, how all my wit fails me just about now. How come I can't make light of any of it—I used to be so funny, Cable."

"There's a time for everything, toots. Rest now. Just nestle with me in our little cave here in the mountains above the sea."

"In the cave where you fucked her—your Asian *princess*? No thanks."

She turned over and went to sleep. She was a woman and she *couldn't* just let it be. Women get pissed either way you go. When you tell a lie they get pissed…when you tell them the truth they get pissed…so like I said, it's best to shut up and get on with living today. Hell, tomorrow you could be dead!

Dinner with Hearst was sumptuous and boring. Fortunately for us, he had some money troubles overseas and had to depart early. The old boy did his business on the phone during the night and slept until noon or so the next day. He told us the U.S. economy was booming but that the stock market was accelerating too fast and real estate values had been falling since 1925. He also mentioned that the average citizen wanting to invest in the booming stock market were borrowing the money to invest and thus caused a risky "flooring," as he put it, if the market hit a snag. He congratulated Pickford, Chaplin, Lloyd and Fairbanks for investing in the entertainment world, which he thought would prosper in both good and bad times. He was unsure about the next two years in the American economy, he said, and wished we'd all take a nice swim in the indoor pool before retiring. Honey, Cherrill, Lloyd, and Chaplin decided to do just that, but Pickford and Fairbanks said they'd play billiards for a while and then turn in for the night. I told Honey that as soon as things settled down for the night I would need to accomplish the task at hand by grappling with the *Augsburg Tilt Knight.*

I liked Marion Davies. She stayed on and talked a while after Fairbanks and Pickford went off to play at the billiard table. She liked Honey. I was trying to catch an off-glance between Chaplin and Davies, but observed none. Maybe it was a myth. But what *was* true was that four years before, a guy named Thomas Ince mysteriously died aboard one of Hearst's yachts out of San Pedro. Chaplin, Hearst, Davies and a few other guests, including the film producer, director, actor-writer Ince, were celebrating Ince's 44th birthday. It was said that due to existing health problems, he reacted to ingesting certain food and drink on the yacht and became ill. From the yacht he was taken by train to Del Mar and then with his wife and eldest son to his Los Angeles home where he died, presumably from heart failure. The other story which had much more sensational appeal and seemed to have more longevity, spoke of a hushed murder at sea , when apparently romantic trouble brewed up a storm, and thinking Ince (donning Chaplin's famous derby) to be Chaplin cuddling in a corner with Davies, Hearst shot Ince in the head. If this was indeed the truth it was swept under the Persian rug and the official certificate said cause of death was heart failure. Many believed that the real truth would never be known—except by the killer. Maybe Hearst had good reason to suspect Chaplin of playing midnight bed games with Davies, maybe not. But this night Chaplin's focus was definitely on Virginia Cherrill.

I told Honey I was going to play cat burglar for a while and excused myself from the table after sucking down the one alcoholic drink we were allowed, which happened to be Benedictine, an herbal liqueur. I said my goodnights, telling the folks I was still exhausted from the trip and disappeared. When the three swimmers went to change I made my way down the dimly lit hallway toward my waiting knight. I stood before the armor on the pedestal and realized how really small our ancestors had been. This guy might've been five-foot four, if that. I took the left arm gauntlet in hand and played with it. Finally I twisted it counter-clockwise and it snapped off. I reached inside and felt for the capsule. Voilá It was wrapped in a very soft doeskin and I immediately put it into my pocket and clicked the gauntlet cuff back onto the arm of the knight's armor.

A marvelous new energy overtook me as I tucked the *Fen de Fuqin* in my pocket. It was as if I had re-connected with it *and* Lei-tao at the same time. I made my way up to Honey's room, only to find her crying on the bed when I entered. "I knew if I didn't sleep with him he'd choose Virginia. Crap, Cable, why does everything always have to hinge on sex?"

"Did he tell you that—I mean, that he'd chosen Cherrill?"

"Duh…he didn't have to. He was playing footsies with her under the water. Even Harold kind of looked the other way. He knew—after all, Lloyd's not just an actor, but like Charlie, a producer and director."

"Well, maybe not everything depends on sex, toots. I'm sorry about *City Lights* but your career has just begun, kid." I came over and comforted her. "Look at the bright side. You're only starting out in a marvelous career. You'll see, other opportunities will present themselves....you're gonna hit the top, babe!"

She reached for me and held me to her. "I love you, Cable. So damn much. Let's just be us from now on, okay?" Then she held me back and looked into my face. "We've got something wonderful going on here, Mister. How about being exclusive so we never have to worry about anyone else coming in between us? I don't know what you did with that Chinese gal—and I don't want to know. I just want a straight shooter, Cable. Isn't that you, Mr. Truth?"

I kissed her. "Yeah, you bet. There's only time in that part of our lives for us—and I'll gladly toe that line for you because you're so good in bed."

She hit me hard on the shoulder. "Damn! Crap! It's that sex thing again, isn't it?" she chided me with a certain kind of Honey Combes smirk.

"Yep. Think of it, our lives wrapped up inside each other whenever the notion overcomes us—can you beat that?"

"Nope." I knew in that moment I'd have to try and make it with Honey as my one and only squeeze. Yet a terrible pain went ripping through me as I contemplated having to tell Adora that we couldn't continue seeing each other. And what would I tell my mother? Her magic, psychic eye scoped Adora out from the beginning and approved without question. And even though I knew a guy could be happy with more than one doll in this world, somehow my heart wasn't in it. After all was said and done, Honey was first and we fit so well, despite the busyness of her career and my discontent with mine. Life is filled with missed timings and bitter ironies.

"Well, I found it."

"Found what?"

"The *God of Our Fathers* thing, the golden capsule. The thing I really came for."

"You sneak. I thought you came to be with me. So you found this capsule thing and now suddenly the world is going to be okay?"

"It's not like that. Supposedly, it holds timeless, ancient knowledge. And it's priceless. I need to return it to the Red Dragon Lady."

"Not her again. Cable, if this is some weird play you're acting out so you can get into some Chinese woman's pants, just tell me. I can take that a lot easier than you chasing down some golden memento that probably belongs in a museum."

"Okay. I'll stop talking about it. I just want you to know that some pretty big players are after it as well as my little Chinese consort."

"Are you in danger?"

"Could be. But for now, you not believing me is more dangerous than they are."

"Okay. I'll go along for a ways. But I can't swallow the whole thing, okay?"

"Yeah, I guess. I'll keep you posted."

New Year's Eve 1928 was a bust at Hearst Castle. All the unfinished beauty and the pretend glory measured by what money could buy, couldn't take a stagnant pall from off the dinner table. Old Billy Boy did come up with some damn good Champagne that was actually *from* Champagne, but we only got one glass at dinner and one at midnight. Hardly a time to get tight and squeeze your señorita. Good sport that she was, Marion Davies was up for playing a game or two. So Mary, Doug, Harold and Marion went to go play cards somewhere. Honey and I had talked about seeing the harbor below at San Simeon and asked William Sr. if he'd be kind enough to see to our transportation in the morning. I must say he was a kindly and gracious host, no matter how peculiar and eccentric in his ways of living life and doing business. We thanked him and retired.

The next morning we walked on the beach near San Simeon just as the mysterious and constant fog began to inhale itself back into the sea. Soon birds were heard in the little Mexican-like haciendas in front of the pier and the little *Sebastian's Store* was just opening. I noticed it was the only private business on the block. *1852* was written above the owner's name. Hearst had built several gigantic warehouses that looked like Spanish missions and a very long pier with railroad tracks going down the middle of it. Steamers from all over the world, so Harold Lloyd told us, would make port in San Simeon laden with treasures from all over the world. Crated and stacked to the ceilings, this compulsive collector of art kept his kingdom a tight ship and ruled over all from the top of the hill above us.

There was a little jutting peninsula we walked out on. Rudimentary trails meandered through brush and woods. Old Hearst had planted hundreds of Eucalyptus trees and word was that the wood and medicinal use of the seedpods were of commercial value. Remnants of an old nineteenth century whaling station stood on the banks of the sea and seals barked in the distance while sea otters played in the calm of San Simeon Bay.

Honey was holding my hand tightly. "I can't believe it, it's 1929. I wonder what kind of year it will be for us?"

"You're gonna fly to the top, babe," I said , squeezing her hand. "And then you'll be able to support me in a fashion to which I will have become fondly accustomed, as the English might say," I joked.

"Now's the time, Cable," she said, as we looked at the receding fog bank pulling back out to sea in the morning breezes. "Now's the time for us to run away and never come back to the old life. We could live like this, on the edge of the sea in a wonderfully fragrant forest near the top of a hill. We'd have a good chance, darling, to forge a good life out of the simple things—"

"—you're dreaming, Honey. You couldn't give up your singing career any more than I could give up the love-hate relationship I have for L.A. and chasing down crooks. Maybe when you make it big, we could have a second home, you know, a cottage somewhere in a place like this. Then we'd have the best of both worlds—doesn't that make a lotta sense? We're both young, babe, and there's still a lot of mileage in both of us."

She took my hand and dragged me along with her. "I suppose so. Maybe you're right. Make hay while the sun shines for both of us, huh? So Honey Combes became Lana Loren who became—became who? That's the part I worry about."

"Well, how about becoming Mrs. Cable Denning—that way you'd have three names to worry about?"

She stopped short. "You mean that? You're finally relenting? I never thought I'd live to hear those words come out of your mouth, Mr. Denning."

"Well, I figure it this way, kid. Love like this doesn't sit around growing on trees, you know. I realize what I've got in you, Honey Combes, and come hell or high water, I think we should try and make a go of it. Whatta ya say?"

"Yes! yes! yes!" She ran to me and hugged me for all I was worth—which to me, wasn't a hell of a lot those days. "*When*, Cable, when?"

"What part of the calendar makes you happy?"

"I *do* know! I've always wanted to be a December bride!"

"Okay, doll—December 1929 it'll be, then!"

She held me, placing her cheek on my chest. "Cable, I've never thanked you. None of this would ever have happened had you not forced your way to the head of my dance queue that night when I was selling myself for ten cents a dance. You encouraged me from the beginning—you said I *could*—and I did—because of you. Thank you, Cable, for giving me a new life…"

My gaze was out to sea, over her head, looking, squinting, seeing into the far beyond. "You're welcome, baby. After all, you *are* my '*golden throat*', ain't ya?"

Honey was elated all the way back to L.A. I could tell my committed confession of love somehow completed her inside. Maybe that's what happens when you finally aren't in a lonely place anymore, and that two can combine to create a life together. Anyway, it sounded good put that way…and who knows, it might even sound good tomorrow.

End Part I

TABLE OF CONTENTS
PART 2

PART 2

CHAPTER 11

GOD OF OUR FATHERS

PASTA AND GUNS

I was rather anxious to make contact with Toggth so I could hand over the capsule to him and get Ravna's monkey off my back by giving him the phony. So each day I looked for a tell-tale sign that things would finally come to a swift and happy ending. Well, sort of...

Sergeant O'Flaherty called me and Mario in one morning after Honey and I got back, for a rather peculiar assignment. It seems there was this very bad guy named *Johnny Porrello* who had been in hiding for a couple of years. The cops found out his whereabouts and wanted us to bring him in. I guess he was such a horrible piece of shit that even the crooked cops couldn't stand seeing him go 'gently into that dark night'. He had been living incognito as a "non-alcoholic" vintner in the valley around Escondido, out of San Diego. The wily sergeant warned us he was dangerous and since at least one of us was sort of in training for a detective's rank eventually, this assignment was a good choice— even if a bit dangerous.

Escondido was mostly a flat land of orange groves and lemon trees. Some grapefruit grew here and there, but we were hard pressed to find Porrello's vineyard. Finally, we were led to a small hilly area east of the main town. On the side of the highway in front of the vineyard stood a small café called *Piero's*. Mario and I went in. The menu pushed wine, cheese and pasta as the mainstays. A cute little blonde number in her late twenties stood behind the counter. She was chewing gum like the stereotypical mobster's moll. "Welcome, gentlemen, and have a seat. Some of Piero's 1927 grape juice—non-alcoholic, of course—as an appetizer?"

Every once in a while I forgot it was still Prohibition. "Yeah, swell," I said. Mario nodded and we ordered some of Piero's vino and some pretty good pasta. "Is…is Piero around?" Mario asked the waitress.

"Who wants to know? And who do you think made the pasta, Little Bo Peep?" the young lady said in a strident tone of voice.

Mario laughed. "Maybe…you never know nowadays. You didn't answer my question—is that Piero out there slaving over a hot stove?" Mario kidded.

"Well, we can call him out and see if he answers to that name now, can't we, gentlemen? I can't say for sure, but underneath the wonderful smell of the food, don't you smell a rat—maybe a dead one?"

"Maybe something died in your larder, Miss—" I said.

"—Theda. You know, like Theda Barra, the vamp? But about that rat—maybe coppers smell like that, too. Don't you think?" she asked, popping her gum.

"Oh, I thought *vamp* had a 'tr' in front of it—wasn't she some kind of over-sexed dish?" Mario said.

"It's sort of a free country, Mister. You can have your opinion about how 'sexed up' a woman can get. But it sounds to me like you've got a little cottage with a pretty wife and kiddies, now, doesn't it?" Then she gave me the once over. "But not you, buster. There's a tough streak in you and I'd hate to get on your mean side. And I'll bet you're still a bachelor."

"Not bad," I said, peeking back at the kitchen. "So, can we talk to Piero?"

"Piero! A couple of flatfeet wanna talk to you."

Both Mario and I had seen mug shots of Porrello and the little guy who came out definitely did not fit that description. He had a slight build and seemed nervous. "So, whatsa happenin' a now, eh?"

"Is your boss in, Piero? By the way, we really enjoyed the pasta."

He lit up. "That's-a nice, caus-a my Mamma she teach-a me…"

"To answer your question, the boss ain't here. Hardly ever comes in, but hangs out up there stamping out the grapes for curious cops. Why do you wanna to meet the boss? He's just a nice guy trying to make a decent living in these prosperous times." She pointed to a pretty nice landscaped dump at the top of the hill with three-stories and a large grain silo on the side.

We thanked the brazen young woman and made our way up the hill. We knocked at the freshly painted front door. Immediately Mario and I knew it was Porrello by the beady black eyes and scar right above his left eyebrow.

"Yeah, are you the guys who want the hooch delivered yesterday? I told your boss I run a legitimate business here— except for that silo. Somehow it got found with a lot of mash in it the other night."

"We don't want any of the bullshit, Porrello," I said, forcing the door open with Mario backing me up. "All we want is you. Now ain't that simple?"

He turned pale. "I don't know what you're talking about— I've farmed up here for years, and I don't know this Porrello guy you're talkin' about—you got your wires crossed, boys. My name's Frankie Lorso." He took out his wallet and showed me his California driver's license with *Frankie Lorso's* name on it. "See? But since you're here, the least I can offer you for bustin' into my house uninvited are a couple of drinks—I mean the real stuff here."

"No thanks, Porrello, we're on duty," Mario said. "Now do you get our drift? We're here to take you in—or have you forgotten so soon?—your rap sheet reads like a who's who in corpses, graft and missing young things that mysteriously get stolen in the night and end up as whores on a street in Hong Kong."

Porrello started to make a run for it. We drew our guns and he stopped. He threw his arms up. "Can't we let bygones be bygones, boys? I can make it worth your while—I mean, really worth your while—money, broads—how about a small percentage of my special 'wine' sales?"

"You know, that sounds pretty good to me, Porrello, but somehow I just ain't in the mood for your brand of evil shit this week." Mario got out his handcuffs and fastened them onto Johnny Porrello's wrists.

"You see, what my fellow officer here is saying, you dimwit, is that someone has to stand up in this asshole of a world opposite crap like you. It's our way of saying you can't always have what you want, including your nice spread here, your booze racket and the hot little number who warms your bed at night."

He snickered. I didn't like his tone of voice. "You cops are dumb. You just don't know the score, do ya? Maybe overnight...yeah, maybe overnight you might hold me downtown. But you know I'll be back tending my grapes in no time while your superiors will be eating humble pie."

"Not on my watch, Porrello," Mario asserted. "And if you do get out by some miscarriage of justice, you can bet I'll be tailing you until I bring you in for keeps. You can count on that."

Mario and I hauled Johnny Porrello in. But a strange thing happened. Just as Porrello predicted, the next day he was out and back home tending his grapes! I went stomping in to O'Flaherty's office, mad as hell. The sergeant looked at me with a rather sheepish look on his face. "I know I ordered ya to bring 'im in, lad. And so ya did. But truth be told, it's out of me hands, Denning. The guys upstairs—they're the ones that tell ya—and bein' that I'm so nears retirement, it'd be foolhardy for O'Flaherty here to be doin' himself in now, wouldn't it?"

I was pissed and disgusted and knew in that instant I was going to quit the force one day soon. The sooner the better. "So what happens to guys like Porrello, sergeant? They live a life of luxury and give murder and graft and white slavery a good name and everyone lives happily ever after? And do you know what we're setting up here? A goddam vigilante force. As soon as my partner Mario Angelo hears about this—well, I prefer not to think about it, sergeant. He just might take matters into his own hands…"

O'Flaherty looked at me, his eyes softened. "Denning, me boy…honest cops like you and Officer Angelo are a rare breed. Seein' that I was one for a bitty time, I can vouch that law and order indeed does not run city hall. So sooner or later you have to wise up, lad—and catch up to the times you're livin' in. Thin line there, me boy. I always said you'd make a good detective. But I was wrong, Denning. You're too honest and they'd kill ya before you could drink your next Jack Daniels!"

I stalked out, all the more determined that my police force days were gonna be far behind me in the not too distant future.

No sooner had I gotten home to my little flat that night and sat in my old comfy chair with a gin and tonic in hand, than I saw a dark red envelope being pushed under my door. I got up and rushed to the door and opened it, hoping to catch the deliverer. I ran downstairs and flew into the street, looking up and down. Nothing. I made my way back up to my apartment, grabbed the envelope and sat back down. Only my name in exquisite black penmanship blemished the front. I carefully unsealed it. I drew out an equally red note and read: *"She still very mad at him over Hatchet Man's death. But chance to redeem. Come Zeng Ping Café, Calle de Los Negros, tomorrow 6:00p.m. Ask for Da Chung. Bring Fen de Fuqin."* The content of the note felt to me like Lei-tao's playful sense of humor, but that didn't make sense either, since it was Toggth who was supposed to collect the *God of Our Fathers* from me, wasn't it? Or did I get my wires crossed? In these days I never knew where the next punch was coming from. I had to follow through but stay guarded every minute. For all I knew it was Ravna shortcutting his way to the capsule—*if* he had gotten wind of the plan to trade out the real capsule for an optical illusionary phony.

WHEN YOU'RE DEAD YOUR NAILS GROW FASTER

Unlike the San Francisco experience, "Chinawon," as some of the locals called it, sat in darker and rougher places. The *Calle de Los Negros* wasn't Chinese, first of all, and the area had been knocked back and forth between ethnic and commercial forces over the past sixty years or so. I hadn't been there since that Friday afternoon when Ardizzone and Blinthe got it on Alameda Street in 'Chinawon'. Near the *Canton Bazaar*, now occupying the old Lugo Adobe house, were the side-by-side shops many in disrepair, but with their colorful lanterns hanging as if symbols of hope for better times… comprised the core of the Asian settlement. And that was the town except for a few open-counter soup and tea cafes. I had forgotten the Southern Pacific Railroad had purchased a big plot of encroaching land for a right-of-way and most of the few hundred inhabitants had been scattered. So, then, I figured, it would be easy to find this *Da Chung* character and get on with it. The damn capsule was burning a hole in my upper breast pocket and it was feeling like a hot football—you never knew who to pass it to next.

I found the Zeng Ping Café, a run-down little food shack with a torn canvas overhang. There were a couple of guys sucking up soup and an elderly Mexican lady with a young girl sitting at the counter. I sidled up between them and sat. I saw no one behind the counter, so I waited. Soon the others had sipped the last of their soup and left. I was about to call it a night when I heard a very odd cackle. Then, through a side door behind the counter came a very small, very old Chinese woman with hardly any teeth. The ones she had were brown and stained with age and chew-tobacco as she approached me, waving a finger. She seemed to be admonishing me for something I hadn't done as she spoke in a high, raspy voice, always concluding with that odd cackle of hers. "You no want Da Chung soup! You no belong here! Bad man! Hurt Chinese Hatchet Man!" she cackled. "You no eat here—I poison you with my food! You have nerve show up here....no money, no woman—where your woman?" the old hag laughed again.

I could barely understand a word she said and was also getting impatient. "Look, lady, I'm here to meet someone—I don't even know if it's a man or woman—can you help me out here? Understand English?"

She continued to rant and rave and cackle. Finally, I'd had it and got up to go. "Oh, I learn engineering and build railroad over Sierra Nevada Mountain as well, impatient man," she now spoke in a familiar voice and when I turned the old lady had gone and in her place stood the exquisite and stately Lei-tao. In the semi-dark of the little joint with its yellow and red paper lanterns swaying in the night breeze, for a moment I fell in love with her. She smiled at me just the way she did the night we got back from the Cave of the Seven Truths. "I was punishing you, Cable, for killing my faithful Wong Lo San."

"I didn't kill him, lady. Toggth did—but I gotta tell you, had he not come in the nick of time, there'd be two halves of my skull still glued to the wall of my apartment." She came closer and checked out my eyes. "He came to kill you?"

"He kept saying I was a bad influence on you or something—that I might ruin you—something about me and my 'sex desire', as he put it."

Lei-tao dropped her gaze. "Oh. Then you are telling me true." She looked around restlessly and summoned me into a nook behind the bar. "Now…the *Fen de Fuqin*—do you have it, please?"

"I might," I said with caution. "How do I know you're the real thing? You could be another shape-changer being shifty in someone else's skin…I've—I've seen it happen, you know."

She smiled at me and came up close to my lips. "What would it take for you to remember the real Lei-tao?"

"Well, let me see now," I teased her. "Maybe a little peck right about, uh, here," I said, pointing to my lips.

She leaned up and really *kissed* me. "You mean like that?"

"Yeah…say, have you been practicing? I don't remember the last 'peck' being quite so 'peckish.'" I chuckled. "And you didn't evaporate into thin air or explode into a red ball of dragon fire."

She laughed out loud. "Oh Cable, you always make me laugh! When you make humor, my whole self lights up! Were you always so gifted?"

"Naw, kid, it's the hurt inside that gives you the edge, you know. So you cover it up with humor. But then again, you—you, uh, immortals don't know about those things, I guess."

Then her face grew serious. "Please…the *Fen de Fuqin*…"

"Toggth told me I was to hand it off to him. Somehow, toots, you don't look like him."

"He's away preparing what is necessary to make the illusional synthesis. He will extract the inner key tablet, duplicate it for

272

later use and I will re-instate the golden capsule with the Tone of Creation." She stopped, looked up at me with those wonderful dark-brown eyes betraying a mystic innocence. "Besides, I wanted to see you again."

"Sure of that now? It took a lot of doing, waking up an errant knight and missing a boring late-night dinner with William Randolph Hearst just for openers—not to mention all the people who have died along the way." I took the capsule out of my pocket and held it in my palm, giving Lei-tao a glimpse of it. "Maybe we'd—we'd better make real sure you're who you say you are. One more of those well-practiced Red Dragon Lady kisses might convince me."

She approached me again. "But I warn you this time, mortal man," she grinned. "This one might give you the Curse of the Red Dragon Lady."

"Now, what in the hell could that be? And don't fool with my head, lady, I've had enough for one lifetime already and I'm not even thirty yet."

"It's that no human female will ever make you completely contented, for in knowing the kiss of the immortals, your soul will long for her all of your days. Do you want to take that chance?"

"C'mon, Lei-tao, let's get this thing over with. I've got a lot on my plate yet, in case you haven't noticed—including how to keep ravenous Ravna off my back until Toggth delivers me the dupe."

"Yes," she whispered. With that Lei-tao, the beautiful Red Dragon Lady, kissed me more deeply than ever before. In a flash of a second I saw red and orange and then black. When I opened my eyes to thank her for one of the best kisses I ever had, she was gone. So was the golden capsule.

I walked up the stairs to my little flat feeling a thousand eyes had been watching me all day. I hesitated at the doorway.

The door was slightly ajar, telling me I wouldn't be alone and the next surprise of the day was awaiting me. I drew my .38 and entered. There in my comfy chair with a low lamp light on him sat Nazar Ravna. "Surely, you were expecting me, Mr. Denning?"

I put my gun away and walked in. "Yeah, more or less."

"I don't mind telling you I've been hard put to keep track of you and the more important whereabouts of the *God of Our Fathers*. You *do* have the capsule on your person, I assume?"

I went over to my dresser that served as my wet bar and poured me a stiff gin without the tonic, lit up a cigarette and faced Ravna. "Wanna drink?"

"I could not stomach that putrid acidity you consume. No, thank you."

"Anyway, you assume wrong, Ravna. I don't have it on my person. And let's not play polite patsy here—your goons have been following me like I was their next breath—and you know where I was this evening."

"This little Oriental shape-changer puzzles me. And why does she risk herself by showing up in person when she could easily send that nasal jack-sprint who works for her?"

I put my tongue in my cheek. "Beats me, Ravna."

"But you know I wanted you dead from the beginning. I really can't abide miscreants like you, Denning. So, for the last time, let's get to it. I know you have the capsule. Hand it over to me and you won't die—at least—not just yet." He got up from my comfy chair. "So...let's have it..."

"I told you, Ravna, I don't have it. It's coming, but not today."

He went to the window and signaled down to the street. "I don't believe you. So, now, we have to do it the hard way—and *then* kill you."

Just then I felt a strange sensation, like a hand reaching into my suit pocket, depositing something. I checked out my pocket. A walnut-sized object lay at the bottom—the capsule! I didn't know exactly what to do, but I knew I didn't want to die at this particular time, so I darted for my open door and fled out into the hall just in time to see two of Ravna's mugs coming up— brass knuckles and all. Ravna followed me out. "Find the capsule, then leave him…almost dead…just a breath or two for another day, perhaps."

Out of nowhere something was slugging the two goons on the stairwell and they went crashing down to the bottom, unconscious. Ravna and I both looked at each other in surprise. "It seems we also have invisible company, Ravna—what's next?"

He pulled his gun. "Hand over the capsule or I'll just do it the crude, violent old-fashioned way ordinary gangsters employ to achieve their goals."

There was no longer a reason to withhold the capsule, since by some magic it had been placed in my coat pocket in the nick of time. "Yeah…sure…okay, Ravna. You win. And you also promised me some dough. Here's your precious golden thing—" I showed him the phony capsule.

"—of course." He reached into the breast pocket of his coat and took out an envelope. "Ten thousand for the finder's fee, but you may not live to spend it, Denning. I hate to be messy and leave tell-tale signs behind me." He reluctantly handed me the envelope. I took it.

"Just don't call me, okay—I really don't wanna hear from you for a couple of lifetimes at least, you weird fucking alien."

I handed him the capsule. He examined it. A knowing smirk went over his face. "Ah….thank you, Denning. You have delivered, at last. Why did your little Chinese virgin give it up so easily? It makes one wonder, doesn't it?"

"I think she likes me. Do aliens care whether or not they're liked?"

"Perhaps some but not all, just as some of us *are* aliens, but not what you think or how you perceive us. We look just like *you*." He approached me, his face growing taut. "And something I've always wanted to do to wipe off your snide, casual attitude, now that we're even." He slugged me hard and I hit the floor, stunned. But just then something pushed Ravna from the top of the stairs and he went tumbling down to the bottom where his two goons lay still out cold. I picked myself up and leaned on the railing, looking down at Ravna and his henchmen. He got up and stood swaying at the bottom of the stairwell, looking up at me. "You're dead, Denning…" he hissed.

"Aren't we all…?" I turned and went inside, nursing my chin.

"You need to select your friends more carefully," a voice said to me from the back of the room.

I turned to see the smiling little creature I had come to like. "Toggth! You old disappearing-act son of a gun! Thanks for saving my butt out there….yet again. Obviously you stuck the phony capsule in my pocket at exactly the right moment—just prior to my assured demise."

"It was close. Our sacred Lei-tao had barely given the precious to me. But I had been doing some advanced preparations and that's why I did not greet you earlier. Now all that remains is for the *Tone of Creation* to be inserted at the right co-ordinances and planetary alignments. Then all shall be restored."

"And on that day, Ravna and his weird Order of aliens will wake up to find that the duplicate has disappeared."

"Yes, that is the down side. There are many dangers yet for you to face, Cable. Not just Ravna. I sense others seek revenge upon you. Keep an eye on Jack Dragna and his clan. Somehow you threaten him."

"Maybe he's just sore because I got rid of a couple of his henchmen free of charge by throwing them off a fast-moving train."

"I will keep watch when I am able. But I also have much to do. So until we meet again, Cable Denning—a most exceptional human being."

"Thanks again, Toggth. And say hello to the beautiful and ever-gracious Red Dragon Lady."

"She is very strange around you, have you noticed? I have this feeling she is trying to find a way to be human woman enough to mate with you—or as you might say, be sexually intimate with you."

"Oh. Yeah, that…well, it's kind of my fault, Toggth. I talked her into a small human kiss one day. She seemed to like it, so each time we get together the kisses seem to be getting deeper and longer."

"That's precisely what worries me, Cable. She's not your kind. She'll throw herself out of cosmic balance if she pursues this playful desire of hers. And it's simply not the proper station for the honorable Red Dragon Lady, who, once turned angry, can evoke the likes of a demon."

"I'll do my share to prevent that. I'll try to watch my boundaries better, okay? Human males are like roosters, they wanna mate with every hen in the damn barnyard." I looked around. I realized I was alone and talking to myself. Toggth was gone.

Maybe I'd never know the truth about the in-famous *Fen de Fuqin*, the *God of Our Fathers*. It goes to show, no one really knows how old something like that was, or where the truth of it actually started to grow into legend. Surely, what I was dealing with had to be pre-Judeo-Christian, and therefore the Bible of the western world was but one stop-off of many, where the original essence got diluted to satisfy a group of men bent on ruling over another group of men.

And something as beautiful and simple as the wisdoms from the Cave of the Seven Truths? Where could that have possibly come from? To give dignity to the individual as well as the whole of creation, and that we *chose* to come here from other planets, solar systems or dimensions—and that this was the dream, and one day we will return because we're not native here. When you really stopped to think about those revelations that Lei-tao allowed me to witness on that day in the 'Cave', it was pretty astounding. That fortunate day not so very long ago.

COPS COME ON SALE SATURDAY NIGHTS

As Mario and I finished up duty the next evening, we were greeted by a couple of plainclothesmen in our locker room that I'd never seen before. "Mr. Angelo?" one of them said. "As soon as you've changed, will you report to Captain O'Malley upstairs?"

Mario and I looked at each other. "What for?" Mario mumbled, taking his uniform off. "I ain't got nothin' to do with you guys upstairs. In fact, you guys don't even know what us downstairs guys do."

"As soon as you've changed, Officer Angelo."

"Tomorrow, guys. I'm beat and I gotta go home to my son's birthday party."

Then one of the officers took out a pair of handcuffs. "I'm afraid this can't wait, Mr. Angelo." I wanted to interfere but the other guy took out a gun and held it on me. "Now, if you'll pardon us."

They took Mario, mandating me not to follow. I showered, got dressed and went flying up to the second floor and stormed O'Malley's office. He wasn't in, but his assistant said to check down the hall at Room #218. There was no lettering on the door, just the number, so I opened it. There sat O'Malley with Joe Lorena! "Sorry to bust in on you like this, guys. I'm looking for Mario Angelo. Some plain clothes goons brought him up about twenty minutes ago."

"Mr. Denning," Joe Lorena said. "I'm glad you're here actually. Please come and sit with us." O'Malley, who was a fat, dark-haired Irishman with squinty blue eyes didn't say anything. "This is a matter that does not concern you, but rather your fellow officer, Mr. Angelo."

"Yeah, I gathered that. Matter…what matter? What kind of a 'police matter' could a hard-working, family-loving guy like Mario possibly have? And yeah, I think it does concern me. I'm his best friend."

"He's been steppin' outta line," O'Malley answered, looking like he'd rather be at the fights than sitting in that chair.

"To put it bluntly, Officer Denning," Joe said, carefully measuring his words and keeping as formal as he possibly could, "your compatriot increasingly defies local police protocol in regard to certain establishments here in the city—namely, the well-established institutions of horse racing, gambling ships and the speak easy trade."

"Not to mention the crooks you have downtown. I speak up against law enforcement policy all the time—so what? I don't get it. If anything, I'm meaner than Mario when it comes to that. I hate the double-standard crap that goes on under the table. It's as corrupt on this side of the table as it is on yours, Lorena." I looked at both of the men. "You know it, I know it—and so does Mario."

"But *you* haven't contacted the State District Attorney's office and bandied around some names and incriminatin' evidence," O'Malley said.

"Son-of-a-bitch, Mario's done that? Why hasn't he told me?"

"Well, perhaps you've been elsewhere of late, Mr. Denning. You know, special leaves of absence and assignments for the department?" Joe Lorena winked at me. He knew…

"Yeah, I guess. But that still doesn't explain…"

"—I wouldn't go no further, lad, if I were you," O'Malley

279

spoke up. "Just leave it alone. Get outta here before I find a reason to put *you* in the clink!"

I looked at Joe. He nodded at me, urging me to agree with O'Malley and leave. "So where's Mario now?"

"He's being held…pending collection of more evidence," Joe said. Yeah, and I knew the kind of evidence these guys would come up with. Once they decided that someone was going over for nosin' around too much, they'd trump up the charges to make it look like treason and espionage all wrapped up in one.

Saying no more, I left and went down to the basement where the holding cells were…like cold, depressing, dimly lit walkways. I knew the cop at the desk and told him to direct me to Mario. I found him sitting in an isolated cell, his head buried in his hands. "Hey, pal." He looked up. "You okay? Those bastards didn't work you over or anything, did they?"

Mario got up and came over to the bars. "No, Cable, but I'm not okay. Thanks for coming. I couldn't take it anymore. Right here, within the force. It's like a disease."

"Well, it *is* a disease, old friend. Power, money and sex kinda make the world go around."

"Someone has to stand up, Cable. By the time Prohibition ends, we won't know the difference between the crooks and the legislature."

"It's already that way, Mario. Gangsters even wear uniforms…haven't you noticed? They don't want Prohibition to end—just yet, as I see it. Too much profit being made by too many. And when they legalize booze, keep your eye on the bouncing ball—just who owns it and who gets left out?"

"It's too late for me, Cable. I know you don't believe in heroes the way I do, pal. But you gotta be who you gotta be. Just like that day when you licked me in the junkyard. You coulda punched me to death, like they were yelling for you to do. But you didn't. Because you were being the decent guy you really are."

"Maybe. Or maybe my knuckles were just sore. Here I thought I was the one with all the guts, spilling 'em all over downtown, making a fuss to help untangle the corruption. But you, Mario, goin' way up over their heads—did you do it?—I mean, contact the State District Attorney?"

"Yep. I thought if I went higher up, the locals couldn't get at me so easy. I'm hoping a letter I sent two days ago with a whole new batch of connections, including O'Malley's bein' on the take in at least six bordellos and four speak easy clubs."

"Mistake, Mario. You can't go head-to-head with these guys. They're smart. They got big brains like Joe Lorena dictating policy from the top of the deck to the goons like Dragna and O'Malley. And so on down the ladder. It's gotta be more subtle. Why in the hell didn't you talk to me first, pal? For God's sake, we grew up together—you know you can trust me to go with you to the end of the line, you stupid cop chump."

"You weren't around, Cable. You've been gone more than you've been on the force lately, remember? And I needed to get the ball rolling. If we don't begin stopping this shit now, my kids'll grow up in a fuckin' sewer of goons on both sides of the law."

"As I said, it's already that way, Mario—what's gonna change it? You and me can bitch and stomp our feet up and down all we want, we can assassinate them accidently on purpose in the streets, send letters of evidence to the State District Attorney until the sky falls down—what's gonna change, huh? I ask you that. We've been out there in the trenches long enough, Mario—it's gotta come from the people, grassroots—then maybe the Feds will step in and clean up the whole mess. But it's the same in New York, Chicago, Detroit, Miami, Frisco—money's the name of the game, buddy—not law and order. And you can kiss the justice system good-bye in the same breath. Judges are paid off just like seals in a circus—throw 'em enough fresh fish and they'll clap their hands right there in front of you, barking a happy sound and twisting the words from a law book no layman can read."

"I don't know, Cable. You know me. I'm stubborn. There have got to be other cops who feel like I do. Why don't they step forward?"

"Maybe they will. In the meantime, they've got you as their poster boy of the month. Do you want me to call and tell Elena and the folks?"

"Yeah, that'd be great, Cable, thanks. And shit, I'm missing Danny's second birthday party tonight."

I left with a bitter taste in my mouth. When I got home I called Mario's wife Rosalie Elena and told her. She was distressed but said she wasn't that surprised because lately Mario had been obsessed with bringing down the Los Angeles Police Department like Tom Mix standing high on Tony's saddle, firing both six-guns at the bad guys.

Then I called Honey and told her I'd come see her tonight. She was delighted. I didn't mention anything about Mario but told her I'd see her later tonight and we could go home together. Then I cranked the phone on the wall to ask for Adora's number. I knew this would be one of the hardest tasks ever put to me. How do you tell a dame you're still nuts about that you can't see her anymore—or worse, someone who loves you so completely you almost stop breathing thinking about it? Elisa answered and summoned her daughter to the phone.

"I cannot believe. Is this *el chico qué me gusta mucho*?"

"Sure is, beautiful. Can you see me tonight? I'd love to take you for a drink or something."

"I like the 'something' I think better than just a drink, eh?" she laughed in her sexy little way.

"Well, I can't stay. I promised I'd ride Honey home tonight after she sings. My partner Mario's in jail for being an honest cop. That's also something I've got to deal with."

"*Oh, lo siento, querido.* When can you come?"

"How about now?"

"I get ready, mi amor. Pronto!"

She hung up and I felt like a heel. Not one stitch of this thing did I have my heart into. Yet I knew the only way Honey and I would have a decent chance, was for me to toe the line. If Adora had come just a few months earlier in my life, maybe before I met Honey, I think I would've spent my life with her. I don't know, just a feeling. Guys get feelings, then push them under the rug so the rest of the world doesn't get to see. Then if someone does, they deny it.

She was waiting for me at the front door to *Todo el Mundo.* She looked stunning, one of those naturally beautiful women you can't stop looking at because the beauty changes every minute, yet somehow stays the same. She was wearing a lovely tan, wide-pleated skirt with a light-yellow blouse decorated with sand-dollar shells. She wore an amber necklace and white low-heels with an off-white scarf over her shoulders. "God, but you're beautiful, Adora Moreno. Don't ever let me stop looking at you, kid," I said as I embraced her.

"Where we walk esta noche? *Tengo hambre…*can we get a 'snack', as you say—maybe at *El Tenemos?*

We walked four blocks to a cafeteria, the kind that bustled all the time with people and noise. But the food was good. We found a place by a stuffed peacock, which stood on the separator between two booths. We talked, laughed, ate and afterward I lit up a Lucky Strike and looked at the young woman I was about to ask to leave my life. But for once Cable Denning's words had no starting place, no way to get from point A to point B and still be honest with himself. So I started with the truth. Adora was quietly finishing her red gelatin desert. "Happy now?" I asked, searching out her eyes.

"*Muy, Querido.*" Then she finished, wiped her mouth with her napkin and took a deep breath. "I come to *la vida*, I greet my life, when I am with you, mi amor. I miss you so. You have many stories to tell—but only tell me what you wish. The rest is *no importante, eh?*"

I steeled myself. "Well, Adora. What I really came for tonight was to tell you I can't see you anymore." Her eyes froze onto mine. "While we were at the Hearst Castle, Honey and I decided—well, decided to tie the knot—you know, get married next December."

Her eyes misted but she remained erect, proud, sitting upright in her seat. "*Sí, mi amor,* I am listening…"

"I don't even know how to say this, Adora. I mean, I care about Honey a hell of a lot—but I don't love you any less— maybe even more sometimes. Yet I can't have two women floating around in my life, one a wife, one a mistress—"

"—*por qué no,* señor? Like I tell your Mamma, *'for always and always I love him…* I will be your *esposa segunda, secreta,* huh?"

I was touched so much that I bit my lip to keep the tears away. "I couldn't live like that, Adora…bouncing back and forth—"

"—you do *now,*" she answered me, putting a lie to any of my pretenses.

I ground out my cigarette in the ashtray. "Yeah, maybe I do at that. But Honey wants kids, you know, a nice house some-where, the times are booming and all—I don't have to tell you what it costs—and me, with a cop's wages. I'm even thinking of quitting the force to become a private dick."

"A private what?"

"A private dick—remember? A licensed detective who works for himself."

She laughed. "Yes, I remember, okay, but it does not mean what you say—it is what you give me *cuando estoy caliente*—when I am on fire for you."

I snickered. "Yes, that, too, Adora."

"Sí. So, *ahora*, you are going to leave me?" She asked in that straight matter-of-fact voice which essentially always crippled me. "And is this to be…*por siempre*—forever? And never again I shall look upon your beautiful, handsome face, *querido*? If this is true, mi amor, how come I do not see it in your eyes?"

Now she *was* making my eyes mist. "Because it isn't there, Adora. It's so damn hard. I just can't do it." I looked down at the table. "I just plain ol' can't do it! But on the other hand, if I don't I'll spend my life being banged from pillar to post—could *you* live like that?"

She smiled a beautiful Adora Moreno smile, somewhere between a sex goddess and Mona Lisa. "I am not born like you, Cable. I am born to love *soló un hombre*, one man, one kiss—you, *el hombre y su beso! Es bastante por la vida*. I wish no thing more, querido."

"That's great, Adora, but life doesn't always get measured out in happy, simple little doses. Sometimes they're big, massive chunks of stuff you gotta get down and digest—make it work because of a thousand things you don't even see coming."

"I cannot be confused for you, Cable. I only *love* you—and love you *only*—and always. What you decide for you…I cannot answer…I can only pray to *La Macarena de Esperanza* that she give me you in this life. *Entonces, es completo. Nada mas*."

In that minute I realized what a mess I had made of things. I didn't even have the guts to say good-bye to a nice, simple Mexican dame who happened to love me. But I had to save face, so I thought. "I'm not saying any of us can control our destinies all the time—or even some of the time—but I'm going to have to try, Adora. I owe it to Honey, I owe it me—and I even owe it to you—what if some young, handsome Mexican guy comes along and sweeps you off your feet. In a few months you'll forget me, huh?"

"*Recuerda, señor*, I've already had 'Mexican', *y no me gusto*—I did not like it."

We walked home in the cool of a Los Angeles evening. When we got to Adora's front door, we stopped. She put her arms around me and brought my face onto her lips. She kissed and caressed me until I thought I'd go crazy from wanting her. "God, I love your passion, Adora. But I can't—I've gotta go. Please…try to understand…I beg you, por favor—make us both strong!"

"Do you love me, Cable?" she asked, looking up into my eyes.

I didn't hesitate as the words spilled out of me. "I love you, yes, love you, Adora, and I adore you, yes, I adore you, Adora—I will never stop wanting you—will you know that—will you think of that when I can't be with you? No one will ever desire you more." I took her into my arms and clutched her to me. Then I turned and walked away.

CHAPTER 12

RADIO DAYS

The streetcar ride out to the *Bella Notte* was refreshing as I stuck my head out of the car window into the night breezes coming in from the sea. I couldn't get over how wonderful I felt after being with Adora. Even though everything I'd planned went afoul, still I was smiling on the inside and outside that someone could love me that much in this world.

Honey's bandleader, Johnny Pillar, had picked up a new trumpet player and when I entered, I could feel the energy heat up between Honey and this guy named Chet James. They had launched into a neat version of Berlin's *Blue Skies*, and by the time it got jumpin', Honey and James were at the top of their forms. The audience loved them and showed as much with tremendous applause and yells and shouts before people went back to smoking, drinking and talking at each other. In those days you could see the constant flash of silver flasks in the subdued light, out of which poured the pure alcoholic spirits that the house dare not legally serve. Since the *Bella Notte* was owned and operated by Dragna's gang, it seemed rather silly that one could go back to a little room by the kitchen, get your flask filled with rot gut alcohol, return to the main clubroom and distribute it into your glass—or the glass of the pretty señorita you were trying to get drunk in the hopes you'd get a benefit performance when you got her home.

I sat up front in our usual saved table. Honey came over to me with Chet James in tow. "Chet, this is another boyfriend of mine—Cable, this is someone I think I'm falling in love with—Chet James, trumpet player extraordinaire."

I got up and shook the nice young man's hand. "I was afraid of this. You see, Honey doesn't fall in love with her sidemen very often—but if you're it—then I guess I'll have to move

287

over. But it's swell meeting you and you play a great horn—Cable Denning's the name."

"Good to meet you, Cable. I hear you're a cop. Buzz is you're also quite a music lover…not to mention an admirer of good lookin' babes and, I guess, particularly if they sing."

"Well, you hit that one straight on, Chet. I'll look forward to hearing more of you—and seeing how your relationship with Honey Combes, Lana Loren here, develops."

He saluted me and left. "Cable…don't embarrass me…after all, I'm supposed to be an engaged woman only *pretending* to flirt with handsome young trumpet players."

"Ya coulda fooled me, lady." I took a swig from my drink and lit up. "So what's new?"

"Well, Charlie Chaplin informed me, as if we didn't know, that Virginia Cherrill is going to play the flower girl for *City Lights*. Hmmm…let me see…but he's having trouble getting the money he wants and the final ideas are undeveloped yet. It might take him another year to get it ready to roll."

"Lucky you didn't get it, then, huh? Just think, that'll give him all the more time to screw his leading lady so they'll know each other a bit better when it's show time."

"Say what you want, Cable. I still think that anything Chaplin does from here on out is going to be famous and classic. He's just that great of a genius." She took a drink and looked me over. "So what about your day?"

"Hmmmm….well, nothing too exciting…went to work, got to our locker, Mario Angelo got arrested, is now rotting in the police corruption jailhouse. Oh, and I had to say good-bye to a beautiful Mexican girl who was in love with me—"

"—Cable! Mario? Wha—what? What did he do?"

"Awww, nothing much, just sent a letter with inflammatory evidence to the State District Attorney's Office in Sacramento.

Seems he incriminated old Joe O'Malley, our beloved and crooked captain. Now he's on their shit list, and frankly, as I told Elena, I don't know how he's gonna get out if it without just plain quitting the force. But do you know what was even stranger? When I went upstairs to find Mario, here I walk in on Joe Lorena having a comfortable chat with big, fat, slovenly Captain O'Malley."

"You mean my Dad Joe Lorena?"

"None other."

"Gees, Cable. You're right. They're all connected. How can you work for all those slime-balls?"

"I can't—forever…"

"And what's this about saying good-bye to some Mexican babe you've had on the line for however long until I wanted to make an honest man out of you? And that's after I had to shoo away your Chinese Tantric sex-virgin."

"She's the nicest young woman you'd ever meet, Honey. I can't quite explain it, but it wasn't just a sex thing. I know this sounds corny, but I loved her spirit—a certain gentleness, or a grace, if you will."

Honey's eyebrows lifted. "Sounds to me you were falling in love with her. I guess I saved you just in time." She laughed. Honey had a way of never quite taking seriously the stories I'd tell her about other women. I don't think she believed most of them were true. "Speaking of which—all this talk of being a hybrid alien—it makes me worry that I won't be able to have children. I never thought I'd say it, but that'd just kill me, my lover man. Maybe they can come up with some other way?"

"Ehhh….we'll adopt an alien who looks just like you!" I quipped.

She laughed. "What'll I do if someday you're not around, Cable?"

Just then the bandleader summoned everyone back. Honey hugged me and left. The song she sang was most appropriate, considering her last statement. *What'll I Do?* Singer Grace Moore had introduced the song with John Steel in 1923, in the New Music Box Revue, when I first joined the force and I was dating Amanda Baxter. I was really hooked on that babe until I found out she and her Dad had a late-night thing going on now and then. I knew incest was much more prolific than one would like to think—certainly in Los Angeles—but when it's someone you care about…it, well, kinda hits home personally.

Honey sang the song with a poignancy I hadn't heard in her voice before. I wasn't sure whether that emotion was aimed directly at me, or the emotion pouring from the open wound she had just experienced when thinking that possibly she would never have her own children. Women are funny that way. And as if my soul didn't have enough punishment, after the applause, my lady launched into a dynamite delivery of *Someone to Watch Over Me*. Honey had sung it while we danced the first night I met her. It was the kind of song where the girl's vulnerability was something you were designed to mend, to make her feel loved and taken care of in this dangerous and nutso world of ours. And my girl sang it with class and feeling. *"Won't you tell him to put on some speed, follow my lead, oh, how I need…someone to watch over me…"* That part bothered me. Why was I dragging my feet? Why was I thinking about Adora half of the time and feeling inside that Honey would just one day suddenly fit into a routine life of boring everydayism with me? And that scared me. Suddenly I felt trapped and desperately fought in my mind to come up for air!

When we got home to Honey's place, Zelda was in the kitchen having a hot cocoa and invited us. The three of us sat at the little nook. I could see Zelda was trying to improve her female image. She had lost a little weight, was wearing some make-up and did her hair with a nice flapper flair.

"So…if it's still okay with Honey, will you take me out to that dinner and dancing you promised a long time ago?"

"It wasn't that long ago, Zelda—I've been a busy and troubled man—plus I'm getting married in less than twelve months."

Zelda looked at Honey and smiled. "Do you still want him—I mean, like forever after and all?"

Honey looked at me. "Yep, I'm afraid so, Zelda. You see, I have this weakness. It has to do with men who are honest, hot in bed and when they tell you the truth, they say it in such a way that you don't believe all of it. But you go along, because you know in the end, he'll be true to you."

"Boy, that's the kind of man I want." Zelda looked back over at me. "So? Are we on?"

"Sure, kid, why not? I've never been a romance coach before. Honey can come along for tips on the sidelines." I looked at Zelda. "When would you like to go?"

"When's your next night off?" Zelda said with great enthusiasm.

"In a couple of days. Both Honey and I have the same days off."

"I don't want to ruin your time together, you two—"

"—Oh, *go ahead*, Zelda. This rascal here may never volunteer again. Oh…besides I haven't told you yet," Honey said, looking at me. "I'm having that dinner with my Dad Tuesday night."

I winced a bit. After what I'd seen down at the station earlier in the day, I had lost a lot of respect for Joe Lorena. How could he be talking out of both sides of his mouth like most of the rats that lived in the sewers he hung out in? I looked at Zelda. "Well, young lady, it looks like you and I are on our own. So… how about Tuesday night?"

"Great! Swell! Thanks, Cable. You'll never regret it. I'm a good student. Can we go somewhere like The *Cocoanut Grove at the Ambassador* on Wilshire Boulevard? I hear the music there is outstanding. And they already broadcast a radio show directly from the nightclub, just like they're going to do at the *Bella Notte*."

"Ok, kid...I think they have some kinda special nights on Tuesdays, so we can go have a look-see." I looked at Honey. "So when's *your* great radio moment coming?"

"Next week is the maiden voyage, lover man. Hang on to your hats, it might be a bumpy night."

CUTTING UP THE RUG AT THE GROVE

Zelda Blodgett was one of those rare dames who could transform from bookworm into butterfly in three easy lessons. When I came to pick her up that Tuesday night I couldn't believe my eyes. There at the door stood this lovely dark-haired beauty in light-peach, red heels and a hair-do that started at her crown and swept slowly around in a swirl down to the nape of her neck. Just as exciting were two very large grapefruits slightly bulging out of that fairly low-cut peach gown. "Wow!" was about all I could say as Zelda greeted me.

"You like? Now, if this doesn't attract a man, what will?"

"I don't know. I think you've got all the flypaper in the world working for you tonight, kid," I said, hugging her as we walked toward the streetcar stop. She got a lot of looks on the whole trip over to the *Cocoanut Grove*. We got there early so we could get a good table. Walking through the lobby, it was like being transported to a tropical island...but then walking into the main room, there were leaning palms all over, placed between a massive collection of round and square tables covered in white table cloths...seating two to six people. There were dignified looking gentlemen standing around waiting to be of service, and one of them showed us to a nice table on a second level. All the tables around the very highly polished dance floor were already reserved. The band, led by a Ray West, launched into a nice Latin number, and so I escorted Zelda to the dance floor. And when I started teaching her some of my very basic Latin moves that I'd learned over the years, Zelda caught on like a trooper and before long we danced like it was old hat to her. We ate and laughed and I could tell she was having a great time.

"I've never had such a wonderful time in my life, Cable. Not even close. Thank you." Zelda looked at me in the candlelight provided at the center of our table and I knew she was beginning to feel things for me she shouldn't be feeling. "Of course, you realize at this point, it's proper for the damsel to fall in love with her charming escort, who also happens to be a policeman—who also happens to be the fiancée of my roommate."

"Yeah, let's not forget that last part." I took a drink of soda water and it tasted so bad I had to have a little booze in it. I reached into my pocket for my flask of gin. I started to pour it into my glass. "Want some?"

"What is it?"

"It's about 70% rot-gut gin. But it sure beats this bubbly shit."

"Sure, why not?" I poured a decent amount into Zelda's glass and she drank it all down in one gulp. "Wowee!" she exclaimed as her eyes crossed. Now some people can hold their alcohol real well, while others, well, they seem to have little tolerance and they become inebriated at the snap of the old flask cap. I learned after three drinks too late Zelda was one of the latter.

Suddenly she was very friendly. "Now, Cable, not only can I thank you from *across* the table, but I can be a little titsy-witsy fly sitting next to you, licking you with all my tongues."

"Well, thanks all the same, Zelda. But thanks from across the table's just fine."

293

"It is, eh? Well, maybe for you, but not for the fair lady who's dressed to the nines for you tonight. Did you notice a lot of guys were—were—hic! eyeing me all night?"

"Yep, sure did. And rightfully so, you're a dish out of those glasses and your old clothes—"

"—would you like to see if I'm still pretty with no clothes on? I'll bet you would. Men love naked women, don't they?"

I felt a bit uncomfortable. "Let's have one more dance and catch the streetcar home. I think I taught you all the good nightclub manners you're gonna need for a lifetime, kid."

"Now tell me, though, you'd love to see me naked, wouldn't you? And then you'd like to seduce me. But I couldn't let you. Because there'd be blood all over the bed." She burped and swayed a little in her booth seat. "I never told anyone, Cable—but I'm a virgin. You are the closest a man has—has—hic!—ever come to loving me. I would give myself to you if you promised you'd never tell anyone—I mean, not even Honey. She'd get pissed, I think…"

I got up as a slow song started playing. "C'mon, kid. One more slow dance to get you to breathe and it's home with you."

She gave me her hand and we made it okay to the dance floor. Then she snuggled her lovely and pungent hair into the nape of my neck, turning every few seconds to kiss my neck, which didn't make me feel any more the comfortable. "This… this is…dreamy, Cable…you holding me…in your arms…I could stay like this for—for—hic!—ever. Don't you just love the sexy Latin music? I swear, I'm…I'm going to buy a whole bunch of—of—Latin American records…will you dance with me at home in—in my room?"

"I'd like to, Zelda. I just don't think it'd be appropriate with Honey there and all."

"Honey doesn't have to be there."

"Oh, yeah she does. I don't want to cheat on her, Zelda. You

294

wouldn't want that, either, now would you?"

The music ended. "No…I suppose not…" I took her hand and we went to the coatroom and got our belongings. We walked out of the club into the fresh night air. By the time we got home it was about 1:00a.m. Wednesday and I had to get up early for work. I didn't want to wake Honey, so I stopped at the door to the cottage to say good-night to Zelda. "Cable… Cable…Cable…I had the best time ever! Are you sure you won't come in and dance some more with me? I promise I won't take my…my clothes off."

"Some other time, Zelda," I said, a bit perturbed. "You have a good rest—and you were great out there on the dance floor."

She waved a forlorn little hand at me. "Good night, good Cable…"

I turned to go when I saw Honey and Joe Lorena turning in toward the stairs. I went to greet them. "Well!" Honey exclaimed, a little drunk herself. "Are you coming from my roommate's evening out—or from her bed?"

"Well," I laughed. "Take your choice. It could've gone either way. Zelda's a hot number when she's got a couple of jiggers of gin in her."

"I could've told you *that*, Mr. Denning. You didn't screw her, did you?"

I started to walk away. I'd had enough of drunks for one night. "Good-night, Honey, Joe—"

"—I can't have babies, Cable," Honey blurted out after me. "Old padre here says I'm definitively a hybrid, like one of Zelda's flowers."

I looked at Joe Lorena. He shrugged his shoulders. "Can we talk about this tomorrow? I gotta get up in about three hours and go to work."

"Sure," Honey whispered half to herself.

I started down the walk. Joe quickly hugged Honey and ran to join me. "I suppose you don't really want to see me anymore, do you? I mean after you walked in on O'Malley and me yesterday."

I kept walking toward the trolley line. "You know, Lorena, I don't expect anything anymore. I used to think decency grew inside some people, like pretty little buds that became good fruit. But you know... the fruit somehow gets rotten inside most of 'em before it can really reach the sunshine. Your life is yours...your business, yours. But maybe someday I'll be able to bring down the likes of gangsters like you and Dragna. If you don't kill each other first, that is."

"Please—put that aside for a minute, Cable. It's about Honey. I think you're the best thing in the world for her. Please help her when this child thing comes up again. She may want to adopt, but you'll have to convince her."

"What's the alternative, Joe? One of your super-duper alien operations like you gave her mother?"

"Yes—and no. It's been perfected since then. It would really work now without endangering Honey. We could take your sperm—"

"—nothing humans make is ever perfect, Lorena. You're asking me to risk Honey's life for some stupid possibility she might have our hybrid kid?"

"It's *not human*, I remind you. Your future wife is half-alien like me. Her potential is staggering, Cable. Will you at least try to look at it like that? A baby from you two would be like a super-child in this world."

"I think we're doing okay right down here on earth. We've been able to produce an Einstein, haven't we...?" Suddenly I got it as my eyes locked onto Joe Lorena's. "That's why he came up with that *Theory of Relativity*, isn't it? He's one of you!"

"A hybrid, Cable—like Honey." I shut down. Nothing more

to say.

We reached the streetcar stop. "Well, good night, Joe…"

"How stupid of me. I have a car, I can drive you home."

"No thanks." I stopped and looked carefully at Joe Lorena. "Look, Joe…when I marry your little girl, I'm marrying a woman I love. Yeah, she'll make her own major decisions alright, but not without me. I don't expect much will come out of you and me. If Honey wants you around, it's okay with me. She has that right. But don't come to me looking for any sympathy just because we're legally related. You're a crook now and you'll always be a crook—so what if you're an expensive one? Or even an alien one? Some thugs just get paid more, that's all. Good night again, Joe." My streetcar came and I boarded. I sat down and looked back. Under the streetlamp I could see the lingering figure of Joe Lorena, some kind of man-being, lost in the middle of a foggy universe, very far from home.

And suddenly I, too, felt far from home. I didn't get off at my stop but kept riding the yellow car until it approached Olvera Street. I got off and ran the few blocks, desperate to get away, desperate to see her once more. There's a compulsion in humans that rips them out of thought into that place of action, responding to something they cannot define, yet are compelled to obey. This was such a moment in my life. It was about 2:30 a.m. when I banged on the front door of *Todo el Mundo*. Finally a light went on under the inside door. A figure in a robe came to the front door and opened it. I rushed into her arms. "Adora! Adora! I couldn't stay away! All the way here I was thinking about your beautiful hair and how it flowed like black silk—and that touching it, makes my whole body come alive! *You* make me come alive!"

"Oh, *mi amor!*" she cried as she clung to me. "Me, too! I miss you! I miss you…*yo te adoro, mi querido!*" We stood there glued together in the cool of that Los Angeles early morning, not speaking for what seemed the longest time. She ran her long, tapered fingers through my hair, stroking me, and when her warm lips sought out my own, I kissed her like it was the last kiss love would ever give us in this world and I would never have enough.

Finally, when I had regained my senses sufficiently, I closed the door behind us and we sat at her desk, she the travel agent, I the adoring customer, eager to be taken away by her on a new journey to paradise. "I—I'm sorry to wake you up. But I was out late at a club—"

"—*mi vida* begins when I see your face, *mi precioso*." Her eyes sparkled as she looked across the desk at me. "You are *mi sueño magnifico, mi obsesion*! Have you come to take me away with you—*por siempre*?"

"If I could, I would—this minute, now, here, Adora." I got up and went around to her side of the desk. She stood to embrace me. I put my hand under her robe and clutched her womanhood with my whole palm.

"Oh, señor, I bleed—I cannot make love—I mean, without *amor y sangre* all over *mi oficina*."

I withdrew my hand. "Oh, sorry. I'm just so pent up for you. I don't know how it happened. I was on my way home—and suddenly I had to let the streetcar keep going until I knew I could leap off and run all the way to you."

She drew me to her and clung to me until her body trembled. "*Yo te quiero, amor.*" There in those hours before dawn, as this beautiful woman and I stood together, I knew I could not speak of past or future with her. We could enjoy only these stolen moments, now…while we are helplessly suspended in time.

IT ALL DEPENDS ON YOU

What'll I do? For the next two days I wondered that and meandered through my job, thinking both about Mario

298

behind bars and Adora, imprisoned from seeing me as I knew her heart yearned to do. To some, life was cheap, but to me it was precious and I saw what it was like to grow old before your time, like my lovely and intelligent mother, swept aside by time to end her days in a ramshackle little house on the wrong side of town. Adora lived simply with the same kind of grace my mother had in her, a kind of spiritual compass, led always to a nobler kind of thought, a lofty version of the human condition where good always triumphed over evil—and love always won-out, because for them, it was the natural way of the cosmos.

The radio broadcast from the *Bella Notte* was a huge success. The National Broadcasting Company established a third network on the West Coast called the Pacific Coast "Orange Network". Through an AT&T phone wire to the greater L.A. area and fed through the main source in San Francisco, people coast to coast could hear Honey singing two of her blockbusters that night. *Brunswick Records* had recorded *Can't Help Lovin' That Man of Mine* and her newly popular hit, *It All Depends on You* with trumpet player Chet James. From the thousands of people tuned in that night, Honey received several offers to appear as a guest on various radio shows, hosted by popular artists of the day, like Rudy Vallee and Al Jolson. Yep, it looked like my *Golden Throat* had made it, and deservedly so, for her talent grew and soon Honey Combes metamorphosed into Lana Loren on the screen in a few old silents. Her management had decided to keep both names separate but active for the time being, so the singer thus remained unassociated with the movie actress.

I was just heading out for some fresh air and a smoke when a familiar voice called out to me. "Cable! Cable Denning!" I turned and looked into the semi-darkness of the club. "Here!"

I walked toward the voice and saw some light reflecting off the glasses of an older man. "Jedediah Penn! Damn! I was just thinking about you! Where've you been, you old son of a gun?"

We embraced. I hugged Polly Parker as well. "We've been off to China. Sorry I hadn't time to tell you. We have much to discuss. When can we meet?"

"Yeah, sure, soon….how in the hell did you happen to come into this club? My fiancée is that gorgeous creature up there with the honey-colored hair."

"You're kidding. Some guys have all the luck. We're staying a little ways down Wilshire Blvd. near Rampart at the *Bryson Hotel* and we came and ate here." He looked up at the stage where Honey stood. "My, my, such fine taste, Cable. Congratulations."

I agreed to meet with Jedediah Penn the next day after work and excused myself to take in that breath of fresh air and a smoke. There were a few other folks out with me, taking in the night air and watching the traffic whiz by. Suddenly I felt a tug on my coat sleeve. "Cigarette! Cigarette!"

I turned to find Crazy Jack nervously shivering in the night air. "Jack! Well, now, isn't this a strange night? First old Jed Penn—and now you showing up…the good penny that you are. How're you doin', old boy?" I did my usual ritual by taking a cigarette out of my pack and handing it to Jack. Then I tucked the rest of the pack inside his shirt pocket. "There. So, as I was saying, how are you?"

"I don't know! I don't know! Jack come—get lady out. Friend caught in jar behind—behind bars—look black to Jack—take lady and friend—go! But I don't know! I don't know!"

People were starting to watch and overhear Crazy Jack talk, so I grabbed his arm and took him around the corner. "Okay, now, Jack…talk! I've come to respect you too damn much, now—you nailed the Chinese thing. So I gotta listen up. So what's this thing about getting Honey out of the club? You've been saying that for months, but she just gets more and more successful here, Jack. I don't know what to think."

"I don't know! I don't know! Jack see trap—zap! Go, now…. take pretty honey-color lady! Take friend, pale in jail…but I don't know!"

"You mean Mario, my pal, don't you? I don't know what to do about him. You see, Crazy Jack, he stepped on the wrong toes and took it further than just a lotta patter, like I do. You see, I'm a coward. Mario puts his life on the line for what he believes in."

"I don't know! Crazy Jack say Cable get him out! Talk in court—make it short! But I don't know! I don't know!"

"What if I can't spring him legally? Whatta we do, an old west trick by backing up the wagon to the jail cell window and ripping it out? Yeah, that'd look swell on my impeccable police record now, wouldn't it?"

Jack began trembling again. "I don't know! I don't know! Friend die in desert heat—save him seat—talk him free…else Jack cry—old friend die! But I don't know!"

"Awww…Jack, I know life's a crap shoot. So I'll really take care of it this time, okay?" I reached into my pocket. I had a ten and two ones. I gave him the ten, leaving me enough for carfare home and some coffee on the job tomorrow. Jack smiled when I handed him the money and shook my wrist with both of his hands.

He laughed. "Cigarette! Cigarette! Good now….like good friend Cable." Then he dashed away toward the streetcar island out in the middle of the street.

Honey and I were driven home by an executive limousine that night. Most of the conversation had to do with booking Honey Combes into major shows and making sure her motion picture career did not conflict with the radio interests NBC might have in her. By the time we got to her place she had begun to drag and so we said our good-nights and I escorted her into the house and into her bedroom. I sat her on the bed and began to undress her. She looked at me with those lovely but tired blue eyes of hers. "Are you seducing me—or trying to be my valet, sir?"

I chuckled. "Tonight think of me as your old pal who happens to sleep with you when the going gets rough."

"Yeah, thanks. And it was rough tonight, wasn't it? But how did I sound? I mean, live is one thing, but on the air at the other end of a radio set—quite another, I imagine."

"Well, you sure moved some of those NBC guys. And at least one of them was at the far end of a radio receiver. I think you sounded great. I never heard you sing *Can't Help Lovin' That Man* before like *that*. I think you got Helen Morgan beat, and she's good."

She put her toes up under my chin. "You always say the right things, Cable. But I do believe I sang the hell out of that tune tonight, know why?"

"Tell me, *Golden Throat*."

"Because I have a man I love to sing it to. How many men do you know support their women as you do me, huh? That's why it's true, Cable—you *can* come home as late as can be, because without you here, it's not a home to me—anymore. I can't wait until we have our own house. God, wouldn't that be wonderful…a place that's got just the two of us written all over it?"

"Yeah, babe. By the way, I went to get some air tonight and ran into Crazy Jack—you remember the guy we took the streetcar ride with—"

"—yes, what about him?" I slipped her dress off.

"Well, he's still alarmed about you working at the *Bella Notte*."

"Crap, Cable, he's still on that? Every time he warns us I get more successful there. It's a gold mine for us, honey bug."

"It's—it's just that he's been so right about everything else—"

She got a bit irritated with me. "—so he can be wrong once, right?"

I didn't say anymore but finished undressing her and tucked her into bed. I did the same for myself and slid in next to her. "Good-night, babe," I whispered, kissing her on the neck. She moaned once and fell asleep.

MARIO'S JOURNEY TO HELL

Immediately after work the next day I went upstairs to see O'Malley. He wasn't particularly glad to see me, but he didn't kick me out and continued reading the newspaper while I talked. "Captain…you know why I'm here. Sooner or later you've gotta give Mario Angelo a hearing. He's got rights, you know."

"Does he, now?" the policeman responded smugly from behind his newspaper. "I'm seein' traitors have *no* rights, Denning. You're a loud enough wheel, but you don't go around submittin' State's Evidence." He pointed to a file at his left hand. "Here. You be takin' a look at the top letter to Sacramento. This'll tell ya how your so-called friend intended to expose some upstandin' citizens—not to mention upbraidin' the very heart of this department itself now, man."

I read Mario's latest letter to the State District Attorney that had obviously been intercepted by the cops before Sacramento could receive it. There was no postmark on the envelope. It mentioned half of the big boys downtown, about a third of the higher ranking members of the Los Angeles Police department—and of course, Dragna and his organization. "Well, it's all here, Captain. So who isn't savvy to what's written here?"

"My point, Denning. You're a good Irishman, and a fellow police officer. With us it's safe, now, ya know. But out there in the bloomin' world? It might be misconstrued—as—as an imaginable truth, now, couldn't it?"

"I want to represent Mario at a hearing, assuming he gets one."

O'Malley looked at me strangely, his eyes widening a bit. "That'd be professional suicide now, that would, Denning. You'd be takin' sides against the hand that feeds ya."

"We grew up together, O'Malley. Don't you have any allegiances to friends?"

"Not ones a-twitterin' on the wrong side of the tracks, Denning."

I thought fast. "I'll make a deal with you. I'll make it look like Mario did all of this because he has been under a lotta pressures lately. And I'll suggest a leave of absence. The thing will cool down after a while—and bingo! everybody forgets."

O'Malley reflected, his beady little eyes darting around the room. "You can do that? If ya can, lad, you'll be coverin' up the wound before it can fester. I'll requisition a hearin' and you would serve as what might be called a *lay counselor*."

I thanked O'Malley and ran downstairs to talk to Mario. He was less receptive.

"So you're making me back away, Cable—you're making me appear to be some idiot weakling from the scum-streets we came from! Are you selling me out, Cable?"

"I'm trying to save your butt, Mario. Look, if I get you off by just telling them you've been under a lot of pressure lately and maybe you were a bit hasty in writing—"

"—but that's not the truth, Cable! All of my life I've known you as the one person I could count on to tell the truth—yeah, what happened to the truth guy—"

"—Mario! In this case, *truth doesn't matter*—they don't wanna hear it! And if I don't get you that leave of absence so you can go back home to your family, celebrate Danny's birthday, love your beautiful wife and be home for a month or so—"

"—okay! Okay! But I won't quit, Cable. Sooner or later, I'll rise up again with that banner of 'right' scribbled across my chest. We both know I've got to do this, and I won't stop until the people who support these bastards realize how bought and sold they are."

"And I'll do it with you, pal," I laughed a nervous laugh. "I told you, Mario, I'd go the distance with you—all fifteen rounds. But we gotta bide our time…and watch our moves. Someone is waiting for you around every corner, so someone *else* has gotta look out for your ass."

He reached for my hand through the bars. "You are my friend, Cable Denning. I won't forget what you're doin' for me."

"Now there's one more thing I gotta know. Where did you mail your second letter from?"

"Here, at the postal drop. Why?"

"Because it never left the station. I saw it on O'Malley's desk. He had me read it—and…the envelope had no postmark. They intercepted it—"

"—damn, Cable, that's a federal offense! Tampering with the U.S. Mail. Shit, man, and you said nothing? How in the hell am I ever gonna—"

"—I told you the whole house of cards was rotten, Mario. For the present, let it be. We'll find other ways, okay, pal?"

He calmed a bit. "Sure, Cable, sure…I just can't stand injustice…"

The hearing room was crowded. About twenty upper-crust cops and half as many hoodlums sat quietly with their hats on their laps as Judge Henry Wyndott entered. Everyone stood. Wyndott was a slender white-haired man with a thin face and piercing blue eyes that looked at you over clear spectacles. "All be seated," he announced in a low-baritone that filled the room. He looked down at the papers in front of him. "This hearing concerns the matter of Mario Ferruccio Angelo, a sworn police officer and six-year veteran with the Los Angeles Police Department, and a filed complaint by his superior officers that claims he acted out of duress and emotional instability in writing a letter containing erroneous information to the State District Attorney's Office, has been submitted to me." He looked up from his glasses. "As such, this hearing is not an indictment, judgment or criminal action suit against said Mario Angelo, but a hearing to ascertain Mr. Angelo's competency in writing such a missive. It also brings to light the question whether or not Officer Angelo is sufficiently qualified to continue at his present post as patrol officer for the City of Los Angeles." He then glanced over at me. "Not as attorney in defense, but providing remarks on Mr. Angelo's behalf, is fellow officer Cable Denning, also with the department since 1923. Please step forward, Officer Denning....I will now entertain your remarks regarding the issue at hand." The judge sat back and folded his hands, awaiting me.

Everyone became dead still. A small lump stuck in my throat. I knew I was winging this one and had to rely on my gift of gab to pull it off. "Thank you, Your Honor. I really don't have very much to say in response to this formal complaint made by Mr. Angelo's superiors except to mention Mr. Angelo's track record of consistent and loyal devotion to the department and the people of Los Angeles for the past six years." I looked around the room. He had arrived late, but in the very back row I spotted Joe Lorena. I just wondered what he could've cooked up for this breakfast show. "To those officers mentioned in this complaint who hail from what we patrolmen call *the bums upstairs*,' you may have forgotten what it's like to be in the trenches every day of your professional life, fighting not just crime, but being there at the aftermath of an accident, arbitrating domestic battles and violence, picking dead people off the street and propping them up against a wall until the meat wagon comes, helping a once-beautiful young woman stagger across a street because life made her a drunk and she's been raped so many times it doesn't matter anymore. Yeah, sometimes the privileges of higher office insulate our superiors from the real world out there." I walked over to where Mario was sitting, looking up at me with large, admiring eyes. "Mario Angelo and I grew up in the mean streets of East L.A., where you got beat up for just walking to school, or disagreeing with the block-bully, or a gang member from across the river who just happens to have a grudge against you, or someone who wants to bash your head in because he doesn't like your looks." I surveyed the room. "A lot of you in this hearing room today came from that side of the tracks. Some of you, like Mario and me, decided to weigh in on the side of the law because we didn't want our kids growing up as hoodlums, or poverty sealing off our fates until the end of the line. And there was hope that justice would be served when we caught the bad guys. Others chose a different path, one where you could shortcut the way to a quick buck at the expense of the common fellow. It seemed to them that crime *did* pay and poisoning people with cheap booze, laced cigarettes, or collecting extra dough on a laundry route, running a bordello or selling pretty white girls off the streets for import to Asia…were okay—stock-and-trade for the other chosen profession. So, you see—"

"—Mr. Denning, with all due respect to your articulation, aren't you going about this the long way around—please stick to the immediate concerns," Judge Wyndott interrupted me.

"Yes, I apologize, Your Honor. So…someone like Officer Mario Angelo, seeing both sides of the coin, and also observing that cops and thugs had a crossover line where they did business together—" A big complaining noise arose from the attendees. "—Mr. Angelo understandably became very frustrated. Since his immediate superiors would not address this double-dipping problem, Mr. Angelo, in desperation and anger, went above the heads of local government and chose to ascertain certain facts and mail them to the State District Attorney's Office. Now…that in itself seems fair—after all, it's a free country, ain't it?" Snickers sounded around the room. "Well, not quite. We're *not* free to do exactly as we like in this world. We're *not* free to say the whole thing stinks and we're—"

The judge rapped his gavel down for the second time. "May I remind you once again, Officer Denning, this hearing is a not a soapbox for your personal opinions. Stick to the facts, *if..you.. don't..mind*." At this there arose a loud sound of approval.

"Your Honor," Mario surprised the hell out of me by standing up. "May I address this assembly? I believe I still do have that right."

"It's unusual, but proceed, Officer Angelo," the judge answered.

I sat down and took a quick look at a worried Joe Lorena. "We have come to live in a land of *disproportionate privilege*…I quote John Adams. You people here have it all wrong—*I'm not the man you should have on trial here*—it's the rotten racketeer over there, sitting comfortably with other racketeers. You call this a hearing. I call it judge and jury in the form of a few men whose self-interests may be challenged by my probing into their illegal and illicit affairs—"

"—Your Honor, I protest the tone of these proceedings," Joe Lorena sputtered as he stood up.

"I was also thinking in that direction, Mr. Lorena. However, I shall allow Officer Angelo to finish his point, whatever disgrace he may bring upon the moment or parties either present or not in this courtroom."

"Thank you, Your Honor," Mario answered. I was proud of him. I could tell he had been reading a lot, boosting his fact lists and dangerously discovering the marital underbelly between Los Angeles politicians and thugs who helped dictate policy.

"Such a mockery puts at risk, not just me, but the many thousands of hard-working honest citizens out there who require fair representation for the taxes they pay. As a cop I've seen them before, and I detest this better-than-thou attitude of roasting the pig on the fire and slowly turning him until he is well cooked and ready to be eaten. Then he becomes harmless, and his voice stops speaking truth. Why? Because he's seen the other end of it, the knife in the back, the bullet hole in the head while crossing a street, the poison in his drink at the speakeasy." The room had drawn silent. "I'm a father of young children. How can fairness be established for ourselves and our children if we ourselves are not accountable for our actions when we know we're violating *ten* laws for every *one* we keep. Please…don't turn this hearing into a witch-hunt to discredit an honest man whose worst crime was believing that most leaders are law abiding. It is true, the pressures on me during the past few weeks have strained my ability to think clearly, but—"

Then Joe Lorena stood up. "If I may, Your Honor, bear witness?"

Old Wyndott seemed to know Joe Lorena. "Yes, Mr. Lorena, you may step forward and bear witness…"

Joe came down the aisle, through the little swinging door and onto the floor beside me. "An officer with Officer Angelo's obvious integrity makes it appear as if his observations and subsequent actions seldom result in mistakes in the field of duty. Therefore, if I may, and out of complete respect for Mr. Denning, who has spoken most admirably as well here today—I would like to suggest that this hearing be a simple matter of realizing Officer Angelo has become overwhelmed in the field of duty over an extended period of time and is deserving of a paid hiatus of no less than thirty days."

"Thank you, Mr. Lorena. And so it is, I concur. I hereby order Officer Mario Angelo to be suspended from active duty for a period of no less than thirty days and no more than sixty, pending a review upon his scheduled return. This hearing is dismissed." And the gavel went down hard with a sound of finality.

There was a big silence and people began to file out of the room. Mario scowled at Lorena. "Well, Lorena, I see you helped me pull my foot out of my mouth, didn't you? Did you ever stop to think I might like it that way?" Mario admonished Joe.

"Not really. It was already decided, gentlemen. I just didn't want either of you to embarrass anyone else or get into it any deeper than you already are. Moral and ethical issues of this sort are sticky and can snag one like flypaper, if you will. You've got to keep watch over your shoulder, you know." Then he walked away to join Dragna's gang of finely dressed thugs.

I walked over to Mario. "Well? That was the most eloquent I've ever heard you talk, buddy boy."

"Thanks, Cable. They shot me down, didn't they? Well, at least it gives us time to regroup. And I'll really enjoy the paid time off with Elena and the kids. When I looked around the room I couldn't believe how many cops and thugs really do sleep together."

"And they're all making a profit," I said in a low voice. "C'mon, Mario, let me buy you a late breakfast."

"Oh, Officer Denning—may I see you a minute?" Judge Wyndott called. I walked over to the bench. "Interesting style...has it ever occurred to you to get yourself schooled and become a legal mouthpiece for the force? Your approach has a refreshing 'ring' of integrity—It might make a difference to a divided jury."

"Thanks, Your Honor. But you heard it right, I'm a trench rat like Mario. Someone has to be out there rooting out the bad ones, eh?"

He did a half-laugh out of the side of his mouth. "Yes—you've got a point *there*. Well, good luck, son." He exited down the stairs into his chambers.

LAKE BOTTOM PROPERTY

That night I stood at the main entrance to the *Bryson Hotel*. The ten story building was structured around a large central courtyard…making it look like two towers. The main entrance was flanked by two pedestals with a pair of lions on each, holding a decorative plaque with the Hotel's name. Inside was decorated with cut-glass chandeliers, Italian marble stairs, nice plush carpeting and richly upholstered mahogany furniture. The tenth floor was dedicated to a ballroom, billiard room and 4 loggias with great views. It is said that the builder spent $60,000 just on the top floor with fine art, rare plants and furnishings. A good chunk of money especially for 1913. It was the only high-rise around until about half a dozen years ago. I knocked at #412. The door opened. Polly Parker welcomed me in, said she was going out for a little air and since I was there, would I watch over Jedediah for a while.

"Cable! Cable!" the old man said with a wonderful enthusiasm from his wheelchair. "We have much to talk about. But first, I've been dying to know—how did things go with the Red Dragon Lady and obtaining the you-know-what?"

I told Jedediah the whole story and he sat as enthralled as a schoolboy being told a bedtime yarn. When I had brought him up to date, he refreshed my drink and I settled back with a freshly lit Lucky Strike. "So now…you say you've got some new stuff for me?"

He looked at me with a deep, warm smile. "Yes, but first, I must ask you whatever happened to that—that exquisite

Latina woman you brought with you on the train. *Adora*. I have thought of her often, Cable. She is an extraordinary creature. Matter of fact, in just the few moments we exchanged conversation, I found myself falling in love with her."

"Well, that made two of us, Jedediah. But since I'm going to marry Honey in December, I had the painful mission of telling Adora I couldn't see her anymore."

"I am very sorry to hear that. How did that work out?"

"Not so well. I botched it from the beginning because my heart wasn't in it. Then, in a weak moment, in the middle of the night I went running to her. You ever experience the feeling? Like nobody else will do?"

Jedediah Penn smiled again. "Oh, yes, yes…I have. I was rather hoping the two of you would merge." He reflected quietly, his hand shaking a bit from a slight palsy he had developed. "One wonders whatever happens to beautiful women like that. Does the rest of the world see the layers of beauty and grace? Or is it likely that most men will see her only as an object of desire?"

"I don't know, Jed, old boy. But I do know if Honey hadn't come along first, I think I would've spent the rest of my life with Adora. And I'm not even the marrying kind!" I laughed, trying to conceal some of the pain I felt about Adora now being out of my life. I cleared my throat and took another swig from my drink. "Okay, now, I'm all ears about your Chinese trip and how it all fits in…"

Just then there was a rap at the door. "Yes?" A second rap came. "Just a minute, please." I instinctively drew my .38 as Jedediah wheeled himself to the door. I dropped back to a corner of the room. Three fairly tall young men in their late twenties, maybe early thirties, stood at the threshold. "Yes. What can I do for you?"

One of them spoke with a slight Italian accent. "Signore

Penn. I am Father Carlo Tortelli. May I come in?"

Jedediah backed off in his wheelchair and admitted just the one man. The other two remained outside as guards or sentinels. Father Carlo Tortelli was very handsome and clean-shaven. One could tell immediately he was well educated and articulate. He had no bad mannerisms and seemed to be sincere. I came out of the shadows as I put my gun away. "This…this is my friend, Mr—"

"—Cable Denning—yes, I know much about you, Mr. Denning," he said, surprising both Jedediah and me. "We both had a mutual acquaintance—one *Isaiah Damianos*?"

"Oh, yeah, I hear he got bumped off. Too bad, I kinda liked the guy, at least once I was sure he wouldn't be kidnapping or doping me up anymore before we could have a decent conversation."

He approached me and we shook hands. It was a good handshake. "You are famous in the *Amadis*, our Order at the Vatican. We are sorry you could not deliver the *God of Our Fathers* to us."

"Well, it wasn't a matter of the highest bidder, you know. Considering I put my life on the line and ran into some pretty mean dudes, it was hardly worth it all."

"We're not bad guys, I remind you. Our procurement would have been for research and preservation of the golden capsule—"

"—c'mon, Tortelli. Don't stand there and tell me your so-called *Church* isn't as political and power-hungry as your competition." He didn't reply, just looked at me and then at Jed Penn.

"Anyway, too bad. The Church would have paid you handsomely. Now it's lost to us. Those creatures are truly Devil-sent and control the politics and money flow of the world."

"You mean the old *Oculus Pyramis Mandatum*? Yeah, they're

about the worst I've come across in my short twenty-nine years. But I'm sure the Vatican comes in there somewhere as a close second, now, wouldn't you agree, Tortelli?"

"Even if that were so, we as a race are lost without all the original pieces in place."

"Don't be so sure all is lost." I lit up a cigarette and smugly looked over at Jedediah. "Dr. Penn here will tell you substance has a way of, well, shall we say, coming and going? Nothing is permanent, agreed?" He nodded. "So perhaps it would not be surprising if one day the 'creatures' you spoke of wake up to find their precious *Fen de Fuqin* simply—poof! vanished into thin air."

I could tell I had piqued Father Tortelli's imagination. "*Fen de Fuqin*. So few know it by that name. Could this be? And if so, that would indicate that what they now covet in their vaults is—is perhaps, ah, perhaps—"

"—a shadow of the real thing," Dr. Penn interrupted. "If I may, Cable here told me of certain actions that transpired between a certain Red Dragon Lady and himself. She's a shape-changer and one of those ultra-dimensional creatures you folks call *angels*. She says the real thing belongs in its proper place, hidden one dimension above us, carrying and sounding the *Tone of Creation*."

Father Tortelli went white. "Mio Dio!" he said as he crossed himself. "Then it is true. The *God of Our Fathers* pre-dates any of our known civilizations."

"Yes, Father," Penn continued. "You people are newcomers, the Jewish meanderings that resulted in the Old Testament, the legends and myths created around the famous 'B.C.' epoch— all new stuff compared to this magnificent cornerstone of the tones that created Creation itself!"

The priest thought for a minute. "Supposing the capsule is in its rightful place. Then there would no longer be reason to seek it out—"

"—for a museum piece or another trinket tucked away in the bowels of the Vatican," I said, knowing how the Catholics were great collectors of such memorabilia.

"Let her be now," Jedediah spoke up. "When something is home, where she belongs and balance is restored, then it is time to quietly bless that moment and move on, gentlemen."

"There *is* one catch, you know," I said. "On that day when the so-called *Tone of Creation* is restored to the golden capsule, the microfilm destroyed, and the phony replica vanishes, I suspect there will be a wrath let loose upon the world. I have a feeling this 'Order' of aliens or whoever they are, does not take kindly to betrayal."

The three of us looked at each other. "Indeed, it is a frightening prospect. But one must ask *why* they sought the *Fen de Fuqin* in the first place. Surely, not as a Chinese souvenir," Dr. Penn said. Then he looked up at Father Carlo Tortelli. "Tell me truly, did you intend to simply lock the capsule away in safe-keeping—or do you have laboratories—and would you have experimented in search of its secrets?"

"I would suggest the latter. Many secretive objects have been scrutinized, studied and implemented through scientific experimentation. By virtue of its alleged power, it only makes sense the Church would wish to delve into the essence of the *Fen de Fuqin*," Tortelli commented.

"In my humble opinion, gentlemen, therein lies the rub. You do remember the *Photonos, Audianos* bit, don't you?" The priest looked stumped. "The God of Light got together with the God of Sound. Their togetherness was supposed to spell out the origin of creation, plus a whole lot of other crap I don't comprendo—"

"—perhaps, if you'll allow me, Cable," Dr. Penn spoke up. I let him take the floor. "First of all, Father Tortelli, have you ever seen the *God of Our Fathers*?"

"No. I've only read vague descriptions denoting its value and complete uniqueness."

"Very well, then. Let me review for both of you. Originally, this timeless, ageless object was not in any kind of physical form. Nor is it to this day, really. Before our traceable history of '*Creation*' occurred, there was an earlier 'Creation', but it did not place the created creatures as *beloved of the Father*, so the legend goes. So when Creative Intelligence wished to personify and spread its seed into form, it favored the *human* model and thus created the Adamic prototype. But the original and much older creatures, not favored by their Creator, became angry and jealous that God had chosen this silly humanoid to express Himself within. The resentment thus built up, evil came into being through the serpent, the takeover of the female principle…what we know as Eve's temptation by the serpent…subjecting the male ultimately to a subservient role. Sex became a power tool for the survival between Heaven and Earth. Then came the ultra-dimensionals and the extra-terrestrials who saw the flaws in the armor of Adamic man, so to speak, and took advantage…obliterating or breeding out the original creatures in favor of the now lesser *Homo sapiens*."

Jed Penn took a deep breath and looked at both Father Tortelli and myself. "Many thousands of years went by and the original Blueprint for Creation remained in a nebulous fourth-dimensional, non-physical form. But about eight thousand years ago a three-dimensional replica was made of it by a very ancient race that happened to be what today we would call the Chinese. You see, the Chinese arrived here on earth as slaves for a superior race of peoples many thousands of years ago. There were several alien visitors at that time, using slaves to mine the riches of the planet. Because there was a lot of slave-stealing among the different mining concerns, each group that arrived created a unique size and *color* of modified humanoid. Thus for one group it was black, tall and muscular… *Negroid*, another was tan-brown and of slighter build, while others were red-skinned. Among the oldest were the yellow slaves. Some synthetic humanoids were called *greys*. White-skins were the thinkers and moralists. They were utilized in many different professions because of their versatility. Some were scientists, mathematicians, engineers, artists—and some, hard-working grunt slaves."

"You didn't mention *white* slaves," Tortelli commented.

"That's because they came later and were horribly genetical-ly altered to resemble their white masters. It was a failed exper-iment from the beginning—but I'm getting ahead of myself."

"Lucky it's a big universe with a lot of room for mistakes, eh?" I quipped, looking out of the hotel window down to the street below. Of course none of it seemed real to me. I had suspended belief so much in the past few months that I really didn't have any idea what I believed.

"There was one very brilliant Chinese whose name comes down to us as *Qin shi Tai Kang*. He reportedly possessed great knowledge of transposition of matter into spirit and vice versa. When his progenitor race discovered the original *Fen de Fuqin*, it resided at the center of the known universe in a timeless, ageless zone known as *The Forever*. Now mind you, none of this was written. As in the Chinese language to this day, it is *symbols* that represent the words. Qin shi Tai Kang knew this and through revelation and divination, was able to dupli-cate in vibrational form, the meaning of the *Fen de Fuqin*. This miraculous piece of doing not only told of Creation's origin itself, but *why* Creation occurred in the first place! Through his exceptional alchemy and magical powers, Qin shi Tai Kang fashioned a replica out of pure gold and 'borrowed' some of the direct energy of the original gyroscope of the cosmos to animate it with equal power and access to its parent."

The priest was transfixed. He stood in the middle of the room shaking his head in utter dismay. "How can such things be? Not even the *Adamos Texts* speak of this."

Jedediah reached to his little stand for a glass and took a sip of water. "So, to make a long story short, this precious was kept in sacred fashion in Qin shi Tai Kang's dynastic clan until he could no longer perpetuate his life. Before he left, however, he fashioned some magic lotus seeds. One of those seeds would give birth to a female protectorate of the capsule, the immortal and sacred goddess, *Nymphaea Nelumbo*. So humans couldn't get their hands on it, he wisely hid the precious on a dimensional plane once removed from this one. The lotus seeds were planted at the bottom of a dry Chinese lake and every time the drought was broken and the rains came, the Red Dragon Lady would be re-born from the lotus and stay in human form long enough to check on things and make sure all was well. If she did not go back to the bottom of the lake when the waters receded, she would be doomed to remain until the next cycle."

I was thinking of Lei-tao and realizing what a really extraordinary being she must truly be! For being such a babe and all, it was hard for me to imagine that she was possibly many thousands of years old. And she wasn't even a human—but some kind of hybrid between a plant pod and a goddess!

"So the *Fen de Fuqin* remained for many centuries undisturbed. Then a mischievous group of evil beings, the *Erggarath*, discovered by accident its whereabouts and stole it. The most powerful single Order on earth, the *Oculus Pyramis Mandatum* wrested it from the *Erggarath*. What no one knew at the time, however, was that if the capsule itself were confiscated, the core of it, known as the *Tone of Creation* could not follow. Therefore, no matter how one might try, without that property, the secrets cannot be ascertained by mortal means. So the Order did the next best thing. They microfilmed the exterior content of the golden capsule, which of course was a series of hieroglyphic-like symbols, and etched it onto a golden replica that contained every single detail of the capsule's communicative symbols."

"So who stole the capsule from the Oculus?" the priest asked.

"Ah, that would have to be my little Chinese girlfriend, Lei-tao," I said. "She's kind of the Virgin Mary of the Oriental set, pure, untouchable but, uh, shall we say, having the pre-possessing nature of a curious woman. Then, of course, I never evoked her wrath, which I hear gives her the reputation of someone you don't wanna be around for a few hundred years."

"So, Mr. Denning, you obtained the capsule from this Red Dragon Lady?" the priest inquired.

"Yeah, in a sort of roundabout way. Then a duplicate was made by one of her very clever little elves and I gave that to Ravna. Now we're all caught up. Isn't that nice? So, now all we have to worry about is the fury that will be set loose on us when the guys back at the ol' Oculus get the bad news they've been duped."

"Indeed," Dr. Penn mused. "Indeed…well, looking on the brighter side, maybe it's getting near that time for many of us to cancel out of the old earth plane existence anyhow. What do you say, Cable?"

"I don't know. I think I'll have to cross that bridge when I get to it. I'm overwhelmed enough. What about you? Well, Father Tortelli, did you find Dr. Penn's tutorial a bit on the thick and unbelievable side?"

He laughed lightly. "Yes, I—I guess you might say that. It's not exactly a story one would hear every day now, is it?"

"No, it ain't…so savor it…you may never hear one like it again. Now that the *Fen de Fuqin* is safe and sound back home, what's your next step?"

"I cannot say. I will report exactly what you have told me here. I personally think it's resolved and we should make no further effort to procure the object—even if we could."

"I hope your superiors…feel the same way, Father Tortelli," Jedediah mused. "It would be tragic for a new search to get underway. It is always costly in many ways, not to mention the people who die needlessly on such a quest—more or less like the search for the Grail, isn't it? An endless, ruthless crusade—and for what? Plunder? Glory? History?"

Jedediah and I shook hands with Father Carlo Tortelli and let him out into the hallway where his two companions awaited.

"Son-of-a-bitch, Jedediah—where do all these people come from? It's like we've got no secrets from *anyone!*"

"We don't. Secrecy in the universe is also an illusion. Come on, Cable, relax...and enjoy the evening. It's later than you think."

He had me draw up a chair closer to him and spoke in low tones. "I saw the lake, Cable!" he whispered. "It really does exist. The area is beautiful, with green plains, meadows, rolling foothills to the East—and dozens of lakes, really. But there is one about two miles from *Qinghai Lake*—one that strangely goes dry, mysteriously drains away its waters, then when the rainy season is abundant, refills." He motioned me to go to a dresser and open it.

"That strange greenish thing." I took out a roughly disc-shape seed pod about the size of a silver dollar. It had symmetrical holes in which, it seemed, to hold the actual seeds themselves. I brought it to Jedediah.

"Now...this little gem, Cable...*Nelumbo Nucifera*...has the outstanding ability to control her temperature, just as warm-blooded creatures do."

"Wha—what the?" I remarked. "How can that be, my dear Dr. Penn?"

"Who knows? But that is why Lei-tao remains relatively warm when she incarnates." He studied my eyes. "Now I know what you're thinking. How can a *plant* also become a *human* in form and function?"

"Yeah, something like that. For God's sake, Jedediah, I held her, kissed her, had Tantric sex with her and felt all the things humans—"

"—you *what?!* Cable, you'll kill her! She was never meant for your use as a common sexual creature in this dimension!"

"Well, sorry about that, but after the second kiss she didn't seem to mind. She just told me regular sex was taboo, that's all."

"Damn, don't you young bucks know how to keep it in your pants? Not all of life is having sex like a damn jump-lizard on a warm fence, you know!"

"If you knew Lei-tao like I know Lei-tao—"

"—it doesn't matter. Keep your hands off, Cable. Believe me, you'll destroy her—and in doing so, upset the dimensional balances."

"Okay, okay, Jedediah. No more touchy-touchy, I promise."

"Good. Now," he continued examining the *Nelumbo Nucifera* pod with me.

"Notice carefully, all the seeds are present in the greenish pod. Lei-tao's seed pod, however, is *red* and if examined carefully, one will find a single seed missing."

"Now don't tell me, that is our absentee little Red Dragon Lady doing her thing back at the ranch with the *Tone of Creation.*"

"You needn't be so smug, Cable. This is serious. We didn't create this vast cosmos, but whoever and whatever did, knew what they were doing. When Lei-tao restores the Tone of Creation to the capsule, things will hum again like they're supposed to in her realm. Maybe even ours."

"I doubt that. Humans always find a way to fuck things up, or haven't you noticed?" He ignored my snide comment and continued.

"So, when I saw the red pod at the bottom of the lake, I left it there but not before discovering that *one seed was missing*. If that one becomes lost or destroyed, Lei-tao has many 'sisters' in the other dormant seeds that will take her place."

"You mean Lei-tao is a clone of herself?"

"Yep, many times over." I rubbed my head.

"More than I can take in one night, Jedediah. So, how about that relaxing and enjoying you were talking about? I'll stay until Polly comes back. I know she works hard and tirelessly for you. You're lucky to have her as aid and companion."

"To be sure, Cable, to be sure...and speaking of which, I must tell you what's in my heart. Sometimes an old man indulges in the moment because it doesn't matter if he embarrasses himself anymore. It's about this haunting vision I keep having about your exquisite Latina, your Adora. I keep feeling her heart. It aches for you. You are like the water that feeds her, my good, young man. She will wither and perish if someone like you doesn't nourish her. Some women were born to be loved and are the best companions in the world. She is such a one."

I squirmed in my seat. Behind the seeming toughness of my look I knew what Jedediah Penn was talking about. I had felt it as well, but kept shoving it down because it was something I couldn't face...something I had pushed away...a lamb I had sacrificed at the altar of relationship in this world. I'm sure I wasn't the first or last who would make such a decision to maintain the moral equilibrium in our so-called "Western Civilization." So, I ask...just how 'civilized' was abandonment—or leaving part of your heart with someone when your real truth lay just beneath the surface, knocking at your chest, telling you that maybe you turned left instead of right?

"I know what you mean, Jedediah. What would *you* do if you walked in my shoes? Don't you think I've tortured myself over it again and again? Out of sight, out of mind ain't what I feel about Adora Moreno, doc. I told you, if it weren't for Honey, I'd play it for keeps with Adora. But it's too late for that now, why torture myself…."

"But that's just it, Cable. You will torture yourself all of your life. One day you'll look back and wonder how you let her get away. It's like having a glove that fits you perfectly, but then just tossing it away because you don't know what else to do with it."

We talked for a while and I watched the old man fade away into the land of snooze. When Polly Parker returned, I hugged her silently and slipped out into the night.

Tomorrow always came too soon.

CHAPTER 13
I'D KILL ANYONE FOR YOU

Some tomorrows don't come around so good. They start out with a bitter taste in your mouth and something in your gut keeps making you nervous and coffee and cigarettes just make it worse. Even the music you hear has a sour note or two in it and somehow you know something's up. Around 9:30 a.m. when I called in, I was instructed to attend the aftermath of a homicide. I was supposed to put my siren on but I just took down the address and with my new rookie patrolman in tow, one 26 year-old wet-behind-the-ears fellow named Davie Spivak, I started out from Alvarado near Broadway. He was nephew to a noted trumpet player, Charlie Spivak, who recorded and played around the clubs back east with noted dance bandleader Paul Sprecht. But young Davie was not too musical and like a lot of the Ukrainian immigrant families, the new rookie took things pretty seriously.

We drove up to 1225 Manzanita Street off of Fountain Avenue. For some reason I noticed the County Coroner's vehicle had arrived ahead of us. I looked over at my spindly young fellow officer. "So, Davie, this is your first murder. Rule one. Expect anything. Humans can be cruel to each other. Sometimes you might think the dead person deserved what he got, other times you'll think the whole world's an unjust merry-go-round and nothing's fair. Lump it and do your job, okay?"

He looked at me with wide eyes. "Sure, Cable. Lead the way."

We walked up to a single little house with a broken down white-washed fence that had known better days and knocked on the door and the coroner's assistant opened it. A pretty young blonde was sitting on the sofa blubbering, her head in

324

her hands. The assistant led me into a tiny bedroom. On the floor sat a white, bloodstained bassinet. There inside lay the morning's horror, the one my nervous gut had been warning about since I got up. This reminded me of what I had just finished saying to Davie Spivak. People stink. An infant child lay naked on a blanket of drying blood, both of its arms and head cut off and placed recklessly on top of the remaining corpse. The smell was that of old blood and feces and it overwhelmed the room. Instantly Officer Spivak put his hand to his mouth and ran back to the patrol car. I turned and walked slowly into the small living room where the woman sat, whimpering. The coroner's assistant informed me that the woman had admitted she had killed her baby. Just then the coroner showed up. He was a burly man with small spectacles and always looked like he had a five-o'clock shadow. But Frank Nance knew his stuff. He summoned me outside.

"Hello, Officer Denning. I noticed your new man's a bit out of breath in the patrol car. Did you frighten him?" he joked.

"Naw, he's just not used to dead babies being dismembered, that's all."

"Oh, gees…" he said as he looked into my sullen face. "You're not kidding…" He took his bag and walked into the forbidding little room. I followed until I stood at the transom. He bent down over the child's temporary coffin. "What kind of twisted mind does these things, Denning? I've seen it a hundred times in my career, but I've never gotten used to it. I just don't understand."

"That makes two of us, Frank." I turned and went to sit down across from the distraught young woman. "Ma'am, I'm afraid I'm going to have to ask you a few questions. Are you up to it? I mean, we can—"

"—*I did it*! I killed my own baby today, okay?"

I took a deep breath. I sat there wondering how the pieces to this puzzle would fit together. For instance, what motivates a lovely young woman, who couldn't have been over twenty-five, to kill her own flesh and blood? What goes on inside that mind? Is it temporary insanity—or were the screws loose to begin with and society just never caught it? I went over to the phone and got the department. In cases like these, if the suspected perpetrator was female, then a female police officer was summoned to the location to take her to a county facility other than the main jail. "Yeah, this is patrolman Cable Denning, badge #71416. Send me officer Rosario if she's available. Yeah—of course—if it wasn't homicide I wouldn't be making this call. Yeah, 1225 Manzanita Street—the coroner's already here. Okay, swell…soon as you can, I gotta get back on patrol." I hung up and looked down at the lady on the couch who now was drying her eyes on her sleeve.

"Will they kill me? If they do, I guess I deserve it…"

"Maybe. You see, ma'am, our laws are full of things they call *extenuating circumstances*. So it's up to the judge and jury."

She looked up at me, soft blue eyes reddened with tears and the unbearable emotion that now sat behind them seemed to speak to me, tell me I did it, I did it, I did it…and yeah, I'm glad I did it even though I'm in pain and I'm divided and don't even know what the hell I'm doing or where I am! But I did it! So now punish me and let me die! She looked down at the dirty, coffee-stained rug. "I killed his baby…because it wasn't mine… it was *his*—and he did it, he got me pregnant so I couldn't see Randy anymore." Then she got this sick, twisted smile on her face. "But you know, I fooled him. I killed his baby, to clear the way for me to be with Randy. Then I'll have *Randy's* baby— and—and we'll—we'll be happy! I know he'll want me even more now. He didn't like me as much when I was carrying my ex-husband's kid. Now he'll want me, free and clear. You know, that's just so swell, and how I like it with Randy—free and clear. And guess what?"

"You tell me, Miss…what?"

"I'd kill anyone for him. He's going to take me to Chicago where his folks want to meet me—and we're gonna dance, whoop it up, go out and have fun, dine in the best places—and find a nice place to live."

"Yeah, that's swell," I said, just keeping the conversation as loose as I could until Officer Rosario arrived.

Then she looked at me more intensely. "You don't believe me, do you? You're a cop. To you I'm a murderess, huh? But I'll be famous for a week or so, won't I? Nobody ever paid much attention to me until I met Randy. He sells shoes. Travels a lot. He's gone right now on the train to Salt Lake City. Then he's coming back for me. I told him it'd all be over when he got back and we could go away. That made Randy happy. He wants me. I can tell. He wants me to have *his* baby. You see, I kept my word, didn't I?"

"What's your name?"

"Donna…Donna Corson…of course that's my maiden name. I would never use *his* name again."

I studied her face. "I…I don't know what to say to you, Miss Corson. But you'll have to go somewhere for detention."

"What's that? Will Randy find me there?"

"Oh, yeah, he'll find you there alright. I don't think you're gonna be movin' to Chicago anytime soon, however."

"As long as Randy can stay with me—can he stay with me there?"

Just then Officer Alicia Rosario appeared at the door. She was a pretty big woman with a tough look. I liked her, though, because she never let emotion get in the way of her job. I introduced her to Donna Corson and let her take over. I quietly walked out of the little house and stood on the porch, listening to sparrows sing in a palm tree across the way. I lit up a Lucky Strike. I glanced into my patrol car and saw my new rookie sitting there upright, looking straight ahead out the windshield.

327

Some guys are cut out for this life, but a lot aren't. Attrition rates among young cops during these years were pretty high. On the surface it was a glory job, but once you got a taste of the underbelly of society, you'd be hard put to justify the existence of human beings at all in this cock-eyed world. For the most part they were self-serving, gave nothing back to the soil they took their sustenance from, and pretended to be some brand of 'civilization,' daring to emulate the ideals philosophers and religionists had scribbled down for centuries. So far, no society had found a way to be part of the natural world without taking from her or to live in harmony with one's neighbor without the ugly head of war peaking up over the brouhaha of human kind pretending to be 'better than' the simple roots they came from.

I got into the Model-T. "I'm sorry, Cable," Davie Spivak said. "Are you going to write me up—I mean, failing my first murder attendance and all—"

"Naw, you didn't fail anything, Davie, me boy. You just saw an opening to the first act of a long play, the one called 'humanity and all its foibles.' You got a lot more tests ahead. You know, pal, we're only five years apart—but it's not the years behind your eyes that count now, but the years out there, out there in the streets, taking a lost boy home, rescuing a dog that's run away from a blind man, picking up a corpse that died during the night of malnutrition, arresting a hoodlum for breaking into a jewelry store by telling you his uncle owns it, picking up a fifteen year-old prostitute who's so full of disease you can hardly get near her she smells so bad…yeah, and so on… you gotta see humor in tragedy, Davie. If you don't, you'll miss the main show, the comedy of errors humans commit upon themselves."

"Easy for you to say. I'm at the other end of those experiences. And I came from a very serious family. I've got to learn to take the punches like you do, Cable, but does it ever get better? I mean, do you get numb after a while and maybe you learn not to take it personally?"

"Yeah, that's right, Davie. You learn not to take it personally." I started up the car and we drove off to the next adventure of the day.

When I dragged myself into my apartment that evening and began throwing my clothes off, I could smell coffee brewing. I peeked around the corner and there sat Mario at my tiny little table reading the paper. "I almost drew my .38 on you, guy. What's up?"

"My first day off with pay...I just wanted to pop by and thank you for getting me off. I've already begun drafting some new indictments against O'Malley, O'Flaherty, Dragna and a few of the big boys downtown—I can smell them all the way from the mayor's office."

"Easy, Mario," I said, afraid for my friend. "You gotta clear some space here until things cool down. You agreed. Right now you're front and center with these guys. We have to remember, if they work in cahoots together, buddy, both sides are the enemy. Let's keep it quiet for a while, okay, pal?"

I could tell that Mario didn't like what he was hearing. But I was hoping against hope that he wouldn't jump the gun. "But I've got a month to trap them into a place they can't get out of. Don't you see? Once I can get a dynamite, registered letter off to the State District Attorney—and this time a powerful article of exposure in the newspapers—the people will rally. There are lots of good and honest people out there. You said so yourself."

"I *did* say that, Mario. But people don't act until they're really sick and fed up with things. Right now everything's looking rosy, the economy is leaping ahead, we've recovered from the Great War, we're our own country again—nope, people aren't quite ready to jump on our bandwagon, Mario. I still think we've gotta wait a while."

Mario Angelo shook his head slowly back and forth in consternation. "I don't agree completely, Cable. It's the rich who are

329

getting richer. Look at Elena and me—my piddly little police salary hardly cuts the rent and food. I mean, her folks have to help us out now and then. They haven't given *us* a raise in two years. But I notice O'Malley's makin' a heftier salary than last year—not to mention the kickbacks he gets from looking the other way when Dragna and his men open another speak easy."

"You got a point, Mario, but it's a sore point. That kind of injustice has been going on since a caveman with a bigger club realized he could clobber his neighbor, take his cave—and his woman—just because he could. Greed, buddy boy. That ain't about to change."

I said goodnight to my childhood friend with a phony smile and trepidation. I had this sinking feeling that Mario Angelo would try too much too soon in this great big grownups' world. Causes were great if you had the right one at the right time. I think Mario was only batting two-fifty on that one.

As soon as Mario had gone, I turned off the coffee and fell into bed. Some days are like epidemics and this had been a hard one on my body and I fell into a restless sleep, filled with dreams about someone I knew of but never met. A guy named Nikola Tesla was trying to talk me into giving him an audience with Lei-tao, the Red Dragon Lady, and I was disagreeing with his premise that she had overcome gravity by something he had invented. Written on his chest in big blinking red letters were the words, '*DYNAMIC THEORY OF GRAVITY*,' and strange electrical bolts of blue lightning came out of his finger-tips. Lei-tao was coming toward me, trusting me to introduce her to Tesla. But as she approached she began to fall apart into pieces and I scrambled around, trying to pull all of her bits together again into a collective whole. But Tesla was laughing as he said he disagreed with Einstein, that people like him would one day "kill anyone for effect" because he sounds brilliant, but he's a child throwing a child's wonderment at us. He kept yelling that space does not bend in the universe because it has no physical properties and that Lei-tao only appeared to be separating from herself. "*Albert Einstein was a metaphysician, not a scientist*", he yelled at me as he began to be pulled into the darkness away from me. "*He was a 'dazzler of objectivity' in the universe—come with me Red Dragon Lady and I will give you everything electromagnetic in your new home dimension—come! Come! Come!*"

I woke up to three soft knocks at my door. I instinctively reached under my pillow for my .38. I got up and sidled to the door. "Yeah—it's late and if you're carrying iron, drop it so I can hear it."

"What is this '*iron*' you say, *mi querido?*"

I opened the door wide. "Oh, Adora! Adora!" I whispered as I pulled her in out of the hallway.

"Oh, señor, you are wet and shaking! *Mi pobre muchacho!*" We held each other only long enough to feel our pulsing bodies fill with desire. I threw off my tee shirt and shorts and began undressing her. I lowered her onto the bed and ravaged her body with my kisses, my hair still wet from my dream-sweats. Her lovely long legs wrapped around me as my manhood plunged into her. She sighed and moaned with such delight that I knew I could never be in this world without her love, without her touch. I reveled in pleasing her and in turn, as she slammed her abundant beautiful breasts into my chest, I could feel her womanhood take me deeper and deeper into her as she surrendered her whole body to me. When I finally exploded into her, I cried like a child who had found his way home after a long, impossible journey. And Adora knew exactly how to field that energy, absorb it into her own being as if she was born with a space for it all of her life.

We lay there in the dark completely spent, completely in love. "How did you know where I live?" I asked. "And it's dangerous out there in this neighborhood at night for a woman by herself."

"Señor…*por favor*…you are talking to first-class travel agent, no? When you buy ticket for San Francisco, I have…I have…I have…" Then her smile faded and she looked deep into my eyes in the semi-darkness. "I have you…I have you…oh, *mi amor*, tell me—I have you…"

I clung to her until I squeezed some of our love juices onto my sheet. "Ooops! That must tell you something—how much of me you have. I gave you all that I have tonight, beautiful señorita."

"*Ah, noche feliz, mi bandido*! You steal my heart and I cannot have it back!" Then she rolled over, took one of my pillows and covered her chest with it. "*Lo siento mucho* I come here tonight. But I wake in a dream. I am wet for you, pulsing. If I do not have you I know I will burst into *muchos pedazos*!"

"And I'm glad you did, Adora. It's just that we can't keep seeing each other—"

She put her finger to my lips. "-shhh…..*amigo, entiendo. Pero*, I have to fool myself, Cable…*pensar* I can come here when I need you—like *este noche*. I must believe that, *es verdad?*"

I rolled onto the side of the bed and sat up, took out a Lucky Strike and lit up. I chuckled to myself. "It's funny, kid, just last night I was talking with Dr. Penn about you. Do you remember him and Polly from San Francisco?"

"Oh, sí, very nice hombre, he speak *español, también*."

"Yeah, that's the man. Anyway, he's as much in love with you as I am. He feels we should be together, you know, the forever and ever kind?"

"I like this man. *Extraño*…it is how I feel also."

"I'm sorry for both of us, Adora, that I just can't be two people. Honey and I are really beginning to grow deeper bonds and it's not like she's some sleep-around or something—but she loves me like you love me—for keeps!"

"*Comprendo, señor.* Forgive me. Maybe I am only a weak woman?"

"No, beautiful Adora. You will never be weak or less than you are tonight to me."

"Can I stay…stay with you…*por favor…sólo un poco más* longer?"

I looked at her with such great love that I felt my own heart pour into hers. "You can stay until the cock crows, doll—"

"—the *who* crows? Am I understanding—I mean—you want me *otra vez*—one more time?"

I laughed out loud. "Well, yes—and no, silly, that means you can stay with me until the rooster crows—"

"Ah….*sí, un gallo en la mañana!*"

Then I put my cigarette out and came back to be with her on the bed. "And yes, I do want you again—and again. I want to be born in you. That's how I feel when you absorb me into your beautiful body, more and more. That's why it drives me nuts to think about you during the day. Or even sometimes when I'm with Honey, I feel my mind drifting to you…"

She pulled me down onto her and once again spread those lovely legs of hers as I fit perfectly between them. Even though I knew this would not be a night of much sleep, it would be a night of ecstasy and healing.

'GIVE ME A LITTLE KISS, WILL YA, HUH?'

March 29th was Honey's birthday and we celebrated it at the club after her show that night. During her performance I noticed some of Dragna's big mugs drift in, including Joe Lorena. As Joe entered, Honey had launched into a new song I hadn't heard her sing before, called Stardust, and it seemed to affect Lorena in some deep-down place. Words had just been added to Hoagy Carmichael's melody…and poignant words they were indeed. I was watching him there in the semi-dark of the club, as he sat on a bar stool holding a glass and I could see tears begin to well up. Maybe aliens had emotions after all. Maybe by the time Honey got to the words, '*the melody haunts my reverie…and I am once again with you…*' he was thinking of Honey's mother, the one he had loved and never got over.

The *Bella Notte* had gone all out for their *Golden Throat* that night and Affonso Amadore brought on a birthday cake five layers high and everyone was invited to have cake and champagne. About midnight Jack Dragna came in with a brunette and two of his goons. He went over to Honey, hugged her congratulations, nodded at me and went into a shady booth to confer with some other hoodlums.

Honey and I were sitting alone at our reserved table up near the stage. "Damn, Cable, do I deserve all this hoopla? I just discovered maybe I don't like all this attention."

"Well, in here you deserve it. You've made these guys a bundle. Just think, from that first day you auditioned with *It Had to Be You* until tonight—look what you've accomplished?"

"It's all your fault, Mister. If I hadn't slept with you that first night, just think, I'd still be out there on the dance floor with countless men fawning over me with their little tokens….waiting in line for me…"

I laughed. "Yeah! Instead, you're a golden-throated goddess of music with a promising career in radio, recordings and soon maybe some films. The films with sound and talking are here, I think!"

"May I join you for a congratulatory drink?" a voice spoke. I looked up. It was Joe Lorena. I still had a lot of mixed feelings about this guy.

But blood is thicker than water, and Honey got up as Joe

hugged her and soon they both sat down opposite me at the table. "Thank you, Joe, this is a happy time for me. My career's going full steam, Cable and I are getting married—and my Dad's here. What more could a girl ask?"

"I'm so proud of you, Honey," Joe Lorena said. "I was really moved by your interpretation of *Stardust*. I'm kind of a popular music buff. I don't think anyone has recorded it with the words yet, so as far as I'm concerned, your version is the one that will set the tone for everyone else."

"That's swell of you to say that, Joe, thanks. Cable didn't slip you some dough under the table to have you say that now, did he?" she giggled.

He looked at his daughter lovingly. "There's hardly a day when I don't think of you and how beautiful you turned out. And it's your birthday and it was your mother who gave you birth—and I know how happy she would be to know her daughter grew up into this talented, lovely—"

"—I—I don't think I can talk about that, Joe," Honey said. "Please…"

"I'm sorry. I suppose I'm just sentimental tonight." Then he brightened up as he lifted his glass to toast Honey. "To you, Honey Combes, the brightest light on Wilshire Boulevard—and soon radio, records and movie houses throughout the land!"

The three of us clinked glasses. "I'll drink to that---and go you one more," I said. "To the lady who'll be the prettiest singing bride in the business."

Honey looked at me and threw me a kiss. "If this is Friday, I think I might love you, Cable Denning."

Just then a drunk Jack Dragna came over by himself and put his arm around Honey. "Honey Combes, this establishment—is—is proud of you. So, what can we do to repay—hic!—repay you? Jewelry, more money, new agent—clothes? What?" Then he bent close to her ear. "Is there someone in your way you don't like? *I'd kill anyone for you, Honey Combes,*" he slurred. "Anyone who got in your way. You know that don't—don't you? Your Uncle Jack's here for you…okay?"

Honey was a bit embarrassed. "Thank you, Mr. Dragna. I appreciate that a lot. But there's no one I can think of who I don't want around at the moment, thanks all the same."

He stood to his full height, still looking down at Honey. "Okay. Just remember, anytime you want someone outta the way—you know who to call, huh?" He looked at Joe and me. "Well, gentlemen, if you'll pardon me, I shall return to my seat." He left. Some gorgeous dish with bobbed dark hair and a red dress stood awaiting Dragna back at his table.

Honey looked at Joe Lorena. "This is what you work with every day?"

"Except Jack doesn't usually drink much. I think he's celebrating your success, Honey. This is unusual for him."

"Well, I hope he never takes me seriously when I say I'm so mad at someone I could kill 'em!"

We both laughed. "Just don't say it around him," I chuckled. "Life, death, rape, murder, torture—all the same to these guys, right Joe?"

Lorena gave me a hard look. "Well, Cable, not exactly. It's that by necessity the syndicate has to have a different set of standards. Society operates on certain assumptions because it is programmed that way—"

"—the most honest thing I ever heard you say. Yeah, the public *is* programmed about good and bad, right or wrong, work hard to support the roof over your head and you might go to Heaven—"

"—Boys! boys! It's my birthday! Let *me* pick the subjects we can get bored about. Hmmm….let me see…what about children?" A sudden wet blanket fell over me. She leaned towards Joe. "You say you've improved your success rate for survival with the method of implantation and going to full-term birth?"

Joe looked at me and then back to Honey. "Yes, Honey. We're near one-hundred percent these days."

"So, correct me if I'm wrong, Joe—but are you saying there's this ongoing process of you alien guys interbreeding with non-alien, human babes? So that on the street, we never know who we're gonna meet?"

"Yes, Cable, that's about it. How else are we going to elevate the state of consciousness for humans?"

"Oh, I just thought that maybe good old Mother Nature takes care of things like that in time. Ha! Maybe I'm just old fashioned, huh? But I wouldn't go around talking this alien stuff around Dragna and his bunch—they might take things personally, consigliere," I said with a lacing of sarcasm on my voice.

"So—I've had just enough to drink to be open minded to this process. I'd love to have Cable's baby—as ornery and cantankerous as he can be—maybe we can filter out those traits, huh?" We all laughed.

"We can do it, Honey," Joe assured her. "You know by now, I would never risk you as I did your mother. You'll have the healthiest baby on the block—no…make that in *town*!"

"Oh, Joe, if it were really true—I'd have to really talk it over with this old cop sitting next to us—but I'd do it—I *would!*"

"I know we've got a day off tomorrow, but how about moseying our way home, Honey bun?" I said, feeling a little tired.

"He just wants sex, I can tell by that tone of voice," Honey quipped.

Joe laughed. "Well, enjoy your youth whilst you may. Which reminds me…if you'll follow me outside, Honey, I have a little birthday present for you."

"That big, huh?" She got up and Joe led us out into the parking lot. There, guarded over by one of Dragna's henchmen, stood one of the best looking automobiles I'd ever seen.

"Happy birthday, Honey," Joe Lorena said as he hugged his daughter.

Honey stood there stunned. It was a rich green with lots of chrome including the spoke wheels and the 'boy Adonis' hood ornament...the top down revealed a nice tan interior. "Joe! No—I can't—I can't accept this—no one's ever given me something like this—I'm—"

"—it's all yours, Honey. A 1929 Packard Roadster just waiting to take you anywhere you want to go—a magic buggy, this one! I think it suits you to a T."

"That was really swell of you, Joe," I said. "I was beginning to worry about Honey taking the streetcar home after work. Now—zip! your world's about to change, little darlin'."

Honey ran over to me and threw her arms around me. "Cable! My very own car!" Then she ran back and hugged Joe again. "This is my biggest and best birthday ever! What woman do you know is this lucky—a loving, generous fiancé, a loving, generous Dad—how did I manage that?"

Joe Lorena ceremoniously gave Honey the keys, and he and the goon walked over to the waiting sedan. Honey watched Joe Lorena walk away into the night. Well, there we were driving home to Honey's bungalow in her brand spankin' new Packard Roadster. "Damn, Cable...who would *ever* have thought my life would go this way? Do you feel you might like him more now? I know I do."

"Because he gave you a car? I don't base my likes or dislikes on *things*, Honey, you know that. I've told you how I feel. Your Dad will always be a hoodlum's mouthpiece as far as I'm concerned. But I won't interfere with your relationship with him or throw a wet blanket on it. Just don't ask me to laugh and puff smoke rings up into the air over a few glasses of champagne when he comes for dinner."

I could tell Honey felt disappointed. For her it must have felt like a kind of fatalistic *déjà vu*, living this moment all over again. And who knows, the layers buried in us might very well pass beyond that dark ecstasy that psychopaths and the truly insane experience. Who knows where and when that line is crossed, when that euphoric numbness allows us to overcome all moral and ethical concerns, so when we smile over the bassinet, chopping off all the limbs of a baby, we can wink at the devil and say it out loud, *"I'd kill anyone for you…"*

CHAPTER 14

MURDER IS A LONELY PLACE

By the end of May, Honey and I were doing really great. May 16th was the first year Hollywood patted itself on the back with the First Annual Academy Awards presentations held at the Hollywood Roosevelt Hotel and hosted by none other than good ol' Doug Fairbanks. The Lana Loren thing seemed to fade away for Honey and the world of film, in light of her fabulous success as a song stylist extraordinaire. We had actually discussed Joe Lorena's offer to have a baby by implantation and bring it to full term using the aliens' advanced facility. Honey seemed to bloom in her career and she increasingly appeared as a guest singer on radio shows. The *Bella Notte* continued to be her musical career headquarters and her audience draw was right up there with the best. Even East Coaster Al Jolson came in one night to see and hear Honey. He was so impressed with her, that he gave her a personally autographed copy of a recent hit of his entitled, *Sonny Boy*. He left her with the advice, so she told me, that if she sang that song to her favorite guy, he'd never leave her.

Despite all my willpower, I could not stem the tide of passion I felt for Adora Moreno. Willing to take a back seat to my busy personal life, she would call me late at night or come rapping at my door in the early evening when she knew I would be in my apartment and not at Honey's. I knew that after December, our late-night liaisons would have to come to an end as Honey and I intended to rent a house of our own until we could afford to buy one. It already hurt me somewhere inside to know I may never again hold that winsome Latina in my arms and feel her womanly surrender as we were both swept into the whirlpool of our desires for one another.

I was barely hanging on by a fingernail in the police force. My new rookie, Davie Spivak, was working out okay but I knew he'd always be a so-so flatfoot, there to get by, and look the other way when he was supposed to and if he stayed with the force, would end up dead in the street or farmed out in old age to a tiny cracker box of a house with a wife and a couple of kids. Our current police chief Davis marked me out for a new patrol assignment, which would begin in June, 1929. It was called the *Dragnet system* and cops were supposed to keep their eyes on cops. Davis wanted to reign in "the lawless streets of Los Angeles," created by goons like Jack Dragna and his kind. But as long as crime paid on both sides of the law, a lot of the corruption would continue on under the heading, "business as usual."

And that's what griped Mario, and worried me most. The department had given him a full thirty-day paid leave of absence, and when he returned, the powers that be never again paired the two of us together as a patrol team. Instead, they stuck Mario in the properties processing department downstairs. Mario was a burly, outdoor type of guy and stuck behind a birdcage all day drove him nuts. But that wasn't what worried me. He had been compiling more and more subversive material to lower the boom on the idiots who ran things downtown, including the mayor. *That* worried me. By the time he had called me in to join forces with him, it had all gone too far and without my knowledge, he had submitted a tell-all article to the Los Angeles Times, a rag run by a guy named Harry Chandler. It was no surprise when Chandler panicked and let City Hall know they had a rat among them, one of their own who had written an exposé against the police force, an indictment against the other rats who ran downtown—and lots of name-throwing levied against the large ring of organized crime that ran everything else. I knew in a minute it would not go well for Mario. Within hours Chief Davis had sent a couple of tough cops over and arrested Mario.

341

He seemed prepared for this move and had a sharp but crooked attorney spring him within eight hours. Milton Silverstein then conveniently disappeared behind a rock before the shooting started. Chief Davis ordered Mario to appear before him and had him resign on the spot. Mario was crushed, for as long as he held a position on the force, he felt he had some clout and therefore a platform to bring his gripes. But nobody saw it that way, least of all the police department.

Now my lifetime buddy was being thrown onto the rocks below, and for the time being, suspended as a man without a country—or a job. It's a funny thing about breaking out of the norm, or the accepted and established authority that somehow nobody agreed to initiate but everyone kowtowed to once it was in place. Now Mario faced the loneliest road in the world, the outcast in search of truth and justice.

It was Wednesday and I started looking for Mario as soon as I got off work. I called Rosalie and her voice trembled when she told me Mario was going to stay with an uncle in Glendale. She also informed me Mario had told her the newspaper publisher had betrayed him and alerted the unhappy recipients of Mario's written wrath. But he wasn't through yet, she said, and he was going to a couple of radio news agencies to spill his beans. Desperate to stop Mario before he did more harm to himself, I called Honey to give me Joe Lorena's phone number. When I finally reached him and told him my predicament, his voice stayed calm. "I don't think you can help your friend, Cable. Bow out of it now. News travels fast and Chandler's pretty close to city hall and big business supports the newspaper. He's out of the crime syndicate loop, but he's got a few cops in his pocket just in case."

"So, Joe, what can I do? Can I get him out of town and make sure he doesn't come back for a while? He's a damn good cop, maybe he can get a patrol post in another city."

"More likely another state, Cable. He's through in California.

In my profession he's called a *songbird,* and nobody likes men who tell tales they shouldn't. If you know where he is, I'd get him out of town in the dark of night as soon as possible. Good luck." He hung up.

I rushed over to Honey's to borrow her Packard. She tossed the keys at me and told me to be careful. I sped out to the address Mario's wife had given me for Mario's Uncle Sesto. 1514 Gardena avenue off of South Central Avenue was near the train station and looked like a cigar box someone had tossed onto a lot. Weeds were grown up over the fence, a half-dead oak tree hung over the roof and the stairs were so rickety I had to step lively not to fall through. I knocked on the front door. Nothing. I pushed on the door. It was open. I drew my .38 and entered slowly. The room smelled of garlic and old coal oil. It appeared Uncle Sesto was not the richest man in the neighborhood. I flipped on a light switch. There on the kitchen floor lay an old man with blood mingled with his receding silver hair. I bent down to check him out. "Sesto—Sesto Angelo? Can you hear me, man?"

"Ay, Mario—il povero ragazzo—you…musta….'elpa him…"

"Yeah, I would if I knew where he was. Who hit you?" I propped him up against his stove. "I need to find Mario pronto, Sesto. His life may be in danger—if it's not too late already."

"*Assassini arresto—aiuto me!*"

I cranked the phone on the wall and asked for police assistance. I talked to a desk sergeant I knew and told him to send someone out to Sesto's. I didn't mention Mario or his predicament in order to avoid stirring the pot any more than it had been already. I picked old Sesto up off the floor, gave him a glass of Chianti and left him in an over-stuffed chair that looked like it came from the local dump. Where to now?

I raced back to Honey's because I knew she needed her car later that night to go to work. Zelda answered the door.

"Cable! You look terrible—and you've got blood all over your hands—did you kill someone?"

"No, Zelda, but someone is about to be killed if I don't get to him first."

"Oh, gees! Is there anything I can do?"

Just then Honey came out in a slip and her hair in curlers. "No luck, darling? Oh! I hope that's not Mario's blood…"

"No, but the next batch could be." I ran to the sink to wash my hands. Honey and Zelda followed. "This red stuff belongs to Sesto Angelo, the uncle I went out to Glendale to see. Remind me, let's not settle anywhere near South Central Avenue. All that's missing are the hogs."

"So what's next, Cable?" Zelda asked. "I'm a pretty good bird dog, maybe I can come along and help?"

"I don't think so, Zelda, thanks all the same."

"No, really, I'm very good at sleuthing—it's like tracing the reasons for sick plants. I always find the culprit."

Honey started down the hallway. "Come in to my bedroom, Mr. Handsome, before you say good-bye."

I dried my hands and walked into Honey's bedroom. "Thanks for the use of your car. That Packard drives like she has a dozen horses under her."

"I wouldn't mind having one man under me just about now." She lowered her slip to bare her wonderful, full breasts. "How about a quickie to take the edge off, Mister?"

"Damn, Honey, I'd like to—but if I don't find Mario before it's too late—I'll—I'll never be able to live with myself."

She pulled her slip back up. "I understand. I'm sorry. I just felt playful, that's all. I can only guess how you feel about Mario, childhood friends and all—and those years on the force together. What are you going to do, Cable? You can drop me off and take my car later, if you want."

"No, babe, that's a couple of hours from now. The only thing I can do right now, is to try and get a hold of Crazy Jack—he's the guy that warned me about both of you, remember?"

"So, far none of it's come true. I wouldn't put too much stock in a bum who smells bad, lives in skid row and has a very nervous tic in his head."

I got a little pissed at Honey. "He's still one of my friends, Honey. Such as they are, they're real and dependable—and that's a hell of a lot more than I can say about the majority of the so-called 'okay' people who roam our streets and eat at fine restaurants."

"I'm sorry, Cable. Go…find your friend. Please be careful and let me know at least something tonight after I get home, okay?"

"Yeah, okay." I started to dart out of the house and Zelda grabbed my arm.

"Please, Cable? I know I can help you. Give me a chance. I just love mysteries. Lost friends are even more fun."

Against my better judgment I nodded my head. "Alright, get a sweater and let's go. But if you're no help in exactly an hour, I'm sending you back home, agreed?"

Honey peeked around the corner. "Zelda…do you really know what you're doing? This man is relentless—and crazy--until he gets his way or gets to the bottom of things."

"I wish I had a man like, I mean, a relentless man who wants his way with me." Zelda looked at me. "Ever since our wonderful dancing date, I've been looking for someone to ask out. But all they want to do is drink—I mean, get me drunk—and then you know what…"

I grabbed Zelda's hand and we left, lickety-split for the streetcar line.

By the time we got downtown to the seedier parts near skid

row, Zelda took my arm and held on tight. "Gees, Cable, these are the places where you hang out?"

"Yep. A cop's work takes him everywhere, kid. From million dollar skyscrapers to—to this, the jumping off place where humanity toils in the debris like grubs. Take a good look."

"Ooooo! I really don't want to. I've been sort of protected and spoiled most of my life. Poverty and filth like this---oooo! It gives me the creeps!"

We walked up the rickety stairs to Crazy Jack's fourth floor digs. I knocked. "No! No! I don't know! I don't know! Who—who....?"

"It's me, Jack, Cable...let me in, I need to talk to you pronto."

"I don't know! I don't know! The photes are coming! You bring the photes? They come now...soon...big...photes—but I don't know!"

"Jack—just open the damned door. I've got some smokes for you."

He opened the door. "Cigarette! Cigarette!" Then he glanced at Zelda who was staring wide-eyed at Crazy Jack through her glasses. I handed Jack a cigarette, lit it up for him and tucked the rest of the pack in his coat pocket as I always did. "Not Honey-color girl—ohhh......ohhhh..." He started rocking back and forth. "Oh....help her, go get her safe—she full of danger—but I don't know! I don't know!"

"Well, Crazy Jack, so far Honey's really been scoring big at the club. I don't see any danger for her there. At least for the present. But you know my cop friend, Mario Angelo—he's in deep shit and I need to find him. Can you help?"

"I don't know! I don't know!" Jack puffed wildly on his cigarette. "Friend die, desert heat...oh, Crazy Jack hurt in head— friend get dead! But I don't know! I don't know!"

In the meantime, Zelda had been taking all of this conversation in with an attitude somewhere between fear and curiosity.

346

"Oh, by the way, Jack, this is Zelda, she's Honey's roommate. Thought she'd like to come along and see where you live."

Crazy Jack opened his door wider and smiled at Zelda. "Pretty lady—come see Jack's house—Jack has mouse—elephant, too! Ha! ha! But I don't know! I don't know! Come see Jack's house?"

Zelda peeked into Jack's putrid mess of a room. "Ah, no thank you, Crazy Jack—if I may call you that. But I really do think you're crazy."

Jack laughed. "I don't know! I don't know! Jack crazy like squirrel—feed squirrel at park—not in dark, come see?" He reached out gently to pet Zelda's arm. She recoiled in fear. "Jack no hurt—squirt! Ha! ha!" he laughed. I could tell this was Crazy Jack's way of flirting, but somehow Zelda didn't quite get it.

"Let him touch you, Zelda. Remember what you keep telling me about accepting someone's overtures graciously? Well, now's that time."

Zelda held her hand out silently, looking up into Jack's eyes. He slowly took his fingers and stroked her arm. "Aha! Crazy Jack touch girl! But I don't know! I don't know! She fear Jack. Jack no fear girl…"

Finally Zelda grew up for the moment. "I don't fear you either, Jack. It's just—just that everything here—I mean, you and where you live and all—is brand new to me. Do you understand?"

"I don't know! I don't know!" Crazy Jack said as he took his hand back and held it against his stomach, as if protecting it. "You like Cable? I like Cable. Cable like you, okay…"

"Yes, I like Cable a lot. He is my friend, too. Is that alright with you?"

"I don't know! I don't know! Jack live in lonely place—see?" He pointed to his filthy one room. Then he looked at me with sullen eyes, his head twitching. "Murder—a lonely place, Cable. No go there. Too late for friend—but I don't know! I don't know!"

"But Jack, where can I find him? Are you sure there's no way I can locate and save him? I've been going nuts all day."

"Jack say—today—friend die, desert heat—too late... Cable...But I don't know! I don't know!"

I thanked Jack and Zelda and I went back down the rickety stairs onto the dark street. "Why does he always follow up with that *'I don't know! I don't know*" stuff?" Zelda asked. "Seems really weird to me."

"Hey, Jack was attracted to you, kid. You should be flattered. I'd never seen him do that before. You must've touched a heartstring."

"Oh, yeah, swell. If that's the kind of guy I attract then I must be crazy myself. Can you see me going around saying *'I don't know! I don't know!* all the time?"

"Maybe..." I kidded her.

She slugged me lightly on the shoulder. "Oh, you! Why can't it be someone like you who falls for me?" She locked her arm under mine as we walked toward the streetcar line. "Cable... could you ever see your way clear to maybe take me out one more time before you and Honey get married? Because then I'll have to leave and find another place to live."

"Well, if Honey doesn't mind, we can go cut up the rug one more time, I guess." Then she looked at my face in earnest.

"But your heart's not in it, is it?"

"I've just got a lot of stuff going on right now, Zelda. Be happy to go out dancing. Didn't you say you had a great time when we went?"

"What...what if there was a teeny, weeny little chance that we could go out and when we got home before Honey—you

348

could—you could—you know…I'm too embarrassed to say it…but you know, maybe we could make whoopee?"

I laughed under my breath. "And…uh, just exactly what would that entail, young woman?"

"Oh, I don't know…whatever happens, I guess. You could start by kissing me goodnight. Then, if you liked that, I'd take my dress off for you and maybe you could touch me—"

"—it's not gonna happen, Zelda. Keep it to the dancing and a coke—and you've still got a deal."

She pouted all the way back to the little bungalow. As we neared the front door I saw a figure lurking in the shadows. I felt for my .38 as we approached. It was Joe Lorena. I gestured for Zelda to go in. I took a deep breath. My intuitions were going nuts. I knew Lorena did not come to bring me good tidings. "Hello, Joe. What brings you out so late?"

"It's your friend, Cable. I thought if I told you up front, you'd handle it like the man I know you are." He came closer to me, his kindly eyes sympathetic and gentle. "They put a contract out on Mario Angelo."

"*Who* put a contract out on him, Joe, you? Downtown? The cops?"

"I'm afraid this time he stepped on big financial toes, Cable. Word is the Jewish mafia out of Chicago got the contract from higher up. Corporations are more dangerous than banks or organizations like mine."

"So, can I get him out? Bribes, getting him out of the area, money—what? I can't just sit back and see Mario get wasted!"

"I told you on the phone, Cable. Let him go. It's too late. Your friend bit off more than he could chew. I wish you had warned him ahead of time."

"Goddamnit, Joe, I did! Several times! I saw it coming. I begged him to cool off until the timing was right. But he wrote some stupid article telling all, so I hear…and now—"

"—I'm sorry, Cable. I felt it fair to you that I was the one to tell you. The ball's out of your court, Officer Denning."

"*Ex*-officer Denning after tonight, pal. I knew the straw would break this camel's back sooner or later. Tonight's it. Finito—over—done with!"

"What will you do? You and Honey both will have to earn some money, you know."

"I've been thinkin' about that, too, Joe. I've been mulling over the possibility of becoming a private investigator. That way I'd be out on my own chasing down errant husbands and wives, girlfriends and lovers, caught in the act. All I have to do is come up with a pretty photo of the happy trespassers for court."

Joe Lorena smiled. "Now, that's not half bad, Cable. I like the idea. You can name your fees, your hours—I might even hire you now and then to trace down someone who's disappeared—"

"—you mean like Mario?"

"Not exactly. More like someone who's confiscated funds that belong to the organization, or someone's wife having an affair with someone she shouldn't be having an affair with."

"By the way, I always wanted to ask you. Did you really love Honey's mother? I mean, being an alien and all?"

Joe became still and folded his arms in. "I was completely, helplessly in love with her mother. You see, Cable, the universe is populated with the same emotional potential for all. Deciding to accept it, is an individual choice. But we all have the capacity."

"I see…well, thanks, Joe, I just wanted to be sure. Honey cares a lot about you—and—and, uh, it would disappoint her if she felt you may not have been the real thing with her mother."

"Good night, Cable," he said and he walked away. "Again, I'm sorry about your friend…"

As I watched Joe Lorena walk away, I knew my life was

about to change. The silent tears I had for Mario, quitting the police force, my impending marriage to Honey, my continued deep feelings for Adora—and the forbidden unknown that may yet be in store for me concerning the mysterious Lei-tao and the *God of Our Fathers*.

Just like Crazy Jack said, two days later they found the remains of Mario Angelo in a ditch, baking in the hot desert sun near Palm Springs. That sorrow alone threw me over an edge of despair and hopelessness. I knew that would stay with me the rest of my life. Yeah, sure I'd get over it someday, but what it meant and how it stayed locked in my craw as a lesson in my life primer book would take a toll that robbed me of any semblance of my remaining youth. Thus at twenty-nine years of age I had grown-up to the real world, and any blinders I might have had stuck to my eyes, I threw away on that day. Now there was only the march of time…then oblivion.

Honey and I attended the funeral at Calvary Cemetery on Whittier Boulevard in East Los Angeles. It was a place where a lot of the old Catholic entertainers were buried, as well as early pioneers in the formation of Los Angeles. Rosalie Elena was shaken to her roots with grief. She grabbed for my arm when they lowered Mario into that cool, hard earth. It was a closed casket rosary service because the assassin put a bullet hole right through Mario's temple and somehow the head began to swell until he was unrecognizable anymore. So Rosalie Elena had only memories now, memories of a vital young man filled with a zest and enthusiasm for life and a wonderful love for those values of home and hearth and family that I seemed to lack.

I used to think murder must be a lonely profession, even if you enjoyed it. Now I felt that both murder and death were lonely places, when all the props were kicked out from under you—and the end result was final. You couldn't return the sales slip for a refund. When you're watching someone you loved disappear down a dark hole of no return, there's something about the finality of it that stops you in your tracks, makes you realize how fragile our mortality really is and that someday it'll be your turn. At twenty-nine years old, holding the hand of a beautiful woman with honey-colored hair who loved you with her warm and wonderful heart and body, it was hard to imagine that trip to never-never land would ever happen to you. Yet it happened to Mario and even though he was 3 years older, that was close enough. It made you think, you either fear life and play it safe or you just plow into it with gusto and your convictions—and if you die in the process, I guess you die doing what you really believe in. So, in the end, is any cause worth dying for? Standing there in the morning Los Angeles sunlight I wasn't sure. Maybe it *was* best to live out a quiet life of desperation like so many. But at least there was a roof over your head, food on the table and a beautiful babe in your bed.

Parked in a limousine not far from the gravesite sat Joe Lorena. As Honey and I said good-bye to Rosalie Elena and her family, Joe got out and approached us. "Hello, Honey, Cable…is there anything I can do?"

I looked back at the gravesite. "Naw, I think you and your kind have already done it, Joe," I said throwing my usual sarcastic barbs his way.

"I told you, Cable, orders for the hit probably ultimately came from Louis "Lepke" Buchalter out of New York and what the press is calling his Murder, Inc ."

"Does it really matter, Joe—you know my Mother taught me something when I was a kid. 'Tell me who you go with and I'll tell you who you are,' was her advice to me. So you can see, birds of a feather, consigliere, eh?"

Joe looked at his daughter. "Do you feel the same, Honey?"

"I don't know what I feel right now, Joe," she said. "All I know is that Cable's best friend was murdered by people who contract with each other to kill innocent people. If you're part of that, then I'm ashamed for both of us."

Joe got a pained expression on his face. "You're right, Honey. That is part of it. I won't lie to you. And I know there's nothing I can say or do that will change either of you from seeing me in that light." He turned to get back into the limousine but stopped and added.... "But I will say, that most of the people who end up on a hit list are hardly innocent, but usually also involved somehow in one of the organizations...especially with the prohibition element. So your dear friend, Cable, was an exception." As he got into the car he said, "Again, my condolences to Mario's wife and family." He got in and the black Lincoln pulled away.

"God, Cable, I want to love him so much. But when I see things like this, I don't know. It *is* like your mother told you, guilt by association. How can I separate out the caring parent from the mouthpiece for the syndicate?"

"You can't. Mario signed his own death warrant because he cared about causes that represented goodness, basic accountability and honesty. But that runs contrary to the bums who run city hall, the police force...and the mob. To me, it doesn't matter whether it was Dragna or the long arm of the New York bosses, they all smell the same and sleep in the same bed."

Honey took my arm and we walked toward her car. Birds sang across the way, flitting out of trees onto tombstones. One wonders if they knew the difference between life and death? Maybe for them being present in the *now* was all that mattered. Don't think about mortality—take it a moment at a time—don't expect anything, just grab that next fly out of the air or that worm out of the ground, sleep on a comfortable branch, sing your best song in the morning to wake you up, bicker with your fellow birds when necessary and mate once a year to perpetuate the species. Hmmm....it all seemed pretty simple to me.

As I helped Honey up on the running board of her Packard,

she turned to look at me. "You do know, Mister, I could never bear losing you. I think Rosalie Elena was a hell of a lot stronger than I'd be. I think I would either melt into nothingness at your gravesite—or jump in after you."

I smiled, trying to make light of it. "Well, it's the Khitan tradition in China and also in India, that when the husband kicks off, they bury the wife with the husband or they toss the wife on the pyre for good measure and they both get toasted while the in-laws look on."

"Talking about in-laws, I need to meet your mother soon—all this time you've never taken me. And you need to meet Bert and Mable Combes."

"Yeah, I'm not really good with in-law crap. You know, it's like I'm marrying you and not them. But I suppose if we gotta—"

She threw her arms around me. "Oh, darling Cable, I love you so! Let's go home, have a stiff drink and make love."

CHAPTER 15

CABLE DENNING, PRIVATE INVESTIGATOR

O'Malley looked at me like I was crazy the morning I tendered my resignation from the Los Angeles Police Department. "Thinkin', I was, you'd be made of stronger stuff, Denning," he admonished me. "We're all very regretful about your fellow officer Mario Angelo, but he was warned, you know, and we can't be everywhere at the same time, Denning."

"Oh, I wouldn't worry your head about that anymore, Captain. We all take the punches different…and you and I are just as responsible for Mario's death as any of the mob bosses or their goons, and you know it."

He looked at me strangely, but then moved on. "O'Flaherty tells me you've been exemplary as a policeman. Yeah, sure, you complain about the system—so do I—but we had real plans for ya. I know for a bloomin' fact that Chief Davis picked ya out to lead that new Dragnet thing he's been dreamin' up."

"I'm goin' where the sun shines brighter, O'Malley. One of these days some semblance of law and order will return to the department—and hopefully, our city at the same time. Maybe downtown will toughen up and suddenly wanna become honest when Prohibition's over. Maybe then the criminal elements of this city will lessen their grip and double-dipping will be harder to come by."

"My, my, but you're hard on us poor, hard workin' folk, Denning. But as I said before, I'll be over-lookin' it, lad, 'cause you're bein' a good Irishman with a lot of spunk. I'll give ya that. Good luck, Denning." He shook my hand and I left his office. That day ended almost seven years of a difficult relationship. On the plus side, I suppose you could call it a crash course in human behavior and just how muddy the lines are between law and order, graft and corruption. But it was time to move on.

Becoming a private investigator in 1929 was going down to city hall, paying a few bucks for a license to operate, proving you've had some kind of allied background and finding a place to 'hang your shingle'. I never checked if I needed a permit to carry my .38, but nobody brought it up.

For $35.00 a month I found an apartment at 6400 Franklin Avenue, Suite B, in Hollywood, that was laid out perfectly to be an office with living quarters in the rear. It was on the second floor and suited me just fine. All I needed was a phone. The largest window looked out over Franklin and my bird's eye view was just swell. I would give up my little flat, hang out here when I wasn't at Honey's and get the business rolling. Trouble was, I didn't know exactly what to get rolling. I knew private dicks did things like take Kodak Brownie photos of people in secret trysts and compromising positions to hold up in court, deliver documents, serve legal papers, trail people who were suspected of miscellaneous and sundry infringements of the law, investigate alleged fraud, verify insurance claims, find missing persons, personal surveillance and protecting persons or celebrities whose safety may be in jeopardy. At least that was the starting list. I had this feeling things of more gravity would be coming my way once I got established.

I had saved a few bucks being a cop and had sufficient bankroll for about six months of operation. If I hustled, I thought, I could get a couple of juicy cases to pay my $20.00 per day plus expenses fee. Hell, with just two clients a month, each case entailing about two weeks, I'd be making enough to start a small checking account that might read, *Cable Denning, Private Investigator, 6400 Franklin Avenue Suite B Hollywood, California.* Yeah, that had a nice ring to it. And in the ensuing days I got my telephone installed, got listed in the Los Angeles

Business Classified Directory. And the new $25.00 edition was just about to come out in August—putting me right up there with only three other private investigators, none of whom I knew and all in downtown Los Angeles. Damn, a few business cards printed up and I was in *business*!

Honey seemed delighted that I had gotten out of the old police force atmosphere, especially after Mario's death. When I called Adora and told her, she was also happy for me. Just talking to her on the phone made me feel desire for her. It was like I had always been in love with Adora Moreno and meeting her in the flesh was somehow a continuation of something we had both lived before. Maybe it was the fantasy of knowing we could indulge each other in deep and sensual pleasures without any of the strings, or maybe it was that whatever part of me belonged to her had a mind of its own and kept me from throwing her overboard. Time and again I had asked her what she derived from our secret and forbidden liaisons—but she always answered the same. "Whenever we can be together, I am completely happy to be with you, mi amor," was always her response. Now I was facing the prospect of not seeing her—ever again.

In early July I took Honey out to meet my mother. When I told her we were getting married, her face fell a little, and although she pretended a smile, I knew instantly she felt a loss that Adora was not to be the woman of my choice. But as the afternoon wore on, she warmed up to Honey and realized I had made a fine choice in my lovely and talented songstress. Still a feeling in the pit of my stomach told me something was wrong with this whole scenario. But what? It was as if I was living out-of-sync in this time zone, trying to be a conventional guy in a conventional world. My mother knew me better than anyone. I guess I was picking up her vibes. She knew my restless heart and inquisitive, penetrating nature. How would it all play out? Could I be Private Investigator Denning and Cable Denning, husband, father, friend and mortgage holder to a new house?

My very first client walked into my office July 18, 1929. Her name was Rusty Wilson, and she was married. Someone had given her my card and she had called earlier in the day to make an appointment. When she walked through my door I could see why a private dick had to watch his professional boundaries, for this gal was a looker with a body that didn't even stop at stupendous. She was about five-seven, dark-red hair, blue eyes and was wearing a maroon skirt and jacket with an off-white blouse underneath. I'd say she was about five years my senior. If I was sizing up that sizzling body right, I'd say she was about a 40-24-36.

"Welcome, Mrs. Wilson," I said as I got up to greet the lady. "Glad you found me so easily."

She extended her hand. It was cool and a bit wet. "Thank you for seeing me, Mr. Denning. May I sit?" She looked me over. "You're younger than I thought."

"Yes, please sit down here, opposite me." I looked over those penetrating blue eyes. "Don't let appearances fool you. I've knocked around more than I like to say. But if you don't like what you see or hear, you can get up and leave any time, Mrs. Wilson, no questions asked. I don't have to apologize for my youth or if my style makes you think you might not be making the best investment here."

She squirmed in her seat a bit at my frankness. "Well, if you put it that way, Mr. Denning, I think I've got to give you the opportunity to prove your mettle."

"So…what can I do for you? You were rather mysterious on the telephone."

"I know this may sound strange to you, Mr. Denning, but I believe my husband is someone else."

I sat at my desk opposite her somewhat perplexed. "Uh… could you clarify that a bit for me? Do you mean someone other than the man you married? Or someone who was never who you thought he was?"

She got out a cigarette. "May I?" I nodded my head and lit her smoke for her. She took a long drag. "Thank you. I need to get this off my chest."

By the looks of her chest, I could vouch there might end up being quite a bit of talk before the interview was finished. "It's okay, Mrs. Wilson. I've seen and heard a lotta strange things in my time."

"Have you—have you ever handled cases with circumstances that cannot be explained? I mean, like things that don't seem… worldly?"

"You might say that—plus six years on the Los Angeles Police force kinda gives you a crash course in human nature and odd occurrences, Mrs. Wilson."

"Oh, I see. Well, you have a nice face. I guess I can tell you. But, please, this must remain in strictest confidence—or else people will think I'm…well, know you, crazy or something."

"Shoot—I'm all ears."

"Well, I've been married for about three years. My husband told me he was a developer of gold mines in Northern California and Nevada. He said his company rented heavy equipment to re-open and reinforce old mines that still had a lot of ore in them."

"Okay…so far so good." I took out a Lucky Strike and lit it.

"But when I asked him if I could go along and see one for myself he became irritated and said a mine shaft was no place for a woman. Maybe I could accept that, but then strange things began to happen. Four nights ago he called me here in Los Angeles and said he was phoning from Reno, Nevada and he'd be home in about a week. That night when I was going to bed, I happened to look out the window down at the street lamp before I drew the drapes. There leaning against the lamp post was my husband!"

"And you're sure it was him? Weren't you a little far away to make a positive identification?"

"Never with Todd. He's six-foot six, always wears a light sport jacket with light-brown trousers, brown and white wing-tip shoes and a straw Panama hat. That was exactly what I saw."

"Well, granted there aren't too many guys at six-six, lady, but still couldn't it have been someone else your husband hired to look and act like him? But of course, that begs the question…why…doesn't it?"

"It gets worse, Mr. Denning. Just as I turned the light off to get into bed, the phone rang again and it was Todd, my husband. He told me he forgot to tell me he loved me. I ran to the drapes and peaked out. That man was still standing there looking up at my window—while he was on the phone to me from Reno, Nevada!"

I took a deep drag on my cigarette and squinted my eyes to look important. I was thinking of my adventures in other dimensions with Lei-tao, Toggth, Ravna, the rather strange news that Honey's sire was an alien from some other star system or whatever—and that he, too, looked just like *us*. So who was to say Mrs. Wilson's husband was like Nazir Ravna had told me, "we look just like you, Denning…" I put my cigarette out and reached into my top right drawer for a bottle of gin. "Would you like a shot of gin and tonic, Mrs. Wilson?" I asked.

She eyed me curiously. "Are you a drunkard, Mr. Denning? My father always told me to stay away from a man who drinks too much alcohol."

I laughed. "Well, Mrs. Wilson, I think I drink moderately. So…do you want one or not—I don't charge for drinks, you know."

She smiled and relaxed her face a bit. "Yes, Mr. Denning. I do believe I would like that drink. Maybe it will relax me."

I poured us both a jigger of gin and added the tonic, handing the lady one of the glasses. "Well, here's to you, kid!" I said, gulping the whole damn thing down at once. Mrs. Wilson, a bit more lady-like, sipped hers. "So…now you've made your opening statement. Was the man standing in the lamp-light your husband or an imposter? And…are you certain the man on the phone had the voice of your husband?"

"Yes, absolutely. I would know Todd's voice anywhere—even on the phone. It's very distinctive. He never learned to articulate *L*'s or *R*'s. I find that curious, but he says he was educated—educated—uh—"

"—educated where, Mrs. Wilson?"

"I—I don't know. He's never said. But to continue, Mr. Denning." She took a larger sip from her drink and sat back, a little more relaxed. "Now, perhaps you must suspend reality as we know it, because that's what I've had to do. The very next night Todd calls me again. I go through exactly the same paces except I don't go to the drapes before he calls. I answer the phone and he informs me he's run into some difficulties with the mining operation in Nevada and he'll be delayed a week or so more. Out of curiosity, I carefully make my way to the drapes, open them a crack and then—then—" Her eyes began to mist in terror. "—then…there stood *two* of my husband looking up at me in the light of the street lamp!"

Carefully, I watched Mrs. Wilson's expression. She seemed to be on the level. "Just so we make things crystal clear here, let me ask you: are you on any drugs or hallucinatory medications that might make you see double or create some kind of fantasy scenario?"

She looked rather indignantly at me. "Mr. Denning! I pride myself on good diet, good exercise and moderation in all things."

"Okay, okay, Mrs. Wilson. Just making sure." I rubbed my chin thoughtfully. "So let me put this thing together in my

361

words and you tell me how it sounds to you. First of all your husband goes away to work in Nevada. Presumably, he calls you one night from that state and while you're talking to him you also happen to see him physically standing below your apartment under a streetlight. What floor do you live on?"

"The second. I don't like ground floor apartments, safety and all, you know. Todd and I have always lived in second or third-floor apartments."

"So you'd have a pretty good view from the second floor. Now, I need to ask another question. Was he in the habit of calling you every night to say hello or that he missed you?"

"No. He hardly calls when he's away. But these two nights in a row he did call. It was not like him, but I certainly welcomed the sudden attention. Todd's not a man to be…be…shall I say, demonstrative?"

"I see. Okay, so on this second night he calls, you're getting ready for bed. You answer and while you're talking to your husband, you quietly make your way over to the drape. How far was the location of the phone from the window?"

"We have a long extension cord on our telephone. It's not a wall type, but one of the newer Bakelite portable dial phones." She looked at me with a slight flush of color coming to her cheeks. "I'm not lying to you, why would I lie to you? Why would I waste your time—or mine by coming here?"

"I don't know, Mrs. Wilson, humans are a strange lot. Sometimes loneliness drives people to strange places."

"Do I look like a lonely woman to you, Mr. Denning?"

I looked her over a second time. Her fingernails were done immaculately, she wore a pair of gold earrings and her hair was meticulously perfect. "You want my truth or a courtesy?"

"I always appreciate the truth." She looked at me with those very blue eyes, as if I were to say the wrong thing she'd crumble right there in front of me.

"I'd say yes, Mrs. Wilson. I think you're lonely and even though you're financially comfortable, I'd guess you feel you got yourself into a lonely marriage, the kind where only one of you is playing the game."

She looked away. "Okay…so if we're telling truths—yes, Todd is often cold and absent, even when we're together. But I don't see what my intimate life has to do with what I came to you about."

"They're all mixed up in the same batch of human behavior, lady. You see, being a cop taught me there are a thousand crossover lines between fact and fiction, love and hate, happiness and despair. You come in here looking for help, right? How can I help if I don't understand what makes you and your husband tick? You know why? Because when you send me out onto that street out there, the more I know the quicker I can resolve this whole thing and save me some shoe leather and you a lotta dough. People hide behind their moral or religious partitions, pretending that all is hunky-dory when all the time they're dyin' inside from lack of sleep, lack of love, lack of friends and missing the one thing in their lives they sought out in a relationship with another person, *companionship with security*. Now you tell me, Mrs. Wilson, I'll bet you're experiencing neither quality companionship nor an all too secure life just about now."

She got up out of her chair. She reached into her purse for another smoke. I came around and lit it for her. "Thank you." She walked away from me, her tall, wonderful body looking just fine in that tight skirt, her buttocks moving like slow pistons on a quality engine. "No one's ever spoken to me like that, Mr. Denning. I can see why you might be very successful at what you do. You're a good psychologist."

"I don't know about that, Mrs. Wilson. I just call it as I see it."

"But you can't see my life from your eyes, Mr. Denning."

363

"Maybe not, but there's a pretty good chance I have a pair of lenses that fit. That's why I'm a private dick."

She flushed. "A private what?"

"Private dick, you know, detective—probably named after police detectives like the hero in those Dick Donovan detective books."

"Oh," she said, clearing her throat and taking a puff on her cigarette.

I sat back down behind my desk. Rusty Wilson followed and came to sit opposite me once again. "So how'd you get the name 'Rusty'? Somehow you don't look like a Rusty to me."

"My hair, when I was a girl. I was born Florence McCready. My mother is Irish, my father was Scottish. I used to be called Flo."

"Do you mind if I call you Flo? You can call me Cable to cut out all the formal crap. I'm not much for stuffy protocol."

"Okay, Cable. Actually, I like Flo better. It's more feminine, don't you think?"

"Definitely." I lit up another smoke, poured us both some more booze and sat back in my chair. "Now, Flo, as I see it, you need someone to sniff out this mystery hubby that shows up in twos—and is supposed to be a few hundred miles away at the same time on the telephone." I was thinking of Lei-tao and the tricky shape-shifting I had witnessed. "I think I need to start in your bedroom."

She giggled under her breath. "I beg your pardon?"

"I mean I need to see the pattern. The phone calls, the guys appearing under the street lamp, etcetera. Is your husband scheduled to call again soon?"

"Why, as a matter of fact he is. That in itself is unusual. He said he needed to talk to me tonight about meeting him in San Francisco for a holiday. Of course I was quite taken aback by that. He's never done that before in the three years of our marriage."

"Maybe he misses you. So, when is he calling you again?"

"Tonight. Can you come? I want you to know, Mr. Denning—uh, Cable, I'm already building a confidence in you. So…perhaps now I can tell you the most horrible part of it."

"Well, thanks for the vote of confidence, Flo. Yeah, I can be there—what time is Mr. Wilson supposed to be calling?"

"Nine o'clock. He said he would be calling at the same time, on the dot."

"So, now, what's this most horrible thing I need to know?"

"Well, first of all, Todd was only six-feet two when we married. Each year he's grown taller. I know because I've had to change out his entire wardrobe each year."

I raised my eyebrows on that one. "Hmmm…so that means your husband has grown about an inch and a third each year."

She took a deep slug from her drink. "Now, here's the part that frightens me so, that I can hardly speak of it, Cable."

"Just go slow, Flo. I'm right here and so far you're hitting a hundred percent on my truth meter."

"So one day the maid was late in cleaning the bathroom and I needed to take a shower. When I entered I noticed a lot of flaky patches of skin all over the shower floor. Todd had left that morning for Reno. I didn't think too much of it at the time. A day later I was sorting out Todd's older clothes to take downstairs into our garage to donate to charity. We keep a big burlap bag. I went downstairs with an armful of his clothes. The bag seemed fuller than I had remembered, so I rummaged around in the bag to make more room. Suddenly….oh, Cable—suddenly…I, uh,…..oh!"

"Suddenly what? You can't leave it hangin' here, kid."

"Suddenly…my hand felt something---ooooo! cold and

leathery. It was large and as I pulled on it a very long scaly skin-thing emerged! I screamed to myself and dropped it on the floor. But then I regained my senses. On a tool bench in front of our car, I found a yardstick. The light in the basement was dim, but I could see well enough to spread this horrible thing out to measure it. It came out to be almost six-foot six!"

Now we had crossed that line into the incredulous. Somewhere in human experience there comes a threshold when one either dismisses what he's hearing or suspends his notion of reality long enough to see it through. I always chose the latter. I thought carefully about what my client had told me. "I have to admit this sounds very bizarre, Flo. But you know what, I believe you. I've experienced a few inexplicable things in my life—enough to know we live in a limited three-dimensional world here."

"Then you really do believe me?" she said, her eyes lighting up. She got up, came over to me and hugged me where I sat. "Thank God! At least there's one other person who believes me!"

I smiled up at her as she withdrew her arms. "So, if you want to hire me on the spot, I receive twenty-dollars a day plus expenses, like carfare, meals and any photos or documents taken pertaining to your case. How's that sound?"

She reached into her purse and handed me five twenty-dollar bills. "Can we accomplish this in five days—and can you start tonight?"

"Didn't you say old Todd boy is supposed to call tonight?"

"Yes."

"Then give me your address and telephone number and we've got a deal."

"What about agreements, contracts—something in writing that I paid you? Even a receipt?"

I opened my center drawer and took out a receipt book. I

scribbled the necessary info and handed it to her. "As far as a contract is concerned, Flo, I work on the honor system—you trust me to deliver and I'll trust you to always tell the truth and update me as the situation requires."

She smiled and then took a last swallow of her gin and tonic. "I think I like you, Cable Denning, Private Detective. I've never known any man to talk as frankly as you do. It's like you don't care, but you do—I mean, when you talk. I must admit, I feel a little disarmed around you."

"Well, don't let that cloud the business at hand, Flo." I got up and escorted her to the door. On an impulse she grabbed my shoulders and hugged me, kissing me on the cheek.

"I'll bet not all your clients do that, Cable, do they?" she cooed.

"Frankly, no…but I'm flattered. I'll see you at your apartment about eight-thirty tonight."

"Please be punctual. We don't want to miss Todd's call."

"I'm always punctual, Flo—unless, of course, I'm dead."

A shiver ran through her. "Please….don't even joke about that, Cable. So far you're the only human being I can trust. I need you to believe in me. You still do, don't you? I feel very vulnerable right now."

"It's okay, Flo. Yeah, I'm with you—and you're in safe hands. See you tonight."

She walked down those stairs from the landing with the kind of movement that wars could be fought over. I had a feeling, however, it was gonna be a hell of a night!

Flo 'Rusty' Wilson lived off Hyperion on Rowena Avenue, between the Los Feliz area and the Silver Lake area. I took the red car out and hoofed it a few blocks over to 3228 Rowena. It was just getting good and dark by the time I reached the building. I glanced up at the second floor and then across the street where Flo had told me her duplicate husbands stood in the light under the lamppost. At 8:25 I rang her buzzer downstairs and she admitted me. I knocked on the door that read "#2." She opened the door and if I had thought this woman to be a voluptuous babe before, what I saw now knocked me six ways from Sunday! She was dressed in a black negligée with a wonderful light-pink over-robe, matching pearl slippers. She had taken her hair down and it flowed like laced marble over her shoulders. Her skin was that tone of alabaster one sees in paintings except without much makeup, one could make out the freckles that trademarked so many redheads. "Cable," she greeted me, "Thank you for being so punctual."

"I told you that's my second name, Flo." I entered and looked around at the very rich furniture and the thick floor-to-ceiling drapes that hung at the two large windows, one of which faced the lamppost across the street. Then I looked back at her. "Wow, lady, I—I, uh, didn't expect such an elegant reception. You're quite a knock-out in that evening wear."

She smiled. "Thank you, Cable. May I offer you a drink?"

"Got any smooth English gin?" I asked, still looking around.

"As a matter of fact I do. I went out and bought some bootleg this afternoon since I knew that's what we were drinking at your office earlier."

"Well, I'm afraid mine was half rot-gut and half raw alcohol." She went to the wet bar and fixed us both a drink. She came over to me and handed me one. "Thanks, Flo. You have a nice place here. It just doesn't look very lived in...no offense."

"It is a bit sterile, isn't it. Todd is so fussy about things being just so. Personally, I'm a little bit more of a scatter rug person. But we make do."

We sat opposite each other for a few minutes. After she finished her first drink, however, she came over to the sofa where I was and sat down next to me. She was wearing an exotic perfume that was transforming some of my organs to some new land of erotic fantasy. "Your—your perfume…is it something…that affects you…the way…it affects me?"

"How does it affect you, Cable?"

"Affectionately, is the best way I can put it. It kind of transports a guy to some other place, if you know what I mean."

"Well, it is expensive, made from genuine whale oils and special herbs. It's called *Caribbean Nights*."

"Phew! I'm betting it could get a guy hooked on a dame right here in the *Los Angeles nights*."

She laughed. "I like your humor, Cable. When I first met you, I thought you a bit gruff and undiplomatic. But now that I know you better…ummm…well, I think I like you."

I cleared my throat. "I—I think we'd better prepare for the business at hand, don't you?"

"Yes," she said. She took my hand and led me to her spacious bedroom. The vanity dresser had a series of four white candles lit and no other source of light. "Welcome to my bedroom, Cable," she whispered in a rather seductive voice. My heart began to pound a little more than normal.

"It's not every day I'm standing in the middle of some gorgeous dame's boudoir. By the way, before I forget it, do you have a sample of the leather-like skin stuff you found in the laundry bag downstairs?"

"Yes, we can get some when you leave tonight."

"Good enough." I was thinking all kinds of things, not the least of which was fighting off a rising penis pulsing in my pants. But I was good at doing my job and that would have to come first.

At precisely 9:00 p.m. the phone rang. Flo played her part well and responded to her husband's comments and questions. While she was talking I slipped quietly in front of the drape that covered the window in question. Ever so slightly, I parted the two wings. Much to my amazement, sure enough, two very tall men stood under the streetlight, dressed exactly as Flo had described, right down to the Panama hats. While she was talking, I slipped out of the apartment down into the lobby, still carefully observing the men across the street. I decided to do a gung-ho rush and came flying out of the building toward them with my .38 drawn. By the time I got across the street they had vanished into thin air!

Immediately my instincts went to Flo's safety and I ran to the front door of the apartment building. The damn thing was locked so I rang the buzzer. I waited to what seemed forever and then Flo buzzed back and I leapt up the stairs to #2. I entered the room just in time to have Flo run and collapse into my arms, her face as white as a ghost. I dragged her over to the sofa, got some cold water and dabbed her pretty face, freckles and all. Soon she revived. "You okay, kid? What happened?"

She clung to me, frightened, trembling. "The minute you left the apartment, Todd knew it and warned me that I had betrayed him and he was coming back to punish me! Then he hung up." She began to whimper like a young girl who'd fallen down and bruised her knee.

"Well, I didn't have the best luck, either. Just like you said there were two guys dressed alike, but by the time I rushed across the street with my gun drawn, they had somehow just—just vanished—damnedest thing I'd ever seen."

Rusty Wilson pulled my face down onto her mouth and kissed me like it was her last kiss in this world. Her warm, moist lips made me forget there was ever anything like danger out there in the unknown and suddenly I was floating with her, holding her in my arms with one hand fondling one of those incredible breasts of hers. She sighed and moaned and lay down on the sofa full-length, pulling me on top of her. "Please, make love to me, Cable. Now. I've been so cold, so lonely—I need to know I'm still a woman, still desirable."

"You're still *very* desirable, Flo. But I don't know if I can do this. I've—I've got this thing about truth, remember? And—and my truth is I'm engaged to be married in December. And Honey and I are kind of tight, you know. I don't want to feel guilty tomorrow."

She stopped and gently pushed me over. She sat up, wiping her eyes. "I'm sorry. I don't want to complicate your life. Nor mine. I'm—I'm just so lost now…confused…I thought I had a husband who—who was…" Then she put her head into her hands and cried some more. I got up and made us both a drink and came back, took out a cigarette and lit one for both of us. "Thanks, Cable. You're a good man. I think you're a rare man, too."

"Well, you were sure right about two things tonight. One, you weren't kidding about triplicate husbands—and this English gin is damn good. Bottoms up," I said and toasted her. In the melee one of her breasts had fallen out of her gown and she tucked it back in. I held her wrist. "It isn't that I don't want you, lady—I do. It's just that—"

"—I know, Cable, you told me. I'll be a good girl. I guess we'd better go downstairs and get you that sample you requested."

"Yeah, good idea."

We gulped our drinks and she put on a heavier robe. We went down a back way into a small garage. She pulled the chain on a ceiling light socket and a dim light filled the room. We edged around her green Packard until we reached a long utility table. Suddenly Flo started. "Cable—it's gone! It was right here. See the measuring stick? Someone took it! Now, I guess, you'll never believe me, will you?"

"Why not, babe, I have so far." I got down on my knees and felt along the concrete floor. Slightly under the table I found a small patch of something that felt like what Flo had described. I brought it up into the light. "Is this the kind of stuff you were talking about?"

She examined it. "Yes! Only it was almost six-feet six inches long and about two feet wide."

"Well, someone doesn't want you to know who they really are—and I suspect it's good old hubby Todd. With your permission, I'm going to take this scrap to someone who might be able to help."

We went back upstairs and she carefully wrapped the item in some wax paper so it wouldn't flake off any more than it had. She gave it to me and I put it gingerly in my vest pocket. "You know, Cable, I was so excited for you in that moment of danger—I don't know what came over me—"

"—it's okay, Flo. Danger and desire often go hand-in-hand. You know, like one triggers the other?"

"Yes. May I at least kiss you a gentle kiss good-night?"

I chuckled. "You know, lady, how are we going to maintain a professional up and up relationship with all this kissin' goin' on?"

She smiled and held me, pressing her cheek to mine, whispering into my ear. "I love the...*up and up* part...if you ever change your mind, I'm just a phone call away." Then she moved her mouth around to mine and kissed me with those warm, inviting lips. I responded and was just about to fall over that edge again when I thought of Honey. Damn! What a conflict, this thing between morality and natural impulse, I thought. She drew her face a few inches away. "I even love the way you kiss, Mr. Detective."

"Well, thanks, doll. But do me a favor next time we meet, will you?"

"If I can, of course..."

"Don't be packin' that perfume! That's a powerful weapon to be carryin' around in mixed company." I said, trying to keep it light...but it didn't work.

"Oh, Cable, please don't go! I feel afraid. I don't want to stay here tonight. What if he or 'they' come back for me? Will they kill me?"

"That's a good question. I don't know. It depends on what they're hiding and what the stakes are. You know, life can be reduced down to two or three easy categories. Money. Sex. Power. In this case, and I can't tell you why, I think it's a matter of power or domination of some sort. You obviously don't need money and you say Todd's a little cold in the bedroom. So, get my point?"

"Yes…so how does that figure in with my safety?"

"He wouldn't be after you unless you knew more than you should. Why they were so careless in enticing you to the window while another one of him was on the telephone baffles me, frankly. They have nothing to gain with you—or do they?" I was thinking of Joe Lorena and how he had used Honey's natural mother for a breeding machine to create a new cross-species. What if the Three Todds were another species of alien wanting to do the same thing with Flo.

"What do you mean?"

"Can you have children?"

"As far as I know, yes. I'm thirty-three now and never really wanted children. I don't think I'm good mother material. I'm kind of a man's woman who also likes to shop or travel the world rather than tend kids."

"I see. Did you and your husband ever discuss children?"

"When we were first married. But he said he couldn't have children and that suited me just fine. But he did press me a couple of times more recently, asking me if I was still fertile, which I thought curious."

My suspicions were beginning to be confirmed. "Okay, doll, here's what I think. I think your husband might be, as you suspected—some new brand of alien. It could be he wants to use you to breed sustainable offspring. They do it by inseminating you artificially, allowing you then to 'grow' the child to full term. The child born, however, is a hybrid, and cannot reproduce itself. So, once they get you where they want you, they will keep you producing like a baby factory until you die on the table."

"Oh, my God, Cable—how can this be? We're living in 1929 America. Don't you think the Government would catch these creatures?"

"What if the Government *is* these creatures, Flo?"

She fell silent and just held on to me, trembling. "Maybe I should conceive your baby, and while I'm pregnant there's nothing they can do to me."

I looked at her with surprise and a sympathetic grin. "You know, lady, you're okay for someone I just met today. But somehow it doesn't feel right to go around having natural babies to stem the tide of other invading species."

"Why not? And look at all the fun we'll have getting pregnant?"

"I thought you said you weren't into kids?"

"*Your* baby, Cable. That's all. One."

"Sorry, Flo, but I'm going to have pass on that one. We've had a few drinks tonight and we're a little tight, not to mention all riled up about the three husbands haunting your abode. I am flattered, however, and I agree with you—most of the pleasure is in getting you in the family way."

We decided to take Flo to a hotel in Hollywood. By midnight she was tucked away and I left her car at the hotel parking. Then I took the streetcar back to Cahuenga and walked up to Franklin to Cable Denning's new private detective hangout. I got in. I was exhausted and I just remembered the bed had no sheets or blankets on it yet. I had picked up the mattress from my old room in my mother's house. It was a bit old and lumpy, but what the hell, it'd do for now. I fell onto the bed with all my clothes on, burdened with the thought that tomorrow I would have Joe Lorena examine the strange piece of leathery skin tucked into the waxed paper in my coat pocket.

All night long the forlorn sound of that lonely sax played in and out of my restless dreams. I was in a very large, oblong room being chased by spider webs that kept entangling me in corners and I'd have to fight my way out by flailing my arms. Soon a very naked Rusty Wilson came running toward me, her mouth open with two viper fangs ready to sink into my neck. I took a shoe off my foot and swung wildly at the gorgeous but lethal woman whose nipples began to bleed green blood as her eyes turned red. I ran toward the far end of the oblong chamber only to come face to face with Joe Lorena in a very tight fitting costume made of some kind of green, glowing rubber, it appeared. He signaled for me to follow him and I did so. But before I could get through the doorway, Rusty's powerful hand grabbed my arm and pulled me back. Joe came again to my rescue and pounded his fist against Rusty's forehead and she collapsed. He then ordered me to take her arm and drag her through the door. The next thing I remember was that I was hovering over Rusty Wilson's great body about to penetrate her. Her snake-like qualities were gone and she opened her legs and welcomed me, but I got nervous and couldn't perform because I suddenly observed the whole room was filled with onlookers watching the curious ritual of mating, or whatever I was supposed to bc doing.

I awoke with a start, sweating, and since I had no sheets, blankets or a change of clothes, I stripped, hung my clothes out to dry and drew myself a bath. I fell asleep in the tub, this time into a restful, dreamless peace.

By about noon the phone had rung a couple of times but I didn't have the energy to answer it. I finally staggered out of the bathtub, let myself drip-dry and eventually got my clothes back on. I went to the phone and called *Syndcorp Imports*, which was Jack Dragna's mafia cover corporation. I finally got Joe on the phone and told him I needed to see him post haste. He said he'd be taking a late lunch, but I told him I'd need a lab with a microscope. He hesitated and then told me to meet him at a house near Griffith Park at 4:00 p.m. I called the *Roosevelt Hotel* to check on Rusty Wilson. She said she had a terrible night and wished I had spent it with her, and when could I see her. I told her I'd come by tonight, after I'd had the you-know-what inspected under a microscope. She also complained that someone was watching her throughout breakfast in the café downstairs. That didn't sit too well with me.

Punctually at 4:00 p.m. I walked to the doorway of 2561 Canyon Drive. It was a quiet neighborhood with hillsides going both east and west not far away. This part of Griffith Park was a box canyon leading into a famous movie-shoot area called Bronson Park. A nice middle-aged woman came to the door. She didn't say a word but led me down into a basement where I found Joe Lorena standing over a microscope.

"Ah, Cable. I was quite surprised to hear from you. But I see you have a problem maybe I can help you with?"

"Yeah, thanks for seeing me, Joe. In a nutshell I get my very first private detective gig with this babe who goes on about her husband not being her husband and it ends up with there being three of them. Long story short, everything she said was true—plus this." I handed him the small piece of leathery skin wrapped up in the waxed paper.

"Well, real life is stranger than fiction, as they say." He took the paper and carefully unwrapped the sample. "I already know what it is—but let me verify it for you." He placed the thing under the microscope and then summoned me over. "Now focus it for your eyes. You see the scales? This is reptilian, nothing more than a snake shedding its skin. Your client has obviously married one of the *lizard people*, an alien race integrated into your species many hundreds of years ago. But now they're having trouble. They seem to have developed an abnormal growth pattern somehow."

"Yeah, I'll say—try about four inches growth in three years. So, are these creatures dangerous—it seems my client has been threatened."

"You bet, especially if they've been found out. They'll eliminate her. More than likely she's already been implanted with a tracer beam, so they can find her anywhere in the world if they want to. I'd send her to Monterrey, Mexico immediately. There's a special clinic we have set up there that can remove the transmitter and free her from this terrible situation."

"Can you set the appointment up, Joe? Money's not a big thing with her, so she can afford to get there and back."

"Normally I wouldn't, Cable, but for my future son-in-law—I'll do it."

"I'm grateful, Joe. This is a lovely, intelligent woman with a lot of moxie. She's too young to die and it'd look real bad on my track record if I lost my first client, now, wouldn't it?"

Joe laughed. "Part of the game, Cable. Welcome to life outside the protective shell of the police force."

"So you say these lizard creatures are integrated into our society? Do they have to replicate the same way you did with Honey's mother?"

"Yes. They are also unable to matc with humans without the assistance of implantation. But I'll tell you, their mortality rate is high because they keep the mothers pregnant constantly until they exhaust them."

"Oh, that's swell. It's exactly what I suspected they might want my client for. You see, Joe, I'm getting more and more perceptive all the time."

"I'm glad, Cable— but don't always trust it…use it wisely."

"And just where do these reptilians show up in our society—beside resurrected gold mines in Nevada and the like?"

"Did you say gold mines? That means deep shafts into the earth—which in turn means they're building a new incubation nest. And where do they show up? They are attracted to big business, government and the military. I suspect their numbers must be increasing. Maybe that's why they are confiscating more and more human females. These guys play rough, Cable. I'll report this to my people."

"It sounds so weird…"

"What do you mean?"

"Your 'people'—I forget just because you look just like us—you're not us, Joe. Sometimes I wish you were. Then maybe I could hate you for being such a son-of-a-bitch. But I promised I'd keep my nose clean because of Honey. As I said, she really wants to love you—but because of your attitude and actions, you keep her on a balancing wire."

"I don't mean to. I really want us to be closer. You must remember, she's got half of me in her, Cable. That *alien race memory* in her will save her from not completely understanding her own flesh, blood and bone."

"For both your sakes, I hope so, Joe."

"Whatever you do, don't engage them. They're a feisty bunch, power-hungry and without conscience. So beware, don't tangle with them if you can help it."

"Are they mortal—I mean can a bullet stop them?"

"Oh, yes, they bleed green blood and perish in a big puddle on the floor."

"Well, at least *that's* good to know." I thanked Joe again and he told me he'd prepare the road ahead for the Monterrey, Mexico trip by plane. I realized I'd have to get over to the *Roosevelt Hotel* as soon as I could. I'd have to stick with Rusty

Wilson until after the operation in Monterrey…which meant more money, but time away from my business and Honey.

I got back to the office and called Honey, telling her my involvement in my very first case was taking me to Monterrey, Mexico. What I didn't tell her was that I wasn't going alone. Well enough left alone, I thought.

Then I packed a few items in a bag and headed for 7000 Hollywood Boulevard and the Roosevelt Hotel. The place was only two years old and the very first Academy Awards Presentations were held this year in the *Blossom Ballroom*. I had put Rusty Wilson on the top floor, overlooking the boulevard itself—I wrapped hard on the door of Room #1200. "Who's there?" a soft feminine voice spoke.

"It's me. Cable."

She opened the door, grabbed me and clung to me the minute I entered. "Oh, God, Cable! The tall creatures—they're everywhere! I couldn't even have lunch! They know who I am—how did they find me?"

"You've got a tracer implanted in you. Get packed, we gotta get out of here *as of* now!"

"Are you coming with me? Please say yes!"

"You're my client, aren't you? I'm pledged to protect you, Flo. So hang on, it's gonna be tough going for a few days."

"Where are we going?"

"Can't say. They've got big ears, too. We need to go while it's still light."

I didn't mean to, but I watched as this gorgeous, mature woman threw off her lounging clothes and dressed there right in front of me. I couldn't help it, but it still got a rise out of me, so to speak, when I saw those perfect large breasts and wonderful pink nipples combined with a fine, white ass. I could swear she was giving me the show on purpose, but it could also have been she was scared and moving under the pressure of my drumbeat.

We got out of the hotel after I paid the bill in her stead, keeping her hidden in a lounge area. We went to get the car and I piled her into the green Packard. I drove us to my office. I grabbed her hand and we walked quickly up the stairs and inside. I went to the phone and called Joe. He gave me the necessary information to get to *Angeles Mesa Drive Airport* in Burbank and to look for a silver two-engine airplane with *Syndcorp Imports* on the side. The plane would be warming up and a pilot named Eddie would greet us. I thanked Joe again and we jumped back into Flo's Packard and drove out to the airport.

Flo was a good sport and trusted me implicitly. Once we parked the Packard and walked out onto the field and greeted Eddie, I felt a lot better. Eddie Contino was a nice guy with a big grin on his face. He loved flying, he told us, although he'd never flown to Monterrey, Mexico before. Once I had Flo sitting comfortably next to me in our own eight-seat cabin and the plane soared up off the runway, I began, in soft tones, to tell her what was up. "Now, remember me telling you that your husband somehow planted a tracing device in you? Well, we're going to a special location in Mexico to have it removed so these bums won't be able to find you."

"What do they want, Cable? The more I see them, the creepier I feel."

"I think, as we discussed, they originally had you sized up for mating material—to conceive and bring to full term as many babies as you could tolerate before you died in the process. Kind of like a female termite or queen bee—just a baby machine."

"Oh, God...and me, who didn't even want kids. How horrible."

"But now I think they want you dead. You know too much.

And unfortunately, when I shooed them away from across the street from your apartment, that offended them because then they knew you had switched sides, so to speak, and you would never be co-operative as a mamma-machine."

She grabbed my arm and kissed my shoulder. "Thanks to you, Cable. You're risking your own life now, aren't you? I'm so sorry, I had no idea—"

"—of course you didn't, who could've? Even *I'm* not in the alien business, you know. I try to run a legitimate private detective agency with integrity and good clients—"

"—I'll make it up to you, Cable. I have lots of money invested—and a fairly large bank account. I'll reimburse you well for this. Just thank you, Cable, thank you so much." She took a deep breath and looked out the west window at the setting sun. "Who knew just forty-eight hours ago that here I'd be with this handsome young private *dick*—short for detective—on my way to Mexico to have an alien apparatus removed from—from….?"

Our brains came to the same place at the same time. "Yeah, that's a good question. I wonder where they plant those things?"

She cuddled closer to me, putting her cheek on my shoulder. "I guess we'll find out. Cable…I feel so safe with you. Ordinarily I'd be frightened at the prospect of being operated on and all, taking a dangerous trip and being followed by other-worldly creeps—but with you—I don't know, it just feels safe. Can you understand anything I'm saying?"

"Sure, babe. I'm a safe kinda guy. So why don't you just lean back with me and let's see if we can get a little shut-eye, okay?" I stroked her hair with the palm of my hand and she leaned over to kiss me…those warm, soft lips clinging gently to my own. I could tell then and there, keeping out from between this lady's legs would be an extraordinary challenge in itself.

CHAPTER 16

VIPER IN A BASKET

It's a funny thing. When you wake up next to someone after a pleasant sleep, somehow that person seems closer to you in your life. That's how I felt when I awoke to feel Flo's head resting on my shoulder as the airplane hummed along. When she finally awakened, she looked up at me with a special smile. Eddie the pilot had left a tray of water, cigarettes, a bottle of tequila and a couple of glasses beside us as we slept. I poured some water for her and she gulped it all down. "Hello, Mr. Denning," she chirped. "I missed you. Even though I think I must have dreamed about you riding up on your white horse, sweeping me off my feet and taking me away to your castle."

I chuckled. "It's nice to know that chivalry isn't dead now, isn't it? I wish I had dreamed about you, but I don't remember a thing. But I *do* recall one thing—as a matter of fact, I kinda went to sleep with that image."

"And what might that be?"

"You getting dressed just before we left the hotel. I didn't mean to look, but I have to confess, the red-blooded American boy got the best of me."

She flushed a little. "Did you like what you saw?"

"You bet, and then some. You're quite a babe, Flo, Rusty Wilson…"

"Do you know you excite me so much I have to go to the bathroom?"

I laughed. "There's a little room at the back of the plane— but I'm afraid it's one-sex-fits-all."

"How do you mean that?" she asked as she stood up and

made her way across my body to the aisle. "I would love for your sex to fit *my* all."

I pretended to be shocked. "Miss whoever-you-are! How can you stand there like that and proposition the man you've employed to protect you—my, my—business relationships must be maintained, you know."

"Easy...I've wanted him since the first minute he touched me in my apartment. I don't think we're going to get out of this unscathed, Cable Denning. I hope it isn't one-sided...that would really hurt—"

"—go to the bathroom—you might feel differently when you get back," I kidded her.

Monterrey airport was small. All three of us left the airplane and we took a wild ride in an open air taxi to a hotel called the *Estrellita* on the outskirts of town. Eddie got a room on a lower floor while Flo and I were assigned one room with two double beds on the top floor. Fat chance, I thought the minute I entered the room, that both of those beds would be used. I had given up any idea of getting through another day without an intensely erotic encounter with this Flo 'Rusty' Wilson. For two days and several hundred miles it had been building up, so that by the time we set our bags down on the floor of our room, we both knew.

According to Eddie Contino, the operation was scheduled for the following evening at 9:00 p.m. Because of both innate laziness and the frequent, oppressive heat, the Mexicans didn't work from about noon to around 3:00 p.m. All business came to a halt, including, I assumed, the staff that kept the clinic going where I was to take Flo. So we decided to jump into a primitive shower that barely fit one of us, let alone both. I gave her a head start and while she was showering, I could hear a wonderful Mexican band playing on a radio somewhere down the hall. "Señor?" a voice called out from the bathroom. "I need a houseboy to scrub my back. Have you seen him?"

"Nope," I answered. "It's—it's his day off today. How about a young gumshoe with a lot of spin on his brush?"

"That sounds fine," she said. I stripped naked and entered the bathroom. The shower curtain was an old piece of canvas, soaked and moldy. But what was behind the curtain certainly wasn't. There in all her naked glory stood Flo, soaping down the front part of her amazing anatomy. It was so remarkable to me, even at my age, that a man should instinctively respond with such fervor to a naked woman's body. I guessed that it was somehow wired into the male sexual system and it was that drive that kept the world populated with the human species.

"Anything you see you like?" Flo asked in a very sensual voice.

"Yeah, just about everything, lady," I said, taking in the marvelous white skin that was glowing wet from the shower. I entered and packed my body next to hers, feeling her soapy body slide against mine. "Okay, so let's get the back done. We can't send you to bed looking like that."

"Looking like what?" she inquired, genuinely concerned, as if I knew something she didn't.

"Looking less than absolutely perfect. One speck of skin that doesn't belong there—and it's back to the factory you go!" I laughed.

She turned around to face the shower wall while I took the washrag and scrubbed her back. "Oh…oh…yes, there, right there. Ah….now…lower, Cable." I dropped the washrag and soaped up my bare hands, rubbing up and down on her buttocks. She sighed and moaned. "Lower…lower…please…the back of my legs…" I bent down as the water pouring from her long, wonderful red hair showered me as I moved my hands around on her near-perfect legs. Then she took my hand and lifted me up to face her, those abundant breasts pressing into my chest. "Now…my turn. She re-soaped the rag and began to wash my neck and shoulders. Soon she had moved down onto my chest and very slowly and sensually she soaped her hands and let the washrag fall, bringing her long, tapered fingers to massage my penis. She lifted my balls and massaged in a circular motion until I came to attention. Then she rinsed me thoroughly and went to her knees, taking all of my manhood into her mouth. I stood there with the shower water running over us, lost in the sucking motion this incredibly sensual woman was performing on me.

"Where in the—the—hell…did you get to be so good with a—a lizard for a husband?" I asked, quite distracted and my speech broken.

She took my very hard, swollen penis out of her mouth. "When a woman desires a man she really cares for…I don't think she needs any lessons, Cable…I just feel…instincts with my desire for you…."

Soon we exited the shower, dripping wet. She took my hand and led me to one of the beds, pushing me down onto it. Then she threw herself down beside me. Suddenly I was thinking about Honey again and my conscience began to bother me. What happened to Mr. Truth Guy? I asked myself. What happened to the man who wants to settle down with one woman and spend blissful years building a meaningful relationship? "I hate to say this at a time like this, but do you remotely remember I'm getting married soon to a peach of a gal—and I'm supposed to be protecting you, not screwing you like we picked each other up in California and now we're in Mexico keeping our dirty little secrets."

She cooled down and sat up on the bed. "Is that what you think of me? A pick-up who's easy—or lonely—or desperate? Well, Mr. Denning, I'll have you know women can turn things on or off a lot easier than can men. So, if that's the way you want it—"

"—I didn't mean to get you mad or hurt you, Flo. I know you're disappointed. But you know, you're like a big test for me."

"How so?"

"Well, like it or not—and even though I've had a lot of years with the police department—you're my very first client as a private investigator. I just opened shop a little while ago. If I fail by seducing the first good looking babe who comes through my doors—don't you see—I'd be setting a precedent for myself? I really think you hired me to have integrity and keep our relationship professional." I scooted out of bed and sat next to her. "I'm sorry...I—I let it go so far. And speaking of truth, I really wanted you—I still want you—and I'd be lying if I told you otherwise."

She put her hand on my leg, looking across the room. "So I'm Cable Denning's very first customer, huh? You're precious, Cable. A unique man. It's true, a lesser man would be on top of me right now having his way with me." Then she got up, went to her purse to get a cigarette and lit up. She did the same for me. She moved like a sensual cat toward me. "But it's tough, Cable. I've gone so long without being made love to. There's something about touching someone you care about and desire, that changes everything. That's what I've felt about you." She took a big drag and exhaled. "But...I did hire you, after all. What do I expect? That you service me as a woman while you're protecting me as a professional?"

"Well, the thought did occur to me—"

She laughed and the tension was broken. She came back down onto the bed and kissed me. "Can I at least do that?"

"Well, it costs more, especially when my meter's running."

"Well, buddy, my meter's been running for you since you first touched me back at my place in L.A."

I glanced over at the other bed. "So...I guess I'd better join the other bedbugs over there—and maybe you should stay here."

She took my cigarette and along with hers, got up and put them out in the ashtray on the little dresser. Then she came back and pushed me down onto the bed again. "I can't let that happen, Cable—I can't spend the rest of my life wondering how much I had missed in not having you." She plunged her lips onto my mouth and thrust her lovely lithe body onto mine, moving her pussy back and forth over my most private parts. "Please—I beg you! Make me feel like a woman, Cable—let me feel what it's like again—take the lady away with you to that exciting and beautiful land—and when tomorrow comes, you can forget it ever happened—forget me as a woman…I promise I'll never ask again….ever….!"

There in a dirty Mexican hotel room, the voluptuous red-head and I journeyed into the land of ecstasy and quelled our desires with sensual fulfillment again and again. Flo was a marvelous lover and as those wonderful long legs encompassed me and urged me into her deepest places. I was glad after all…I was glad that I had allowed that instinct to release itself, for none of it was wasted—that one lovely woman is as genuinely enjoyable as the next. It's man's illusion that so many differences exist in his current pleasure model, that two people can exchange on a par level and give equally to one another with no promise of a tomorrow. Finally spent, we slept wrapped up in each other's arms, lulled by the faint hum of the ceiling fan.

I woke up horny for that knock-out dame beside me, but she was fast asleep. Her breathing was slow and almost non-existent. I thought it would be a naughty but nice way to wake her up by some slow sexual stimulation. I slowly moved my hand up her leg into her thighs, brushed lightly over her mound and started for her stomach. I was shocked to feel that somehow during the night her belly had distended to the size of a small watermelon! I continued playing out my game, reaching her two mountainous breasts and fondling them with sweet tenderness. She began to stir and sigh. I moved back down over the swollen belly and cupped her pussy with the palm

387

of my hand. She opened her eyes. But there was something strange about them that I couldn't put my finger on. It was as if they had changed to a slightly more greenish-blue than I had recalled the day before. "Hello, there, sleepy head," I spoke softly.

She smiled and rubbed my hand more firmly into her womanhood. Then suddenly she cried out. "Owww!" Then she threw off the sheet and looked at her stomach. "God, Cable, what happened?! My—my stomach—it's all swollen—what did we eat yesterday—I don't understand!"

I was trying to wake up and do some thinking at the same time. I tried to make light of it. "You were saying you wanted to have my baby—and we did make love about a hundred times unprotected. I just didn't know they grow in there so fast!"

She tried to laugh. "Owww! Damn! These pangs, it hurts, Cable!"

I didn't waste any time. I threw on my clothes and went downstairs and got Eddie Contino out of bed. "It's Mrs. Wilson, Eddie—we've gotta get her to that clinic now—and I mean *now*! Contino didn't say a thing but put his clothes on hurriedly and we both went up to get Rusty. As we burst into the room the window closest to the bed was open and the dirty yellow curtain was blowing in the morning breeze. Rusty Wilson was gone! Furiously I ran through the three rooms, checked the closet and looked out both windows, one overlooking an alley, the other the street out in front. Nothing! I was about to run out with Eddie when I spotted something on the open bed. There scattered in a small area on the sheet were unmistakable fragments of the slick, leathery skin Rusty's husband had shed back in L.A. I swept them up into my palm, threw them in my pocket and asked Eddie to get us to the clinic as soon as possible. We rode through donkey dung, vegetable carts, chickens and goats in the street and erratic drivers so anxious to commit suicide that I felt like jumping out and walking the distance. Finally the taxi pulled up in front of a very modern building and we flew out. I went immediately to the main desk, but it took Eddie to explain who we were. We were shown into a large waiting room where just the two of us stood. Soon a middle-aged man with a large moustache and thick glasses presented himself.

"I am Dr. Zellini—your young woman is not due until 9:00 p.m.—you are aware of that."

"Yeah, we are, Doc, but you see the lady in question has disappeared. Maybe forty minutes ago from the hotel *Estrellita*."

"Oh. That's unfortunate. We'll have to notify the authorities. In Mexico, that isn't easy. In the meantime, I think one of you should communicate back to California and explain the situation."

"Good idea." He led me to a phone in a private office. I asked Eddie to make sure the good doctor notified the local cops. I called *Syndacorp Imports* collect and asked for Joe Lorena. He came to the phone, I told him exactly what had happened. He remained calm and told me the lizard people must have traced Rusty Wilson to the hotel and struck the minute I was out of the room. He warned me about any of several things that could happen, but at any rate, I'd best consider my ex-client dead. He also urged Eddie and I to get back to California as soon as possible. We spent all of the morning and most of the afternoon jumping on possible leads—like had anyone seen a gorgeous naked woman running down the street chased by a bunch of lizard men who were six-foot-six or taller? Or how about a woman wrapped up in snake-skin being carried into a hearse by very tall men who all happened to look alike? I kinda liked that one.

Finally we were directed to the main police station and met one Captain Mendoza. He had a pencil-thin mustache, dark burning eyes and nice silver temples with salt and pepper hair. "Señores...welcome to Mexico! I am sorry for your predicament." We thanked him and he presented us with a piece of paper written in Spanish. "*Tristemente, aquí* we have a young *mujer* close to your description lying quietly in the morgue downstairs. She died just one hour or so ago. *Lo siento*, such a *mujer bonita, también.*"

Mendoza took Eddie and I down three flights of concrete steps. When we reached that place where the stiffs hang out, I could smell the unmistakable mix of rotting flesh and formaldehyde. "And you're sure she died just an hour or two ago?" I asked, my gut senses bugging the hell out of me. "And what did she die of?"

"*Ay, señor, misterioso*—we cannot find a mark. *Venga, señores*, you will see."

We entered a dimly lit room where four autopsy tables stood. A kindly looking little Mexican man with a clean-shaven face and green smock greeted us. The two Mexicans exchanged some fast Spanish lingo and then the pathologist turned to us and led us to a table where a body lay under a sheet. With the large stand-out breasts and the distended stomach, I could tell before he lifted it that it was Rusty Wilson. When he uncovered her, both Eddie and I were taken aback. She looked absolutely lovely, as if she were asleep…not too pale and everything seemed untouched. "We cannot explain the swelling *aquí*," the little man said, pointing to Rusty's stomach. "She is not carrying *un bebé*. También, in the *pasaje vaginal* we find abundant remains of *spermatozoa*." Eddie threw me a knowing look, but I kept shut on that one.

"It is as if she *está muerta…pero…ella se ve pacífica*—and asleep," Captain Mendoza said.

"And you're sure there's no pulse, heartbeat, low-scale breathing or any other sign of life?" I asked.

The little pathologist covered Rusty's body with the sheet. "I am sure, señor. Sometimes young people stay fresh for several hours."

We thanked the men, stopped by the hotel for our bags and got a ride out to the dust-blown airport. It was getting dark by the time the mad hatter's ride from hell was over and we got out of the car, somewhat shaken but alive. Eddie Contino had been obviously shaken by the day's events. It wasn't exactly my favorite day, either. Not only did I lose a client—but my very first goddam one! And when a guy makes love to a gorgeous dish the night before and they have some fun times together— and bam! suddenly she's lying face up in the local morgue, it can take its toll on life's expectations.

"Gees, Denning," Eddie was saying. "How in the hell do you live your life on the edge like that? I thought she was a babe, too—and when a tough break like that comes along—"

"—she's not dead, Eddie."

"She's not? Coulda fooled me, buddy. I've seen a lotta stiffs in my time. She looked pretty, but she looked dead, too."

"Call it a hunch. You came in at the middle of the movie, Eddie. What I already went through with this dame *before* we got to Mexico is a whole book's worth." I looked at him as we started walking toward the plane. "How much do you know about—about things in the Dragna gang, or Joe Lorena? Or are you just a pilot…a lackey?"

"Yeah, that's me. See nothin', hear nothin', say nothin'. It ain't a good idea to be too curious in my line of work."

We got to the airplane, but when Eddie checked the fuel gauge from inside the cockpit, he came out storming. "What's up?" I asked.

"Son-of-a-bitch Mexicans! I told 'em to fill 'er up before we got back tonight."

"Well, there's still a guy hanging out at the tank truck by the tower." We walked over and found the man didn't speak any English. We hunted down the one clerk left in the terminal and he translated we wanted fuel and fast. But, it seemed in

Mexico, there's no such thing as fast.

Finally we rode out with the tank truck to our twin-engine silver bird. The attendant began pumping the fuel into the wings. Just as he finished and Eddie got into the cockpit to fire up the engines, I thought I saw some figures coming toward me. Only the sweep-light from the airport tower provided some light, but it seemed to me the figures were running toward the plane. I called to Eddie and he jumped out of the plane, this time with his .38 in hand. A chill went down my spine as I beheld what looked like a tall naked woman being pursued by three very tall hooded creatures. But just like my dream, as the female approached, I could tell it was Rusty Wilson and she was heading right for me full speed. I had one of those rare moments in my professional life—I froze. I couldn't even draw my gun as Rusty approached. But as she got closer I saw her mouth open wide and two deadly viper-like fangs extended from her eye-teeth, her eyes had turned a luminous green and she hissed a low, guttural sound at me. For a split second she hesitated, as if some old part of her remembered who I was—but it didn't last, for as the three creatures behind her stopped to observe, the tall, lithe female started to strike at me. Suddenly Eddie Contino's .38 emptied into Rusty's torso and blotches of green blood began to appear. She fell to the ground within two feet of me as I went to my knees, drew my gun and started shooting at the three other creatures. I hit one in the back of the head and it reeled, fell backward and came crashing down onto the tarmac.

I was down on my belly, face to face with the once beautiful body of Rusty Wilson. Her face was broken and distorted. Poor thing, I thought, she must have gone through hell in the last twenty-four hours. From human woman to corpse to resurrected alien reptile-woman! I picked myself up as Eddie approached me. "You alright, Denning? Shit, man, why did you hesitate? That thing was gonna do you in, man!"

"Thanks for saving my ass, Eddie. I thought it was the real

Rusty Wilson at first." Then I looked at Eddie's surprised and astonished face. "Plus I didn't want to kill my meal ticket. She was my client, if you'll remember."

"Who the fuck wants clients like that?" He looked over at the airport. Some activity seemed to be stirring. "We gotta get the shit outta here—c'mon."

"What about her? And the dead giant lizard I shot?"

"My orders are to leave with just our butts! Let's go!"

We boarded the plane and Eddie checked the wind direction with his finger out of the cockpit window and we took off, heading into a light evening breeze. I collapsed into one of the eight vacant seats. From that day on I had a lot more faith in my nightmares, not to mention my intuitions. My brain was so muddled with questions and unsolvable conundrums that I asked Eddie for the whereabouts of all the booze the plane was carrying and helped myself to a goodly amount of it. Several hours later I was drunk and asleep on the runway at *Angeles Mesa Drive* airport. Eddie had gone ahead to the terminal to make a phone call while I tried to pull myself together. When he returned he said he'd been instructed to bring me directly to *Syndcorp Imports'* headquarters.

As we drove along I kept hearing that lonely sax playing out there in the night, picturing Rusty Wilson in that black negligée and her warm, inviting face and body calling to me. I could still hear her voice coo and purr as she quietly fell for me on that sofa. Romantic love was the one thing that stopped you in your tracks in this world, that reminded you that vivid time-outs were worth the while and knock-out dames with intelligence and sensual leanings made it all worthwhile, somehow. But now I had lost her—and lost my very first client in the worst way a private dick can...*death*. That was the one thing that had no return policy, no re-engagements, no sweet talk on fancy telephones in the middle of the night from a penthouse above the roar of the city.

Eddie Contino bade me good-bye and said he was sorry about the way things turned out and better luck next time. Personally, I hoped there would never be a next time that was anything like this one. As I walked down a hallway I saw Joe Lorena approaching. He looked serious and a bit drawn. "Cable, please, come with me."

We went into a small private lounge where I saw Joe take a drink of some orange-yellow concoction I didn't even want to guess at its content. He poured me a gin and tonic. "Thanks. So...looks like I blew everything, Joe. I'm sorry. These lizard creatures were everywhere down there. With that damn device still in Rusty Wilson, they knew where we were every minute."

"It's not your fault, Cable. You're young and inexperienced in my world. Plus everything changes. Nothing remains the same. I learned just hours ago, that Mrs. Wilson's tracer implant was not just a transponder, but it was a *transformational didactic enhancer*—in other words, the lizard folk were experimenting with her, slowly turning her into a new species of them: a female who is loaded with deadly venom and can kill anything organic within seconds."

"Let me get this straight. One lizard guy marries her, implants her with this enhancer thing. Slowly she changes into a new version of one of them. So they never intended to use her as a baby machine?"

"Well, not exactly. Our sources tell us only about five-hundred females between the ages of eighteen and thirty-five were fitted with such a device. Didn't you notice anything unusual when you woke up with her that morning? And by the way, I hope this won't turn into a habit of promiscuity, Cable—it would devastate Honey to know about this."

"No, Joe, I didn't intend it to happen. I'm sorry...sorry for everyone. But, yeah, that morning her stomach seemed distended as hell. The night before it was perfectly flat."

"Precisely. That fits what we've learned. The warm sperm you released into her that night triggered the acceleration of hundreds of reptilian eggs previously planted in her ovum. Once so stimulated, they possess the ability to grow rapidly. So when you awoke and saw her stomach swollen, she was actually pregnant with hundreds of female lizard-like creatures just like her. The male lizard people, the tall ones, watched you exit the hotel room to find Eddie Contino. In that minute, your job was finished and they kidnapped her to a safe place like a morgue, to go into the necessary state of suspended animation."

"You mean I was a breeding patsy the whole time?"

"That's why they didn't interfere before you had mated with this Rusty Wilson, poor soul."

"Then how did she die? I mean, I saw her on that slab, Joe, not cold, but according to the pathologist with no pulse, heartbeat or other vital signs."

"There is a pre-state where the parent-host goes dormant. But what you didn't see was her rapid recovery after she awakened from that suspended animation and deposited her eggs."

"Wha—what?! Deposited what? You mean she just laid her eggs somewhere and left the scene?"

"Yes, just like any other reptile. There is little maternal protective instinct in these creatures. However, if laid in a safe place and hatched out, they are far from helpless. In fact, like most vipers, they are poisonous the moment they come into the world."

"Oh, fuck…that means dozens of those little shits are growing up right now in crooks, crannies and warm canals in old Monterrey."

"Well, not quite, Cable. We managed to find a laundry room where your client had laid her eggs. We destroyed them all… *this time*. But we won't always win. There are too many of them."

"So, a final question. Why did she and her triplicate husbands named Todd, come flying after Eddie and me at the airport?"

"That's easy…you knew too much. They like to be secretive, cover their tracks. That's why you were ordered out of there immediately." Joe Lorena took another sip from his strange drink and I lit up a Lucky Strike. "You're going to have to look over your shoulder for a while, I'm afraid, Cable. They might be back for you. But then again, we don't really know if that is their modus."

"Shit, Joe, I'm beginning to understand your way of looking at things…now I see why you're in the middle of Dragna's dung heap."

"It's the best way I can operate and still hope I can do some good. Jack's organization has constant infiltrations of aliens. We have eliminated a lot of them, but there are at least five traceable genera functioning on the earth at this time. And not all of the really bad ones are aliens, I might add. Some earth beings are badly bred and their brain connections are, what I would call, badly wired. These, among your kind, are just as dangerous as the aliens."

"Yeah, I can think of a couple in my time. The young woman who removes the limbs off her living baby, the doctor who sells out his soul for a sealed golden capsule, or even someone like Frank Leggore who would kill anyone who got in his way without conscience. I'm happy to put people like that away for good. They can't belong…there's no place—"

"—yes, Cable…no place." He looked at me with those kindly eyes of his. "So, future son-in-law, I hope you have a clearer picture of what I do and why I'm in what you term, *the middle of a dung heap*. What is a life worth if you can do no good while living it? What value can you put to living if you do not strive to improve just a fraction of it?"

For the first time, I looked at Joe Lorena with admiration. "I see it now, Joe." I got up and shook his hand. "I smell pretty bad from the trip and need to clean up, call your daughter and tell her I love her. Oh, and I think I'll tell her, uh, one other thing."

"And what's that, Cable?"

"That I think her Dad and I are going to get along just swell." Joe moved toward me with his arms extended and I hugged him.

CHAPTER 17

THE TRANSFIGURATION OF LEI-TAO

It was late morning. The heat of August, 1929 was exacerbated by the arrival of the Santa Ana winds, which swept down from the heated mountains to the east of Los Angeles and came flushing down the canyons at night like someone had opened the ovens of Hell. Legend was that on a night when the Santa Ana's blew, ancient tribes that lived on the land thousands of years before, released those whose deaths were due to foul play and allowed them to avenge the wrong doing.

My business was beginning to take off pretty well and I stuck with simple cases that included tracing down errant husbands, wives, girlfriends and lovers and snapping the all-important Kodak shot of the tryst in action. A few protection and escort cases came in, a missing persons case now and then but nothing I couldn't handle. I was doing okay and making a living from my happy little office on Franklin near Cahuenga Blvd. Honey and I were doing great and despite an occasional slip with Adora Moreno, who I was still somehow addicted to, I was playing it straight against the line. I even went out and bought some new sheets and blankets for my childhood bed in the back, a new toothbrush and some large towels so at least I'd feel dry after my showers in the morning.

Honey's recordings were doing well on the radio. This hot August morning, I was listening to her Brunswick recording of *"Blue Skies"* cut with her new great trumpeter, Chet James. She had become smooth, professional and her records sold at sheet music and piano stores very well. I was trying to find a phone number when the phone rang. "Yeah, Cable Denning Agency here…"

"Cable? Is—is it really you?"

A young female voice was at the other end. "Yeah, it's me, who's this?"

"Ginny—Ginny Fullerton—remember me? I finally made it, Cable—I'm living and working in L.A. now, I finally got away from Big Bear Lake and my Mom and Dad and all…you know. I think Dad will miss me most. He was furious when I told him, but I'm old enough to be my own woman now, right?"

"It's good to hear your voice, Ginny," I said, actually glad to hear the fresh, youthful energy exuding from this lovely young woman. "How in the hell did you find me?"

"Well, when I went downtown to your old police head-quarters, a nice sergeant said you had quit to become a private 'dick'—" she snickered. "Isn't that rather offensive—I mean that he called you that?"

"Well, not really, Ginny. You see, 'dick' has come to mean detective. I was curious myself and read up on it. It might've started before the turn of the century with British underworld slang meaning *to watch*…or maybe even from a series about Scottish detective, *Dick Donovan* from around the same time that was popular here in America."

"Oh….uh huh. Well, I was probably thinking of something else. And, by the way, I haven't forgotten you or that wonderful afternoon at my aunt's place."

"That was a long time ago, Ginny. I'm—I'm getting married in December—to a gal named Honey Combes, a famous singer…"

There was a long pause. "I didn't know. That was the girl you talked about when—when we did it." Then she brightened up. "Well, you always told me there wasn't much of a future for me in your life. I guess a girl can keep trying, huh? It's just not that easy…I mean having the best, Cable, and then settling for less. Are you sure you can't see me now and then? Do you live with your fiancée?"

"Not until the wedding. But, Ginny, I don't mean to throw a wet blanket on things, but—but—it's just not gonna happen. I'm an older guy, remember, and you're looking for a stud who's twenty and horny all the time."

"No, I'm not, Cable. I'm looking for you. Please...? Sometime soon? How about just going out for a drink some night—like we're friends or something? You know, I do think of you as a friend, too. You've always been so respectful—and good to me. Damn...I'm droning on like a pussycat in heat, aren't I? I'm sorry..."

I really liked the kid. And she was a fine young woman, certainly not a sleep-around. "I'll tell you what, Ginny. I'll take you out to dinner some night soon to celebrate your arrival in L.A. We'll carry on like two old pals with a couple of drinks and some good food, how's that sound?"

"You'd do that for *me*? Oh, Cable, I can't wait! When?"

"Do you have a phone?"

"Well, not exactly. I'm living in a rooming house with seven other girls. There's a community phone downstairs and anyone will take a message and give it to me. The number's HOllywood 4441. I live on Virginia near Wilton Place."

I jotted the number down. "Well, you're not that far away. I'll give you a call soon—I promise."

"I'll hold you to it, Cable. I can't wait.....bye..."

We hung up and I looked around my office. Why in the hell was I always getting myself in deep shit with women? I was remembering that young, supple body of Ginny Fullerton's, those firm stand-up breasts, a fresh, warm pussy that gave so willingly, maybe even innocently. I was reflecting on the plea-sure of it all when the phone rang again. "Yeah, Cable Denning here..."

400

A man's deep, dark voice said, "Cable Denning...I want to kill you..."

"What's that?—I'm not sure I heard you right."

"I want to kill you...you must be dead to my eyes. If I permit you to live, all will be lost. You are a carrier...vermin...a pestilence that haunts the world. You are a disease and must be controlled."

"Look, Mister, I don't know what you're talking about, but I'll tell you this. I don't scare easy, and if you're bluffing, it's a cheap bluff. So why don't you quit wasting my time and just go away, I'm a busy man." I hung up.

Immediately the phone rang again. "That was rude, Cable Denning. You treat people unkindly. You're a taker, and that's what takers do. You ruined the only thing that was ever precious to me. Now you must die for it. If I permit you to live, you will keep on taking again and again. If no one stops you, your evil will spread like the Devil's poison. You do not respect the sacred. You have no sanctity in you for the pure and good."

"So, assuming I'm this evil piece of shit you're describing, just who am I supposed to have done this to—certainly not you...some female most likely...someone you knew...remember, buster, I'm a detective and I can usually put two and two together pretty damn quick. So, you've got a grudge and you wanna settle it by killing me, right?"

"It's the evil that you are—that makes your heart corrupted. You are born cursed and those you touch die because you are cursed. I cannot allow this. Where you go, death and evil follow."

"Well, I don't think my mother would agree with you, Mister. Those of us who came up the hard way remember the school of hard knocks and what it's like out there. So creeps like you are just another layer of crap that's accumulated on the road."

There was a slight pause. "Your mother was innocent. Your

father came as the Devil and inseminated her that you should be born with lust through fornication and rootless pleasure. Through your wanton lusts, you have left a pile of broken souls, hearts cursed by your touch in the name of wanton pleasure, nothing more than wanton pleasure."

I thought for a minute. If I hung up he'd just call again. I'd have to bring it to a head somehow. "So…in the old days, if someone offended you—"

"—*if thine eye offend thee, pluck it out*, Cable Denning…"

"As I was saying, in the old days if someone offended you, you challenged them to a duel. Are you willing to honorably face up to a fair fight—or are you also a slinking, cowardly piece of slime riding on the coat-tails of Prophecy?"

That seemed to stop him for a minute. "What do you know about Prophecy? What you must know is that you shall not sustain when the Rapture comes and the dark, evil ones will be left to rot in the forbidden places of Hell and Damnation."

"You know, buddy—I have no use for Bible-slingers. I've never been religious, so if you want my attention for the next thirty seconds, you're gonna have to do better than that. So, forget the Bible shit and tell me why you want me dead."

"The depraved can never embrace God. They have turned the worm and through their abominations have caused disgrace upon the world. That is why I must kill you."

"So…when is this event supposed to take place? Will you make an appointment to kill me—or will it be a slimy, cowardly act that smacks of the same evil intent that you accuse me of. Don't forget the *do unto others as you would have them do unto you…and let him who is without sin cast the first stone*, Mister Self-Righteous."

Again, there was a long silence. "You are admonished henceforth unto blasphemy, for your lack of contrition has sealed your fate."

402

"You know, I have one more thing to say, and then I'm going to hang up, buster. Somewhere there is a statement that says, '*I love you just the way you are, and I love you too much to leave you the way you are.*' You see, buddy, I love whatever is good in me just the way it is. And if someone wants to change something in me that isn't all that great, then the only way it can be done is through *love.* Now, you can take all the rest of the killing and murder crap and shove it!" I hung up. The phone didn't ring back.

In some ways life is like a walk on a tightrope, you never know when you're going to lose your balance and fall off. The recent experiences of my life had left me battered inside, in a place where your vision of reality and fantasy merge—what's real—what isn't? How do we know the impact of those "thousand natural shocks to which the flesh is heir," as Shakespeare said. But little traumas add up, things popping up out of the ordinary that take you on an adventure you didn't count on. From the time the *God of Our Fathers* entered my life, nothing would ever be the same. Nor would it be calm and cool and predictable like many people exist—by rote and habit, one day pretty much like the one before it. Meeting Lei-tao still sat inside my head like something I dreamed last night, one dimension removed from the commonplace reality I had come to expect as human existence. But it taught me something very powerful…i.e., *never expect anything* and believe only half of what you see. For most of life was an illusion pasted together by governments and religions to contain their populations. God knows what *they* knew and weren't telling.

Mario's death hit me hard as well and I still missed him. The women who came into my life blessed me like a kaleidoscope of beautiful colors, each a different flower in a field named 'Call Me Lucky.' From Honey to Adora to Ginny Fullerton to Rusty Wilson, I had tasted the sweetest and most intimate moments humans can share. I'd always be grateful for that. Every once in a while someone so unique comes along that you become addicted to the sight, sound and feel of her. That was how I felt about Adora Moreno. But I knew also, if I lived to be five-hundred years old, I'd never be able to put my finger on the 'why' of it all. Maybe beautiful women like that were sent into my life to help balance out and heal the darkness and violence that are always in the middle of things like a monkey wrench thrown into the mix to make sure you don't get too comfortable with this life. So this unsettling, unaccountable thing roared out of the unexpected, shooting up like a black geyser of evil—that flip side of God's coin in the universe. There was something perverse about that, I thought.

I was as restless as those winds from the Santa Ana Mountains and knew I couldn't stay in my office, waiting for the next phone call that could be anything from a distressed lover to a mysterious stranger threatening my life. So I made my way to Bronson Park, a place I would go for natural sanctuary through the years. There was a nicely maintained trail meandering through oak trees, tall grasses and a little brook that babbled its way down toward a huge culvert and then disappeared somewhere under the city. Further up, there was another road that was well traveled. It was just about a quarter of a mile from that point where one could find the *Bronson Caves*, probably man-made from an old rock quarry a few decades ago. Many scenes for movies were shot in and around the caves. Damsels in distress, rowdy miners, cowboy chase scenes and the like showed up time and again on the silver screen with that familiar background. But most of the time it was a peaceful quiet walk. There was one place I liked particularly well. If one didn't turn right to go to the caves, but continued straight up the canyon, soon the thickets, wild purple thistles and fallen trees were joined by the sounds of birds and crickets.

I found a nice old rotting log and sat, the Santa Ana's whipping up the grasses and whistling across the tall hills above. And then a vision appeared in my head. I was being transported to a penthouse somewhere in the city. On its highest point sat an apartment with a lovely patio emptying out onto a terrace with dozens of strategically placed potted plants. It was nighttime and that sexy, lonely sax was playing as I looked over the edge at the city far below. I turned to light up a cigarette and my eye caught a woman in a white negligee holding a champagne glass in her hand, leaning up against the outside of her door, looking at me. She gazed at me with that 'come hither' look, her head slightly tilted down, her eyes boldly looking into mine. "Come…come over here, lover man." I walked over to her. She was a doll, medium long auburn hair, pouting red lips, probably about five-foot four with a great shape. She was wearing nothing under the negligee and her full breasts stood out at attention, pink sensual nipples protruding through the silk, a dark, welcoming mound between her legs. Her eyes were molten amber and began to fill with tears as she spoke. "I've waited for you so long to come and dry my tears. At midnight I come out here and wait…telling myself that someday you'll come and dry all my tears, and whisper to me the promise of love I see in your eyes." I wanted to speak but couldn't. She took my hand and tipped her champagne glass to my lips. I took a sip and she smiled. The sound of the sax began to burn into my brain, getting deeper and breathier as it wove an erotic spell around the two of us. "I go to bed every night with a prayer that you'll make love to me…but it must only be you…will you whisper to me that it's you? And when you do, I will take your hand and lead you to my warm, waiting bed." I walked into her open arms. My lips made their way to her ear. But I couldn't say it—I couldn't open my mouth!

Suddenly I was shocked out of my reverie by a strange yet somehow familiar voice. "Just frolicking in that sperm-filled brain of yours…I always wanted to know what young mortal men were pre-occupied with beside sexual conquest. Now I know…*nothing*…"

There sitting on a small log in back of me sat Toggth! "Damn it, man, you scared the shit out of me. And what's the big idea of breaking up that great fantasy I was having?"

"Well, since I created it in your busy head, I thought I'd enjoy it with you for a couple of minutes. I conjured up a beauty for you, didn't I?" he laughed and jumped off the log and came around to look at me.

I laughed along with him. "You rascal, Toggth! Good to see you. But why was she crying?"

"Ah, just a little extra touch of mine. You see, human desire desires *itself*—it's *you* that you love. But you maintain the illusion that happiness is found in another person. That poor, wretched beautiful woman will wait out her lifetime, thinking that a physical union with a man will bring her happiness. At best, it will take the edge off of her desperation until the day she realizes *she is complete within herself.*"

Something in what Toggth said rang a truth-bell in me. "So…man is complete without woman…and woman complete without man?"

"Well, as your saying goes…almost a cigar, Cable. But not quite. You see, if you are in possession of your whole self, then those sensual intimacies and saying you love someone, fulfills the wonderment of companionship, but not from a place of need or desperation. It is natural for man to seek woman, and woman to seek man. You mortals are programmed that way… mostly, I might add, for procreation as the slave-race you came from."

I responded with a dour expression. "I'd rather not discuss that, Toggth. So, tell me, what brings you by to break the peace of my sanctuary?"

"Sorry…but I have three things we need to talk about."

He stood in front of me, those warm eyes of his looking into mine. "Okay, shoot, mister, I'm all ears."

"First, you might be pleased to know the *Tone of Creation*

has been restored within the *Fen de Fuqin* and all hums well in the upper dimensions."

"That's good news. And how is the beautiful Lei-tao?"

"We'll get to that in a minute. Second…I feel through the forces of energy, there will soon come a disturbance. I suggest the *Oculus Pyramis Mandatum* will discover our little trick on them and retaliate with a vengeance."

"Oh, that's swell. I just lost my best guy friend to murdering thugs, my first client in my new P.I. profession turns out to be a victim of the lizard people and gets killed on an airport runway in Monterrey, Mexico, while turning into a green, snake-like monster—and now you tell me all hell is about to descend upon us once the so-called 'Order' discovers our ruse—is that all that's bothering me today, Toggth?"

"Not quite, Cable. Or at the very least, it's bothering me."

"So, now what? Something I did or am about to do?"

"It's our sacred Red Dragon Lady. She's been depressed. Completely unlike her. When I asked her about it, she confided in me that she missed *you* and wished you wouldn't have kissed her with your usual sexual intent and appetite. Remember, she's very sensitive to vibration—and she allowed your desire vibration to enter into her. Now she's confused and somewhat obsessed with—with—how you might say, I fear, following it through."

"And what does that mean?"

"It means she wants to experience being a sexual, mortal woman with you. This can never take place, Cable. It would unbalance the entirety of her jurisdictional dimension. Don't you see? In all her thousands of years, this threatens to be her undoing, a trespass we can ill afford."

"So what can I do to prevent it? Remember, Toggth, I'm just the lowly mortal here—and you guys are the all-powerful— why can't you handle it from your end?"

"It's not that simple. Here's how I suspect it will work. In realizing her obsession, Lei-tao's wisdoms will tell her she cannot appear to you in an absolute physical form—unless she has powers of which I have no knowledge—to modify her vibrational make-up. If that is so, she must enter into your psyche in a *dream state.* Now, if she does that, you must prepare your psyche before you go to sleep each night to visualize a golden gate at its entrance. She will try to enter there, you must tell her, 'no,' and she will leave. She cannot force the uncooperative will."

"Now, how in the hell can I remember to do that every night? That'd drive a guy crazy, just thinking about the pressure and consequence if it fails."

"I know of no other way, Cable. Please, much is at stake here. Will you cooperate?"

"Yeah, sure, I'll do everything I can. I suppose if I write a note to myself on my pillow or something, I'll do your little golden gate thing."

"Thanks, Cable. I like you. And I want us to like one another. My responsibility to the great Red Dragon Lady is for life. If I fail her, all else in her domain fails."

"Where is she now?" I asked, trying to keep track of all the nutso things that were occurring in my life lately.

"As far as I know, sulking back at the Cave of the Seven Truths. She's reviewing the content of those Great Truths, so she may be somewhat fortified when the temptation hits her that she wants to be with you at all costs. I *do* think Goddesses have a female quality *that* is difficult for me to comprehend. They can be a bit erratic in their thinking process."

"Hmmm…well, I'll keep my eyes peeled and my ears open. And if she comes thumping at my dream state door, I'll send her packing—politely, of course."

"Thanks, Cable. I must be off. Let's be vigilant. Also, I'll help keep an eye on the *Oculus Order* and try to warn you when the unfortunate discovery is made."

I shook Toggth's little hand and we parted. The afternoon had worn on and the Santa Ana winds had increased in velocity. I walked down to the streetcar line and took the Hollywood Boulevard car over to Cahuenga and walked up to Franklin. As I went up the stairs to my office, I gotta funny feeling in my gut. I couldn't quite put my finger on it, but something was up. I unlocked the door to my office. I had drawn the dirty yellow venetian blinds so the room had an eerie yellow, subdued hue to it. I needed a drink. I went to my desk and opened the upper right hand drawer and took out my cheap rotgut gin. I bought it off of some bathtub bootlegger named Zoot Carradine. He also made a horrible rum and an even worse vodka from rotten potatoes he dug up somewhere by the hundred pound sack. I poured the gin into the old well-used glass I kept on the desk and lit up a Lucky Strike from my favorite green pack with the red logo. I sat back, thinking *what a life I was living!* For a fleeting moment, I was even thankful for all the good things that had come my way. But the other part that niggled at me came from some of the words my mysterious and threatening morning caller had used. *Where you go, death and evil follow*, he had said. In a way he was right. It did seem that so much of my life led me into dangerous situations that often resulted in dark and terrible discoveries—not to mention people getting killed. I mean, what were the odds of someone like Mario getting killed if it weren't for my supporting him in his cause—or Rusty Wilson dying a terrible death by turning into some horrible viper-like thing and getting shot dead in Mexico? Yeah, sure, I meant well—but it didn't turn out that way. Why was I always putting myself and others in danger's path? Could I actually have, unknowingly, been the cause of all these things?

Just then the phone rang. "Yeah, Cable Denning here," I said, still distracted in my head.

There was a slight pause. "Is this the famous private detective?" a warm, medium-high female voice spoke.

"I don't know about famous, lady, but you got the private detective part right. What can I do for you?"

"I think I need your....*services*...but I cannot come to you." There seemed to be a very slight accent to the voice, not unlike one I'd heard before. But where or when, I couldn't recall. "Would you be able to meet me at my lodgings around ten o'clock tonight?"

"Isn't that a bit late for a meeting with someone you don't know, especially a private dick?"

"A private what?"

"That's slang for private detective."

"Oh. I wasn't sure what you meant." I could tell she was fishing. "Well, if you think that too late an hour, how about nine o'clock?"

"I get twenty-bucks a day plus expenses. In your case, being a house call, it doesn't matter whether or not you become my client, I'll still have to charge you."

"That's fine. Can you come? I'm—I'm in a rather awkward and desperate situation. Please consider that, Mr. Denning."

"How did you hear about me?"

"Well, you seem to be quite popular with some people. I have heard through other sources...some...some of your rather unusual cases under extraordinary circumstances."

"Uh-huh...give me your name and address—you don't live too far away, do you? Streetcar service goes off in some areas by midnight."

"I'm in a brand new building at Wilshire near La Brea. 5225 Wilshire Blvd., apartment #1206."

I knew the building. It was a pretty fancy complex and the twelfth floor probably meant some expensive real estate. "And

410

your name, please?"

The dame was beginning to intrigue me. I always loved that first rush of a new adventure. "Ona…Ona Stephens…" she answered.

"Alright, Mrs. Stephens, I'll—"

"—*Miss* if you don't mind—I'm unmarried."

"Boyfriend, bodyguard, houseguest? Anyone else I should look out for as I approach your apartment? Dog?"

"No. Just me…I'm alone."

"Then how do you know you can trust me—or, for that matter, what I look like?"

"Believe me, Mr. Denning, I trust you." Then she queried me in a rather playful tone of voice. "So, tell me, what *do* you look like?"

"Well, I'm about five-ten, kind of rough with dark eyes and a cleft chin. I usually wear a trench coat and a dark brown fedora."

"Do you have a kind face?"

"What's that have to do with whether or not I make a good private investigator, Miss Stephens?"

"Nothing, I guess. May I expect you then at 9:00 p.m.?

"Yeah, lady, I'll be there."

"Thank you." She hung up and I scratched my head. I wondered if that phone call was the reason I had that funny feeling when I climbed the stairs to my office earlier. Or maybe some dames were just bashful, maybe she was ugly and didn't want to be seen in public. Maybe someone was after her and she feared for her life. I had a feeling I'd find out in a few hours. I went into the back where my small but adequate living quarters were, stripped, showered and shaved. At least I'd try to keep a decent image of Cable Denning, *Presentable* Private Detective up and running.

About 9:00 p.m. I was pressing the indicated buzzer at 5225 Wilshire. Almost immediately the response tone buzzed me in. I took the elevator to the twelfth floor and got out. I had packed my iron just in case. One of the unspoken rules in the private dick's manual was never to go out without your .38—I had learned that just being an off duty cop....you never know what you might come up against out there.

I knocked on the door of apartment #1206. When the door opened I was slapped with a heavy dose of déjà vu. There in the same white, see-through negligée with a glass of champagne in hand and those same pink nipples staring me in the face, was the very woman in that great vision Toggth had conjured up earlier...just before he appeared out of the vapors and shook me out of my marvelous patio reverie. "Mr. Denning. Please come in."

I entered with this funny feeling I knew the doll. She escorted me to a sofa and asked if I wished a glass of cham-pagne. I couldn't refuse a bit of the bubbly, especially in these Prohibition days when most of it tasted like carbonated straw. I had a feeling Miss Stephens' alcohol would be first class. And it was. "Good to meet you, Miss Stephens." I toasted my glass in her direction and she toasted back, but I noticed she did not drink. "Well, here's to you, lady, and may all your troubles be small ones." Her eyes were locked onto mine and I was feeling a bit uncomfortable. I took a big sip and put it down on the glass coffee table. "You know, there's something I have to tell you. Are you an open minded person? I mean, if I told you about something out of the ordinary that happened, are you— would you be, uh, receptive to it?"

"Oh, you might say that, Mr. Denning. Please...go ahead..."

"Well, I took a walk in Bronson Park earlier this afternoon. I sat on an old log and, uh, suddenly my mind was transported to a penthouse, and I found myself looking down at the traffic far below—I mean, it was much higher than your building here. I turned around to light a cigarette and you....*you* were standing at the threshold to your patio door, dressed exactly as you are now, only it was around midnight. You called me over and spoke to me and said—"

"—I've waited for you so long to come and dry my tears..." And my jaw dropped as I just sat there looking at this babe.

"You—you *are* you, whoever *you* are! How in the hell—"

"—come..." She urged me off the sofa and took my hand. The minute our flesh connected I could feel a familiar rush go up my arm. What the hell was going on? She led me to a door that exited out into a spacious patio. Again, I could've dropped my teeth, for the flower boxes and tubs of shrubbery were exactly as I had seen them earlier in the day! "Now...do you remember this? Only it *was* midnight and I told you if you whispered to me the promise of love I see in your eyes...that I would take you to my warm, waiting bed." She gazed at me with such abandon, I thought she'd pull me into those eyes and I would disappear.

"Hey, toots, I don't know who you are or what magic spell you're casting here, but you'd better come clean, because I'm getting a nasty headache trying to figure this one out!" I turned and went back inside and she followed. I sat down on the sofa and she sat next to me. Then Miss Stephens' voice disappeared and a more familiar one emerged from this beautiful lady. "Cable...it's me...I had no other way to get you here—I had to do it secretly—Toggth would get so angry with me if he knew—"

"—Lei-tao! What the—how?—how come you don't look like you—I mean, you're in the shape of some stylish white woman?"

"I was eavesdropping when Toggth visited you this afternoon. I tuned into the erotic vision he created for you. He did it to derive his own pleasure from the experience. So I just duplicated it."

"But why? We both already know the score, Lei-tao. You're not supposed to engage in intimate earthly activities that involve—"

"—loving you? Why not? *Why not, Cable!!* I've lived a life of discipline for a time beyond your imagining, without even once experiencing what it's like to be a female who enjoys pleasure in the carnal, sensual worlds—with a man like you who will take me—and—and open me up with passion and force. Why can't I have that? Even if just once?"

"Because if Toggth is right, it'll crumble your whole dimension—according to him, that vibrational jurisdiction, as he tells it. And then you have to go back into the lotus pod for another fourteen thousand years until you are called again. That's your role, that's your fate, your destiny, Lei-tao. We've all got fates, destinies—name me one person whose life is their own—one they can do with as they please or have control over?"

She lowered her voice. "It won't happen that way. I've perfected a way to transmigrate my cells and genetic coding to match a human female's. Oh, Cable, I've never felt like this. Your smile lives with me—and it's not like me at all! Remember, I'm the Red Dragon Lady, always in control. But I can't work this out alone—no matter who I am or where I am or what I do, I see your face, I hear your voice. Can't you see, I can have you safely now. I can love you completely…please hear me, Cable—please hear me—I'm in *love* with you! It's not ever going to change, Cable, not for me!"

That stopped me in my tracks. I withdrew and became silent. She bent over, got the champagne bottle off the coffee table and refilled my drink. "You're not drinking?"

"You know it is dangerous to me, remember?"

"Oh, yeah, I forgot." I was defeated before I had begun to fight this ravishingly beautiful woman with the wisdoms and wits of a goddess. "So what do you want me to do, Lei-tao? I gave my word to Toggth—he's your overseer—I always try to be a man of my word. Put yourself in my shoes—what would you do?"

"Toggth's wrong, Cable. He doesn't know I've mastered the transfiguration process. And I can reverse it." She looked down to the floor. "*Then* I can go back, return to my little lotus pod for another umpteen thousand years. That's the price I pay." She got up and took my hand, pulled me up from the sofa and led me to her bedroom. "This…is that warm bed, Cable…the one I invited you to in your daydream."

"I don't know if I can do this, Lei-tao. It's true. Originally I was the one at fault. I initiated all the kissing stuff, partly because it's my male animal habit—and partly because after our tantric experience in the Cave of the Seven Truths, I was hot as a pistol for you. I wanted to experience what I knew I could experience with no other woman—or goddess—ever…"

"That part, my desire for you *is* irreversible, Cable. No one, nothing can stop my wanting you." She came up to me and clamped those luscious lips of hers onto mine. "If I don't have you I'll perish anyway—so what's the difference? One less goddess in the dimensional atmospheres?"

At least in that statement she made sense…I guessed. "Oh, Lei-tao. And if you're wrong? I'd never be able to forgive myself, babe. Because I know I started this whole damn thing—"

She put her finger to my lips, sat me on the bed and turned off the lights. Only one red candle burned from her dresser. Then she slipped off that very translucent gown of hers and the Red Dragon Lady's perfect body shone in the semi-darkness, shape-shifting before my eyes from Ona Stephens to Lei-tao. She got on her knees by the bed where I sat and took the champagne glass out of my hand. "We don't need alcohol to make us perfect together." Her eyes misted in the faint red glow of the candlelight. "I love you, Cable…and if that is my sin, so be it…"

I pulled her up to me and pressed her lips onto mine. She began unbuttoning my shirt and soon we stood face-to-face, naked together. In the glow of the red candle the transfiguration of Lei-tao began, the process from goddess to human woman, filled with passion and desire, trespassing all protocol demanded of her world, only to have to return into the humble pod of a lotus seed on some distant tomorrow.

"Oh, Cable…please…do whatever you do to any other mortal woman—do that to me…force me, ravish me, touch and kiss every part of my body, inside and out. Force my breasts into your mouth and kiss me until my lips bleed!" She sat upon my chest, rolling in a seductive rhythm, allowing me to feel her thick, wet womanhood slide up and down upon my own body. Soon she had rolled over and opened her arms to me. I came into them and we bonded in such a powerful way that my whole spirit was elevated as my heart beat furiously with desire for this exquisite and rare beauty. We lost all sense of time, in the descent, deeper and deeper into layers of ecstasy and fulfillment. Our bodies were wet with perspiration and yet the frenzy continued until every ounce of available energy was spent from our bodies.

Finally we lay quiet for the longest time. Then with such a secret joy in her voice, Lei-tao whispered into my ear. "Mr. Denning…you have just made me the happiest of creatures—anywhere. And…you impregnated me with the perfect daughter who will become the first immortal woman in constant human form."

I was trying to come out of the erotic trance we had been in. I heard her words, but I'm not sure they registered correctly. I sat up. "You what? Mind repeating that, doll?"

She arose and put her arms around me. "I just conceived our

child. You have honored me, Cable, with a companion daughter for all time. Never again shall I be lonely in the carrying out of my tasks as protector of the Cave of the Seven Truths and my jurisdictional dimension. I will have a rightful heir now."

I was angry and sympathetic at the same time. Suddenly I got it that all these many centuries, Lei-tao had been lonely, circulating there among the stars, trapped in a seedpod at the bottom of a Chinese lake. She had been seeking companionship, but now she would have her own replicated child, a daughter, to feel the magic that only motherhood can bestow upon the female psyche. "You…you didn't tell me that part of it, kid. Shouldn't you have consulted me? So now I'm going to be a cosmic father—or what? You sure are a barrel of surprises. Oh, by the way, you were wonderful—I mean, as a lover—and I'd always want you to know, no matter what, I really did desire you, lady, big time. I'll take that part of the responsibility."

"I am sorry I didn't tell you. But I was blinded by the longing, the desire for you that tore me to pieces and I was afraid if I told you I was receptive and could conceive tonight, you would run away."

"Well, yeah, that's a distinct possibility…"

"But no matter how it ends, I will love you for always, please believe me. Are you angry with me?"

"I don't know what I am anymore, Lei-tao. Should I be? Do immortal Red Dragon Ladies do things like you just did as a matter of course—or am I the privileged exception?"

"No, Cable. Only a foolish Red Dragon Lady in love would do what I've done…obsessed with desire for the object of her affections."

"How—how do you know you'll have a daughter and not a son?"

"You helped determine that for me, my lover. Your seed honored the divine feminine tonight."

"Well, don't ask me to understand that."

"I won't." She tittered lightly, threw her arms around me and rocked us slowly on the bed. "I will come visit you as my tummy grows…so you can feel our child stirring inside. Won't that be so—so…" She broke down and began crying. "Oh, Cable—I can't live with you—I can never live with you or be your wife or mistress or even your lover, ever again."

"Yeah, babe, I know…I'll be dead a few thousand years before your turn rolls around again, right?"

She clung to me. "Daiya Guang says love is timeless…and that it always recognizes who it embraced, combined with, adored…though many thousands of years may pass."

"And who's this Daiya Guang?"

"My mentor and teacher. Each Red Dragon apprentice must be schooled many thousands of years until she is ready."

"I see. Do you understand how nuts all this sounds? I dwell in a practical everyday world where lifetimes are measured in so many thousands of *days*. And then…phht!…you're gone! A meat wagon picks up what's left and the remains get buried or cremated. It's anyone's guess what happens to the part that wasn't physical. Soul? Spirit? Cosmic Consciousness? Believe me, babe, I've heard 'em all."

"But what about the Cave of the Seven Truths, our wonderful tantric exchange, the magic experienced that day? Can you discount that?"

"No, but I can't explain it, either. It'd put me into overload if I tried."

She kissed my back and shoulders. "All I know is that I am in love with you tonight and tomorrow, and the next day—and I will miss you too much for me to bear it!" she cried. "With the *Tone of Creation* in place, my work is finished now and I will soon be called back…back into the lotus pod, back into the lake."

"And what happens to our daughter?"

"She will…she will…I don't know…I was selfish, wasn't I? I just assumed she would be in my jurisdictional dimension at the Cave of the Seven Truths until the lotus returns…"

"For fourteen-thousand years? That's a hell of a long wait. Didn't you say something about a first immortal woman in constant human form?"

"I must consult Daiyu Guang. She will know…Oh, Cable— what if my selfishness doomed her to a life—a life of—confusion?" I held her in my arms and lowered her back down onto the bed.

"Well, let's not worry about it tonight." A thousand feelings went through me, but I was exhausted and eventually the goddess and the gumshoe allowed all thoughts to perish, and we drifted off to sleep, a deep contentment upon our faces.

Sometime during the wee hours of the morning Lei-tao began to convulse and vomit. I staggered to the bathroom with her and she threw up red and green liquid until the toilet bowl looked like a gruesome version of Christmas morning. Then she informed me she had to go back to her dimensional home at the Cave of the Seven Truths and get Toggth to make her up a special potion to cure her. I helped her dress and she was so weak that the best she could do was let me hold her in my arms. As I was doing so, her body faded from within my embrace and all that was left was the slight scent of her on my chest where her cheek had been moments before.

CHAPTER 18

THE DEVIL WEARS A DRESS

It was September 1ˢᵗ, 1929, and the rent was due. I made my way back to my office feeling guilty as hell. Why had I let Lei-tao talk me into this strangest of seductions? If ever a guy proved he was ruled by his balls, it was me, a primitive male creature addicted to the feeling of that exciting hunt and chase until finally the quarry is cornered and that erect appendage between his legs merges victorious and the woman's moans and sighs of pleasure become the reward for all his trouble. But this time, I feared, it came with a terrible price. I just didn't know what it was yet.

Honey had come after work to see me and left a note under my door. She said she kind of wanted to see her future husband a lot more and that Nick Mortenson with the *Columbia Record Company* was prepared to sign her after her *Brunswick* contract expired in January, 1930. This was good timing, as there was rumor that *Brunswick* was going to be sold to *Warner Brothers*, moving their headquarters to New York and possibly a renewed contract with them would no longer be honored. *Columbia Records*, on the other hand, just lost their main rival in *Edison* and was looking to expand. I was happy for her. Honey was a woman punching her way successfully through a man's world, doing what she loved best. That was to be envied. If we were lucky, some of us found a niche we sort of fit into in this life—in my case, it seemed it was to graduate from policeman to private investigator—barely a step up, really, from the everyday grind found in the force.

I picked up the phone and dialed Honey's number. "Hello?"

"Yeah, doll, it's me."

"You were out last night when I came by. I hope it was business, Cable. I'm you're almost-wife, remember me?"

"It was business, babe, sort of. I mean I had to go to a client who was in danger and she couldn't come here to the office."

"Oh? And was she comely and alluring?"

"Yep. She came to the door in a white see-through negligee and not much else. It's hard to explain, but earlier that same day while I was walking in Bronson Park—"

"—why don't you ever walk with me in Bronson Park? I'm off during the daylight hours, you know."

"Well, the Santa Ana's were blowing and I had a very disturbing phone call earlier. I needed to clear the air by myself. You can understand that, doll, can't you?"

"I don't know what I understand—or believe—anymore, Cable. So who was the new client—some bimbo, I suppose, who was instantly attracted to the mystique of a private dick—every pun intended."

"Very funny. Actually, remember the Chinese Red Dragon Lady from San Francisco I got sort of involved with?"

"She's here in town?"

"Was…here in town. She had to go back late last night."

"After you screwed her, Cable?"

"Well, not exactly—if you'll recall I told you she was sort of this other dimensional creature and we had tantric sex—"

"—Cable, if you're going into that crap again, count me out. Now, look, buster. I'm your fiancée, right? If you're screwing around *before* we get married, what will you be doing *after* we're married?"

"I'm just tying up loose ends, Honey. You know, it's been a pretty good chunk of my life this momentum of babes through the years and the old dog's trying to learn new tricks and all. I'm sure you realize putting the brakes on isn't all that easy."

"Well, it better become a lot easier in less than four months, my love. You're just lucky I'm not the jealous type. Besides, I love you, you incorrigible playboy. And you need to toe the mark with me. What if I went around fucking all the guys that hit on me in the club?"

"I'd be pretty pissed. Might even call the whole thing off…"

"So I rest my case, Cable. Now, will you come over tonight so you can take it out of your pants for *me* for a change? If it's clean, that is—and not tainted with some other woman. You do know a girl can feel those things."

"She can?"

"Yep. So…what time?"

"I'll be there when you get home from work—before midnight, anyway. Okay?"

"Cable….I love you…truly…truly I love you and want you. Don't run out on us. We've got a beautiful thing going, let's not ruin it."

"I'm sorry, babe. Yeah, I'll be better at it, I promise. I mean, we have been doing really well lately, right?"

"Yes. Let's build something together, my darling. See you tonight when I get home from the club." I hung up, feeling like a cad.

Just then I heard a terrible explosion coming from the street below. I ran to the window. A car had blown up where it stood at the curb. Women screamed and men rushed toward the little Model-T to save the occupants. But it was too late. The intense heat consumed the interior of the car in no time and any passengers would be sizzle-roasted in seconds. Finally a fire truck came and it took them two hours to extinguish the hot metal remains and another half-hour for a tow truck to hall it away. What a lousy event, I thought, just outside my office window. I was exhausted from the night's adventures with Lei-tao and thought I'd take a catnap.

Suddenly the front office door opened and in walked someone I had hoped I would never lay eyes on again. Nazar Ravna, immaculately dressed as usual, entered. "Well, I see you've come up in the world, Private Investigator Denning," he said, with a sardonic tone just under the pretended pleasantness. "I don't blame you. The police force is an abominable place to work, isn't it?" Then he wandered over to the window behind my desk and looked down at the street. "It's a good thing you don't own an automobile. They seem to have a tendency to just…poof!… explode these days." He laughed a terrible laugh. "Someone got their wires crossed—or…did someone cross the wires?— regardless, someone may have thought that was you in the car that went up in flames a few moments ago. But I see they missed their mark. Perhaps…it was only…to…warn you…fire a volley across your bow…if you know what I mean…"

"So that was you, was it? And who was the poor bloke you roasted to a crisp?"

He looked at his manicured fingernails. "Who knows? Who cares?"

"I can't say I'm happy to see you, Ravna. In fact, I was beginning to feel like I had a life again, business is good, my pending marriage to—"

"—pending…I like that word, it's so…so *tentative*…as if we hang suspended day to day on a string…uncertain…fearful of that next unknown moment. Ah…so much of this short little life is…is *pending*, don't you think?" He came and sat opposite me at my desk. "May I?"

"I hope you're not expecting me to take you out to lunch. I'm kind of short on funds these days."

"Oh, no, I wouldn't expect that. Our last, how shall we say, 'altercation' involved you pushing me down a flight of stairs on top of my men. I may appear pleasant at the moment, but I am not a forgiving man, Denning."

"Let's get the record straight, Ravna. *I* didn't push you down those stairs. Something or someone else did. But, I sure wish I had, after receiving that hefty punch you threw."

"Oh, that was only a down payment, Denning. Do you recall my last words to you that day?"

"I'm not in the mood for chatting or listening to your threats, Mister. Just get on with what you came for and be done with it—and leave like you came in—through that door over there."

"Testy....you're still so testy, Denning." He took a deep breath. "Well...now that you force my hand...you see, a strange thing occurred in our vaults at *Oculus* headquarters. You do remember the golden capsule that caused us so much difficulty? And I finally wrested it from you not all that long ago. It must have a mind of its own, Denning, because it has—just—simply disappeared! And I was wondering if you had any knowledge of its whereabouts?"

"Look, Ravna, enough people have died defending or trying to obtain your precious golden capsule. Maybe it does have a mind of its own, I don't know, maybe it just decided it didn't like you and your 'Order' and wanted to go home. Ever think of that?"

"How quaint. I like that. In your uneducated clumsiness, you do have a way with words that warm the heart." He cracked his knuckles. "I was thinking...oh...perhaps of more nefarious or deceitful things. Like perhaps the capsule you transferred to me that day was not—uh, *the real thing*, shall we say?" He got up and walked around the room, running a finger over my furniture. "You need someone to come in and dust, Denning. Cleanliness is next to—oh, well, you know...." He came back and stood over me. "What I'm suggesting is that...perhaps... someone—perhaps not even you—contrived a way to fashion a *copy* of the *God of Our Fathers*. If that is the case, then we were both hoodwinked. If, on the other hand, you *knew* that what you handed off to me that day was not, shall we say, the genuine article, then, my most unfortunate man, there will most certainly be consequences. Would that not be fair to expect if indeed you betrayed my trust in you?"

"You're trying to skin the wrong cat, Ravna."

"Am I? We find it curious to discover that you and that Chinese Red Dragon Lady have rendezvoused subsequent to your receiving the *Fen de Fuqin*, as she calls it. How might you explain that?"

"We happen to like each other. I don't sniff around your personal life, Ravna, so leave mine alone. And I'd appreciate your leaving just about now. I never told you this, but you bore me. You know why? Because you're layered with deceit yourself—not to mention ulterior motives, criminal intent and that certain careless disregard for human life, which I detest. Ever since that day you killed Anne Banning and dumped her body in my apartment with Adora watching—"

"—oh, your little Mexican whore. Yes, she's actually quite attractive and quite pleasing under the covers, I'm sure. You wouldn't want to lose her now, would you? It could be arranged…so easily…along with her petite little sister and that fine upstanding mother of theirs."

I was so livid toward this walking piece of crap I could have strangled or shot him on the spot. "You know, you treacherous son-of-a-bitch, we've been through this before—remember San Francisco? You touch them, Ravna, and I'll save the Order a lot of trouble by killing you with my bare hands here and now." I was trembling. I went to my desk and took out my bottle of gin and poured a big one. Then I lit up one of my Lucky Strikes. He stood there watching me. I took out my .38 and pointed it at him. "So what's it gonna be?"

He observed me quietly, always composed, always focused. "You smoke and drink to hide your fears, you know. Your womanizing ways are another, shall we say, 'escape hatch' of avoidance for your inferior and tortured personality. You play a child's game, Denning. Shooting me will avail you nothing. It wouldn't even be *my* order for the Moreno women to be targeted for murder. It comes from higher up. And even we are not certain it is they who hover, ready to pounce. We are not alone in the quest for our now missing precious capsule. When certain powers are angered, no telling where they may retaliate. Perhaps your fiancée, the most attractive Honey Combes will be next. Or the fetching little country girl you seduced who pants around you like a bitch in heat. *Someone* has to pay…and no one is certain who it might be. If we could find her, we'd even kill that Chinese slut who's been holding out on us. It all leads to her, you know. But if she's one of those shape-changing creatures, it makes it difficult to round her up, let alone dispatch her. We don't have access to those dimensions, do *you*? I've always wondered where you went with her when you were making me wait while you played footsy in Chinatown last year."

I sat there uneasy as hell in my chair, as if I was being grilled by some monstrous thing that had no connection with human feelings. But I had nowhere to escape to. And somehow I had to fight back, I couldn't let monsters like Ravna get away with the attitude that he and his kind were all-superior and the rest of the world inferior underlings fated to servitude and stupidity. "You know, Ravna, you really don't know how to be nice, now, do you? If you dug into that empty void that's your heart, maybe you'd realize some things can be won with kindness—so instead of us killing each other, why don't you just bow quietly and leave here—and never come back. It's definite, you're a piece of shit without a conscience, I don't like you—and that makes it official in my book. You're like the bad penny that always shows up just when it isn't welcome—and you, Nazar Ravna, are never welcome."

He smiled a wry smile. "Your wit and humor are always disarming, Denning. Actually, I do like that." Then he grew grim. "You do recall I vowed I'd kill you somehow, someday after I was pushed down the stairs that day? Well, for the moment, I'm willing to let bygones be bygones. I'll make a deal with you. You come up with the real *God of Our Fathers* and I promise not a hair will be touched on the head of anyone you may consider off limits to us."

I thought for a minute. What if he wasn't bluffing? What if he really knew the phony was a phony, as Toggth suggested might happen? "How do you know the capsule I handed to you wasn't the genuine article?"

"Simple. First of all the symbols and the mathematics didn't quite 'jibe' under laboratory tests. Something was, how do I say it—absent. Secondly, the golden microfilm, which was supposed to duplicate the capsule's symbolic key-code was missing from the capsule's interior. A fatal omission, Denning—which is why you are my number one suspect, along with your little invisible shape-changing pals."

"Oh, I'm sorry to hear that," I said, tongue in my cheek. "How do you know someone in your organization didn't do a switcheroo on you?" Just then, with the worst possible timing, in walked Adora. She glanced and half-smiled at me, and then looked intensely at Nazar Ravna. I saw she recognized him immediately and her voice trembled. "Oh, *lo siento,* Cable. I was coming by to—see—"

"—Adora!" I called from across the room, getting up from my chair. "I think we'd better talk another time. I'll call you later."

"No, no! I insist," Ravna interjected, raising his voice. "This is a propitious occasion. Your little señorita should hear what I have to say." He looked at the luscious and beautiful Adora. "Young woman, you might as well know—perhaps you can help convince your hard-headed lover here—that his life hangs in the balance, depending on how he answers my questions this very day. May I ask, what do *you* know about the *God of Our Fathers*?"

She looked at me wide-eyed and then back to Ravna. "*Dios de nuestros Padres?* I never hear, Señor. I know nothing of such a one."

"She's on the level, Ravna. I've purposely kept her in the dark--from knowing anything—just so when occasions like this popped up she couldn't figure into your equation."

Ravna studied my face, then Adora's. "Somehow, this I believe is true, Denning." He glowered at Adora. "So, young wetback, on your way. And I warn you, never breathe a word of seeing me in here to *anyone—comprendes?* Or your clandestine lover boy here will end up with flowers on his chest at the local mortuary."

Adora looked back at me. "Go on, babe, skedaddle, I'll call you later."

She turned quickly and went out the door. "Every once in a while you surprise me, I mean, for a scheming killer without a conscience."

"She's no use to us dead, if you're alive." He went for the door, then turned back to look at me with his intense, beady black eyes. "That's the deal, Cable. You find the Chinese woman, get me the real *Fen de Fuqin*—and I promise to leave you and yours alone forevermore."

"Your promises are about as good as yesterday's toilet paper. You'll have to do better than that. You see, once a crook always a crook, as far as I'm concerned, Ravna. It doesn't matter if you wear rags or high-class Florsheim's, what's inside is still rotten."

"I warn you, Cable. I'll be back for an answer within a couple of weeks. Then the bodies will begin to pile up until we get a commitment from you. Try as you might, you'll never deceive the Order—they made the rules—and…they enforce them."

He exited as he had entered, quick…determined. I took a deep breath and settled back into my comfy chair. Shit! This was all I needed now. They had discovered the fraud quicker than I thought. Just then the phone rang. "Yeah, Cable Denning here."

"Cable…have you forgotten?—it's me, Ginny. After we talked a couple of days ago, hearing your voice made me miss you. Can you see your way clear to make an appointment for our dinner date?"

I was dead tired by now. I just needed to be alone with my thoughts. "Okay, kid. Hmmm….let's see…how about next Friday night, the 11th? I don't have a car yet. Give me your address and I'll take the streetcar to pick you up."

"Oh, Cable, that's wonderful. Thank you. I know you're a busy man and all. And almost a married man, huh? Well, anyway, my address is 5653 Virginia Avenue. It's just east of Wilton Place. What time on Friday? I get home from work about 6:30."

"What if I pick you up about 7:30?"

"Yes…perfect, Cable. I'm looking forward to seeing you again. It's been ages."

"Yeah, it has been at that, Ginny. Well, I'll see you Friday about 7:30."

We hung up and I staggered into my little bedroom and fell onto the mattress. I was out almost immediately. But I was having dreams from the get-go. Restless dreams, dreams in reds and oranges and indigos, where suddenly a hundred Lei-tao's appeared running all over, scattering little umbrellas that contained lotus seeds. But somehow I knew they were my sperm seeds and all the different Red Dragon Ladies were trying to catch the seeds and tuck them under their kimonos. A golden dragon appeared from out of nowhere, elegant, beautiful, powerful. His deep jade-green eyes looked me over. He opened his mouth and spat green fire at me, but when the flames reached me, they didn't burn. Instead, they felt good, like a healing blast of magical energy that lifted me above the scattering women. The dragon tossed me up behind his neck and I hung on to huge golden spikes as he flew me up to the front steps of an iridescent castle high atop a snowy mountain, which constantly changed colors—wondrous pastels from light blues to pinks to lovely greens, salmon reds, maroons and indigos.

After he eased me to the ground, the mighty dragon gently nudged me with his nose to enter the castle doors. I pushed softly and the two gigantic doors swung easily open. I entered cautiously. Beautiful music was playing somewhere. A *liuqin*—a Chinese stringed instrument Lei-tao told me about that sounded like a mandolin. When I walked down a long hallway into a great room, I was astonished to find eight beautiful women sitting, dressed in long, light-green dresses and all playing the *liuqin* in concert. The music filled me with peace and lifted my spirits. The leader of the ensemble was a lovely young woman with short, black hair and a yellow tight-fitting outfit. But no one noticed me and I stood there in the middle of the great room, transported by the music. Mystified, I watched as the women began to ascend toward the ceiling and soon disappeared through it, although I could still hear their wonderful musical strains…

Then a voice spoke behind me. "Welcome…to my palace…I hope *Hanu Long*, my golden dragon, did not frighten you. I am Daiyu Guang."

I knew I had heard that name before. "No…your dragon was kind…and even the green flame felt good. Seems to me I've heard your name before—"

"—I am Lei-tao's teacher. You know why you are here. Lei-tao has violated the precepts of her station. Such an act upsets the balances in all our dimensional planes. You might say it is a *chain reaction*. Using secrets she has learned, she modified her female body to accommodate her ovum in order to receive your seed. But you must realize, this cannot be, nor can the embryo reach maturation."

I stood opposite this lovely creature, who measured no more than five-feet. Everything about her was delicate and her face shone with goodness and her dark, almond eyes spoke only kindness toward me. She wore a golden tunic with a glowing light-golden cord belt and golden pearl slippers. "I'm sorry for all of it. It was my fault. When I helped her replace the *Fen de Fuqin* and we experienced tantric sex in the Cave of the Seven Truths, I kind of went overboard and began to desire her as a man would desire a normal woman. I thought I could bring her a pleasure she'd never had before—"

"—or was ever intended *to* have, Honorable Mr. Denning. But at the risk of your own life, you have helped us all restore the *Tone of Creation*. We have watched as you are again threatened by the evil ones. We can help. But only to a certain extent. Your dimensional world is not ours, you must surely understand."

"Yeah, I do. I just wish there was some way I could make amends for what I helped cause."

"The burden lies in the heart of Lei-tao, Honorable Mr. Denning. She has to come to terms with being accountable to her own kind. The child cannot and will not be born."

I took a deep breath. I could still hear that magnificent music playing high above us. "That music…I know the instruments…especially the mandolin-like sound of the *liuqin*. It is so…so tranquillizing…"

"Yes, music heals, Honorable Mr. Denning. You must return to your world, now that I have told you the truth—which we know, you embrace with such devotion and dedication."

"Yeah, well, thanks, ma'am." I didn't know what else to say. It was as if I couldn't be polite enough around this exquisite little being. "May I call you Daiyu Guang?"

"If you like. I must send you back now…we will do what we

431

can to assist you…be kind and understanding to Lei-tao…"

"Will you punish her?" I asked as I could feel myself being pulled back down the corridor of the palace.

"No…*forgive her*," came the answer.

Suddenly I was rolling and moaning on my bed, dripping wet from sweat and tears. "*Mi amor! Mi amor! Mi pobre muchacho!* It is okie-dokie, Cable. It is me, Adora." She was dabbing my face with a cool, wet cloth.

"Adora!" I reached up for her and pulled her down to my mouth. I kissed her until there was only wetness between us. I could never have enough of this beautiful woman who flitted in and out of my life like a magic fairy. "I had this incredible dream!" I finally said, trying to sit up in bed. She sat beside me. "I was in this castle or palace that was completely Chinese and beautiful. A golden dragon flew me into the clouds and to this place, you see, after a bunch of Red Dragon Ladies—" I stopped. What use would it be to tell anyone. "Anyway, it wasn't a nightmare, Adora, but a beautiful dream."

She smiled at me. "Beautiful like you, *mi amor*. What can I do for you?"

"Just lay here beside me, quietly. Listen to my heart and tell me I'm still here, alive and really looking at your incredible face, *mi querido.*"

I scooted over and she rolled her wonderful body close to mine. We just lay there in the early afternoon, not speaking, not touching…only content to be in each other's presence.

Just before sunset I awakened to feel Adora's soft, warm lips gently touching my cheek. I turned my head to look at her and the smile she gave me melted away all possibility that danger could even exist in this world—or maybe it was just our world. It seemed safe and protected by some unseen god whose hands pushed us together ever so delicately, smiling to know that we had found each other in this life.

Then she got up and sat on the bed. "Cable…*yo temo, mi favorito*. That *hombre terrible* who comes *esta tarde*. Does he come back to hurt us?"

I sat up and put my hand on her shoulder. "Naw…he just wants something I used to have," I said, underplaying it. "On that San Francisco trip, to Chinatown—you remember—after they tied you up and dumped Anne Banning's body in the middle of our room? Well, since *they* haven't got it, they think I know more than I do—"

"—do you, señor?" she asked, checking out my eyes. I could never lie to Adora, her warm brown eyes went right to those deepest places in me. "Yeah, babe, I do. Much to the curse of it all, they *know* I do, somehow. And they're willing to do whatever it takes to get it. I bought some time today. Maybe a couple of weeks."

"*O mi querido!*" she cried and held on to me. "*Venga con me, mi corazón*—we go to Mexico—I have an *abuela en la ciudad de Ensenada*. They never find us…Cable…"

"Thanks, Adora, but there's no escaping these guys. They're everywhere. We just gotta lay low. Besides, you forget, I'm getting married in four months." I winced in saying what I had to say. "And I keep telling myself—and you—that I can't see you anymore…but neither of us seem to believe that, do we?"

She lifted her long skirt, pushed me down on the bed and mounted me. She bent down and kissed my lips while undoing my pants. "Make love to me, *mi amor*! Never stop making love to me!" she sighed breathlessly. Soon we were lost once more in that perfect ecstasy that this rare and beautiful young woman always brought to me. I could no more refuse her love than stop the oceans from coming to the shore. The Fates were perverse, I thought. They had given me ecstasy through the forest of agony. When would the other shoe drop, I wondered?

It was about 10:30 p.m. when I dragged myself over to Honey's. I saw a light on and knocked on the door. Zelda

Blodgett answered. "Gees, Cable! You look terrible—those dark circles under your eyes. You need some of my aloe vera plant rubbed on them."

"Hello, Zelda. I'd go for a stiff shot of gin—or whatever you and Honey are drinking these days."

"You know I don't drink—except that time when you took me out and got me drunk at the night club. And Honey? I don't think she drinks alcohol much either. Bad for her voice. I make sure she has a glass of warm water with a squeeze of fresh lemon and honey before she goes to work—if I'm here, that is."

"Yeah, well, I'll scrounge around for what I can find. How've you been?"

"Well, I'm still date-less, and boyfriend-less, if that's what you mean. I just don't seem to connect with the guys at school. I think I told you that already. I just loved our time together. I'll bet you make all girls feel like real women when you talk to them, dance with them—and—ahem!—you know…"

I felt like teasing the straight-laced little bookworm. "No, I—I don't know exactly what you mean, Zelda. Fill me in."

"You know…the sex thing…I mean, the overture stuff… kissing, undressing, feeling skin to skin, touching private places, feeling your temperature rise and your pulse quicken—like plants have a rather dull life compared to humans."

"I think you're right on that one. But you know, I wouldn't mind being a plant just about now in my life…"

"What do you mean?"

"At the moment I've got a lot of pressure on top of me and being a plant—you know, sunshine, water, a little fertilizer and some tender care—they've got it made."

"I never thought of it that way, Cable. I kind of feel that way, too, though. I would love a man to be on top of me, smile his sunshine on me, water me with praise now and then, fertilize me—ummm, pretty often—and hold me with tender love

434

every night."

Poking around the kitchen cupboards I found a half-full unmarked bottle of gin I had left ages ago. I got a snifter. "Do you want a shot?"

"Sure, why not? I'm safe with you. I can drink and tell you the things I'm feeling and you won't take advantage of me, right?"

"Well, I wouldn't go that far, kid," I teased her and laughed. "All depends how horny I am and who's around to take care of it."

Zelda blushed. "I offered that to you...last time we went out...and you wouldn't even come in and dance with me some more." I poured her drink and she gulped it all down. "Oh! Whew! That burns! So where does that leave us? I still dream of our night together—and I dream about you, Mr. Denning... very naughty stuff, I'm afraid." She pushed her snifter in my direction and I re-filled it. "It's so hard to get started. I mean, if I dress up and go out to a place where Honey started for ten cents a dance, I'm just going to attract the wrong kind of guy. So where do I find the right kind of guy? I get feelings just like any other girl, and I really get tired of just satisfying myself with my fingers—ooops! I didn't mean to say that, sorry..." she said, turning a very bright red.

"It's okay, Zelda. It's natural. I wonder if plants masturbate?" We both let out a howl of laughter and Zelda fell over toward me, laughing on my shoulder. Then she pushed her lips onto mine and kissed me with a gin-scented kiss. "Whoa! What was that about?" I asked, pulling back.

"Oh....pent up passion, Cable. Uncontrollable, stupid, pent up desire—the kind that fantasizes about you—and it's stupid because all you ever did was take me out once for dinner and a dance!" She began to weep. That was all I needed. So we spent the next forty-five minutes drying her tears and re-affirming that one day Mr. Right would come along for her.

A little after midnight Honey came through the door looking pretty beat her self. She saw us in the kitchen and entered. She sized up the situation. "Getting my roommate drunk again, eh?" she chided in her wonderful light-hearted way. "You know, Zelda, as soon as we're married, I *am* getting a ball and chain for this guy here. Wherever he goes, seduction follows." She came over and kissed me. Then she looked at Zelda. "I'm not, however, going to kiss you…"

"You're looking a bit crimped around the edges tonight, doll," I said.

"Yeah, well, that has to do with seduction, too. Some millionaire mafia playboy has been targeting me for his next bedroom playmate—and the club is too scared to call him off because he brings in so much business."

"Do you want me to cool his britches outside of the club?"

"No, Cable, I don't want you involved. I'll handle it. Affonso does his best, but he's only the manager of the club. The back room belongs to the big players—and owners." She looked at both of us. "So, lover man, I'm beat and going to take a long bath. Which of us will you bed tonight?" she tittered. "One of us will be clean, the other smell like a plant."

"Honey! That's not fair!" Zelda fought back. "It's true, I always talk sex around Cable. But you know it's—it's really—"

"—yeah, I know, Zelda. Relax. So, Cable, you either take a bath with me or warm up the bed—which will it be?"

"As tempted as I am to see you nude and play with you in the tub, I think I'll be the bed-warmer tonight." I was thinking about my late afternoon tryst with Adora and the thrill of it still buzzed in my groin. Honey went on and I said good night to Zelda. I watched her walk slowly down the hall toward her little room. In a way I felt sorry for this attractive young woman hidden behind glasses, books and plants. "Zelda…I'm not sure there's a definite answer for your predicament, but if I were you, I'd look for someone who's already a professional in the plant world—that way you'd really have a lot in common."

She stopped and turned around to look at me. "Damn, Cable, you know, I never thought of that. I've been looking in school for Mr. Right—maybe I could get a summer job in a lab or something and meet him there!"

"Now you're talkin', kid," I said with a big grin. "Good night."

I stripped and crawled under the covers. I was exhausted from the long and wearing day. I was thinking about Nazar Ravna and that insane *Oculus* order of his. For them, it was like a game of pin-the-tail-on-the-donkey and I was the jackass getting pinned. I decided not to worry Honey about the events of the day. There had to be a way out. Then a light went on in my head. Crazy Jack! I'd check with Crazy Jack! That little guy was hooked up to something, like Madame Palladino, he was plugged into other dimensions beyond the veil of our common everyday experience. That made me feel better.

Honey came in and started combing her lovely honey-colored hair in front of the dresser mirror. She was looking through the glass at me in the bed. "You know, Mr. Denning, you're really a fine looking young man."

"You mean, for a young old gumshoe, that is, eh?" I chuckled.

"Maybe…but I like your looks. Smooth looking but chiseled at the same time. It's almost as if your parents couldn't make up their minds who you'd look like. But it doesn't matter, I like what I see…"

"Well, thank you, Miss Combes, alias Lana Loren."

She finished and came over, got on her knees on top of the bed and sidled over to me. "I've composed a song for you. Wanna hear it?"

I was moved. "Really? No one has ever done that for me, babe. Yeah, sure, I'm all ears."

She stretched out on top of the bed, resting her head in the palm of her right hand. Well, promise you won't laugh. I can get pretty sentimental when it comes to you, Mr. Private Dick."

"I promise."

"It's not really finished yet. But here goes. '*Will you dance with me, til the music stops playing…dance with me, never let me go…will you kiss my heart and say that you love me, so I'll know… Long ago I dreamed that a boy like you would come…and dance with me…freeing my lips to say I adore you, that I'm for you…and hope you might adore me, too…*' That's all I've got so far," she said as she stopped singing.

"That's great, darlin'! Sing it again…see if I can follow along…" She began singing and I joined in as best I could in my quasi-baritone. There in the mid of night on a little street in nowhere, U.S.A., my betrothed and I sang. When we finished, we laughed together. I grabbed her and brought her lips to my own. "Thank you…I love you, lady…"

"You're welcome. I'll finish it someday." She turned the light off and slid into bed with me. "You know, lover, once upon a time you said I was like a goddess when you made love to me. Do you still feel that way?"

"You bet I do, babe. And I still feel like I'm one of the luckiest guys in the world. Any man who has you, holds the best this world has to offer in his arms, Honey Combes."

"That's nice to hear, Cable. We don't say those things much anymore. I hope that isn't a preview of married life. I couldn't stand it if our love making ever got worn down, worn out and old hat."

"Yeah, me, too. It's up to us. I know I've been a bit remiss lately. But all that's over now. We're planning our wedding, our lives together, and we're happier than we've ever been."

"Oh, Cable…yes…yes…" She said that and rolled over on top of me, kissing me. Then she ground her pubic area into mine until she got the right response and moved her tongue down the middle of my body until she was holding most of my erect manhood in her mouth. Soon we had merged into that wonderful lighted moment and it reminded me of one of the most excellent reasons I loved my future wife, the beautiful Honey Combes, the magnificent Golden Throat.

FRIDAY'S CHILD

Crazy Jack wasn't in his apartment. So I went searching the streets looking for him. This part of skid row was seedy, unkempt and filled with every imaginable kind of human—or maybe non-human—that one could imagine. Characters on every corner, having slid through the slats of life to this, a daily cacophony and parade of panderers, alcoholics, prostitutes, drug pushers, marginally functional people like Crazy Jack who were only a few steps away from a nut house—and the usual assortment of those who fed off of each other for survival. It seemed strange to me that Skid Row was located so close to Main Street and its environs. Seems it's an area that should bring visions of a wholesome America and white-washed homes and businesses, clean streets and moral upright citizens living the good life. But no, this was the slum, the bottom of the barrel.

I turned a corner and passed a bar. The stench of dirty sawdust, beer and stale tobacco smoke filled my nostrils. Suddenly I felt a tap on my shoulder. "Cigarette! Cigarette!" I turned to see Crazy Jack's anxious face and darting eyes. "See Denning! Think of Cable...is Crazy Jack...but I don't know! I don't know! Cigarette!"

"Jack! Good to see you, old boy. In fact, I was just looking for you at your place." I reached in my pocket for a pack of Lucky Strikes. In the usual ritual, I took one out, gave it to this poor nervous creature in front of me and tucked the rest of the pack into a half-torn suit jacket he was wearing. "I need your help, Jack. Let's walk..." He followed me like an obedient dog as he puffed away. We walked a block before we found a quiet little area with a brown lawn and lumps of animal crap everywhere. "The bad guys are back, Jack. Frankly, I'm feeling a bit wary about the whole thing. I mean, it could get real ugly. What do you think?"

His eyes widened until the whites predominated. "I don't know! I don't know! All go boom! Soon! Drain away, go away—sign—awww....not good! Money boom—zoom!" He made a gesture like he was kicking something invisible high into the air. "But I don't know! Cigarette good! Lucky Strike, ha! ha! good!" Then he began to move back and forth like a pendulum of a clock. "They kill—car go boom, too! But I don't know! I don't know!"

He must've psychically picked up on the car bombing below my office the day before. "Yeah, they thought it was me. These same goons blew up a car right in broad daylight. Remember when I went on the train to Frisco? And you directed me to the Lark? Well, it's that same batch of idiots who want this golden capsule with some kind of mystic code—"

"—danger, Cable! Danger! But I don't know! I don't know! All...everything...comes boom! ...the *photes*—the photes are coming! Go away, Cable Denning...run! Oh....cry....cry..." Crazy Jack began to sob and sat down on the sidewalk where we stood. "I don't know! Jack cry...cigarette." He reached for my pant leg and pulled back and forth on it, sobbing. "Jack like Cable...hide...they find you every—everywhere—but I don't know...I don't know...!" I bent down to help the distraught man. He took my hand and his twitching, blue-grey eyes looked into mine as if he were looking for something. "But

440

Cable Denning not run…not like him…but I don't know! I don't know!"

"What's this thing about money going 'boom-zoom' or whatever you said? I don't get it. The nation's more prosperous than ever before. Life is good for a lot of Americans. The banks are lending, Wall Street, the Spring Street Financial District are booming—people can buy houses and cars—shit, Jack, we're in the middle of prosperity."

Jack was shaking. "I don't know! I don't know! People jump—boom! windows—look! Up there!" I looked up at one of the tall buildings he was pointing out. I saw nothing except pigeons chasing each other on a ledge. I chalked it up to hallucinations and thought it had not been a good day after all to seek out Crazy Jack. I took a few bucks from my pocket. "Here, Jack, buy yourself a hamburger and a milk shake."

He gave me one of his nervous half smiles. "Cable always good to Jack! Get straw-colored girl from bad place…" Then he did a strange thing. He took a hand and cupped his crotch. "Oh…they like—ouch! hurt Cable Denning—but I don't know! I don't know!"

"*Who* wants to hurt what, Jack? You're not making a lot of sense today. I know you've always warned me about Honey being at the *Bella Notte*, but it's a gold mine for her. And this crotch thing…does it have to do with seeing too many babes—or what?"

"I don't know! I don't know!" He reached into his torn pocket and took out another Lucky Strike. "Cigarette! Cigarette! Good…" I lit his smoke and he put it in his mouth. Then he took both hands, palm open, and rubbed them across his belly. "No baby…come…Ha! Jack cannot have baby! But I don't know! I don't know! Ha!"

I left Jack sitting on the sidewalk, smoking and mumbling to himself. Poor bereft misfit, I thought. He never had a chance in this world. Somewhere in his brain wires got left out or crossed and he'd forever be in the ranks of the disenfranchised of the society in which he lived. Yet he had this uncanny psychic thing. Still, I could not make heads or tails out of his blithering this day.

Ginny Fullerton lived in a freshly painted large two-story affair that was populated by young single women. I discovered that when I arrived to pick her up. A rather tall, breathy sounding young thing stood smoking on the stoop of the house. The porchlight was on and she was wearing a yellow kimono and slippers. "I'm—I'm looking for Ginny Fullerton—do you happen to know her?"

"Are you kidding, Mister? You can tell a country hick a mile away. I suppose she's sweet and all—but between the two of us—very naïve. I don't think she's cut out for city living. Who are you?"

"I'm...I'm, uh, her dinner date."

She looked me over. "How does Ginny rate a stud like you? She doesn't seem the kind who puts out easy—you must have a magic charm or—"

"—look, lady, I'm not really interested, if you don't mind. Just tell me where to find Miss Fullerton."

"Now it's *Miss Fullerton*—well, *sorry* there buster." She ground out her cigarette in an abalone shell on the porch railing. "So I guess I'm a little out of line, talking that way to your sensitive masculine ears. Get used to it—girls are bitchy and filled with envy, and don't forget jealous and possessive. You couldn't be much older than me, now, could you? I'm good at sizing up guys—"

"—now look, whoever you are, I need to—"

"—you *do* want to know where Ginny's...bedroom is... don't you? Second floor, third door to the left. And there are house rules. No men after ten p.m. So let me finish. It's a hobby of mine, sizing up guys for gals. Now you…hmmm…let me see…you work for yourself…or maybe—yeah, you have that clean-cut cop look. Are you a cop?"

"Good guess," I said impatiently. "Used to be."

"See? Monica knows her stuff. Now…as far as your taste in the fairer sex…me, not included, because I don't dig guys. Hmmm…I'd say you like variety and don't force yourself. You make 'em want *you*, right?"

Just then Ginny appeared in the doorway to save me. "Cable!" she exclaimed, happy to see me. Then she looked at Monica. "Oh…I see you've met Monica. I'm sorry…she should be locked up—"

"—keep your trap shut, ya *hick*! I was just sizing up your new lay here—and I guess you could do worse. I enjoy minding other people's business. You know why? Because most of the time they haven't got the guts to be honest. Someone has to point out to them that they're just not all they think they are."

"Well, I can't say it's been pleasant talking to you, because it hasn't. I let you foam at the mouth, Monica, because women like you, no matter what side of the sex fence you're on, give the female gender a bad name. And sooner or later you put your foot in your mouth. So, happy chewing…" I said as I took Ginny's arm and we walked toward the street and the streetcar stop.

When we were out of earshot from Monica, Ginny breathed out a deep breath. "Sorry about her. She's everybody's pain in the ass. I think she's a little unbalanced or something. What do you think?"

"She might have gotten a warped outlook from her child-hood, is my guess. She got sexually all mixed up and must have found men repulsive. But when she looked at her own sex, that wasn't so hot, either. So she's a fence rider and sour that she doesn't know how to find emotional or sexual fulfillment."

"Who does?" Ginny answered. She stopped us and gave me a big hug. "Anyway, I'm so happy to see you again."

She was wearing a light-blue dress with nice reddish heels, an off-white light coat and her hair was done up in a bun. "Likewise, doll. You look very becoming tonight, Ginny," I said, checking her out.

"Thanks, Cable. Not too bad for a backwoods girl, huh? Where are we going?"

"Well, if you're up to it, there's a new club on Beverly Boulevard near Virgil...not too far from here... decent food and I hear there's a great band for dancing, as well. Are you game?"

"I'd go anywhere with you, Cable, you know that. And besides, I'm single and fancy free. God, I was reading that women in some other countries have no rights at all. I know there can be a double-standard here, but these women have to keep covered up when in public—even their faces—and a husband has the right to kill his wife if she commits even the smallest infraction."

"Yeah, you're talking about a lot of places. India, China, the mid-East, even Latin America—any place where a male's need for superiority under the guise of politics and religion suppress a woman's rights as a human being. Islam, Hindus, even some Christian societies, make the woman barely more than a baby-making machine and a cook."

"That's terrible. I'll bet if we had a baby, you'd give me full rights in the household, huh?"

"Don't be so sure," I chuckled. "You can't judge a book by its cover. I might be this outrageous male chauvinist pig and tie you to the bed, take you constantly at my whim and beat you when you're bad."

She giggled as we boarded the streetcar. We sat and she grabbed my hand. "God, Cable, I have to say it again. Thanks for keeping your word."

"That's me, babe, Old Stick-to-it Denning here."

We rode along in silence for a while. "Interesting name for a night spot…did you say Rooftop or something like that?"

"*The Roof Garden*…well, if you can believe it…it is actually at the top of a 14 story storage building. It's called the *American Storage Building* and you have to take an actual freight elevator up to the very top. I guess it is sort of a speak-easy with music for dancing provided by George Redman and his Roof Garden Orchestra. They do a remote radio broadcast in the evening. That's actually where I heard about it."

"You mean it is actually a real storage building?…to store furniture and boxes inside? I wonder why someone would think to put a night club up there on the top of *that*?"

"Well…you know we are living in a restless world these days…and people are always trying to think up something unique to get an edge over their competition."

"You're so smart, Cable. Most men are so boring because they *think* they know a lot, but you really do."

"Thanks, Ginny, I'll take that as a compliment. You're no dummy yourself, for a country hick, that is."

She lightly punched me on my shoulder. "You!"

We arrived at 3636 Beverly Boulevard and if you didn't know better, you'd never guess there was a night spot on top of this formidable 14 story building. We found the elevator and were eventually transported to the sights and sounds of the 'Nite Club De Luxe'. We walked into a crowded, noisy den. It was a place where people came to drink, smoke and yell…trying to talk to another person above the din. The Roof Garden Orchestra had just started…featuring a hot jazz guitarist and they were playing an up-tempo version of Honey's *Makin' Whoopee*. Ginny and I sidled to the bar, got a waiter to find us a table and twenty minutes later we were sitting about three tables away from the bandstand. Ginny was glowing in the candlelight and her fresh, young face was alive with curiosity and you could tell this was the first time she'd been to such a place. "Oh, Cable, I love it! It's like soaking in a new rain… it feels so refreshing to hear people let their hair down, enjoy the music and all."

"That's sort of my take on it. Music and this atmosphere bring a certain life to me, too. I wouldn't wanna be without it in my life."

"I understand…me too." She took my hand again. "You know, when you were talking about tying me to the bed and having your way with me, I got this rush. I wanted to say right then and there that I love you, but I didn't want people in the streetcar to hear it." She looked at me with those peepers of hers. "But I do, Cable. I really do. It's not puppy love or anything like that. It's the grown woman part that longs for you when I can't get you out of my mind and days go by—"

"—Ginny…I'm sorry…I'm very flattered by what you're saying. But you're forgetting a couple of things here, aren't you? One, I'm getting married in about four and a half months— and second, you promised you'd accept me on my terms—like good old friends, right?"

She shut down. I hated to do that to this very pretty young thing who had somehow become enamored with one of those fantasies women often have to idealize her Prince Charming. She sipped her fizz and I got my flask out and poured a little gin into it. "This will make me feel better?" she asked, looking at me with all sorts of questions in her eyes.

"I don't know, but maybe it'll help you forget. Tonight's our night, kid, let's enjoy. Would you like to dance?"

She lit up. "Yes, I would. We haven't danced since that time in your little cabin in Big Bear, remember?"

"Yep, that was a fun evening, wasn't it?" I took her hand

and we went out onto the dance floor as that sexy jazz guitar launched into *It Had to Be You*, a song Honey had auditioned with at the *Bella Notte* a year or so ago. Ginny merged her body into mine and we fit just fine. Her back was a bit stiff, so I put my open hand at the bottom of her waist and told her to relax. She did and I could feel her warmth invade me like a cup of nectar being poured over my body.

As she put her lips on my neck, I got a chill. "Cable," she whispered. "Why is life so incomplete, so frustrating? Here I am with you. I'm very happy, but I'm crying inside at the same time."

I spoke in a low tone. "I'm not sure I can answer that, doll. I think we are intended to be or do something—and it just isn't always as we've planned. That's life. I could tell you stories, but I won't bore you."

"I wish you would…" she said, still nuzzling at the nape of my neck. I was thinking of the bittersweet irony of loving two women. I loved and was crazy about Honey, but in that minute when the jazz guitarist twanged out the music to the words, *'the mere idea of you, the longing here for you, you'll never know how slow the moments go til I'm near to you…I see your face in every flower, your eyes in stars above…it's just the thought of you, the very thought of you, my love…,'* Adora's face was in front of me and I realized I was in love with that smoldering little Latina who lifted her skirt to sit on my chest and opened my heart to some version of unconditional love. The test for me was *who* would I want to end up with on a desert island--and hands down, it came up Adora. The music stopped and we sat back down.

As the evening wore on, Ginny was feeling no pain from the lousy gin I had been pouring into her carbonated fizz. "You're a truth guy, right?" she spoke up, a little inebriated. "Truth is, it's very diffi—diffi—difficult—hic!—to be with someone— someone you don't have a future with. I mean, if this were a—a normal relationship...I would know I'd see you...again—hic!—and you'd be taking me home to make love—make love to me..."

I'd had a few drinks myself and slurred over the thoughts that would have brought a cohesive end to the conversation. "Yeah...if it was a normal relationship...but you *don't* know, kid...and no woman should have to live—live on the edge all the time, never knowing if or when her intended might—might drop by to be her passionate lover for the night..."

"I'd even settle for that with you, Cable. Just to know you'd—you'd make love to me...like you did at my aunt's house..."

"Forget it, kid." There was a lively version of *I'm Sitting on Top of the World* being played by the orchestra. "Tell you what...we need to put some *life* into our step—not this morose romantic slush...let's kick up our heels, young lady, okay?"

She took my hand again, but as we got out onto the floor the fast song ended and immediately after the applause, a love song started up. This time it was Jerome Kern's *'Can't Help Lovin' That Man of Mine'* from a wonderful musical play, *Showboat*. It was 1927 when it came out and I remember taking Amanda Baxter to see a preview concert version downtown at the *Alhambra Theatre* on Hill Street. The music was exhilarating, powerful, beautiful, and poignant—all the things good music should be. I thought it was Kern's best work. I also remember sitting there in the dark with Amanda Baxter's hand feeling up my leg toward my private parts. She was a sensual dame who had been sexualized by her incest-motivated father. But I didn't know that at the time.

Ginny broke me out of my reverie. "I love this song, I even know some of it. She began to sing in a breathy, warm voice into my ear as we slow danced on the crowded floor. '...*he can come home late as can be, home without him ain't no home to me, can't help, lovin' that man of mine...*' See? I do know some of it."

"Yeah, kid, that was fun! You're pretty—pretty sexy when

you sing, you know."

"I—I am…?" she stuttered, still a bit drunk. "Then you should desire me, Mr. Denning—here and now—here—here and—hic!—*now*!"

"Right here…on the floor?" I kidded her.

"Yep. That way—that way I'll have—hic!—proof that you made love—made love to me."

I laughed. "I like you, Ginny Fullerton." I don't know what got into me, but in the crowded darkness I moved my hand up Ginny's leg to her crotch and squeezed. I could feel her body collapse in surrender.

"Oh! What—what—hic!—are you doing, Cable? You're going to kill me…aren't you—with love? But don't stop…I would never want you to stop." She started breathing heavier. "Take me home, please. I'm feeling—feeling a bit, uh, dizzy… hic!"

We rode toward Ginny's rooming house pretty much in silence. She held on to my hand and wouldn't let go for a second. When we got off the streetcar and heard it clang away down the street, she turned to me. She took a deep breath and grabbed my neck, bringing my head down to her lips. She forced them onto mine and the wet warmth went through me like a sparkler on the Fourth of July. "I—I have to tell you, Cable…my—hic!—*my* truth, Mr. Truth Man. I can't let you go home without—without having you—and letting my body be filled with your—your…you know…"

The cool night air sobered me up a bit. "Ginny…oh, Ginny. You see what a mess we've already created? I'm not—not as strong as you might—might think. I'm a sucker—a real sucker for a babe's warm, wet kiss. So…there you have it…but you gotta send me…on…my way…"

"I can't, Cable, I can't."

She took my hand and we walked toward her rooming house

449

and climbed the front steps. When we got to the big front door I stopped her. "You have a ten o'clock curfew—and it's—it's way past ten, lady," I said, fighting my growing desire.

"Mrs. Murphy sleeps with…with toilet paper in her ears. She's also hard of hearing. Girls bring their guys up all the time," she said quietly. She led me into the hallway and we climbed a flight of stairs up to the second floor. She stopped at the third door at the end of the hall and used her key to open it. She took my hand and led me straight to her bed, which was a pull-down, now opened in the middle of the room. She smiled at me. "Women…women scheme…all the time, Cable. I'm like—like—hic!—the *spider woman*, luring you into—into her web."

"So I see," I whispered.

She immediately took my coat off, began unbuttoning my shirt. By the time she unzipped my trousers there was an active member already standing at attention inside my shorts. She got down on her knees and gently took it out, sucking it into her mouth. It was hard to believe this young woman was as inexperienced as she said she was, but maybe some things are just instinctive—and this was one of them. Soon she stood up and took my hands, placed one on a breast, the other on her crotch. "This is for you, Cable. I've—I've saved it for you…all this time. No one has touched me—or had me since—since that day at my aunt's place."

I began to undress her in a frenzy and soon we lay on her squeaky little bed wrapped up in each other. As with the first time, there was no doubt Ginny Fullerton and I had a chemical animal response to one another. Maybe there was no other way to explain it, but she was so *easy* to make love to and her young, pulsing womanhood brought out all my primal instincts as I penetrated her. She began to yell, but I put my hand over her mouth to quiet her. She moaned and groaned until finally her voice grew higher and higher in pitch until she let go like the bursting of a dam whose waters had begun to overflow the dyke.

Finally an hour or so later we lay spent in each other's arms. I could tell her appreciation for the moment had overwhelmed her. Finally she whispered to me in the darkness. "Cable...I *came*...again...what is it about you?" By now most of the alcohol had worn off and her speech was less halting. "I had the funniest feeling..."

"Yeah, what was that?" I asked, a little curious.

"I could feel something—like, uh, a 'click' in me as you filled me with your beautiful love...like we were one for a minute and—and—never mind, just a woman's feelings..."

"Well, it sounds pretty special to me, whatever it was." I freed myself from her body. "I hate to say this, but I hope you were safe—you know, we made love without—"

"—it's okay, Cable. I would tell you if—well, I wouldn't want to put you through all that, your getting married and all."

"I gotta go, Ginny." She didn't respond, but lay there in the dark, stretched out on the bed. I got dressed and bent over to kiss her good-bye. She was crying and I felt the taste of salty tears on my tongue. "What is it, babe? I thought this is what you wanted?"

"Trouble is, I want it all the time," she sobbed. "I don't expect you to understand. I'm sure it's a woman's heart thing. I'll get over it." She sat up and put her arms around my neck. "Thank you, Cable. I'm—I'm sorry if I pushed you over the edge. I...I just didn't know...what else to do, I wanted you so." She tittered under her breath. "So you see, I can be selfish and thoughtless like any other woman. I didn't mean to offend your relationship with your fiancée. But, God, Cable, sex is so powerful!"

"Tell me about it. Look at me, doll. You can't take all the blame. I jumped in there with both feet. But you know what,

Ginny. In some crazy way, I'm glad I did."

"I'm *very* glad you did, big boy," she said in a sultry tone. "Is there any chance of a rematch sometime? I know you like boxing. But wrestling can be just as much fun. But I guess that's asking too much, isn't it?"

I winced. "I want us to be friends, Ginny. I really like you. And I want you to call on me if you need me for other things, like if you get in a tough jam or life wants to break you in two, or you need a friend to talk to."

There was a brief silence. "I love you, Cable," she whispered.

I hugged her once more and went out the door, tip-toeing past Mrs. Murphy's door.

THE HORRIBLE DR. SCHUMACHER

It was already September 7th, 1929. Time has a way of escaping through your fingers and one day you know you're gonna wake up old. I was already feeling that at twenty-nine and my birthday was just around the corner on the 13th. I had slept soundly the night before and thoughts and feelings of Ginny Fullerton kept bouncing in and out of my brain like a ping-pong ball looking for what side of the table it belonged on. It was Saturday and I knew it would be a big night for Honey. So I decided not to call her since she told me she had a few new songs to get straightened out with her accompanist.

I was fiddling at my desk, trying to figure out how to tie together all the loose ends I had in my life. For a guy, it's two things, usually. Work and dames. One keeps you sane, the other drives you crazy. Women were always a delightful mystery to me, as unlike a man as an oak to a redwood—but they were still trees. Somehow you had to make it work, but you couldn't live easily with them, and you sure as hell couldn't live without them. They presented that enigma in a man's life when he has to make up his mind to be married and do his best to toe the line of fidelity, or fuck around until he can't anymore and wake up old and alone. At twenty-nine, my balls were still restless and drove me into untenable situations for the sake of a fine, intelligent, good looking woman who happened to have a great body and was daring enough to live on the edge of eternity with me when we explored the unknown dimensions of the he and she world.

Just then my office door opened and in walked a familiar face. I thought hard to place it. "Mr. Denning…Father Tortelli. Do you remember me? It was Cable, right? We met that night at Dr. Penn's hotel."

"Oh, yeah, come on in. Excuse me if I don't call you 'Father,' but I ain't religious, never have been. Come in…sit down."

"You can call me Carlo." I reached for my Lucky Strikes and offered one to the priest. He took it. "Thanks, Cable." I lit the cigarette for him. He sat back, took a deep drag from his smoke and looked at me. "May I ask you a rather personal question?"

"Yeah, sure, go ahead, shoot…"

"Do you believe in God, Cable?"

I was taken aback. That question always put me on the spot. Try as I may, I could never quite get a clear picture. I knew I couldn't accept the religious concept, the stereotypical mythology of some big guy on a throne in the heavens, doling out judgment from fire and brimstone. Or the clear-cut partialism this character expressed, as in '*my people.*' The rest of us must be the expendable majority, then. "It's a loaded question, Carlo," I answered the serious priest. "Opinions about a 'God' in the universe are as varied as a babe going into a dress shop and trying to select a style and color that fits her best."

He laughed. "I never saw it that way, I must admit," he said. "But it is true…most of the world's population never heard of Jesus Christ."

"And that's another whole can of worms," I said, taking a drag on my cigarette and exhaling slowly. "Haven't you left out Buddha, Mohammed, Lao-tzu and the rest of the prophets?" I snickered. "I was always a Moses fan as a kid. You know, some big bearded guy climbing a mountain, talking to a burning bush, God trying to explain himself with the *'I am that I am'* statement and Moses aging fifty years as he receives the stone tablets containing the Ten Commandments. Now, to me, that's drama!"

He laughed. "You're right. There seems to be a lot of melo-drama in the Bible, doesn't there?" Then he drew serious. "Before they killed him, Father Damianos was coming around to the viewpoint of an ordinated cosmos, unending…never-theless prescribed by intelligent design. He must have felt that the *God of Our Fathers* held that knowledge."

"I won't argue there. So, what's all this have to do with your visit?"

"Well, truth be known, you have been under our surveil-lance, and we know someone from the *Oculus* has visited you—and most likely threatened you."

"Well, Carlo, why aren't I surprised? Everyone else seems to be watching me, why not the Church?"

"It isn't intended to be malicious, Cable. We fear that the *Tone of Creation* you spoke of will be stolen with the golden capsule—and God's world will be thrown into chaos."

"But isn't that kind of the prophecy of your Bible? Chaos comes in and out as the king of the hour again and again in history, right?"

"Yes, but not on this scale. This could threaten the entire human race."

"So what? I've never been that crazy about people anyway, Carlo. Personally, I think humans are parasites and take without giving because they're out of balance with nature."

"What a cynical view for such a young man! How old are you?"

"Twenty-nine in a few days. And you?"

"I'm forty-two. I've seen a lot more than you have, Cable."

"Have you? Have you seen the struggling masses, Carlo? I don't mean in India or China or Africa, but right here on our soil—the poor lost and disenfranchised of the world? Broken down lives that dwell in the shadowlands of survival, with broken down brains and emotions, some nuttier than Aunt Martha's Christmas fruitcake. The decaying old, the sick, the crippled, the panhandlers who day in and day out compete for the next dime someone will hand them, the toothless prostitute who plies her trade, her dirty, festering body passing on the diseases men have given her along the way. While all along, the millionaires high above this sewer of humanity sit and laugh with cigars and champagne, count their money and make a phone call to sell out their own mother for the next buck—because they're diseased, too, Carlo, only their disease is an obsessive, addicted mentality bent on using whatever crooked scheme they can to feed off of the unsuspecting dupe who gives his few hard-earned bucks to the crooks who are happy to take it. Yeah, crooks and criminals, the ones who go free most of the time, because they wear a new pin-striped suit, men's cologne and shiny new shoes. But you know, they're rotten inside, they smell of corruption and their hands are dirty with the chaos *they've* created out of lack of concern for their so-called fellow man. Have you seen that, Carlo?"

He fell silent, finishing up the last puffs on his cigarette. He bent over my desk and ground it out in my ashtray. He took a deep breath. "No, Cable, I've not seen that. The Church protects us and keeps us too busy to float among the masses. We leave that up to the parishioner priests."

"A pity. I would consider it a classroom must, like Humanity One. And so you see, that's why I'm not crazy about humans. I think they're a remnant race of beings, left over from some experiment gone wrong many thousands of years ago."

His brow furled. "Where...where would you get that notion?"

"Oh, I don't know. Part of it is that I've seen things, Carlo. Taking that trip with Lei-tao to the land of the Cave of the Seven Truths, the tantric sex, some kind of teleportation—and how other dimensional creatures live—naw, humans just don't add up. At least in their present state."

"I can't tell you how impressed I am, Cable." He looked around my disheveled, dirty office. "You, a common gumshoe eking out a living in a strange world of misfits—you should have experienced all this? And if I may, do you recall what the Seven Truths are, as the Chinese lady explained them to you?"

I thought for a minute. "Yeah, one being we are mighty spiritual beings who deserve dignity and purpose. Second...let me see...we chose to come here from somewhere else. Oh, yeah, someone else chose us to be here, as if this wasn't our native planet or whatever. We're all gifted and wanted to be here *now*, the reason for which escapes me. Six, we existed before in some other world or dimension and seven, we will return one day to our native home and hopefully leave behind some kind of meaningful contribution *here*—anyway, that's the best I can recall the way it went."

Father Carlo Tortelli's eyes widened and his mouth dropped open. "Cable! That's evidence of God if I ever heard it—but a modern explanation—may I write it down?"

"Be my guest. I don't know about the God thing, though. What if some incredible mind is simply having fun, creating all this diversity whether we like it or not—no choice—like being born...did you have a choice?"

"Free will?" he asked as I gave him a piece of paper and a pencil. He asked me to repeat the Seven Truths...and so I did as best I could. He thanked me as I remained quiet, looking out my window at the traffic below on Franklin Avenue. "So, as I was saying, what if it's free will that allows us to come here?"

"Who in their right mind would wanna come here? Born in misery and poverty, maybe you grow up to adulthood, screw or get screwed, reproduce your own brand of little rats, then grow old and die. *That* you'd wanna come here for?"

"I think there's something else. Isaiah Damianos told me once that he suspected that *love* was the *instructor of choice* for the earth existence. Here we were to learn *love*. All kinds. Then, when we have accomplished that greatest of all feats, perhaps we return to that native land you were talking about. It goes along with Jesus saying, '*In my Father's house there are many mansions, I go there to prepare a place for you...*'"

"And don't return, I hope. I don't know. It's a hard sell. Even with love, not everything goes hunky-dory, you know. It can be pretty dark shit, Carlo. And I'm not sure there's an answer to any of it."

"Well, to paraphrase you, you're in pretty dark shit, too, just about now, Cable. Do you not think they will kill you in an instant as they did Isaiah? They're bigger and more powerful than even we are."

"I don't know the answer to that, either. Maybe not as long as they think I can access the *Fen de Fuqin*." I cleared my throat and lit up another Lucky Strike. "So, let's get down to it. Really, why are you here?"

"We know Nazar Ravna visited you. We also know he wants the capsule. He probably doesn't know about the *Tone of Creation*, does he?"

"I don't think so. He wants the scribbling on the capsule itself—and the golden-etched tablet it contains, but maybe no longer does."

457

"What happened to that?"

"A creature named Toggth, a friendly little genius, took it out when the *Tone of Creation* was restored to its rightful place."

"Hmmm….I see. So what are you going to do?"

"Your guess is as good as mine, Carlo. Ravna's 'Order' wants something I no longer have access to. He's given me a couple of weeks to come up with it. Then I guess we can write Cable Denning off the books of the living. Got any suggestions?"

Carlo Tortelli looked sad. "We'd hate to lose you, Cable. I see you as a fighter for justice, fairness and the upholding of the law. A man of the truth, eh? I think a good priest does the same thing, don't you?"

"Are you a good priest, Carlo? And, you know, outside of homosexuality and molesting young altar boys, how do priests vent their pent up sexual drives? I always wondered about that…"

He looked at me strangely. "Some masturbate because they're afraid of physical human contact. Others leave their frocks at home and frequent bordellos. I guess that about covers it."

"Thanks for your honesty. I like that trait in a person."

"So, Cable, I have these concerns for you. What will you do?"

"My hunch remains the same. If Ravna and his gang suspect I may still have some link to Lei-tao and the magic of the *Fen de Fuqin*, then I think they'll keep the door open and not bump me off because I still might have value to them. After that, I can't say."

Father Carlo Tortelli got up. He reached across my desk to shake my hand. "Best of luck to you, Private Investigator Denning. We'll…we'll, uh, nevertheless keep an eye on you, if you don't mind. I remind you, you have value to us. And after all, we are the Flying Priests, highly trained in the art of—of… shall we say—getting the job done?"

"And if I did mind? Would it stop you or the Church?"

"No…probably not. We have a vested interest in the *God of Our Fathers* as well. Take care, Cable, and keep your back covered."

He got up and left. I stood there behind my desk asking myself what possibly could be next? The phone rang and it was Honey asking if I'd come out to the club tonight to hear her and we'd drive home together. I said I'd be there, but I wasn't sure what time. It was okay with her and we hung up.

Night and the city have a strange relationship. They kind of belong together, as if the city is nothing special during the daylight hours when grey and whitewashed buildings, streetcars, automobiles, smoke and thousands of little ants called humans buzz this way 'n that in the streets. But when the sun sets and one by one the lights set the city ablaze with towering monoliths glowing in the dark, rows of neon lights brighten up the streets and moving streetcars, automobiles and trucks, one and two-eyed creatures of the evening, add to the spectacle and fanfare of a new night being born. But when I heard that lonely sax wafting through the night air, it always came from the not-so-lit places…the haunts for beings of the shadowlands whose own stories would fill the pages of history with tears and sagas of loneliness, abandonment, abuse, confusion—and the feeling of isolation when someone loses their way out there in the jungle. But it was my city. I was bred and born into it, fought my way to the top of the pile of hoodlums I grew up with—and here I was, battling in a love-hate relationship with a mess of concrete and air, noise, pollution and forgotten souls. Only the *music* was right, and it breathed perfection, kept its magic intact, singing its song of joy, laughter, heartache, misery and ascension, and freed millions of hearts otherwise shackled to oblivion.

I left my office about 9:30 p.m. I was about to cross Franklin and walk to Cahuenga Blvd. where the yellow car would take

459

me out to Highland Avenue and I would transfer to the red car and go out to the *Bella Notte* from there. But I never made it to Cahuenga Blvd. As I stood at the curb, a large black Cadillac pulled up right in front of me. Immediately two thugs dressed in black, grabbed me and tossed me into the back seat at gunpoint. Then one of them hit me good with a blackjack over the noggin and I was out.

Things were grey and black, a whirling tornado was spinning in my head and when I came to I had the king of headaches from the back of my neck to my temples. I tried to move, but realized I was strapped to a gurney. There were some strange looking long, tubular lights hanging above me and as my blurred vision began to clear, I could see I was in some kind of clinic or the like. The smell of hospital room chemicals permeated the air.

Finally someone came in. A big, burly guy with no smile at all lifted my head and gave me a sip of water. "Where—where...uh, where am I?" I asked. The big guy said nothing and left.

Then a familiar voice from behind me spoke up. "You are, Mr. Denning, in one of our most advanced facilities, underground somewhere in Los Angeles."

It was Nazar Ravna. "Ravna! What the hell are you doing? I promised Honey I'd be at her club to hear her sing tonight," I said.

"I'm afraid that was hours ago, Denning. The nightclub has long since closed and your desperate little fiancée is most likely frantic and looking for you by now. Isn't that nice? I love to stir things up—"

"—so, you lousy piece of worthless shit, what is it this time? What are you gonna do to—"

"—not *me*, Denning, but rather Dr. Schumacher. One of the most famous surgeons in the field of microbiology. Dr.

Schumacher is the world's leading authority on the castration of mice and rats for laboratory experimentation. Of course, she also is just as deft at the removal of the testicles of other, larger creatures."

"What in the hell are you talking about, Ravna? Get me out of this thing and let's talk."

"Cannot do, I'm afraid. You see, what we are about to inflict upon you is rather like—hmmm....how shall we say, *punishment*, first for talking so crudely to me the other day when I kindly visited your office—but we're punishing you most of all because of your association with those meddlesome priests of the Catholic persuasion."

Then a chill ran through me. These guys really *were* nuts! "So...you're intending to castrate me, is that it, Ravna?"

"Precisely, Denning. We thought that eliminating surely the main source of trouble in your life—mainly your sexually prolific nature—we'd tame you down a bit. Dr. Schumacher assures us that a castrated rat is so much more docile than one whose male hormones are still carelessly rampant."

Just then a dark-haired woman dressed in white approached, coming from out of another door across the room. She looked me over. She stood about five-foot five, was very thin and her complexion sallow, as if she'd never been in sunlight. Her hair was slicked back with what appeared to be petroleum jelly. She had a decidedly German accent. "Vell, vell, vell, Herr Denning. Herr Ravna has told me much about you. I believe him to be correct zat you are due for corrective surchery. I am Dr. Else Schumacher. You see, ofer-actiff pituitary leads to ofer-breeding tendencies. Herr Ravna tells me you haff been much too actiff in spreading your seed to so many fine, young vomen. Ve cannot permit zis sing to continue."

I was looking up at this little vixen with the cold blue eyes in disbelief. "You actually do these things? Have you any idea of

461

the emotional trauma, let alone the legal implications of such a heinous act?"

"You…vorry about your little moral issues…I vill concern myself vis obeying za rules…of correct…medical procedure in such a case…as zis. I haff little or no regard for your emotional velfare—especially since breeders such as you, Herr Denning, must be curtailed vile zey are still—in zeir prime years."

Now I was sweating—and flabbergasted. It was like a surrealistic dream and I was floating through it, suspended somewhere between rationality and the unbelievable. "You're not kidding, are you?" I asked, swallowing hard. If this dame was on the level, it would be the end of my family jewels—once and for all!

Dr. Schumacher looked over at Ravna. "Za qvestion is, Herr Ravna, should ve or should ve not use anesthesia?"

"You must recall, Dr. Schumacher, none of this was my idea in the first place. It was Dr. Udter's recommendation. And the *Oculus Council* approved it. He mustn't lose his mind and must be saved for other purposes. That also is an order. Even if he is minus…certain parts…"

"Yes, I do recall. Perhaps, zen, ve should administer a little numbing agent insomuch as za pain won't be as…debilitating… ya?"

"Yes, Doctor, I think that would be wise."

"Vell, Herr Denning, ve haff decided to leaff your penis but take bos of your gonads—und giff you a sedative. Dat vay you vill be able to tolerate za pain vizout loosing your sanity."

"Yeah, well, thanks for nothing, you sell-out Kraut! And you, Ravna, after all we've been though, why in the hell are you doing this? I always thought there might be a thin layer of civility in you—"

"—because I don't like you, Denning. You're pompous, haughty and definitively need to be subdued into submission.

Dr. Schumacher, will you kindly prepare the patient?"

"Ya, Herr Ravna."

No one can tell this story, not even to yourself, let alone someone else. The horror that I was living and feeling this minute felt like a trap door had just opened and I was in free fall. And for a man like me, which was worse—death or castration? I guess one could always follow the other. I didn't know how I'd feel after losing my balls, or how I'd respond, since so much of my life was living with and responding sensually to females. I knew that harems employed eunuchs to protect the sultan's precious concubines. I don't know, maybe I'd be okay with it after a while. Protecting people in my line of work didn't always have to be sexual. In fact a lot of it wasn't.

Dr. Schumacher bent over me with a needle that squirted a queer yellow fluid and soon she had jammed it into my arm. Slowly, I could feel my anxiety lesson as my brain began to go to sleep and my body stopped trembling. The doc lifted the surgical gown up, exposing my genitals. It was getting blurry, but I could still hear Schumacher's voice. "Oh, now ve can see vhy ze vomen vere so…so enamored vis Herr Denning here. It is a handsome penis und qvite large scrotum. Such a big pouch, ya, indicates an over-active production of semen. Vell, ve vill take care of zat!"

"Get on with it, Dr. Schumacher, this is not a sight-seeing tour of male anatomy. Simply do your job and get on with it," Ravna growled.

The doctor said nothing but went to a small table by the operating gurney and picked out a selection of surgical knives and cutting blades. Then she stood over me with gloved hands and smiled. "It von't be long now!" she said in a sickly, jovial voice.

The last thing I remember is a ruckus in back of me, and a series of gunshots ringing out. I heard Ravna yell out and Dr. Schumacher let out a howl as a bullet went through her brain and she collapsed on top of me, one of her surgical knives missing my leg by inches!

The next thing I knew I was riding in the back seat of a car humming along on a highway. As I came to, I saw Father Carlo Tortelli smiling at me. "Cable...can you hear me?" He called to the front of the cab. "I think he's coming around. Would you grab the flask in the glove compartment, please?"

Soon, I was tasting a pretty fine liqueur in my mouth, and Carlo's hand was feeding me. "Carlo...where...where am I?" I felt between my legs. Everything was still there. "I'm—I'm still intact—what happened?"

"I had a feeling they were gunning for you after we talked this morning. So Father Banducci, Father Grandino and I decided to watch you, just in case. We followed the black Cadillac out to the underground lab and got there—how would I say it?" The priest chuckled. "In the nick of time, I think would be appropriate."

"I owe you one, gentlemen," I spoke up. "What about Ravna and his weird accomplice?"

"*Morto*...dead, I'm afraid. There was no other way. Ravna had two of his goons planted outside of the entrance, so we had to take care of them first. We almost didn't get to you in time. Now wouldn't *that* have been a pity, Cable?"

"And then some, Carlo. Just think, I would've had to become a priest or eunuch in a harem." He laughed. "I am indebted to you. Where are we going?"

"To the safest place you could go right now."

They propped me up as they walked me up to Honey's little cottage. They knocked on the door. Honey answered with only a robe on, her face gaunt and worried. "Cable!" she cried out as she ran to me and embraced me. Then she looked at the three priests. "I knew when he didn't show at the club he was in trouble—but did he offend God or something?"

"No, signorina," Carlo answered, smiling. "He almost underwent a life-altering operation at the hands of—well, suffice it to say he's alright, safe and sound and needs your love and affection for a couple of days."

Honey took me inside and invited the priests in and offered them coffee. They thankfully accepted. I was still woozy and sat at the table teetering a little. "Thank you so very, very much, Fathers. I don't know anything about what has happened and I'm not going to ask. I'm just thankful to you all," Honey said, her face still a bit drawn.

"Aren't you Honey Combes—the singer who recently recorded *It All Depends on You*?" Carlo asked.

"Yes. That's me, I guess."

"I'm a big fan, Miss Combes…I love good musica."

"Thanks. Just call me Honey. What can I do for you?"

"May I have your autograph—or even an autographed record, if you could spare it?"

"Are you kidding? The three guys who save my fiancé's ass deserve the best. I'll be right back."

Just at that moment Zelda came wandering in. "What's—what's all the commotion? It's four o'clock in the morning, you know." She looked at the priests. "Oh, God, did someone die? Cable?" She looked at me teetering at the table.

"Yeah, Zelda. I'm okay. Just had a close shave, that's all. These three swell priests saved my butt from—well, from the removal of some of my most valuable possessions."

"Oh, Lord, Cable! I'm so glad you're here—and okay." She was dressed in her flimsy nightgown, the yellow one through which her nipples stood at attention—and if she should happen to lean over too far, all of heaven would be able to view those ample breasts of hers.

Honey came back into the kitchen with an album in hand.

465

"This is my latest two-record album. It has four of my favorite songs. *It All Depends on You, Love Me or Leave Me, Makin' Whoopee* and *Red, Red Robin*. I hope you'll like them. I autographed the inside…here…."

"Molte grazie, Honey," Carlo said.   "

"Thank *you*, Fathers. And here I thought the bum was out makin' whoopee somewhere. We're going to be married in December."

All three priests congratulated us. Then Carlo grew somber. "Since we more or less know one another, I think it only fair to tell you to take any and all monies out of investments and stock market speculations. There is advance word of an imminent financial collapse."

We all looked at each other. "In the middle of a prosperous time?" Honey said, looking curiously at the gathered priests. "Besides, Cable and I haven't made any investments into stocks, bonds or the like."

"But my father has," Zelda chimed in. "He invested all the family earnings into some stock investments—the money he's received from his inventions, including the world's largest strawberry."

"I'd advise him, then, to withdraw as soon as he can and keep the money under a mattress somewhere," Father Tortelli responded. Then he cleared his throat. "Well, we must be on our way. It's late."

"How can I get a hold of you?" I asked. "I want to take you guys out to lunch or dinner or something swell—for saving my—my, uh, butt tonight."

"You can't. We'll contact you, Cable. Good night, now." Honey and I escorted the three priests to the door. We watched as they made their way down toward the street and disappeared.

Honey was still looking toward the empty driveway. "There but for the grace of God, eh, Cable? You're really in trouble, aren't you?"

"Nothing a good night's sleep won't cure," I grinned.

"Cable! Please! Don't lie to me! I know you've been keeping things from me besides old girlfriends. If you can't tell your own wife-to-be, then who can you tell?"

"No one, toots." We closed the door, said good night to Zelda and went into Honey's bedroom and I started undressing. She noticed the welt Dr. Schumacher's needle had made on my upper arm.

"And that was part of it, wasn't it?"

"Honey...I can't talk about it tonight. I'm dead tired."

"When I first met you I thought the life you led was exciting. Now I think it's just dangerous. I don't know if I can live that way, Cable. What if we do have children? What would I say—oh, your father may or may not be home tonight—he's in a gun fight in a warehouse somewhere—"

"—Honey! Some other time, please? Let's get to sleep."

As we got into bed she tried to drop it, but I could feel her restless body next to mine. And what the hell was this stock market thing Carlo Tortelli was warning us about? For Christ's sake, it was a booming era!

CHAPTER 19

THE EXCHANGE

It seemed to me the more things that happened to me, the less I knew about life. Nothing stays simple. Everything changes. I could feel Honey's attitude take on a different color as our wedding date approached. Maybe she was having second thoughts about being married to a gumshoe that constantly lived on the edge of danger—not to mention mysterious dimensions I had never really explored with her. She always shut me down when I mentioned the Cave of the Seven Truths and Lei-tao and all the stuff that happened on that adventure. In a way I couldn't blame her. Some dames like a calm, predictable life at home, without all the unsettling crap my profession brought to the dinner table. But then, of course, we seldom had dinner—because of *her* career.

I worked hard that week…handling all the miscellaneous cases that came across my desk. Things like catching Mrs. Fletcher's husband in bed with her sister and taking the all-important Kodak quickie, while they were having their quickie, going to court to verify photos I had taken regarding a divorce proceeding, escorting a beautiful blonde from the East coast to her boyfriend's lair in the Hollywood Hills, and last but not least, serving eviction papers on a poor, wretched couple who had fallen on bad times and couldn't pay the rent anymore. The landlord was a merciless Turk who owned seven houses in the neighborhood, one more bug infested than the other. I knew the type. Continue to collect the dough until the houses were condemned, then move on.

On Thursday the 12th Adora called and wanted to see me and help me celebrate my birthday. I told her I was up to my ears and tomorrow I was going to see Honey at the club and she had prepared a little shindig for me to help celebrate my twenty-ninth year on planet earth. I could feel her pain when I said I couldn't see her. You know why? Because I was experiencing an equal pain. I just wanted everything complicated to go away—take Adora's hand and run across a meadow somewhere, take her into my arms and make love to her in the grass beside a bubbling brook. But I told her my truth, the one that said I didn't know when we could be together again. Soon, I hoped. She hung up and I could hear the tears of disappointment. I knew this couldn't go on much longer, but I didn't know how to cut it off. It would be like cutting off a leg. She had made my heart feel like when the sun bursts out from behind a cloud after the rain. She was sunshine and I was in love with her. There was no way around it.

I had hoped against hope that after Ravna's death at the hands of my benefactor priests, the *Oculus Pyramis Mandatum* would release its stranglehold on me. Life always contains a certain number of unresolved items, dangling participles with question marks that never quite settle to resolution, but sit in your craw like a group of unsettling thoughts, reminding you that you're in a crap game and when you spit on the dice and roll them against the bank, you never know what numbers are going to come up.

It was getting on to sunset as I sat in my desk chair smoking a Lucky Strike and sipping on a gin and tonic. Suddenly I got a chill all over and something made me look toward my bedroom. There, standing at the threshold, stood Toggth. He did not look happy. The little creature approached me. "She seduced you, Cable, and you succumbed. Now she is with a child that cannot possibly be born. What happened? We talked about it. Why couldn't you have simply walked out on her when she shape-shifted into that alluring hussy who trapped you?"

"Well, hello to you too, Toggth," I said, trying to make the situation amenable. "I know the whole thing…I was taken in a dream to the palace of Daiyu Guang, her teacher. She filled me in."

Toggth seemed puzzled. "Oh. Daiya Guang summoned you?"

"Yep, and I heard the most magnificent music…"

"The *liuqin*…music of the astral spheres." Then he looked at me with those wonderful eyes of his. "But I'm still angry with you. Why, Cable, when you knew it could destroy her?"

"The human animal drives are incessant. It's like desire bangs up against your brain, Toggth, until you can't stand it anymore—and you're addicted to the feeling of that warm, pumping motion when she opens—"

"—I don't need the details, Cable. Somehow she must abort the embryo. What you *don't* know is that in Lei-tao's womb, the fetus will grow exponentially faster than in a human female's.'

"So what do you want me to do?"

"Stay out of the way. She came to me and told me she was ill. She was convulsing because your seed is incompatible with hers. Our sacred Red Dragon Lady suffers greatly. You must let go of her *in all ways*, even with your mind. Do you understand?"

"I'll—I'll do my best. Shit, how could I have known—"

"—you said that before, too. Just forget you ever knew her. Forget the *Fen de Fuqin* and all that it has to do with. You were not supposed to know as much as you do. Lei-tao loved you, an emotional wave-form her kind are not allowed. Now you see the trouble it has caused."

"Not that it amounts to a hill of beans, but you probably know the *Oculus* came looking for the *Fen de Fuqin*. They were going to punish me for being so arrogant toward them by castrating me. Luckily, I was rescued by three priests—"

"—yes, the *Ordium Sanctus Breva*. I know who they are. I

am glad they saved your—your reproductive pleasure parts, but they have gotten you into a lot of trouble, haven't they?"

"Oh, I don't know. Most times the pleasure is worth the pain. Just not in Lei-tao's case. I am very sorry for that…"

"I must leave you now, Cable. We will see if we can save Lei-tao. Rarely, does the lotus pod lose one of its own."

We embraced and I watched the little fellow vanish into thin air in the middle of my office. I felt lousy. My philanderings had brought such a burden upon this beautiful young creature/woman who crossed over traditional lines to dare to love this stupid, crazy mortal man. I would miss her and hoped against hope she would be saved.

It was a restless night. I got tired of office work, phone calls, smoking cigarettes and drinking booze. I became listless and tired inside, like I was already an ancient traveler on his last legs. I brushed my teeth and fell into my little mussed up bed. Soon I was deep in a sleep and I was watching Lei-tao approach me. But she was naked and exuding a moving green substance that glowed from her body. She came to me and smiled. We were in a very large room. Far across on the other side there was a purple bed. Lei-tao pointed to it and started across the floor to stand in front of the bed. To my shock, lying also naked on the bed lay Ginny Fullerton! Lei-tao called to her silently and Ginny got up and stood before the Red Dragon Lady. A strange humming noise began and I could swear I heard a very beautiful music from a symphony of liuqins that filled the room. A strong magnetic field of blue and purple began to form between the bellies of Ginny and Lei-tao. Soon the colors merged and an undeveloped fetus emerged from Lei-tao's stomach, breathing in the amniotic fluids now exchanging between her and Ginny! The fetus slowly moved from Lei-tao's stomach…two feet or so away, into the womb or stomach of Ginny Fullerton. I got it now: Lei-tao didn't want her child to perish, so she was transferring it into a human woman, one who had recently made love to me and had my vibration on her, and someone who could most likely be pregnant herself via a natural course of events. When the glow and exchange subsided, Ginny lay back down on the purple bed. Lei-tao floated over to me and smiled down on me, nodding her head slowly up and down. She bent over me to kiss me good-bye and I knew in that instant it would be the last time I would ever see her.

LAST CANDLES ON THE CAKE

Friday the 13th of September was anything but unlucky for me. It was a wonderful day, filled with a clean sky from sharp northwest winds sweeping off of the ocean a few miles away and a happy surprise when Honey came into my office around ten in the morning with a tray and some breakfast. "Good morning, birthday boy," she caroled as she entered my dingy bedroom.

"Wow! Babe! What a surprise…I didn't think I'd see you until tonight."

"Well, now, this is breakfast and lunch—tonight you get dinner, some ice cream and cake—and me for desert when we get home," she said in her usual warm, but direct way.

"That sounds like a swell deal, babe. Come here!" She put the tray down and fell into my arms. I embraced her and kissed her.

"Cable—your beard! It's going to get me all irritated and red—and I want to look perfect for you tonight. Know what I'm wearing?"

"No, but I have a feeling you'll tell me."

472

"A brand new gold sequined gown, the kind with the large scales, tight-fitting to the ankles? I've got gold heels to go with it and a marvelous strand of pearls Chet's mother gave me."

I stopped all motion for a minute. "Chet's mother? Your trumpet player? Why would she give you her—her jewelry—unless there's something going on between the—"

"—damn it, Mr. Green-eyes! There *is* something going on between Chet James and me—great music! Chet's not into girls, so his Mom felt that the pearls would go to better use if I had them. Simple. Get it, Cable?"

"Oh…he doesn't dig tits and pussy, huh?"

"Nope, just the hardware you got between *your* legs, lover man."

"Oh…I—I, uh, didn't know. Sorry if I was jumping to conclusions."

She brought my coffee over to me and put the tray on my lap. "At least I don't go around chasing guys up to the eleventh hour of my marriage," she said, a little offended.

"Okay, babe,…please, let's drop it."

It was a stand-out night at the *Bella Notte*. Honey sang two songs that night. *You Were Meant For Me* was a huge success with the audience, reminding us that Honey was the best in the business. But toward the end of the evening when the place was still packed, Honey Combes touched me to the core when she quieted the audience and spoke over the microphone. "A couple of years ago I fell in love with a young policeman who became a private investigator. He's one of those men who gets women right—right *here*—" She put her hand on her heart. "He's also the kind of man a simple country girl like me can love because a part of him is all man, while another part is a boy, still wondering why he has to grow up." The audience laughed. "So, to the boy part in my man, I dedicate this song." The audience applauded. When Honey began to sing Al Jolson's *Sonny*

Boy to me, I felt like crawling under the table and melting into droplets of booze on the hardwood floors. From the first words, *'When there are grey skies, I don't mind the grey skies,'* the audience was blubbering—as was I. Again, Honey Combes had made me the luckiest guy in the world—and only because of one thing—only because she loved me—and somehow that would have to be enough for a lifetime.

September went by in a flash and it was October 1st, 1929. My rent was due again. I hadn't heard from the *Oculus*, which brought much relief. I hadn't seen Adora, either, and that was tough. We spoke on the phone and I kept trying to ween us off each other. Some days it was okay, others it was a losing battle. I was playing with my dirty gin glass when the phone rang. "Yeah, Cable Denning here."

"Cable…? It's—it's Ginny…I know it's been a while, hasn't it?"

Her voice seemed subdued, a little out of spirit. "Good to hear your voice, Ginny. How goes your world?"

"Not so good, Cable. I think I'm pregnant."

I became dead still. No man wants to have that bomb dropped on him unexpectedly. "You—you what? Would you mind repeating that?"

"I said I think I'm expecting our baby. Yours and mine."

I became a little flustered. "I thought you told me—"

"—I must have been wrong, Cable. What are we going to do?"

"How far along are you?"

"Well, from the night we made love. About a month or so—but you know what? It seems to be growing so fast—I mean, my tummy is already beginning to puff out—and I've had this strange greenish discharge…but it doesn't feel like an infection or anything."

"Have you seen a doctor?"

"Yes. He confirmed everything."

I lit up a Lucky Strike, took my bottle of gin out of my desk drawer and took a big swig right out of the bottle. "I—I know a couple of doctors who will—terminate the pregnancy—"

"—no! I could never do that, Cable. Selfish as it seems, *I want your baby*, even if you *are* getting married in three months."

"Damn, Ginny…we gotta talk…not on the phone…I'll come see you tonight after work—what time?"

"About seven? Thanks, Cable. I really need you about now."

When I came to pick Ginny up, the evil and nasty Monica sat with a naked leg slung over part of the railing, and if one cared to peek further, her yellow loosely tied robe revealed she was wearing no panties. "Oh, the private dick cop again. You come around sort of like a dog, don't you? Sniffing out the fresh young stuff. Let me see…you're Ginny's gigolo, aren't you? She's been acting strange lately. You know what I think?"

"I really don't care what you think, lady," I said, bristling at this obnoxious woman.

"I think you knocked her up. Happens a lot around here. All you need is some alcohol and a couple of coat hangers, you know."

Just then Ginny came out of the house. She didn't say anything but walked straight to me. She hugged me and we walked away from the horrid Monica who stood there with a smug look on her face.

We walked to a café a few blocks from Ginny's boarding house. She looked pale, drawn and lacked the old verve I had come to look for in her. We took a back booth and ordered simple. I took a big breath and exhaled. "Damn, Ginny, I don't know exactly what to say. Your news kind of knocked the wind out of me." I reached across the table and took her hand.

"But I'm not going to desert you, kid…we'll see it through, somehow."

"Cable, it's my own fault. I could swear I was safe…I mean just three days before we were together I was over my period. I can always tell when I'm more, uh, more receptive…and it wasn't that night."

I was beginning to piece together that dream Lei-tao must have implanted in me, and the reality sunk in that Ginny must be carrying the Red Dragon Lady's child! "I believe you, Ginny. Sometimes things happen that just don't have a reasonable explanation. Maybe you were visited by some magic prince who impregnated you during the night or something," I chuckled, trying to keep things from getting too heavy.

Ginny's face changed color. "Why would you say that? I know this sounds really weird, Cable—and you don't have to believe me, because I barely do. But a night or two after we were together, I had this dream—like I was naked in this big room and a beautiful young woman—also with no clothes on—with dark hair and wonderful glowing, brown eyes came over to me. She was like—like a glowing green all over and I could feel her energy pull at my stomach. She asked my permission for something, but I can't remember what it was. I came and stood close to her but I didn't feel any fear. She smiled at me and I loved her smile. Then I saw that her tummy was big, like she was expecting a child and the next thing I knew I woke up with this feeling in *my* stomach. Do you remember that night when we made love how I told you I felt some kind of 'pinch' or 'click' inside me? Well, that's how I felt when I got up to go to the bathroom that morning, only it was a much stronger feeling in my stomach."

"And you definitely want to keep it," I said, still hoping.

"It's *us*, Cable. It'll be the only way I'll ever have—to know something that came from us will be with me always."

"How are you going to support a kid? You can't work and raise a baby. And you know I'm not exactly rich. What do you intend to do?"

"I already told my aunt. She was very understanding and not angry with me. I guess being a nurse and all. She said I can come live with her and she's retiring in about three months—and she'll be home and would love to care for our baby while I work during the day. Then maybe on weekends once in a while—you—you can come see your son or daughter?"

It felt like a terrible, twisted rope to me, something that got knotted up that wasn't supposed to. "It's a funny arrangement, kid, but I guess it's lucky for both of us that your aunt is so willing—"

"—I told her you don't make much money and couldn't pay much to help out. But I didn't tell her you're getting married in December. That would have upset her. But do you know what scares me, Cable?"

"What, doll?"

"What I said over the phone. The baby's growing so fast—it's like I can feel my stomach expand every day. I've never had a baby, but I don't think it's supposed to grow that fast unless I'm—I'm having a giant or something. Do you have huge men in your family?"

"Nope, just plain, medium guys like me." I thought quickly. "Maybe that dream you had—you know about the strange green woman with the stomach—maybe there's something to it, I mean, more than you think?"

"Naw, I don't believe in that stuff. My Dad, being a preacher and all before, thinks anything outside of the Bible is the devil in disguise or something. I think that's part of what drove my Mom nuts—and maybe to drink too much. I don't know what to tell my folks. Sooner or later they'll have to know—"

"—cross that bridge when you come to it, Ginny. Right now,

you gotta take good care of yourself. Is there anything you need right now?"

"Yeah, you…it's like the baby makes me want you even more." She looked away and out the window. "I know things can't go on like they were. It's my fault, I kept chasing you, as I said, like a bitch dog in heat and now look where it got me—"

"—don't hammer on yourself, doll. Things are what they are now. We'll deal with it, okay?" I smiled at her as best I could. "Chin up, eh?"

She gave me a half-smile. "Thanks, Cable, for coming here and seeing me. I knew you wouldn't run, but I also knew it's a pressure you don't need in your life right now, especially with you marrying your girlfriend and all…"

I escorted Ginny home and told her to call me if she needed anything. I hugged her at the doorway to the rooming house and I could swear that little creature in her stomach reached out to me and pulsed against my own gut, as if it knew I was its sire. I started for the streetcar stop across the street. I noticed a tall, slightly rotund man in an overcoat wearing a dark fedora waiting a few feet below me on the island. His face was intense and he had burning dark eyes with large unkempt eyebrows. His temples were silver and I figured him for about fifty-five or so. We both got on when the trolley came. The man seemed to be checking me out. I decided to get off the streetcar a couple of blocks early at Argyle and walk the extra distance to my office. When I exited the streetcar, he followed. I made the mistake of darting down a little alley that ended at Dix Street. He was hot on my tail. Half way down the alley he yelled to me. "Only they who sin with guilt run from the Lord!"

I stopped and turned toward him. He came running at me and I could see as he approached he had withdrawn a long, shiny knife from under his coat. "I'd stop if I were you, Mister." I drew my .38 and took a bead on him. "I wouldn't want to mess up the alley with your blood."

He kept coming until the whites of his delirious eyes were but a few feet from me. "I told you I was going to kill you. I have come to lift the abomination from the world. Your bullets won't stop me before God permits me to cut you down, smote you with his thunder for your trespasses against his commandments."

I did recognize the voice as the crazy who had threatened me on the phone some time ago. "Remember what I said to you then, stranger, *let him who is without sin cast the first stone*."

He stopped within six feet of me, glowering at me in the dark alley, a dim bulb from a transom light barely lighting his face. "*For the righteous shall serve as judge to the fornicators, as the unrighteous will not inherit the Kingdom of God.*"

I hated Bible slingers and this guy was a fanatic. "So, buster, you'd better tell the accused just what and who he's offended."

"Ha! Your abominations leave you weakened in the face of God's hand."

"Well, not exactly—I'm giving you a chance to show me you're not completely crazy—just a little left of upset and demented…" I taunted him. His eyes grew wild and he started for me again, then suddenly stopped, the knife flashing in his hand.

"*Just as Sodom and Gomorrah, which likewise indulged in sexual immorality, did serve as example by undergoing punishment of eternal fire and damnation.*"

"You got one more chance before I fire and blow your shoulder off—who are you and what am I accused of—and with whom?"

He seemed unstoppable. He rose up to full height and spoke like from a pulpit on Sunday morning. "*He shall strike the earth with the rod of his mouth and with the breath of his lips, he shall slay the wicked!*"

With that he lunged at me. I was a lot faster and dodged his advances, but he came at me again, slicing away with his very sharp blade. But as he came, I sidestepped him and clunked him on the head with the handle of my .38. He fell to his knees but kept helplessly slashing away. Finally I bashed his knife hand and he let out a yelp. The knife went clanging to the alley floor. I picked it up, tossed it into my pocket and trained my gun on him. "Now, buddy, suppose you tell me what this is all about, huh?"

He began sobbing, rocking below me on his knees. "You deflowered and committed sinful acts with my Ginny! You defiled her in the presence of God without benefit of matrimony and left her to have your way with other Jezebels who would partake in your…your abominations!"

So that was it! Ginny's Dad was the old ex-pastor! I got it and kicked him over onto the alley floor. "You stupid son-of-a-bitch. Your daughter is a grown woman and can make her own decisions." I suspected he did not know about the latest development of Ginny's pregnancy. "Whatever she has done, for whatever it's worth to you, she did with love—"

"—never! It was *lust* that brought her to you! I know my Ginny. You are evil incarnate and she fell under your spell. You seduced her like you would a harlot, cast upon the wicked shores of fornication—"

"Whoa there, old man! Let's not make the judgment crap too thick. Now…I'm going to let you get up and walk down the alley. If I ever so much as see you around me or Ginny again, or if you call me with your liable threats, *I will come looking for you*, hunt you down and kill your ass! Is that understood? My plate is kind of full right now, Mister, and I don't have time for gospel-slinging idiots."

He slowly got up on his feet. He said nothing but walked away down the alley, back toward Franklin Avenue. My heart was racing and sweat poured down my face and my chest was wet with perspiration. I followed the big man until he got onto a yellow car heading south and I went on toward my office.

It was about 9:30 when I climbed the stairs to my humble abode. When I reached the top landing, I could have cried at the sight I beheld. There sitting on the floor, leaning against my office door was Adora! She had dozed off. I went to her, bent down, took her head and clutched it to my breast. "Babe... babe! I'm so happy to see you...thank you...thank you for coming to see me."

"*Mi amor!*" she exclaimed. "I could not live another day without you!"

Her lips clung to mine with a desperate passion and I returned the joy I felt with her by holding my own lips to hers for the longest time. Finally, I lifted her up, took her hand and opened the door.

Once inside I locked the door behind us and we stood in the middle of my office as the phone began to ring. We stared in the semi-darkness at each other, neither of us wanting to let go of the magic of our fingertips touching in the dark. I knew in that instant part of me was inseparable from this beautiful señorita whose love filled places in me no other had ever come close to.

I let the phone keep ringing as I took her hand and led her into my little bedroom. She was breathing hard as if she had been suffering all day on a cross and now she was cut down from the agony to face her beloved, who adored her, the one who would heal her wounds. She immediately took her dress off and dropped it to the floor. She was wearing nothing underneath. I said nothing but sat at the edge of the bed and took my shoes off while she unbuttoned my shirt. "*Usted está mojado, mi querido. Que pasó?*" She noticed my perspiration....

"Not much, I—I just met some weird guy in an alley who was knifing for me." Finally the phone stopped ringing.

"*Ay! Fue aterrador? Oh...mi amor, la luz de mi vida!*" I wasn't sure what she said, but somehow it didn't matter. She grabbed my body and pulled me to the bed, unzipping my trousers and pulling them off. She was trembling and moved her body over on top of mine, placing her warm lips onto my still sweating head. "*Yo ayudo…ay, te amo, te amo…!*"

"Whatever—whatever you're saying, Adora, yes, yes, yes! I do want you—and I can't let you go—no matter how I try, I'm stuck on you, kid!"

She wrapped herself around me and soon we were merged into each other, as our lovemaking reached new heights of delight and fireworks. It had become the glue that held us together and I knew I would never want to be without it or Adora Moreno.

CHAPTER 20

LUNCH ON THE MOON

Adora stayed all night and we had slept the sleep that lovers sleep. I awakened to subdued sunshine coming in through my faded yellow pull-shades and the phone incessantly ringing again. We kissed and embraced and I sent her into the shower as I staggered to the phone. "Yeah, Cable Denning here," I said, my voice an octave lower than usual.

"Cable? Cable? Is that you? It's Ginny...my God, Cable, my father came late last night and..." she cried, her voice faltering. "He—he told me he tried to kill you! He was inconsolable. I tried to explain we did what we did, you know, and I consented to our making love. That made him all the more furious and someone called the police because he was yelling in my room."

"Where is he now?"

"In jail—my father's in jail."

"He probably needs to cool off for a while, Ginny. He'll be okay. I don't think I hurt him all that bad."

"Thank you, Cable. I'm—I'm so sorry he attacked you. Did he injure you?"

"Nope. Just made me sweat a lot. Look, Ginny, I've got a big day ahead of me and I've got to run. Don't worry about your old man. He was probably just more attached to you than either one of you thought. Without realizing it, he may have been re-directing his devotion for the one lacking with your mother. I've seen it before. Just makes it worse that he is a Bible slinger—and an ex-pastor to boot."

"Yeah, I guess that's right. Well, please call me—soon?"

"Will do, babe, so I'll see you—"

"—oh, and Cable...my stomach's even bigger today! It ached
483

a bit and I didn't go to work. Please call me later."

"Yeah, sure, Ginny." We hung up and I looked around the disheveled room. It was much like my life, cups, dishes, files, reminder notes and stale-smelling ashtrays, full to the brim, were strewn about. Just then the beautiful Adora came out to greet me, her face glowing in the golden morning light. She was wearing a light-pink dress with black, patent leather shoes and coral necklace hung around her neck.

"I am standing here, mi amor. But I cannot get my feet to walk. I do not want to leave you. I am torn apart to leave you, mi querida. What am I to do? *Ay, tengo dolor, mi precioso.*"

"What can I say, beautiful? You gotta go home and help your mother and sister at *Todo el Mundo*. I promise I'll call you in a day or two. By the way, come here, you…"

She smiled as I drew her to my still-naked body. "I'm glad I still have the blinds drawn…because this…*this* is the best way I know…to hug you…"

She melted into my arms and kissed me as if she would have to leave her lips behind, if she had to go. "*Hasta la vista, mi amor.*" I gave her a buck for the streetcar and she glided out of my office. I stood there semi-paralyzed, finding it almost impossible to change gears and face another day in the life of Cable Denning, P.I. A life that at best was a string of dangerous misadventures. Only my little Mexican doll brought sanctuary to me—like a canteen of refreshing water on a blistering summer's day in the middle of this torturous desert called—L.A.

I connected with Honey and told her I'd be up to my ears in backlogged work for a couple of days, but I'd come over and spend the night with her soon. She grumbled a bit but her own career was going great guns and she told me *Columbia Records* had definitely made a bid to buy out her *Brunswick* contract. I told her I was glad for her and would talk to her soon. No sooner had I hung up the phone than it rang again. "Yeah, Cable Denning here."

"Mr. Denning? This is Dr. Marvin Kalmisch over at Hollywood Hospital? I understand you know a young woman by the name of Ginny Fullerton, is that correct?"

"Yeah, sure—is she okay? What's happened?"

"Well, if you can, I would advise you to get here as soon as you are able. Miss Fullerton is undergoing the most bizarre physical events I have ever seen. I thought you may be able to shed some light on it, since the lady in question mentioned in her delirium that you were the father of her child."

"Yeah, doc, I'll be right there!" I tossed on some clothes and ran out the door. I had to see this thing to the end and Lord knows what bizarre things poor Ginny's body might be suffering!

The hospital was at Vermont and Fountain and the yellow car stopped right in front of it. I ran to reception and asked for Dr. Kalmisch. Soon a burly man of medium height and glasses came out to greet me. "Mr. Denning?" He shook my hand. "I'm glad you're here. Please…follow me."

He led me down to a basement corridor where special rooms existed, I assumed, for the containment of 'special' patients. It looked more like a looney bin than a hospital. We entered a room with an orange tag taped to the door and the name "Fullerton" written on it. Ginny lay in a bed being attended by three nurses. Gobs of greenish fluid were being sponged off of her naked body and she was twitching back and forth on her bed. The doctor took me aside. "Frankly, Mr. Denning, we are baffled at the color and prolific amount of the amniotic fluid—"

"—amniotic what?" I asked, totally puzzled.

"*Amniotic* fluid. It is a special water, if you will, contained in the sac in which the baby is suspended and is able to breathe—and, we believe, maintains the pre-respiratory balances of the fetus."

"Oh. So the weird green stuff isn't normal, I take it. Ginny did mention to me over the phone that she had a green discharge."

"The green amniotic fluid with a consistency of a very light cooking oil is well...unheard of, Mr. Denning. Such things simply don't occur with humans. And yet...we are standing here witnessing the impossible. That's why I was hoping you might shed some light on the subject, having known Miss Fullerton."

I glanced at Ginny's naked body and quickly observed that her stomach was no longer distended. "All I can report for sure is that she complained of some kind of unusually fast expansion of her stomach. She even asked me if I had giants in my family—that's how fast she was swelling out."

"What is amazing is the fact that she was not even into her first trimester. But that isn't the only thing that baffles us, Mr. Denning. Follow me."

We wound down even more stairs until we entered a laboratory where a very frail looking Oriental man greeted us. "Oh! This is man?" the little fellow in the white medical robe inquired.

"Yes. This is Dr. Arthur Okamura, Mr. Denning," Dr. Kalmisch said. "Arthur...Cable Denning." We bowed in acknowledgement.

"In Japan, where we believe in many strange things, none more strange than what we find in Miss Fullerton, Mr. Denning." He led me to a gurney that had a sheet covering a small, oblong object. "In one moon cycle, Miss Fullerton gave birth, if I may use term, to fully-developed—ah, *something!*"

"What he means is that the fetus was not human—well, not entirely. I know I'm sounding ridiculous, but take a look for yourself," Dr. Kalmisch said.

Dr. Okamura lifted the sheet from the object on the gurney. My breath stopped as I beheld a light-yellow pod, blotched by green stains, perhaps no more than eighteen inches in length and six inches across. The alien object had a knob at one end where it looked like the umbilical cord had been attached. A small groove went from that point to the slightly larger "head" of the object, which lay open and to my shock and amazement, a tiny human-like head with beautiful shiny black hair rested in the cavity! I had no words, but stood there knowing in my heart it was Lei-tao's last attempt to bring something that represented "us" into the world.

Finally the little Japanese doctor spoke up. "I studied botany for a time at university. This…what we see here, Mr. Denning sir, is technically edible seed of plant genus known as *Nelumbo nucifera*, found prolifically in the Orient and in Colombia, South America. For most of us, it is recognized as Lotus seed and is eaten raw by millions of people." Then he pointed to the little skull and the abundant, lovely black shining hair. "But… as you can plainly see—a human-like creature has been formed from within seed-pod itself." He started to cover it up.

"Please!" I said. "One minute…please…" I wanted to cry and in that moment realized how nature herself fought to keep perpetuating her own— against all odds strove to modify and mutate until she had produced something new. That was her game. The adventure of new species from old, populating a universe of oddities no human mind could even begin to understand. The two men stood there with me. "Okay. This will sound crazy—even impossible. But this is my understanding of it, okay? I don't want either of you fine doctors to go through the rest of your lives without at least hearing what I have to tell you about this thing. Sometime ago I met a Chinese woman who, for the want of better words, was born of a lotus pod at the bottom of a very cold lake in China. I could go into greater detail, but the bottom line is that a beautiful other-dimensional creature came forth from this lotus pod. We met and I crossed into her dimensional world with my own carnal desires. She succumbed and fell in love with me. She wanted to have my baby but when she modified her physiology to

487

accommodate conception, she became violently ill and could not survive giving birth to a human hybrid child. So, her solution was to transfer the fetus while still in it's very early stages of development, into the womb of Ginny Fullerton, whom I had recently been with intimately. No one knew how rapidly the fetus would grow." I stopped, took a finger and ran it through the black, luxuriant hair of the little head poking out from the seed. "Sometimes love is selfish, even though it doesn't mean to be. It only means to express itself because one someone cares a hell of a lot for another someone. Even if it crosses over the line of the impossible, love finds a way, and if it dies in the process, the original intent and feelings remain."

Both men stood there looking at me, their eyes wide in disbelief. "I'm a Jew, Mr. Denning," Dr. Kalmisch informed me. "Sure, I go to Temple and hear the ancient scrolls read and we are asked to believe many fanciful and mythological tales. But science? I see no science in the religious codes that men make to maintain an orderly society."

"That's too bad, doc. Neither did I until I met Lei-tao. But all that changed for me. Now I'm a believer. Your proof lies right here on the table. Take it or leave it."

"And it was your sperm that fertilized this Chinese vegetable woman?"

"Yep. She was a shape-changer and appeared to me as some babe..." I stopped. I saw the uselessness of it all. "Well, suffice it to say, gentlemen, I was the donor of the sperm."

"You will be asked to maintain the highest priority of secrecy about this, Mr. Denning," Dr. Kalmisch said. "Even if some aspects remain scientifically unexplained, you understand we must destroy this thing."

"Who's gonna believe me? Neither of you do. So let's drop it. Will you bring me to Miss Fullerton's room? I need to say good-bye to her."

"Yes, please follow me," Dr. Kalmisch said.

We entered Ginny's room and she was propped up in her bed. She recognized me and gave me a weak smile. "Cable… Cable…" I came over to her and took her hand. "I'm sorry, Cable, I lost our baby, didn't I? She grew so fast, my body couldn't keep up…"

"It's okay, Ginny. You're a bit weak just now. You need to rest up. I'll check up on you every day. If you're good and don't chase after the doctors, maybe some flowers and a box of candy will come your way, huh?"

She tried to giggle. "Oh, Cable, don't make me laugh! It hurts…but…I love you…and think you are…you are…the best man…I've ever known…" She closed her eyes and one of the nurses signaled for me to go. I exited out into the hallway, climbed the stairs and eventually made my way back to the waiting room. I entered the smoking room where expectant fathers puffed away in their nervousness. I looked out through the glass windows at the reception desk. A medium-tall woman with dark hair run through with lots of silver was talking to the receptionist. I lit up. The woman seemed nervous and began to take out a cigarette. The receptionist pointed her to the smoking area where all the other nervous people stood around in a cloud of smoke. She entered and lit up. I noticed the book of matches she was carrying said "Big Bear Lodge" on the cover and when she glanced at me, I could see Ginny's eyes. I approached her. "Are you by any chance Ginny Fullerton's mother?"

She looked at me with a stern countenance. "Why, yes, and who are you?"

"I'm a friend of Ginny's. Have you seen her yet?"

She pulled me away from the other people to a far corner of the room. "No…I'm trying to get up the nerve—to—to see my daughter. She ran away from home, you know. But I knew the city life would ruin her. My husband followed her—and now—now—"

"—Yeah, I know…he's in the local hoosegow. Yeah, I know the story, Mrs. Fullerton."

She focused her eyes on me more intensely. "So you…you must be him--the man responsible for poor Ginny's predicament, then."

"Yeah, I guess you could say that." I wouldn't have dared to bring the Lei-tao episode into the equation. "Your husband tried to put me away for good, but it wasn't my time to exit yet, I guess, so I had to subdue him until he gained his senses. He's gotta watch that religious stuff, you know. Fanatics like him can cause a lot of trouble."

She relaxed a bit. "He's the one who drove me to drink, you know, Mr.—Mr.—"

"—Denning, Cable Denning, Mrs. Fullerton."

"Mr. Denning. He raised Ginny with his Bible thumping hell and damnation and I was too weak to fight him. He was violent, you know."

"Well, it doesn't surprise me. So while you boozed it up, poor Ginny got the dirty end of the stick. And since you were unwilling to sober up or give your husband what he wanted in the bedroom, he zeroed in on Ginny as the object of his affections, didn't he? And when she came to the city, he went crazy with possessive jealousy—you know, no man can have her except me—type of thing."

In a sudden rage Mrs. Fullerton slapped my face. The entire waiting room froze and looked toward us. Then she recoiled. She began to sob. I gave her my handkerchief. She took it. "I'm—I'm so sorry…I didn't mean to do that, but truth hurts a lot sometimes, Mr. Denning."

I ran my fingers over my cheek, which was still burning a bit. "Yeah, sometimes, Mrs. Fullerton." I took a deep drag, exhaled and then put my cigarette out in an ashtray over by the staring, silent people. "What's the matter, folks, not used to a little human drama? Well, bone up, you expectant fathers, your time is coming. Happy diaper changing!" I said as I started for the exit.

Mrs. Fullerton followed me. "Please…will you accept my apology? I haven't had a drink in three days and I'm a bit on edge."

"You need to mend the fences with your beautiful daughter, Mrs. Fullerton. She's a special little lady—and you're damn lucky she made it this far with an okay attitude toward life—no thanks to you or your fanatical husband."

Tears came rolling down her cheeks. "You're right…I've decided to stop drinking and take Ginny home with me. I don't know what to do about Jeremy. He's so bitter. Part of it is my fault—"

"—you know, Mrs. Fullerton, I've found that when things need fixing, you just gotta step-up and tell folks the truth. You know how to do that? It's simple, just put one syllable in front of the other—and pretty soon you'll feel yourself having a coming out party, a much needed cleaning up inside. It works every time."

She grabbed my arm. "I know you were good to Ginny. I also realize you were the man she looked after in Big Bear a couple of years ago. She fell in love with you, was obsessed with being with you. I never felt like that. In a way I envied her and it made me drink even more. Now I want to make it up to her, be a mother to my daughter, help her grow up—"

"—she's already grown up, lady. The best thing you can do now is show her some kindness and good, healthy love…the kind that fits…the kind that gets buried through the years because we're hurting too much inside with our own selfish, feel-sorry-for-ourselves kinda pain, smarting in that place you used to call your heart. You've been into self-pity so long you haven't noticed you've neglected the things you should have loved and cared for all along. Good luck with Ginny, lady." I took her hand off my arm and walked out into the dirty sunshine of another Los Angeles day.

"WHEN I GROW TOO OLD TO DIE"

Moving into early October, Honey was about to sign a contract with Samuel Goldwyn to make a movie with Ronald Coleman entitled *Condemned*. At the moment the lead female role was between Honey and a pretty little gal named Ann Harding. Goldwyn, who was reputed to be feisty and stubborn, liked Honey's looks and was opting for her, while Coleman preferred to work with someone familiar. He probably didn't want to be upstaged, either, by a beautiful honey-colored blonde singer who was gaining a lot of popularity on the airwaves of the times.

Ginny went back to Big Bear to live with her mother and convalesce. I knew the hospital had been ordered to destroy the fetus and so Lei-tao's story faded into the past for me, somewhere between a beautiful reality experience and something I dreamed last night. As our wedding date approached, Honey and I were doing well and I fought to stay away from Adora, not always winning. My heart hurt when I thought of the day I could no longer feel this exquisite young woman's body melt into mine, or hear her musical feminine voice in my ear. But I also knew that nothing stays the same and the only permanent thing in the universe was *change*. So I limped on with memory and regret, like most humans, going through the motions of existing on a strange planet, eking out a living the way successful private dicks plied their trade. Grabbing what I could when I could, to pay the rent and put a few bucks away now and then for that proverbial rainy day people always talk about.

Even though I began hearing even more rumblings that the financial markets were over extended, I thought little of it. It had been a phenomenal year for economic growth in the good ol' U.S. of A. I was hard pressed to see how the system would be compromised to where it would affect the general population in a negative way. Money was always made and lost in the world's biggest gambling casino…Wall Street. In my opinion, the financial markets were where the rich played and speculated. For the little guy like me, it was hardly a dot on the map of everyday life.

The thing that nagged at my insides most was the fact that I had not heard a peep from my nemesis, the *Oculus Pyramis Mandatum*. Their silence after Ravna's death only meant one thing to me: they were regrouping and strengthening a plan to come descending like hordes of locusts at a later date…threatening me in some diabolical way to re-secure the *God of Our Fathers* for them—on pain of death, or worse, if I happened to fail. I felt I probably had to tell Honey the truth about how serious this shit could go. In a way, it was unfair that she should live under a lie—not realizing she's loving a man who indeed may not be around to see their first wedding anniversary. So I decided I'd have to confront *myself* in front of my future wife, spill the whole thing and start with a clean slate.

Sunday October 6th was the first day Honey and I could sit quietly in the morning and have a pleasant breakfast together. Maybe it didn't exactly tie in with a rough 'n tough guy image, but I missed little things like that. You know, that first cup of coffee with someone you love to be with, someone you love to look at and talk to because you know she's intelligent, witty and cares about you, too.

As we finished a couple soft-boiled eggs with toast and Honey filled our cups with fresh coffee, I thought it the best time to break the news to her. "Babe…there's something I need to talk to you about."

She looked at me with that intense 'I-knew-it-all-the-time look. "Yes? Will I need paper tissue, a fire extinguisher or a gun?" she joked.

"Well, depending on how you take it, maybe all of them." We laughed. "I mean, some of it you kind of know, but I haven't told you the rest of what I think you should know."

She sipped from the top of her coffee cup. "Here I am, darling…"

"Well, you sort of know that I was involved in procuring that golden capsule and all. You know about the Red Dragon Lady—and I realize you don't want to go there. And that's okay. But what you need to know is that behind all of this crap that's been going on is a maverick organization—a secret order called the *Oculus Pyramis Mandatum*."

"Hmmm…Latin…already sounds dangerous," she ribbed me.

"These guys are the real thing, as far as playing rough, Honey. They threaten and kill people who are in their way and they have no compunctions about removing someone who has something they want. Now…for a short while you know I had the golden capsule, the one I retrieved from Hearst Castle when we were there. I told you I'd keep you posted. But you didn't seem that interested—"

"—I wasn't. And I'm still not."

"So, how can I tell you that there will be some big curve balls being hurled at my plate one of these days soon? And when *they're* up to bat, they're big hitters. They play for keeps, Honey."

She studied my eyes. "You know, Cable, I've seldom seen traces of real concern or fear in your eyes. But right now I do. Who else besides these bad guys and the Red Dragon Lady wanted it?"

"You remember the three priests who saved my butt that

night? Well, the Catholic Church has its own hit squad of pretty rough players…Carlo Tortelli and his flying priests are three of them. And as I saw it, they take no prisoners."

Honey turned some thoughts around in her brain. Now I saw the half-alien part of her come onto the playing field. "Okay. So at least three parties want what you say you already gave back to the rightful owner, the Red Dragon Lady—so what's the problem?"

"What I didn't get to yet, was that a phony replica was made and I gave that to the *Oculus* guys to keep them off my back. When they discovered the ruse, they came after me. A guy named Ravna, who I originally met in San Francisco, visited me in my office and said he'd give me two weeks to get my shit together and deliver the real thing to him. I didn't have it, nor did I have access to it any longer. Angry and desiring to scare me—which they did—they kidnapped me and took me to some weird underground lab where a very twisted sister named Dr. Schumacher was going to castrate me as 'punishment' for having deceived them—"

"—Cable! You're not kidding, are you?" Suddenly Honey's face grew fearful as if she could feel the evil just got sucked under the door when I talked about the Order. "Darling! I had no idea!" Then she returned to her jocular self. "But then again, since we've continued to have great sex of late, we can assume they did not succeed in that plot—"

"—no, it was Carlo Tortelli and his two buddies that killed Ravna and Dr. Schumacher that night, along with a couple of other goons protecting the joint. I tell you I was seconds from being under Schumacher's knife. Then they brought me here. But it's only a matter of time before Ravna's replacement will come hunting me down."

Honey got up from the table and went to the little kitchen sink and looked out the window at the sunny California day. "You know, Cable, I've discovered that loving someone is a funny thing. Although you know in your heart it's constant, there are days you wake up wondering why you love that person. Maybe some of it has to do with hormones, I don't know, my period, how I've been received on stage the night before, my frustrations with my movie career, how frustrated I get with you, how our schedules conflict and we catch as catch can late at night, mostly in bed when we're both tired out from the world. We laugh and make light of it because sex still covers up a lot of what lies beneath. But being in a marriage, I think, is very different. I think it may start with love, being in love with someone—but soon *trust* has to enter the picture." She turned to look at me. "And you know, all fooling aside, I've never completely trusted you. I know you're kind of truth—oh, and maybe you do tell a few white lies now and then. But I kept hiding things from myself, fears that you'd come home and give me some venereal disease or smell like another woman's perfume or something. Do you understand what I'm saying, Cable?"

I played with my coffee cup and half smiled up at my beloved Honey Combes. "Yep. Everything you say is true. We play Russian Roulette every day and don't know it. But I wish I'd heard you say these things before."

"Why? It wouldn't matter. You're always going to be you, Cable. At the start it was fun and games, we laughed and played. But when we got serious about wanting to be together, it was like all of that slowly drained away out the window. I hoped against hope you'd settle down with me, stop seeing your little Mexican señorita—and God knows who else—I mean, I have no clue what you did with that Rusty Wilson woman in Monterrey, Mexico—before you say she died a terrible death. Did she—really? You have a knack of tucking away little secrets you think won't matter to me or to the rest of the world. But you know, Cable, it does matter. I love you completely, with my whole heart. Isn't that ever enough to cement a relationship and loyalty in marriage? You remember that night when I sang Jolson's *Sonny Boy* to you? Well, I meant it, every word. You *are* a boy-man, despite your strengths and the gutsy face you turn to the world out there. But to me you're the man I love, and the boy who won't grow up in some very important ways."

I felt very uncomfortable. But she was right. I was a professional philanderer, playing dames against the odds, thinking I could juggle them all as the occasion presented itself as if I were still sixteen chasing down young skirts in the streets of the ghetto I came from. "Maybe there's a piece missing in me, babe," I said, looking down at the table, unable to face Honey's intensely direct blue eyes.

"Maybe…yeah, maybe there is, Cable. And where does that leave someone like me who *can* love and *can* commit? Remember what I said a few weeks ago—what if I went around fucking all the good-looking studs that come into the club and proposition me? Men have a real hard time reversing things. But if I did that, I could never come home to you. I'd hang my shingle out somewhere and say, 'Five-hundred bucks a fuck, you drooling Johns'. But I don't do that, do I? Because I'm in love with you and want to share my body only with you, mister. Whores are a type of woman. Are you a type of man who whores around and finds danger as an aphrodisiac so that the variety of women equals the variety of your dangerous escapades?" She stopped, came back to the table and sat down. She took a deep breath and exhaled. "I'm sorry, Cable…these things have been on my mind for a long time. But I didn't mean to dump them all on you this morning…" She reached her hand across the table and touched mine. "I guess I've hurt for a long time. And sometimes it seems I'm facing a glass mountain with you. I can't climb it because I just keep slipping back down."

Her eyes began to tear and I got up and came over to comfort her. I dabbed her tears with my napkin. "Truth is truth, doll…even if it's uncomfortable, I had it coming…all of it. If

I was on trial right now and I was also judge and jury, I'd condemn me on the spot and kick me out of your life."

She grabbed my arm. "Oh, God, I could never do that. You're still magic to me, Cable. Even with all that I just said, you bring me joy, laughter, happiness, incredible intimacy—and you're a man I can talk to. Most girls can't talk to their men like I can to you. That's worth a lot. I'm not throwing the baby out with the bathwater here—I'm just throwing out the babes who've been *in* your bathwater!"

We both laughed and it broke the tension. "You'd still want me after all that?"

"I wanted you before I even started saying what I just got through saying. Chalk it up to a hopeless romantic, but I still think we can be the happiest couple in town—won't you give us a full and fair chance, Mr. Private Eye?"

I pulled Honey Combes up into my arms and kissed her with everything I had, bad coffee breath and all. She melted into me and I caressed her beautiful blonde hair in my hands. "Yeah, babe. Starting here, starting now—this could be the start of something great!"

She took my hand a led me into the bedroom. "I just don't want you to fuck me this morning, Cable...I want you to look at me...and *love* me when you enter me. I want to feel the connection between down there—and our eyes. After all, lover, it's my heart I offer here...do you accept?"

We stripped naked and lay on the bed in the morning sunlight, caressing each other. I was wondering if I could truly make love to my woman and look into her eyes at the same time without losing my erection. Some guys are like that, you know.

It took me a week, but I finally broke it to Adora that I seriously couldn't see her anymore. On the day I told her, it killed something inside of me but I ignored it and went on with my promise to myself and Honey to make a good life with her. It broke Adora's sweet heart. When I stood there telling her, she went numb and looked into my eyes, unbelieving.

On Saturday the 19th of October, Honey had to go in to the *Bella Notte* early for a photo shoot. She had then planned to have an early supper there with me, and just dress and get ready at the club for her performance that night. I was looking forward to seeing her with an extra enthusiasm that afternoon for some reason or other. Maybe my newly pledged commitment to her made me feel good about us, and maybe when a man has only one woman to think about, everything runs smoother. But that wasn't entirely true, for somewhere deeper inside me I had to fight off the reminders of Adora's face and smile, her warm gentle voice and soft body knocking at the door to my heart.

On a sudden wave of appreciation for Honey, I had written a note to her and carried it to the club that late afternoon. I also brought something else. For the first—and what would turn out to be the *only* time in my life—I put myself in debt and bought my babe a brand spanking new engagement ring. It set me back close to a thousand bucks, so I'm afraid it would also have to serve as our wedding ring. The jewelry store I bought it from agreed to allow me to make small monthly payments. Hell, at ten bucks a month I'd be paying for that ring forever! The owners, a very funny, typical Jewish couple named Abe and Golda Sachs hoped I'd be able to pay it off sooner than the almost ten years it would take to own the damn thing outright. But I wanted to go all out with a babe like Honey.

When I arrived, she was extra glad to see me and when I hugged her I could feel her blend into me as never before. "Cable…I've been thinking about us all day. I can feel you've turned a corner and I want you to know how happy I am. I think at last I'm going to have my cake and eat it too—you, my career and maybe even that transplanted baby that Joe was talking about, huh?"

I laughed. "Yeah, babe, I'm all for transplanted babies, but just remember, I ain't gonna risk you nohow for no one, huh?"

We sat at a private table and Affonso Amadore personally came and served us. "Cable…you woulda beena so proud of your *bella signorina*! She looka so…ummm…*magnifica* for the magazina cover!"

"How much did she have to pay them for that spread, Affonso?" I chuckled, knowing it would get a rise out of both of them.

"Signore! Theya pay her! Whatta you thinka, eh? Is she not-a one of the mosta singers *magnifica* in all-a thisa bigga country?"

"On second thought, maybe you're right, Affonso. Maybe she *is* the best—and pretty little packages like Honey are hard find." He cleared his throat and left us.

"It really is the cover—me on the front with an article and everything…"

I looked at Honey. "The cover yet…my, my…you certainly are coming up in the world, doll."

"No less than *Photoplay*, my lover man. The byline's going to read something like… 'Sizzling young singer breaks Hollywood's mystique with two careers'. Your wife will shine for you, Cable…" Then she reached across the table and took my hand. "For *you*…you aren't threatened or intimidated by all this success I'm having, are you?"

"Are you kidding? I'm the guy who started it all, remember

500

me?—the guy with the bright idea to have you audition here?"

"Yes, and I'll never forget it."

"By the way, I've got a little token here to seal the deal, babe." I took the ring out of my pocket. It was in a little square velvet grey box. I handed it across the table to Honey. Her eyes brightened and misted at the same time. "Just in case you might think I haven't jumped in with both feet."

She took the box, opened it and stared at the small but elegant diamond ring. "Oh, Cable! Cable! You never cease to be a wonder to me—how lucky can I get?" She got up, came over and kissed me a big one. "Damn, I wish I could take you to bed right now—I just feel better…better than I ever have about us, Mr. Private Detective."

I smiled. "Well, don't be getting any big ideas about flirting with too many of your customers or I'll have that ring altered to fit your nose."

She laughed out loud. "Damn, I love you, funny man."

"I also wrote you a little something. I don't know what got into me, but I thought it was about time I told you in writing what I really thought of you," I kidded her. I reached into my breast pocket and took out an envelope. I handed it to her and her eyes brightened.

She opened the envelope, took out the card and began to read out loud: "*Dear Golden Throat, Dames like you come along but once in a great while—try a century or two--but I'm not betting on it, so I grabbed you while I could. A long time ago a babe with a great smile asked me, 'Do I look like a dog to you?' she said. 'I could never belong to someone, Mister,' she told me then. That was the first night I loved you. If I was given the whole world to do over again without you in it, I'd toss it out for those quiet few acres by the sea you keep talking about. You're a good teacher, kid, and I've learned that love comes in a lot of colors, but yours is pure gold… so I think I'm gonna love you until the last streetcar leaves town… Cable.'*

Honey was in tears when she finished reading, her mouth curving down as she tried to stop herself from crying out loud. "Oh, you big hunk of a mushy romantic! Now look what you've done! I'm going to have to re-do my makeup." She got up and came over to where I sat, bent down and kissed me again solidly on the lips. "Thank you, Cable. No one ever wrote me a love note like yours—I will treasure it for always…as long as I live…"

"Awww…don't take it so seriously, lady, I copied it off another greeting card in a dime store where I got this one," I said, making light of my single-handed accomplishment.

"You poop!" she exclaimed as she sat back down. "It's just like you to put yourself down. But I know you wrote every word. And I know you that well. I can feel you, Cable, all the way from my toes to my heart."

"Yeah, well, here's to us, Honey Combes," I said as I lifted my glass to toast my fiancée.

I left the *Bella Notte* right after our supper, telling Honey I had a lot of homework to do for a court hearing in the morning. I got back to my office and went right to my desk drawer and took out my bootleg bottle of gin and poured a big one. I lit up a Lucky Strike and sat back, feeling pretty damn good. My stomach was full, I had a roof over my head, my business was really picking up—and I was going to marry the classiest dame this side of the Nevada border.

But I was kind of exhausted from all the shit that'd been flung at me lately and all that food made me sleepy. So I flopped down on my crumply old bed. I began to doze. I wanted to hear some music and so I turned my little box radio on. The band was playing a soppy version of *The Man I Love* and I thought about Honey. Yeah, life was gonna be just swell!

But almost immediately I began to have one of those restless, foreboding half-dreams, when you're in a semi-state of consciousness and you toss and turn and no position seems

502

comfortable. I was back at the *Bella Notte* and Honey was getting dressed for her evening performance. It was so vivid. She was standing in her slip, fitting one of her gowns over the front of her body and looking into her full-length mirror. As she was checking things out, all of a sudden a dead man appeared at the transom. It was Frank Laggore. His face was twisted and scarred, one eye was partially closed, and he held a .38 in his hand, brandishing it at Honey. "The comely Miss Combes, I presume…" he said in a raspy, twisted voice.

Honey's eyes stared at the specter in disbelief. "Mr. Laggore! I—I thought you were—were—"

"—dead? By the hands of your boyfriend? I heard he always bragged about having nine lives. Well, I've got *ten!*"

"How—how did you get here? And why *aren't* you dead? Cable told me you'd had an accident aboard a train or something—"

"—accident? Ha! For bein' the so-called *truth man* he says he is, you do know that son-of-a-bitch is a liar—"

"What do you want? You scared me before—*before* you were—were—" Honey had to look away from that ghastly face of his.

"—You mean…before I was thrown from the moving train to scrape along the rails—bumpity bump!" Then he drew deadly serious. "Do you know how that feels? Huh? To lose consciousness and wake up a misshapen, grotesque monster?"

"Mr. Laggore—may we talk about this some other time? I do have to get ready for my performance tonight. I'm very sorry for your disfigurement and I'm sure it was terrifying and very painful—"

"—painful?" He lunged forward and took Honey's arm. "Painful…was only part of it…" He took his cold gun barrel and nosed it down between Honey's breasts. "The other part was wanting you, Miss Honey Combes, star of nightclubs and radio—Lana Loren, some fucking starlet who fucks a stupid private dick who could never appreciate her—never give her what I could've!" Then he yanked her slip straps off of her shoulders.

Honey was scared and began to tremble. "Don't *do* that! You don't want a woman who would kick and scream and fight you off every second—I'd *die* before I'd let you have me, you crude pig!"

Laggore glowered at Honey. "You might just have your way, Miss Combes. What better way to get back at the man who made me like this…this thing— a ghastly, ugly creature hiding in the shadows!"

"And you want to blame Cable for it? I know him, he wouldn't have started something with you unless he was provoked—and I know you and that other terrible man who got thrown off the moving train ganged up on him—you were out for his blood! You would have killed him if he wasn't better than you—in or out of bed, Mr. Frank Laggore!"

"I wouldn't tempt the devil if I were you, lady—you're still a whore as far as I'm concerned, like all women, giving out to the highest bidder. Well, whatever Denning had, it wasn't worth it!"

Honey came back now with her own brand of anger. "He's worth a million of you, you dumb Dago! And don't you think I know, it was all because of *me* that you went after Cable. It was never that golden thing Jack Dragna was going to get paid big bucks for. Don't you think I could feel you look at me those nights when Cable wasn't here? Don't you think I could feel your lust like a hot knife cutting through me, your eyes staring at my breasts, sitting at the little table at the foot of the stage wishing you could look up my dress and have what Cable has anytime he wants it!" She took a deep breath as Laggore backed away from her. "I always wanted to tell you what I really thought of you—that you were disgusting and slimy and the phony politeness in your voice hid the truth—you were always a monster—only now the outside matches the inside!"

Unable to control himself any longer, Laggore emptied his gun into Honey, some bullets penetrating her body and shattering the glass on the mirror behind her. Honey screamed, and then whimpered in pain, holding her abdomen as Laggore stood there frozen and half smiling, his gun smoking. Honey's eyes widened in disbelief and she staggered to the floor and collapsed.

I woke up, sweating and restless. But I knew it was a nightmare. Maybe I'd better call the *Bella Notte* just in case. It was still early and Affonso Amadore assured me everything was okay and Honey was resting in her dressing room, getting ready for her Saturday night show. So I went back to work at my desk. After about three hours I had finished my preparations for a court case and held out the photos I had to present the next day at a hearing. Some elegantly dressed man was screwing a little hussy in his own home while wifey was away. She suspected it—and I snapped it with my trusty Kodak!

Just then a news bulletin came over the radio. *"A tragedy to report tonight! Honey Combes, the noted singer and rising Hollywood actress was shot tonight by an unknown assailant at her regular place of work, the Bella Notte nightclub on Wilshire Boulevard. Reports are sketchy, but it is believed that Miss Combes has been transported to the Los Angeles County Hospital—"* I was numb as I dashed up and turned the radio off. I stood there in the silence, unable to accept or believe anything. Then on impulse I grabbed my coat and hat and went running out the door. I fled into the street, desperately looking for a taxi. Finally one came and we rushed straight down to Marengo and State, where the L.A. County Hospital was located. I knew the joint well. As a policeman I had visited it many times checking on shot up thugs and goons. But now—my own Honey!

Frantically I ran into the building to reception. I was immediately directed to a "closed" area and I ran down the corridor looking for Room #11. I bumped into a nurse who told me I had to wait for the doctor before I could enter. But I couldn't do that and I burst in the door. There with blood seeping all over her pretty green sequined costume, her face distorted in pain, lay my beautiful Honey. "Sir! You are not allowed in here! Please, I must ask you to leave immediately!" a tall man with silvery hair demanded.

"No way, Mister, that's my fiancée!" I ran over to Honey's bedside. "Honey! Honey! It's me, Cable—can you hear me, babe?" I grabbed her hands.

She barely opened her eyes, squinting up at me, still writhing with pain, blood seeping out of several wounds, one real bad one in her chest. "We can't stop the bleeding—she's been shot six times, all of them in crucial abdominal areas. I'm Dr. Evans." He motioned me aside. "Frankly, I don't think we can save her—she's lost too much blood already and I think one bullet nicked her right coronary artery. I'm sorry…"

I dashed back to her side. "Honey…please…please…don't go, babe, stay with me here, okay?"

A faint light went on in her eyes. "Cable…I love you, Cable…oh…what—what happened?… I'm cold, Cable…hold me…hold me!"

I threw my arms around her as the nurses tried to pry me off Honey's body. By now her green dress was sopping wet with blood and she looked so pale I almost didn't recognize her.

I ran around the room like a maniac, screaming at everyone. "Can't you do something? Stop the bleeding!…she's tough, she's so young… strong! She can survive… country girls are stronger, aren't they? Let's give her a warm bath, wash off the blood—then she'll be okay! Please! Somebody!"

The doctor leaned over Honey and put his stethoscope to her chest. He listened. Then he looked up at me and shook his head. Honey was gone. In one final exhale of breath, my beloved Honey Combes was dead…like a big light that went out in my world. I gritted my teeth and went back over to her lifeless body. I bent over and kissed her still warm lips. Her eyes looked up at me with that glazed stare I knew so well.

I was blubbering. "…I love you, babe…and you know… I'm—I'm right behind you—it won't be long—I wanna hear you sing *Sonny Boy* again—really soon…" Then I thought of my guilt. "I'm so sorry…sorry, Honey…"

The doctor urged me away from her body. He gently escorted me out into the hallway. "There is never an answer to this senselessness, sir. But I suggest you go home and let it sink in. Don't be afraid to grieve. Talk to friends, a priest…be comforted in knowing at least she didn't suffer long. And now she's at peace."

There was nothing I could say as I felt my feet carry me toward the exit. I stepped out into the cool night air. A breeze from the ocean carried that familiar smell of salt water and dampness. I put my hat on and started for the streetcar line. Why hurry home now? Why take a taxi? Why not just walk all night and drink and smoke until I can't feel anything at all anymore?

Just as I was crossing the parking lot, a voice called out me. "You're next, Denning," a man's voice called out from the dark. Then he approached me, his gun drawn. "Surprised, Mr. Detective?"

Like a nightmare from hell there stood Frank Laggore! Only it looked like some scarred, distorted version of Laggore. But I knew the score as the fiber I was really made of firmed up and I faced the son-of-a-bitch. "It was you, you bastard. You… killed her, didn't you, Laggore?"

"Yeah, I did. She preferred you to me—and now we're even." He came out into the light. His face was terribly scarred. He ran his fingers over his cheeks and nose. "This is what happens when someone throws you out of a moving train and you skid along the spikes and rails for a while. It kinda tears up your face—and no surgery will ever make it go away, Private Dick!"

"Don't slip up, Laggore—because you'll be dead before you reach the pavement. You didn't have to kill Honey. You shoulda come for me. Only spineless cowards like you kill women, you worthless fuck!"

"Over there, Denning." He pointed to a coupe parked a couple of rows over. "We're going for a ride. You—you are going for your last ride."

I steeled myself. I was trembling inside from Honey's death. But I couldn't let him know that. So I said nothing as he put the gun barrel in my side and forced me forward into the back seat of the automobile. Two goons were in the front seat, so he climbed into the back and held me at gunpoint. We drove for what seemed thirty or forty minutes. We ended up at Angeles Mesa Drive Airport in the middle of the night and drove out onto the tarmac until we stopped beside an old silver biplane. This was the same airport that Rusty Wilson and I departed from on our way to Monterrey, Mexico. I was beginning to wonder if the fates had it in for me, bringing me back that unpleasant memory. Laggore pushed me out of the car and we walked toward the plane. "Why don't you just shoot me here—now, Laggore. It's better that way, like putting a wounded animal out of his misery. I wouldn't wanna live in this cesspool of a world with you in it, anyway."

"Have no worries, Denning. You will be dead soon enough. It's just that I have special plans for you." He pointed to the plane. "You see, my boys here are gonna tie you up to the stunt man's guy wire above the top wing. You're gonna be a stunt man tonight. At about three thousand feet or so, the rope will be cut—and the fall will—will, uh, you know—spill your worthless guts all over the ground below. I had a lotta time to think about it, hiding in dark corners while my face and body began to mend. So now it's all about making you sweat before you die. Brilliant, don't you think?"

"Shut up and get it over with! I think those scars make you look more like what you've always been inside, Laggore, sinister, dark, mean and without conscience. So don't spare me any mercy, you worthless maggot!"

He hit me hard on the side of my skull with his gun butt. It hurt and at once I could feel the blood pour down the side of my face. He yanked my hat off and threw it to the ground. "You won't be needing that, either. The famous Cable Denning fedora. Nix on the trench coat, too…in fact, one of my boys could use both of those items, even if they are dirty and used."

"Before I go, how about one more Lucky Strike? Don't dying men get a last smoke before the firing squad does its thing?"

"Not my brand, Lucky Strike. I'm a Camel man…you lose." Then he took his gun barrel and popped the buttons off my jacket, one by one. "Do you know what fun it was to empty my gun, bullet by bullet into your little songbird whore? I made sure she saw me first and that I saw the whites of her eyes before I let her have it. She looked so surprised, Denning." He chuckled with delight. "Like—like, uh, 'why me?' was written all over her pretty face as she crumpled right there before me. You know, dead is dead—and she just lay there…*dead*. You shoulda seen it, detective!" My teeth were clenching and in that moment I woulda risked getting killed just to get at Laggore. "I made sure I didn't mess up her face, though—she really was quite striking. But she wouldn't fuck me—she was filled with some silly illusion that you were something special, but I know about all the dames you were ballin'." Then he shouted into the air like an insane idiot. "But you're not! You're not, Denning! I was the special one—me, Frank Laggore, Primo Capo, senza misericordia!" He brought his voice down to a whisper. "I…I…who was born with nothing…made a place in

509

the mob for myself—I was headed for the top of this pile of shit—until *you*! You killed me...while I was still breathing. I'm gonna enjoy snuffing you out—and guess what?" He laughed. "You will not be breathing when you splatter to the ground, Denning—finito!"

Out of nowhere shots began to ring and Laggore's two punks folded up onto the tarmac, dead. Laggore spun around wildly, looking for the killer. "Jack—is that you? I knew you wouldn't have...approved...but even if she was a moneymaker for you...she's really better outta the way, you know. I'll make it up to you, Jack. I'm back, Jack! Here to stay—" I slugged Laggore's gun hand and the revolver went clanking to the ground.

Just then three more shots rang out of the night and found their mark in Laggore's body, one hitting him squarely in the middle of the skull and he dropped like a potato sack. Out of the darkness came a figure with his gun drawn. *Oh, shit*, I thought, *I'm next*. But as he approached I couldn't believe my eyes. "Joe! What the hell?" He came closer and put his gun away. He looked terrible, his face sunken, his eyes sad and tearing.

"She was my daughter, Cable. He killed my only daughter! I lost her mother through stupidity, but I lost Honey through ignorance. And you lost her because you neglected her. Your friend Crazy Jack knew. He had warned you again and again. Now...it's too late...for all of us..."

"I'm—I'm sorry, Joe. It's been a hell of a night."

"I'm sorry for you, too, Cable. My tears are part of the ones you can't cry yet. But you will. I know you loved Honey and she was nuts about you."

"What'll Dragna say when he finds out you killed Laggore and two of his henchmen?"

"Who cares, Cable? I have to go away. I may never see you

again. You see, when one of my kind kills a human, it's an automatic given that we be re-processed. We are pledged not to kill. I broke that rule." He approached me. "Can you drive? If not, I can take you back to your office."

"Shit, Joe, I can't go back to my office. Not tonight. I've gotta walk—and walk, and then walk some more until the reality sinks in."

"I understand. So…can I leave you off somewhere?"

"Yeah, how about Honey's place? I have a few memories to clear out."

Joe Lorena ended up being one of the nicest men I would ever know. We sat in the car in silence in front of Honey's place. When it was time to go, I reached out my hand to shake his. Instead, he reached for me and hugged me tight and sobbed for a minute. Then he withdrew and smiled faintly at me. "Goodbye, Cable Denning, Private Detective. May you heal from all this and see yourself in the stars some perfect night, a night when this memory has faded and you recall your life. And in the balances, you'll recall that to have really loved—even if suffering the painfulness of its loss—it was far better than never to have loved at all."

I got out and he sped away into the night. I slowly made my way to the cottage. I used my key and opened the door. Sitting at the kitchen table with the saddest of postures sat Zelda. She had been drinking. "Cable!" she cried as she came running to me and threw her arms around me. "I heard on the radio. I went down to the hospital. But I was too late. They said you'd been there."

I walked over to the table and stood, looking at the sink, still seeing Honey fixing our morning coffee. "Yeah, Zelda, I came in near the end, in time to…to hear…I heard…heard her last…her last words…"

"Oh, God, Cable. Stay here tonight. Can I fix you something?

Like something hot or a drink of gin? Hell, even *I'm* drinking! I don't think you should go back to your place tonight. Or maybe not even here. Do you want me to stay with you?"

Zelda's voice was concerned and kind, but I couldn't absorb much of it just then. "Maybe I'll collapse on Honey's bed for a few minutes. I just need to walk, that's all. I'm supposed to be in court in the morning. But I don't think I'll make that." She took my hand and led me into Honey's bedroom. I lay on our pillows and I could smell Honey. I began to sob. Zelda kneeled on the bed and came over to me. In a most maternal fashion, she covered me with her ample body. She felt warm as I drifted into a restless oblivion.

I can't remember much about the funeral. Hundreds of people formed a circle around my Honey's coffin on a sunny Los Angeles afternoon. It was fitting that Hollywood Memorial Park Cemetery abutted Paramount Pictures off of Gower and Santa Monica Boulevard. Honey might have liked that, yet I think her spirit was waiting for me on a few acres of land down by the ocean in Northern California. I think her heart was roaming hills of green grasses and soft breezes, daisies and blue skies with bluebirds chirping over the next rise.

I stood next to Zelda, Affonso Amadore and the entire staff of the *Bella Notte*, Chet James, her favorite trumpet player, and Honey's foster parents from Northern California. I didn't have what it took to speak to anyone that day, but the folks looked like the salt-of-the-earth type, lean and hard-working, sun tanned and windblown from life on the land. In the distant background I could see Father Carlo Tortelli and his assassin priests. Conspicuously absent was her father, Joe Lorena. But I knew why. His grief would not have permitted this parting shot fired over the bow of a tragic life. I could hardly bear up under it myself. My mother was also unable to attend due to illness...I think she was grieving for both of us. The preacher said something that hit me pretty hard that afternoon. "It is never fair when one we love is taken before her time. But who is to say what God's time is for someone—or what is fair in the eyes of God? If it is true that the good die young, then Honey Combes created happiness for all who saw her beauty and heard her sparkling voice, either in person or on the radio or phonograph. Think instead, that this good-bye is not forever, for we all travel close behind…"

"…we all travel close behind…" Yeah, that was the statement that stuck in my mind. He was right. Maybe some curtain pulls away on that day we leave this dismal human existence and we rejoin those we knew and loved. I don't know. It was a comforting thought.

I looked away as they lowered Honey's casket into the cold, damp earth. I could not imagine that such a beautiful creature would decay and shrivel into the world of the forgotten inside a pitch-black wooden box. But it was a reality I had to face. As people broke up and I made my way toward the streetcar stop on Santa Monica Boulevard, Zelda took my arm. "Can I drop you off, Cable?" she said, her eyes red from tears.

"Thanks, Zelda," I said, allowing her to lock her arm into mine. "Yeah, we can ride together, I guess."

"Gees, Cable, I loved Honey so much. I think you knew that. I respected her, too. That's why I never pressed you to—to do other things—with—with me, like you know…"

"Yeah, kid, I know."

"Sometimes it takes a long time for something like this to soak in. I still can't believe she's gone." We walked toward the streetcar island. Behind us a voice called out. It was Jack Dragna, and I walked toward him, leaving Zelda behind.

"Denning…" he said as he caught up to me. "I want you to know I'm—I'm sorry. Truly sorry. Honey was a wonderful young woman and a great find for the *Bella Notte*. I also want you to know I had no knowledge of Frank Laggore's plans. You know I would have stopped him. And I lost Joe Lorena in the bargain. Can't figure that one out. Was he particularly close to Honey?"

"Yeah, he was her father," I answered.

Dragna's eyes widened. "You don't say…" He shook his head. "You don't happen to know where he went, do you? He's just disappeared. The boys went to his flat. His clothes, money, furniture—everything's there, untouched. As I said, I can't figure it."

"After he wiped out Laggore and his two goons, he'd probably had it with guys like you, Jack. Smart as he was, I don't think he could take *Murder, Incorporated* anymore and had to jump ship. That's my guess. Or maybe he did himself in, I don't know."

"Yeah…ya never know, Denning, ya never know."

Of course I wouldn't tell Dragna that Joe Lorena was an alien who had to return for re-processing for having killed humans. "See ya around, Dragna…" I said as I took Zelda's arm and started to walk away.

Jack Dragna half-heartedly saluted me and began to back away. "Again, Denning, my condolences. If there's ever anything I can do, you know where to reach me down at the docks."

"Yeah, thanks, Jack. I'll be seeing you…" He walked away. Zelda stopped and looked at Dragna disappearing down the sidewalk. Then she looked at me. "Who was that guy? I got these really funny feelings about him."

"Ah, forget it, Zelda. He's a big-time racketeer, head of the local Mafioso. The days of his kind are numbered. He was Joe's employer."

"Gees…you sure hobnob with dangerous people sometimes, don't you? I mean, people like that probably even kill other people all the time, huh?"

"Yep, if they get in the way."

That incessant melancholy sax was wafting through the tunnels of my pain-ridden brain as we boarded the red car. It was singing a sad version of *The Man I Love* and it made me want to cry for the world, and then run from it—*leave me alone with the music! Let me be! Let me suffer my way—and then let me heal when finally one day, no more pain can come!* Invisible voices kept saying they knew how I felt—but no one could know how I felt! This was my cross—bring on the nails, I was victim and executioner, and while you're at it, hammer the last nail into my head—then toss the dice and let me collect the robe of sin and redemption. Then maybe peace would come. At least I needed *that* break in life.

We ended up with me taking Zelda home to the little cottage she shared with Honey. I walked her to the door. "Well, Zelda, here's where I get off. Whatta ya gonna do now?"

"Move to a less expensive apartment or rooming house or something, I guess. I don't know what I'm going to do with all my plants, though."

"Well, if you're really pressed, you can drop a few off at my office, as long as they look good. The place *is* kind of bare. But I don't wanna fight through a vine-filled jungle to get to my phone."

She laughed that wonderful laugh of a young woman. "I've always thought you a very funny man, Cable. But do you mean it? That you'd be willing to house sit some of my plants?"

"Well, there's one catch. You'll have to come once a week or so and water 'em, because I might forget."

"Oh, sure, as long as I live close by. I'd like to live close to you. Maybe we can go out to dinner and a dance again sometime."

"Don't count on it, kid. I'm a little raw around the edges these days, in case you haven't noticed. It'll be a while before I get kick-started back into circulation. Right now I'm kinda living on my nerves—and I don't know how long they're gonna last."

"Well, maybe I shouldn't bring over my plants quite yet." She came up and hugged me, kissing my cheek. "I'll give you my new phone number as soon as I find a place. You're still over on Franklin, right?"

"Yeah. And by the way, thanks for holding me that night after…it—it felt good."

She let go of me and looked into my eyes. "If you only knew, Cable, how many times I've longed to hold you all night—and the fantasies I had about us—you probably would never want to see me again."

"I doubt that, kid. In fact, I'm flattered…remember what I said, find yourself a young man hanging out in one of those white-coat labs. I'm sure you'll both be singing the same tune before long."

I walked away, leaving Zelda Blodgett standing at her door. Life is a minefield of ironies, I was thinking as I boarded the streetcar and headed for Franklin and Cahuenga. That lonely sax was playing in my head again and I realized its song was my pain, the unhealed saga of the human condition, fraught with pitfalls, day to day existence, misery, relatives, money, politics, war and if you're lucky, love…coupled with great music sung by a babe in a low-cut sequined gown in some smoky joint in the middle of the night, bathed in a dingy spotlight. Yeah, some things you just have to shove deep down inside and hope to hell they never erupt and tear you apart someday when you're not looking. As for me? I think what's left of my heart will travel on for a while, picking up little pieces of happiness here and there, until maybe memory and regret take a back seat and when I breathe in the sea air on an overcast night in this city I hate to love—it won't hurt so damn much.

A fire engine's horn blasted through the night, its siren the desolate reminder of our mortality, and as I rode past the uncounted faces in the store windows or walking the sidewalks, I knew they, too, had an expiration date stamped on

516

their destinies. I got off the trolley and started to make my way to my office building. I felt like a stranger walking to a new life I had no clue about, an insipid nobody without an identity. Maybe no one knows why or how you carry on when all the props have been knocked out from under you and life becomes a numb motion of sameness and desperation. So I drink, smoke—maybe someday even have the courage to walk down into that smoky nightclub I was talking about, listen again to some hot babe warble a few great tunes amongst the din of clanking glass and loud voices trying to tune out the unbearableness of life. Avoiding the recognition that life is a one-way ticket that has been punched by the conductor— eventual destination?—a local cemetery.

And love? Honey had taught me a lot of things, but above all I learned that goodness comes from the deepest and simplest places inside—places branded into the makeup of a person where common decency still holds court and tells you that if someone like her existed in the world, the world can't be *all* bad. The same could be said for Ginny Fullerton—and most definitely for a little Mexican babe named Adora Moreno.

I got to the top of the landing, a little winded from too many Lucky Strikes and rot-gut gin. I turned the key and opened the door. The sound of that damn sax was still filling my head like a haunting memory that won't go away—and—the phone was ringing. "Yeah, Cable Denning here…"

THE END

ACKNOWLEDGEMENTS

COVER IMAGES:

Cable Denning: Kenneth A. Cox Photography

Black Dragon: Zyman Photostream

Honey Combes: Elevate Costumes Australia
www.elevatecostumes.com.au

Lei-tao: Provenance unknown

Lotus Flower: Provenance unknown

Watchful Eye of Oculus: Rick Weiss

Editing and research Consultant: Frances Moss
Original Cover Designs: Frances Moss